In the Face of Evil

Based on the life of Dina Frydman Balbien

Second Edition – September 2012

Collaborated with Dina Frydman Balbien.

Cover photo of Dina taken in Atlantic City after war, approximately 1946-1947.

ISBN

978-1-77067-080-8 (Hardcover)

978-1-77067-081-5 (Paperback)

978-1-77067-082-2 (eBook)

Published by:

FriesenPress

Suite 300 – 852 Fort Street

Victoria, BC, Canada V8W 1H8

www.friesenpress.com

Distributed to the trade by The Ingram Book Company

What people are saying about
In the Face of Evil

"This book is the outcome of three miracles. First, the mother, Dina Frydman, lived through the Holocaust, surviving an unbelievable, all too true set of tragic experiences that wiped out her entire family: occupation, ghetto, work camp, slave labor, Auschwitz, Bergen-Belsen (in its final stage of total collapse and chaos). Miraculously, she came through with her goodness, honor and affirmation of life intact. This book reflects those qualities.

Second miracle: for decades, in an incredible feat of memory, Dina relived and told her stories, recounting them with pitch perfect recollection, including a vivid gallery of portraits of friends, family, victims, persecutors, and with vital scenes of the kindness and cruelty of strangers, the love and incapacity of family, the support and saving help of friends.

Third miracle: Dina's daughter, Tema Merback, absorbed these stories and reproduced them in this authentic, gripping, moving account. What the mother could not do—put her testimony in a book—the daughter has done and without losing any of the fire, or the suffering, or the heartbreak, or the moments of relief and of despair. In the end this book communicates an irrepressible, overflowing life force and decency and hope in the face of the most inhuman crimes ever.

As authentic, as compelling, as devastating as a survivor's account written at first hand, this book snatches memory and life from the jaws of oblivion and gives them as a gift to its readers. This book was a mitzvah to write and a mitzvah to read."

—Rabbi Irving (Yitz) Greenberg, Founding President, Jewish Life Network; Founding President, CLAL: The National Jewish Center for Learning and Leadership; Chairman, United States Holocaust Memorial Council, 2000-2002.

"Reading *In the Face of Evil* brought to mind two aspects that couldn't be more vivid. Simply, it is a period of time when there were no iPhones, nor iPads, or Facebook; the pronouns mostly used were 'we and us', as in family—something that is missing in this current world of ours. Reading *In The Face of Evil* allowed me the honor of hearing the voices of a family that stood the test of time. I could smell the odors described, hear the noises, and yes, feel their pain. I recommend this book to every High School student, their parents, and most importantly as a reminder for the State Department and Pentagon, which deal with similar tyrannies."

—Peter Kash is an international bestselling author and has visited Dachau and Auschwitz and the Warsaw Ghetto. He is currently completing his doctorate thesis in Jewish Education at the Azrieli School at Yeshiva University.

Table of Contents

Prologue .... **xi**

Part 1

Radom, Poland Summer of 1939 .... **1**

Chapter 1 — An Ordinary Family 3

Chapter 2 — Welcome to the Sabbath Queen 17

Chapter 3 — A Threatening Storm 43

Chapter 4 — Germany Attacks 51

Chapter 5 — "The New Order" 59

Chapter 6 — Change is for the Best 75

Chapter 7 — Crisis Strikes Again and Again 81

Part 2

The Ghetto Years **97**

Chapter 8 — Life Changes 99

Chapter 9 — Adventures in the Ghetto 117

Chapter 10 — A Time to Say Good-bye 131

Chapter 11 — A.V.L. 145

Chapter 12 — An Accident 151

Chapter 13 — The Jewish Hospital 159

Chapter 14 — Nadja Tells a Tale 167

Part 4

Szwarlikovska Street **219**

Chapter 21 — The Workers' Camp 221

Chapter 22 — Jacub 227

Chapter 23 — Farewell, My Love 233

Part 5

Pionki, Poland 1943 .... **237**

Chapter 24 — Slavery 239

Chapter 25 — "*Chervonutka*" 247

Chapter 26 — Farewell to Arms 251

Chapter 27 — A Train Journey 255

Part 6

Arbeit Macht Frei

Summer 1944 .... **257**

Chapter 28 — What is This Place? 259

Chapter 29 — Auschwitz, Birkenau II 261

Chapter 30 — *Kaddish* 267

Chapter 31 — Run as Fast as You Can 273

Chapter 32 — Satellite Camp Hindenburg 277

Chapter 33 — The Last Christmas 287

Chapter 34 — Death Has a Name 293

Part 7

The Road to Recovery **303**

Chapter 35 — Castle Langdenberg 305

Chapter 36 — Stuttgart Displaced Persons Camp 319

Chapter 37 — Aglasterhausen International Children's Center 329

Chapter 38 — Lady with a Torch 347

Epilogue **353**

Acknowledgements **357**

About the Author **358**

"To forget the Holocaust is to kill twice." —Elie Wiesel

The Oath
Avraham Shlonsky, Israeli Poet

In the presence of Eyes
Which witnessed the slaughter
Which saw the oppression
The heart could not bear,
We have taken an oath:
To remember it all,
To remember, not once to forget!
Forget not one thing to the last generation!

In the Face of Evil is dedicated to and in remembrance of the 1.5 million Jewish children and the more than 4.5 million Jewish teens and adults who were exterminated under the murderous regime of the Nazis.

I also dedicate to and acknowledge my mother, Dina Frydman Balbien, the bravest person I have ever known. She is my inspiration in life and the heroine of this book. Her endurance of the Holocaust has never dimmed her positivity or belief in humanity. Writing the story of my mother's survival during World War II was a journey that has transformed my life forever.

Prologue

Seventy years have elapsed since the end of my childhood and the beginning of World War II. The destruction of community and family that followed the German invasion and conquering of Poland precipitated and forced me into an unnatural adulthood. The odd windfall of this calamitous event is a searing imprint of memory. Faces and voices have followed me my entire life offering up their advice and counsel, whether desired or not, shadowing each step as I steered my course through the seas of life. At times they have proven to be more real to me than yesterday's events. Often, these friendly ghosts have capriciously danced through the corridors of my dreams as real and alive as the last day that I saw them. Like the story of "Brigadoon," the mythical community of book and song that reappeared every hundred years and for one shiny bright inexplicable moment sparkled through the mists of Scotland, so has the vanished world of Radom, Poland returned to me in dreams and at times in waking just as it was long ago. The joyous community with its various degrees of religiosity, the marketplaces and shops, the places of learning, the observance of holidays, the intellectual liveliness, and of course the devotion and celebration of the Sabbath are all safely locked inside the reels of memory that play like a film in my mind, alive again.

Although I have tried at times to put the war behind me for both mine and my children's sanity, like the tattoo that I bear, it is burned into me and has colored every moment of my life. With the passage of time there have been endless books with their endless revelations as to why or how such a nightmare could have occurred, but in the end the only lesson learned is that it happened. The Holocaust happened and millions perished through systematic slaughter. A world of people with their joys and sorrows disappeared and with them went a way of life. The apocalypse has long passed and the years have flown by like the clouds in a windblown sky. Soon there will be no survivors left and the keepers of the memory will be just that, a memory. So it has come to me, the bearer of the torch, the last to remember their sweet sojourn among friends and enemies before I, too, leave this world of bitter sweetness. The tale has now been written of those who lived, that they may endure and that you might know them.

Dina Frydman Balbien

Part 1

Radom, Poland Summer of 1939

Chapter 1

An Ordinary Family

From the window of our apartment, I look down on the bustling streets. The morning sun shines on my street, Koszarowa Ulica, a busy thoroughfare in Radom's Jewish quarter. Placing my hand on the window, I feel the warmth radiate through the glass. The bright August morning pours into my bedroom, casting away the shadows of a doubt-filled night. The ordinary ebb and flow of life seems to continue in a reassuring cycle of sunrises and sunsets.

Across the street, the shopkeepers are opening their stores. Michal the baker comes out and looks at the sky. A smile spreads across his plump face as he brushes some flour from his prominent nose. Mrs. Rabinowicz greets him, and with a last wistful glance at the sky, he follows her into his bakery.

The birds' songs crescendo in the tall chestnut trees lining the street, adding to the symphony of daily life. People hurry through the busy streets in pursuit of their daily callings. Bicyclists weave among the horse-drawn carriages, or *dorozkas*[1], the principle form of transportation throughout Poland's cities. Life seemed normal enough on this warm summer day in 1939.

I rub my eyes in an effort to dispel the dream that still plagues me, trying to make sense of the visions of the night. It has been two years since my beloved *zaida*[2] passed away. Last night in my sleep, he came to me. Reaching across the barriers that separate the living from the dead, he touched me in an urgent gesture to communicate. Standing at the foot of my bed, silently beckoning me to acknowledge his presence, he hovered; his large immaterial body shimmered before me. His eyes, the color of blue ice, bore into me through the veil of death. He conveyed a warning I could not fathom. The ghostly apparition had disturbed my peaceful slumber and I had brusquely shooed my grandfather away, reminding him that he belonged in the afterworld of the dead.

I awoke with a horrible feeling of guilt and remorse. Why had I not reached out to him full of the love we once felt for one another? I had not asked him why he was there. Instead, in the imaginary landscape of my dream, I had told him to leave and not to return. How could I have sent my beloved grandfather away? I tried to brush the vision from my mind and replace it with the happy memory of my grandfather as he was in life, Jekiel *starke,* meaning Jekiel the strong in Yiddish. Rhythmically swaying in his rocking chair, he impatiently waited for our cherished daily routine—when I climbed on his lap and kissed him. Together we would rock as he told me stories of his youth, the security of his arms enfolding me, his white beard tickling until I was reduced to giggles. The fond memories of a favorite grandchild encircled me in a blissful cloak of warmth and safety, shielding me from the terrors of the dream.

1 Horse drawn buggy, Polish

2 Grandfather, Yiddish

My zaida, a pillar of our community, was sorely missed by all. Although my brother Abek and I were too young to attend his funeral, I remember my parents' description of that saddest of days. Seldom had there been seen such an outpouring of respect and honor for a citizen. My grandfather had been an important patron of an orphanage the Rothschild family had founded in Radom a century before. It was one of many institutions established by charitable benefactors to provide for those less fortunate. The Jewish community was well organized in caring for its own.

The funeral had been a solemn affair on a gray rainy morning. A special dorozka, drawn by white horses, pulled the funeral bier containing my grandfather's coffin. Behind in sorrow had walked my parents, grandmother, and sister, along with my uncles and aunts, cousins, friends of the family, and dignitaries from the community. Following them walked more than a hundred children from the orphanage, flowing in a slow dignified river of grief to the old Jewish cemetery dating from the tenth century. There, my grandfather was laid to rest, surrounded by ancient tombstones, testaments to the Jewish community's continuance and prosperity in Poland. For centuries the Jewish people had been persecuted and exiled from kingdom to kingdom until finally they had found a safe haven, given asylum by a benevolent Polish king.

My grief is an empty void within me and now I have driven away the ghost of my zaida. Turning from the window, I wonder if he will ever return to my dreams.

I hear my grandmother call from the next room, "*Dinale, kym a wek fin fencter est za speit ci gain ci shuleh.*" ("Dina, get away from the window, you are going to be late for school.") I hurry into the spacious kitchen and grab my grandmother from behind, squeezing and kissing her firmly on the cheek, "Good morning, Bubysy, it's the most beautiful day!"

"Good morning, Maidele, come and eat your breakfast. Did you sleep well?"

"No, I tossed and turned, from strange dreams, I guess."

"What dreams, tell me about them maybe we can make sense of them? They say that dreams are a premonition of what the future holds."

"Don't worry, Bubysy. They can't be very important because I can't remember what they were." How could I tell my grandmother I had spent the night wrestling with the ghost of her dead husband? She would attach all kinds of superstitious meaning to my visions.

"I am sorry you didn't sleep well, sweetheart, but at least today is Friday and you can sleep late tomorrow."

Nodding, I give her a reassuring smile. I do not like to upset this sweet woman whose life is solely dedicated to her children and grandchildren. My grandmother lives with us, as had my grandfather before his death at age 72. The two had made an incongruous couple, visually at least. He was a strapping giant of a man well over six feet and she a tiny bit of a woman barely reaching his chest. Spending time with my grandfather had been my greatest joy. Perhaps a bit jealous, my grandmother sometimes felt I occupied a little too much of his time and she would banish me outside when I was overtiring him. Several years before, in a moment of childhood frustration, I had retaliated and struck back at her. Resentful of being cast off from his lap and forced outside to play, I had pushed my grandmother and she had lost her balance, falling down the stairs in front of our building. Fortunately, she was only bruised and not harmed, but I had received a severe punishment and was not allowed to play outside for a week. My father, who never spoke above a whisper, was furious with me, banishing me to my room until my grandmother was well enough to get out of bed. My grandfather, who always sided with his beloved granddaughter, forgave me without reservation, sneaking into my room to keep me company, his pockets laden with forbidden treats. The incident had filled me with a well-deserved sense of guilt. I was especially obedient and loving of my grandmother thereafter.

Snatching a freshly baked roll from the basket, I sit down at the table next to my younger brother Abek, tousling his tight blond curls.

He brushes my hand away from his hair. "Mamashy says you have to take me with you and Fela when you go to the movies tomorrow."

"There is no way that you are coming, Abek! Fela and I have been planning this for weeks and we don't need you to ruin our day."

"You have to take me. Mamashy said so!"

"We'll see about that!"

Abek looks pleadingly to Bubysy for her intervention.

"Dina, don't torture your brother." Grandmother places a bowl of fresh blueberries and cream in front of me and I begin to eat. Kissing Abek's forehead, she continues, "If your mother says Abek can go, than he will go." She smiles at Abek, smoothing his curls, "That is enough arguing for one morning. Now eat your breakfast *kindele*[3] and off you go to school."

The effort to define my place in my family is a constant dilemma for me. I crave confirmation of my uniqueness as the middle child. My first-born sister, who is sixteen, is clearly the standard against which all comparisons are made, both in intellect and beauty. My younger brother of seven holds the lofty position of being the long awaited son and baby everyone dotes on. At ten, who am I next to these two bright planets in the universe? Sighing, I resign myself to the inevitable intrusion of my brother on my weekend plans. Bounding from the chair, I grab my book bag.

---

3 Children, Yiddish

My grandmother kisses and hugs me, her last words dissolving in the air as I dash through the door.

"Remember Dina, straight home after school—it is Shabbat and your parents will be home early."

As I run down the stairs, I think of my mother and father who had left in the early hours of morning to open our butcher shop on Rynek 13, a few blocks from our home. I pictured my mother sweeping the front steps of our store, greeting the passersby on the street. Always cheerful, smiling, and welcoming, my mother has a devoted following of customers in the gentile community and is admired as a successful businesswoman in the Jewish community. In Poland, it is unusual for a woman to work, but my mother loves the independence that working affords her. Maintaining a home is a huge job in itself, but mama prides herself on perfectly balancing her family and working life. In their large store, the tiles scrubbed to a dazzling sheen, my parents work side-by-side providing for their many customers.

The morning light half blinds me with its brilliance as I walk from the cover of our courtyard into the busy Friday pedestrian traffic. My neighbor and girlfriend, Fela, waits for me on the street. "*Dzien dobry*[4] Fela, sorry I'm late, were you waiting long?" Smiling, Fela raises her thick brown brows and questions, "*Nu*? So, what's up?" Fela had an uncanny ability to read my moods.

I shudder remembering the ghostly specter of my grandfather, "I had a dream last night that was so real; my zaida came to me and I sent him away. I can't get it out of my mind, I feel sick about it. Do you think he will ever come to me in a dream again?"

"You are a goose. Why did you send him away?"

Turning and walking toward school, we cut through the slower moving people on the street.

"I was frightened; I'm not used to being visited by ghosts. He just stood at the foot of my bed glowing... trying to tell me

4 Good morning, Polish

something. I don't know why I sent him away. I should have welcomed him instead of shooing him away. Why do you think he came to me?"

"He probably misses you as much as you miss him. Besides, it was a dream. Your grandfather loved you so much; even his ghost would forgive you anything." She takes my hand and gives a reassuring squeeze. "He'll be back, don't worry. Just don't tell him to go away next time." We walk in silence as I contemplate my doubts.

Changing the subject, anxiety grips Fela's voice. "I wish it was only ghosts that I am afraid of. Day and night, all my parents talk about is Hitler. 'Hitler's henchmen are beating the Jews.' 'Hitler's henchmen are seizing Jewish businesses.' It is like a broken record with a needle stuck. All I hear, day and night, is the name Hitler!"

"I know, it's horrible. My parents talk of nothing else but what Hitler is doing to the poor Jews of Germany and Austria. Every night they sit by the radio listening to him scream his hatred for the Jews. Tata says that he is afraid the Germans want Poland."

Fela nods, her face a mask of foreboding. "I know. Ever since *Krystallnacht*, it has gotten much worse. Do you think the Germans will try to take Poland?"

I reply in a low voice, "I hope not, but Tata says that nothing can stop them if they attack us."

The unforeseeable future shadows our steps as we walk in the dazzling sunlight, a sharp contrast to our worries. Fela and I know more about the current situation of the world than either of us would like. It is hard to ignore the constant barrage of bad news that swirls about us. A gloom settles over our conversation as we arrive at school.

Waiting for my teacher, Mrs. Felzenszwalbe, to arrive, I am consumed by the unusual dream of my grandfather. How I missed the man who had paved the way for the good life that my family enjoyed. My grandfather's struggles as a young man making his way in the world, like so many Jews of his time, is a study in hard work and industriousness. Traveling and developing a relationship with distant farmers, he began importing cattle from Russia and selling them in Radom. He achieved early success and was well respected in the community. A short time before his death, I was allowed to accompany him to the livestock market where he purchased beef at the large outdoor marketplace. My grandfather had suffered a wound in his heel that turned to gangrene. Unfortunately, the doctors were not able to save his leg and it had been amputated below the knee. Consequently, he walked with the aid of crutches. I attended him on this trip to carry his briefcase. I could not have been more delighted; it was a special honor to be chosen from his many grandchildren to accompany him. It was an adventure into worlds unknown, to observe the sights and smells of the marketplace. The grainy smell of hay and even the pungent aroma of cow manure combined with the earthy smells of the farmers and throngs of people created a heady mixture for a sheltered child. The Polish farmers had come from their surrounding farms to town with their cattle, calves, and other livestock. The large outdoor emporium was crowded with people. Varied languages filled the air, as vendors and buyers tried to outdo each other and obtain the best possible price. Their hands gesticulated and their voices rose to be heard above the din of the crowd. My grandfather walked among the stalls, stately and dignified, greeting the farmers who vied for his attention. As we ambled through the crowd, he eyed the animals, stopping now and then to examine the eyes and mouth of a healthy looking beast. Finally, having found a cow that met his expectations, he engaged in a lively exchange. After a minute or two of haggling, he walked away saying over his shoulder, "Too much money! Come, Dynka." I had run behind him trying to keep up.

"Zaida, are you angry? Wait for me!"

Slowing his pace, he patted me lovingly on the cheek, "No, Dinale, I'm not angry. It is the nature of trade, the way business is done. Commerce is like a game, where you have to anticipate your partner's next move. Like in chess, each person tries to outwit the other. Now stay close to me. I don't want to lose you in this crowd."

As we moved away from the farmer's stand, I heard him call behind us.

"Pan Frydman, Pan Frydman, please sir, come back!"

The farmer, sensing failure and the possible loss of a sale, came running after my grandfather, his arms waving, calling him back to his stall. After several minutes of fierce negotiations, they both smiled and shook hands, finalizing the bargain. We purchased the cow whose fate was sealed on its journey from farm to market. Several times that day, I witnessed the ritual of market etiquette and the game of commerce engaged in by two willing partners of buy and sell.

As I daydream of my grandfather, the rising volume of my classmates beckons me back to the present. Hitler. Czecho-Slovakia. Poland. Invasion. The words of war flutter around me like leaves falling from a tree in a winter's wind. None of us has ever experienced war first hand, but our parents' growing fears are alive within us. We are keenly aware of the danger facing all of Europe from Germany's aggression; it is a daily discussion taking place in every home across the continent.

Mrs. Felzenszwalbe enters the classroom and the childlike exuberance of our voices fades to whispers.

"Good morning Pani Felzenszwalbe."

"Good morning children. Please take out your math notebooks to begin today's lesson."

Happy to focus my mind on something other than my fears, I open my book and the thoughts of war recede into the background.

Mrs. Felzenszwalbe controls her classroom with a strict manner and a warm smile. Her deep blue eyes reflect the intellect of a probing mind and a life spent educating children. Her students respect and adore her, making for few behavior problems among us.

Adjusting her glasses, she sets about the morning session of mathematics and we begin our calculations in our notebooks. All thoughts of the belligerent nation of Germany are forgotten. The Jewish and Polish communities in Poland live in segregation, as encouraged by church and state. Excluding business relationships, our daily contact with the Christian community is minimal. My friends and my parents' friends are Jewish. However, my mother enjoys close professional ties within the Christian community as she deals exclusively with non-Jews at our butcher store. The students at my school are Jewish, but the curriculum is Polish, designed to meet the standards of every other public school.

I love school and try hard not to fall short of my sister's performance, as she left a good impression on Mrs. Felzenszwalbe. On my first day of school, to my dismay, she singled me out and asked, "Dina Frydman, is Nadja Frydman your sister?"

Embarrassed as all of the students had turned to scrutinize me, I stammered, "Yes, Pani Felzenszwalbe, she is."

"If you do as well as your sister, I will be very happy with you." Angrily I had complained to my mother how it wasn't fair that I should be compared to Nadja in front of the whole class. But Mrs. Felzenszwalbe, like the best of her profession, soon inspired me, opening new vistas of thought and reasoning. I studied diligently to gain her approval.

After school, Fela and I make our way through our neighborhood. The shopkeepers are closing their stores and hurrying home to celebrate Shabbos. Peacefulness descends upon the streets and the sweet perfume of freshly baked *challah*[5] and the fragrance of stewing meats and ground spices permeate the air. It is hard not to be caught up in the holiday magic of Shabbat. The turbulent storms of the world seem hard to imagine amid all the normalcy of everyday life and simple routine as our neighborhood prepares to greet the Sabbath Queen.

Fela and I stop to pick up my brother from his *cheder*[6] after school. The young boys emerging from the red brick building are loud and boisterous. My brother's enthusiastic greeting enfolds us as he spots Fela and me in the crowd of parents and siblings. "*Shabbat Shalom,* Dina! *Shabbat Shalom,* Fela!"

"*Shabbat Shalom,* Abek," I take his hand and we begin the walk home. "How was school today, Abek?"

"It was great. The Rabbis are teaching us the story of the golden calf. Remember when Moses went to Mount Sinai and God gave him the Ten Commandments and when he returned, the people had melted all of their jewelry and molded it into an idol of a calf? The Jews were dancing around worshiping the golden calf as if it were a god."

"Yes, silly, of course we know the story of Moses."

"The Rabbis said that for forty days Moses prayed and begged God's forgiveness until finally on Yom Kippur[7] God relented and forgave the people for worshipping a false god. God then commanded Moses to have the faithless Jews melt the golden calf and remake it into a golden tabernacle so that he could dwell among his people. He forgave the fickle Jews and showed them that their God was merciful. He also promised the Jewish

5 Traditional woven egg bread, Yiddish

6 Private religious school for Jewish boys, Yiddish

7 Sacred High Holiday for the Day of Atonement

people that he would dwell among them and return them to the land of Israel where they would live forever in the land of milk and honey. I told the Rabbi that maybe it is time for the Jewish people to go back to the Promised Land. Maybe that is why the Nazis have gained power. Maybe they are a sign from God that it is time for the Jewish people to go home."

"Your teacher must have been stunned, Abek," says Fela.

"Yes, so what did the Rabbi say?"

Abek stops walking and assumes the Rabbi's posture of contemplation, "He scratched his beard and rolled his eyes as he pondered what I said. Then he said he would have to think about my theory over the weekend and discuss it with the other Rabbis. He proposed that we continue our discussion on Monday. He also added that it was an interesting way of looking at the Nazi threat." Abek's face lights up in a proud grin.

"Yes, well, you certainly gave those Rabbis something to think about." I can't help but be impressed with my brother's reasoning. "We all know how smart you are. In fact, you are so smart, I have decided you can come to the movies with Fela and me tomorrow."

"I can? I can? Oh thank you, thank you Dina!" His small hand presses mine in gratitude and I am reminded of how young my brother really is.

"Please stop fussing, Abek, before I change my mind."

"I promise I will behave Dina. I promise I won't talk during the movie."

"You'd better not talk or I will never take you to the movies again!" I try to mask my amusement and portray a stern demeanor, but I cannot help but love my little brother whose birth has been such a godsend. Childbirth is dangerous and my mother had suffered several miscarriages between my sister and me and again between Abek and me. His birth has insured that the Frydman name will continue. My father has three sisters and all of their children carry their husbands' names. My sister and I are Frydmans only until we marry.

Abek, beams with pleasure, his crown of curls bouncing as he runs ahead. I smile as I ponder the future: my brother and his sons will carry on the Frydman name forever.

Chapter 2

Welcome to the Sabbath Queen

Arriving at the courtyard of our building, I inhale the many aromas of holiday cooking. The delicious scents waft through the air from the apartments, each competing for prominence.

"Please tell your parents *Shabbat Shalom*," I say as I hug Fela.

"*Shabbat Shalom*, Fela," Abek yells, bounding up the stairs as he waves good-bye.

"*Shabbat Shalom*. Abek, see you tomorrow!" Fela calls to the place from which my brother has disappeared.

"I'll meet you in the morning at nine and we can go to the apple orchard, okay?" I say, following Abek up the stairs.

"Nine is good." She waves and is gone.

Entering my home, I am greeted by the flavorful fragrance of holiday cooking, sending pangs of hunger to my stomach. My mother stands at the stove, busily preparing our Sabbath meal. The kitchen is warm and my mother's cheeks are flushed from her efforts. She bends to enfold me in the warmth of her arms as

I kiss her, inhaling the sweet perfume that lingers in her hair and neck. Rising to her full height, Mama is an unusually statuesque woman who stands several inches taller than her husband. Her hair is black as a raven's wings and her eyes are washed pale as a sapphire sea. Solid and steadfast, the force of her nature is obvious—like a tigress, she protects her family.

Mamashy's childhood had been cut short and through no circumstances of her own, she was forced into adulthood. Mama came from a small city called Brzeziny in western Poland. It was not far from Poland's second largest city, Lodz. Brzeziny is a rural farming area with a large population of ethnic Germans. Her father, a butcher by trade, had begun to go blind when Temcia, my mother, was a teen. In a desperate effort to forestall the inevitable, my mother took my grandfather to Berlin to one of the leading eye specialists in Europe. In those days, it was a major endeavor to travel and required the proper travel documents. Permission to leave and to return entailed a tedious process of bureaucratic red tape. Relations between Poland and Germany were strained as always and even traveling by train was a major bother. The expense, of course, was high, but anything to save my grandfather's vision was worth the effort. Sadly, it was all for naught. The prognosis was grim but definite. The doctors could do nothing to save his eyes. A short time later, he went blind and my mother was forced to become a breadwinner for the family.

Her perfect German, spoken without an accent, served her well. Entrepreneurial and of financial necessity, she developed her own little business. She traveled to the farmers on the outskirts of Brzeziny, speaking her perfect German or Polish and taking their orders for specialty items they could not resist. She saved them the time and effort of traveling to the city to shop, freeing them from a lost day of work on the farm. The *Volks-Deutshe*[8] looked forward to my mother's visits, for she always

8 Ethnic Germans

brought them little gifts of sweets. As she bicycled up the road to their farms, the children would run to greet her in anticipation of the goodies in her basket. Later, she would return with a team of horses, driving a wagon laden with the farmers' goods.

I picture my fearless mother with her hair blowing in the wind as she flew across the country roads in her wagon, her hands firmly grasping the reins. Like a heroine in a movie, she stepped outside the acceptable bounds for a woman at that time. Creating a business of convenience for the farmers, she garnered a small profit and contributed to her family's survival. My mother's earnings and her older married sisters' contributions assured that my grandparents were secure financially. Even now, my mother and her five sisters send a monthly stipend to their elderly parents in Brzeziny.

Always hungry for my mother's attention, I never miss an opportunity to spend time alone with her. "Mamashy, tell me again the story of how you and Tata met."

"Dina, I have told you this story a thousand times," she laughs.

"I know, but please Mamashy, please tell me one more time."

Smiling, she sets aside her spoon to tell me once more what I love to hear, "Well, one day a *szatchin*[9] came into your grandfather's store telling him she had the perfect girl for your father. Your grandfather called your father over and the matchmaker repeated her praise of me, the wonderful Temcia Topolevich. Your father asked sarcastically, 'and where does this most perfect of females live?' The matchmaker answered, 'Not far at all, in Brzeziny.' Laughing, your father asked, 'Why do I have to go all the way to Brzeziny to find a bride? Aren't there any girls in Radom that are good enough?' The matchmaker shrugged her shoulders and said, 'Trust me Joel; would I send you to Brzeziny if I didn't think that this Temcia was the perfect girl for you? I have looked high and low for a girl to fulfill your and your

9 Matchmaker, Yiddish

parents' desires. I have found you a diamond; do you want I should let you settle for a dull stone? It is your parents' wish that you should meet the right girl and marry. What can I do if this girl happens to live in Brzeziny?' With this your grandfather interjected, 'What is the big deal? We take a bus ride to Brzeziny, take a walk in the park. You pass each other on the path, take a good look… nod hello… smile, and you either decide to meet formally or we go home. Not such a big investment.' Your father reluctantly agreed and the anticipated day arrived. It was a beautiful spring afternoon; the roses were bursting from their buds and the fragrant petals lay strewn across the pebbled path, the gentle breeze lifting them on the air until they floated down like feathers, dotting the emerald grass. I wore a stylish blue lace dress the color of my eyes and I carried a matching parasol that I twirled in the sunlight. At the pre-arranged time, your grandfather and father walked toward me. Your father wore a beige suit with a red tie and a brown fedora that accentuated his brown eyes. He looked so handsome. We acknowledged each other with a nod and smile as we passed. Your father turned around and called out to me, halting my progress, 'Miss Topolevich, would you do me the honor of walking with me?' We strolled down the garden path, your father and grandfather on either side of me. Of course, your father fell head over heels in love with me the second he saw me. I thought he had the kindest of eyes. Seeing the immediate connection between your father and me, your grandfather urged us to walk ahead alone while he sat and watched the chess players that gathered in the park on Sundays. We walked together quietly for a time, both of us shyly eyeing the other. I will never forget how nervous we both were, but everything about your father pleased me and I felt myself falling in love with him. We sat on a park bench enjoying the quiet of each other's company. Then he took my hand in his and suddenly the words began to flow between us, as natural as a river journeying to the sea. We shared so many common values and dreams. We knew we could build a good life together. Within a few days, your father and his parents returned to Brzeziny so the Frydman and Topolevich families could meet and the marriage could be formally arranged. We were engaged, our pictures taken, and the wedding was planned. The matchmaker had done her job well and earned her commission. Ever since then, our marriage has been blessed with mutual respect and admiration. Of course, the greatest confirmation of our love was the birth of our three beautiful children."

It is no wonder that my father fell madly in love with this self-sufficient, proud young woman when first he set eyes upon her. My mother fills the room with her presence. She is known for her beauty and intelligence. Her clever business sense adds greatly to her in-laws' and her husband's successful business; but it is her laughter, a rich contralto of vibrant tones, that fills our home with magic. Like the beautiful operas she favors and plays on our phonograph, our home resounds with harmony and music. Mama is the perfect counterpart to my more serious and studious father. In an unusual example of equality in the home, my parents are partners in every facet of life.

"Oh Mama, I love the story of your courtship with Tata."

The *lokshin*[10] coming to a boil rouses her from her reminiscence, "Yes, it is a lovely romantic tale. One day you too will fall in love with a handsome young man and have beautiful children and I will have the pleasure of being a doting grandmother. Now Dinale, enough tales of the ancient past, please hurry and tidy yourself for dinner so you can help me." With a nostalgic sigh, she picks up her spoon, continuing with the preparation of our meal, "Now go, shoo!"

10 Fine egg noodles, Yiddish

"Yes, Mamashy." Always obedient to my mother, I rush to ready myself for dinner.

In the dining room, my grandmother is busy filling a cut crystal carafe with wine the color of claret. Wrapping my arms around her, I kiss her on her cheek, "*Shabbat Shalom*, Bubysy."

"Dinale, my darling maidele, *Shabbat Shalom*, how was your day?"

"Fine, Pani Felzenszwalbe was strict as ever, but I got an A on my math quiz."

"Good for you. Your Tatashi will be so proud. Be sure you tell him about your accomplishment at dinner."

"I will. Fela and I walked home together and we can't wait to go to the movies tomorrow with Nadja. I know you are right, Bubysy, about taking Abek. I told him he could come with Fela and me."

"Your brother ran in the house to tell me. I'm so proud of you. You have one brother and it is only right that you should behave properly toward him and include him. Now hurry and get dressed. Your father will be home soon."

Dina's parents' engagement photograph. Standing from the left, Dina's mother Temcia is resting her arms on Joel's shoulders. Dina's Uncle Alexander and Aunt Nachele are standing, and her grandfather Jekiel is seated. The photo had been sent to America to Jekiel's brother who had immigrated.

Looking around the spacious dining room, I linger looking at the Sabbath table dressed in white linen and finery. My sister set the table and it glitters with its abundance of Hungarian porcelain and silver. Two large heavy silver candlesticks stand gleaming, ready for sundown and the blessing that signals the beginning of the family meal. My father will soon return from *shul*[11] where he was welcoming the Sabbath Queen with prayer and thanking God for his blessings.

In our bedroom, my sister is sprawled on the bed, her head buried in a book. Without looking up, she asks, "How was school?"

I plop down beside her. "School's fine, I got an A on my math quiz."

Smiling, her eyes still glued to the page, "Good for you Dina."

11 Synagogue, Yiddish

"What are you reading?"

"A speech Jabotinsky gave last year. He wrote it especially to rally the Jews of Poland. To warn us of the approaching evil and to beg us to get out of Europe before it is too late."

"What does it say? Read it to me."

"If I read it to you, Tata will be so angry at me. He will say that you are too young to have such worries."

"You have to read it to me; I promise I won't tell Tata. Please, Nadja, please read it to me."

"Oh, all right, but you had better not tell Tata." "I promise I won't."

Snuggling close to my sister, I listen as she reads, "... it is already three years that I am calling upon you, Polish Jewry, who are the crown of world Jewry. I continue to warn you incessantly that a catastrophe is coming closer. I became gray and old in these years, my heart bleeds, that you, dear brothers and sisters, do not see the volcano that will soon begin to spit its all-consuming lava. I know that you are not seeing this because you are immersed in your daily worries. Today, however, I demand your trust. You were convinced already that my prognoses have already proven to be right. If you think differently, then drive me out from your midst. However, if you do believe me, then listen to me in this eleventh hour: In the name of God, let any one of you save himself as long as there is still time. And time there is very little."

She closes the book, her brows furrow with worry as she sees the dejection on my face. "I told you that you were too young to hear this, I shouldn't have read it to you."

"What does it mean, Nadja?"

"It means that we should leave Europe and end the Diaspora. It means that we should return to our homeland in Palestyne."

I look at the face that perfectly reflects my own. The wide set indigo eyes so like my mother's and the fair hair of my father.

"It's so weird, but Abek told the Rabbi at his school the same thing. He asked the Rabbi if maybe the Nazis weren't a sign from God for the Jews to go home to Palestyne."

My sister's eyes appraise me as she considers my revelation, "Abek is a smart little boy. Come, we had better get ready for Shabbat. Tata will be home soon." Lovingly, she touches the dimple in my chin, an inheritance the three of us share from our father. The Frydman chin, an identifying feature every Frydman possesses, the gene passes down from father to son and daughter alike. Throughout the generations, it never fails to appear.

My sister stands and looks in the mirror, smoothing her wavy blond hair and straightening her dress that clings to her developing body. Standing beside her, I reflect on our faces, so much alike, yet so different. My chubby cheeks and curveless body are clearly the reflection of a ten-year-old child of innocence.

Looking at my beautiful sister in the mirror, I wonder if I will ever blossom into such a beauty. She is popular with her many friends who congregate in our home on the weekends to listen to records and dance. My relationship with my sister is a typical love-hate sibling rivalry. She loves me, but I seem to be a terrible nuisance. Six years separate our births, yet we share a room and a bed. She yearns for privacy, but I impose myself on her and her friends. Once I had intruded on a soiree and even dared to ask one of her boyfriends to dance. The young man, not wanting to offend, had complied. I was ecstatic as we turned about the room dancing and I pretended not to see the murder in my sister's eyes. She was smoldering with rage as I danced with her boyfriend, who towered above me. Finally, unable to bear another minute, she ran from the room and complained to our mother. To my chagrin, I was removed from the room, the door shut in my face.

On Shabbat there is peace between us and together we approach the kitchen as my father returns from shul.

"*Shabbat Shalom,* Tata." Running to my adored father, I wrap my arms around him and look up at his beaming face; his warm brown eyes alight with pleasure.

Hugging and kissing the top of my head, he asks, "Dinale, *Shabbat Shalom,* my darling daughter. How was your day at school? Did Pani Felzenszwalbe reveal to you the secrets of the universe?"

"No, but I got an A on my math quiz."

"Such a smart girl, I am truly a lucky man to have three brilliant children."

Tata pauses and sighs, his expressive eyes lined with darkness and worry.

"Tata, you look so tired."

"I'm fine; it is the world that is not. Come, let us pray to God and celebrate Shabbat."

Taking our places around the beautiful table, we wait for my father to be seated. Our family eats dinner together every evening, but Shabbos is especially meaningful and ritualistic. My mother stands to bless and light the candles, her head covered with a beautiful turquoise silk scarf. She covers her face with her hands and sweetly sings the *benchet Lecht.*[12] Then my father blesses the wine and we all take a small sip. His baritone voice resonates as he blesses the challah. He closes his eyes and prays for our greatest wish—peace. "Amen," we murmur in unison as he breaks off pieces of challah and passes a piece to each of us. As is his custom, my father opens to a page of the *Tanach*[13] and reads to us a short story from the Bible. It is comforting to think that in every Jewish home, these ancient traditions and prayers are taking place at the same time. I picture a million prayers tak-

---

12 Blessing over the candles.

13 Sacred book of Judaism consisting of the Torah, Prophets, and Hagiographa.

ing wing and ascending, the holy letters floating through the ethereal mists to the heavenly throne of God.

With the scent of my mother's cooking drifting through the house to tempt us, my sister and I rise to help carry the first course to table. To begin, my sister carries the whole carp, cut into separate servings. My mother has simmered the fish in a broth of carrots and onions and it steams with a sweet fragrance as she serves each of us. During the fish course, the conversation is kept to a minimum while we carefully dissect the fish from the bones in our mouths. From the age of three, we had been taught how to carefully bone our fish. Yet each of us has experienced the horror of a bone getting caught in our throat and having to be saved by a chunk of challah and a firm pat on the back.

Masada Jabotinsky Club, 1939. Dina's sister Nadja is seated third from left. On the night of the deportation to Treblinka, Nadja's boyfriend ran into her home in the ghetto and rescued the photograph, which he carried for the duration of the war.

Having survived the fish course and its obstacle of small bones, we resume the conversation in earnest.

"Nadja," my father asks, "What do your friends at Club Masada Jabotinsky say about the impending threat of Hitler and the Nazis?"

"We are greatly worried, Tata, and believe that the only future for the Jewish people is in the land of Palestyne. Many members from other groups have already left for the Promised Land to work on a *kibbutz.*[14] Tata, I would very much like to make *aliyah.*[15] I could pave the way for all of us to immigrate. All I need is your blessing."

"Joel, I will not lose my eldest child," my mother interjects. "Not with the Nazis nearly at our back door. We must remain united as a family and face the coming days together. Besides, Nadja is an exceptional student and we have always considered her a perfect candidate for university. Her teachers all say she should study here in Radom and then go to university in Warszaw. Who knows? Perhaps she might even study in Switzerland. Joel, you and I have always shared that dream for her."

My father sighs, the lines deepening in his face, "Temcia, please, I have no intention of separating the family at this precarious moment and sending our teenage daughter to an uncertain future in Palestyne. It is out of the question; however, I understand her feelings and respect her right to express them."

"But Tata, you yourself once dreamed of leaving Poland and immigrating to America," my sister pleads. Nadja and her friends, all members of a club that encourages immigration to Palestyne, believe the future of the Jewish people lies only in Palestyne. For her, "next year in Jerusalem" is not just a prayer recited in the Exodus, but her dream and mantra.

---

14 Cooperative village or community in Israel where all property is collectively owned and work is organized on a collective basis.

15 When a Jew returns to live in the land of Irael/Palestine.

My father exhales, pausing, his eyes focusing on the distant memories of his youth. "Yes, it is true that I once dreamed of leaving," he hesitates, "but it was not to be. Remember Mama?" He turns to his mother, drawing her into a shared remembrance. "Remember, when I tried to convince father to let me go? He said it would kill him to lose his only son and he was too old to start again in a new land. He had built a good life for us in Poland and in the end, his argument prevailed. I couldn't bear the thought of leaving you. Since I couldn't convince you to abandon your life in Radom, I remained. I have never regretted that decision until the rise of Hitler and his cronies. When I read his manifesto in *Mein Kampf* it was clear that Hitler's insanity toward the Jews is dangerous. I never dreamed he would rise to power in the sophisticated intellectual climate of Germany. Krystallnacht—the Night of Broken Glass—shattered the lives of German Jews and any illusions I had. Perhaps I should have stood up to father and left."

We are all reduced to silence by my father's unusual confession. My brother breaks the spell, "But Tata, if you didn't stay in Poland, you wouldn't have met Mamashy and we wouldn't have been born!"

My father's eyes clear as he returns to the present. Patting his precocious son on the head, he exclaims, "You are right, Abek. Where would I be without my three musketeers?"

My grandmother seizes the opportunity of renewed levity.

"Joel, you read too much. It cannot help to read about every atrocity committed by the anti-Semites. What kind of conversation is this for the Shabbat table?"

My father is a keen follower of current events and reads several newspapers in German, Polish, and Yiddish every day. The stress of the Nazis' rise to power has taken a terrible toll on him. Over the years, he has followed Hitler's steady rise and grab for power in Germany, often complaining to his friends of the threat. These same friends would look at him as if he were crazy, "Joel, stop worrying, what is happening in Germany is not going to happen here in Poland." Now, of course, that danger is clear and threatening.

"Mama, this is a far worse threat than some random pogrom. The Nazi threat could affect the safety of every Jew in the world. It is important that the children understand what we are facing, regardless of their ages."

"Son, calm yourself, it will do no good for you to make yourself ill."

"Mama, I'm perfectly calm. Please don't worry." My father's voice rises in frustration. "Nadja deserves to voice her views and I want to encourage her quest for knowledge."

My grandmother worries greatly about my father since his heart attack of last year. She and my mother had vigilantly cared for him. Sometimes my grandmother reminds me of a witch-doctor. Her knowledge of herbs and their medicinal attributes seems more effective in its cure than the doctors and their medicines. Often, I accompany her into the countryside, following her with a basket that she fills with wild herbs of anise, arnica, basil, chamomile, cloves, fennel, laurel, mint, mustard, sage, and wild beet, each with its own particular medicinal properties and application. Once home, she grinds, dries, or cooks the stems and flowers, producing pungent odors throughout the house. These ancient remedies, passed down from generation to generation, become mysterious poultices or syrups that have the benefit of curing whatever wound, ache or illness suffered. Unfortunately, sometimes the noxious cure is worse than the ailment.

None of us could forget when my father was confined to bed and my grandmother had suggested that the cure for his heart problems entailed my father drinking a particularly vile concoction mixed with his own urine. My mother and grandmother argued for days over that idea. Finally, after a particularly heated discussion, my grandmother prevailed. They were unaware that I was listening from my favorite place to spy on adult conversation, under the table in the kitchen. Imagine my mother's surprise when her youngest daughter piped in, "I'll never do this; don't you ever try this on me. I would rather die than drink urine!"

Their argument forgotten, my mother and grandmother broke into uproarious laughter, clutching each other. My mother tried to regain her composure to discipline me. "Dina, come out from under the table. You are such a busybody. My goodness, no one is going to make you drink any *pish*!"[16]

The more I listen to my sister's arguments, the more my own desire to leave Europe is fired up. "Tata, I too want to live in Palestyne. What if I went with Nadja? Then she wouldn't be alone."

"Me too," interrupts Abek, "I want to go, too!"

I glare at my impudent brother. "Abek, you are just a baby. You couldn't live a day without Mamashy."

"It's not true," my brother whines, "Tata, tell her that it's not true."

"Dina, stop teasing your brother, I want this conversation to end *now*," my mother warns, with irritation in her voice.

My father smiles at his beloved son. "Abek, don't worry. Dina and Nadja are not going to leave you."

"Girls, come help me serve the rest of our dinner before it is ruined." My mother stands as she turned to us. "I will not have us arguing at the Shabbat table. It is disrespectful of God."

My grandmother, who wisely always sides with my mother, adds, "Joel, Temcia is right, the family must remain as one. Your dear father, blessed be his memory, would have insisted that we are stronger together than apart."

My mother rises and Nadja and I follow her into the kitchen. Returning to the dining room, my sister and I carry the white

16 Urine, Yiddish

china bowls rimmed with gold. We are careful not to spill the chicken soup swirling with delicate handmade noodles. We resume our seats and within moments, the aroma of chicken broth cleanses the room of negativity.

"Mamashy, it is your best soup ever," I compliment her with the enthusiastic concurrence of everyone at the table.

My mother blushes with pride, reminding me, "Dinale, you say that every time you eat my soup."

We all laugh at the truth of her observation and I smile in the glow of her approval. Finally, my mother and grandmother serve the braised brisket, surrounded by glazed baby new potatoes and honeyed carrots. It is a meal fit for a king and prepared with love. We sigh with communal satisfaction as our stomachs fill with the luscious food and fine wine.

My mother prides herself on her incredible cooking and baking skills. You can smell the sweet aroma of sugar baking from a block away and my friends are always begging to sample the fruits of her oven. Once a week, she bakes challahs, rolls, cakes, and cookies for the week ahead. The cakes are laden with fruit and the cookies dripping with sugar.

Tonight, honeyed cake and tea from a silver samovar grace the table. Again, a sigh of satisfaction arises from each of us as we finish the meal, leaving not a crumb on our plates. My favorite part of Shabbat is when we sing in Yiddish, Polish, or Hebrew. I close my eyes, trying to reach the high notes of tonight's song, *Beltz, Mayn Shtetele Beltz,* a popular song written by Jews who had immigrated to America.[17] Singing slightly off key, we do our best to maintain the melody, our bodies swaying in rhythm.

Azikh tu mir dermonen	So when I recall to myself
Mayne kindershe yorn,	my childhood years,

17 Written by Alexander Oshanetsky and Jacob Jacobs.

Punkt vi a kholem	just like a dream.
Zet dos mir oys	It seems to me
Vizet oys dos hayzele,	how does the little house look,
Vos hot amol geglantzt,	which used to sparkle with lights?
Tzi vakst nokh dos beymele,	Does the little tree grow still
Vos ikh hob farflantzt?	Which I planted long ago?

Rerfrain:	Refrain:
Oy, oy, oy Belts, mayn shtetele Belts,	Beltz, my little town of Beltz
Mayn heymele, vu ikh hob	The little house where
Mayne kindershe yorn farbrakht	I spent my childhood!
Belts, mayn shtetele Belts,	Beltz, my little town of Beltz
In ormen shtibele,	The poor little room,
Mit ale kinderlekh dort gelakht	Where I used to laugh with other children.
Oy, eden Shabes fleg ikh loyfn	Every Shabes I would run
Mit ale inglekh tzuglaykh	with all the other children
Tzu.zitzn unter dem grinem beymele,	to sit under a little green tree,
Leynen bay dem taikht	read by the river bank
Oy oy oy Belts,	Oh oh oh Beltz
Mayn shtetele Belts,	My little town of Beltz
Mayn heymele, vu kh'hob gehat	My little home where I had
Di sheyne khaloymes a sakh	So many fine dreams.
Dos shtibl is alt,	The little house is old
Bavaksn mit mokh	overgrown with moss
Dos shtibl is alt,	the little house is old
In fentzter keyn gloz	no glass in the windows

Dos shtibl is alt,	the little house is old
Tzeboygn di vent,	the walls are bent
Ikh volt shoyn zikher	I would surely
Dos vider nit derkent	not recognize it again

Once we exhaust our repertoire of songs, we are whisked from the table to prepare for bed. My mother, sister, and grandmother remain to clear the table and restore the kitchen to orderliness. My brother and I brush our teeth and wait for my parents and grandmother to come and kiss us goodnight. Once the comforting rituals and kisses are complete, my brother, who sleeps in my parents' room, is asleep in minutes, while I lie listening to the muted conversations that drift from the kitchen. Beneath my snowy down comforter, I try to fight off sleep, waiting for my sister to join me. Finally, I feel her slip beneath the covers. Turning to cuddle with her and warm her feet, I beg forgiveness for whatever transgression I might have committed recently and she lovingly forgives me with a hug.

"Nadja, I whisper, "Do you think the Germans are going to attack Poland?"

My sister sighs snuggling closer. "I'm not sure; maybe they are just rattling their swords to scare us. If they do attack, it won't be good for any of us. Maybe, just maybe, if they do invade, the rest of the world will denounce them and declare war on them. If we're lucky, we can survive their domination until we are liberated by the democracies that are sure to come to our rescue."

I yawn and my eyes grow heavy. "I hope you are right, I don't want our world to change." Seeking the comfort and safe harbor of my sagacious sister, I nestle in her arms and nod off to a peaceful sleep.

In the morning, I jump from bed, disturbing my sister's peaceful slumber. "Dina, stop with the jumping, I'm trying to sleep."

"It's Saturday, Nadja. Get up, sleepyhead. It's a beautiful day, the sun is shining, the birds are singing, and we are free to do whatever we want." I giggle as I throw a pillow at her.

"Go away!" She buries her head beneath the covers as I race to get dressed, eager to meet Fela in the courtyard. Saturdays are carefree days for us to play as children. Fela and I planned a morning walk to the apple orchard behind our building.

As promised, Fela is waiting for me downstairs. Walking arm in arm through the courtyard, we make our way onto the sidewalk, my eyes adjusting to the light. The shops are closed for Shabbat, but the streets are full of people walking to synagogue or en route to visit friends and family. Fela and I slip into the stream of passersby and make our way to the apple orchard. We love the orchard, with its massive trees laden with sweet fruit. The orchard is our secret haven where Fela and I give voice to our dreams.

We pick some apples and then sit down, planting our backs against a tree. The dappled morning light filtering through leaves dances around us in a rainbow of colors and shadows. Taking a bite from my apple, I wipe away the sweet juice that runs down my chin. "Mmm... these apples are so good," I say, wiping away the sugary liquid with the back of my hand.

"I know," says Fela. "I love this orchard. It's so peaceful. Sometimes I feel like there is no other world than this, our secret hideaway where nothing bad can happen. I feel the same way when we visit my grandparents' cherry orchard in the summer."

Laying my apple aside, I confide, "I can't wait to grow up and do whatever I please. I am definitely going to live in Palestyne. When Nadja goes, I will find a way to follow her, even if I have to run away. Last night, I told my father I want to go to Palestyne with Nadja. So, what do you think of that?"

Fela looks at me with the eyes of a sage. "You are dreaming. There is no way your parents will ever let you go. Ten year olds don't leave their families to go halfway across the world. You can tell your father anything you like, but there is no way he will ever let you go. I bet he said no to your sister and she is sixteen."

I sigh, nodding, knowing she is right. Why dream when the world is falling apart? As I fight the frustrations warring within me, I suggest, "Fela, let's make a pact between us, a sacred promise."

She looks at me, her eyes narrowing, a slight smile teasing the corners of her mouth. "What kind of promise?"

Jumping up, I pull her to her feet. I begin to dance around in circles, spinning her with me as I shout, "That we will be friends forever and that after the war, if there is a war, we will go and live in Palestyne, and we will pick olives and live on a kibbutz, and swim in the blue waters of the Mediterranean, and marry handsome boys with olive skin, and… oh, I don't know… we will just live and be happy!"

Fela and I spin around and around, the sound of our laughter filling the air with the delicate music of our youth. "Promise me, Fela, promise me!" The orchard is a dizzying blur of light and shadow flying around us as we spin faster and faster.

"I promise, I promise!" Fela shouts now infected with my enthusiasm. "We will be friends forever, and plow fields and plant crops, and marry farmers! Whatever you want—just stop spinning. I am getting so dizzy."

Our laughter echoes in the quiet of the orchard. I let go of her hands and we fall dizzily to the ground, my eyes to the sky, my heart pounding within my chest. The trees and sky spin around me out of control until my eyes adjust and slowly my balance returns. I cannot help but think that the world as we know it also is spinning out of control and silently I pray that it, too, will regain its balance.

We lie under the blossoming apple trees for an hour, eating apples and watching the clouds as they race across the August sky, content in each other's company. I jump up, offering Fela my hand and pull her to her feet. "Let's go, or we will be late for the movies and I better make sure that the nudge, Abek, is ready to go."

"I almost forgot about the movies," Fela says, brushing the dirt from her dress, "Abek's a good boy, I don't mind if he comes with us. We better hurry, though. I have to run home and get some *zlotys*."[18]

My sister has promised to take Fela and me to a movie, a special treat. I am madly in love with Shirley Temple and never miss one of her films. She is the biggest star in the world and all of her movies are subtitled so we can understand them. I, like millions of girls around the world, dream of being Shirley Temple, with her dancing ringlets and doll-like face. It is the perfect Saturday treat for us and it allows my parents to have some private time together, which they certainly deserve.

"I'll race you back," I challenge.

"Go!" Fela yells, as she takes off like the wind, her hair streaming behind her. Picking another apple, I run after her as fast as I can, knowing I can catch her.

The Little Princess is such a wonderful story about Sarah Crewe, a little girl who refuses to believe that her father has been killed in the Boer War. With courage and tenacity, she endures terrible hardships, determined to find her dear papa. A timely tale for all of us, it ends with her reunion with her father. Sarah's perseverance, her love and belief that she will find her papa, drives the story. Her ability to rise above and weather the obstacles in her path makes this film particularly poignant. A desirable escape from our world suffering through a depression and on the verge of war, the movie evokes strong emotions. Fela and I sniffle away. We are totally engrossed in the fairytale on the screen.

18 Polish currency

Even Abek manages to remain silent instead of voicing his usual observations throughout the film.

After the movie, my sister, brother, and I walk arm-in-arm to the ice cream store for a special indulgence, a delicious ice cream cone made with the freshest of cream. The ice cream store is filled with families and young adults enjoying the warm summer afternoon. Nadja leaves us sitting by ourselves with our cones at a small table while she says hello to her friends across the parlor. I scrutinize the behavior of the young adults and their flirtations. Fela asks, “Is that your sister’s boyfriend, Mikal?”

Licking my cone, I shrug my shoulders. “I think he is one of them. She has so many. All the boys seem to be in love with her.” Fela sighs. “It must be wonderful to be so beautiful and have so many admirers. Do you think we will ever be surrounded by handsome young men competing for our attention?”

“I don’t know about you,” I teased, “but I will have so many admirers that I will probably have to shake a stick at them to fend them off.”

“Oh Dina, you are such a silly goose. What do you think they are talking about?”

“Politics, of course. That’s all anyone ever talks about now.”

“What do you think the Nazis will do to us if they invade and take Poland?”

“I don’t know, but I hope they expel us. I hope they send us all to Palestyne. I don’t want to live where I am not wanted.” I am repeating the words I had heard so many times from my sister at the dinner table. I watch my sister, surrounded by the eager faces of her friends, all eyes glued to her and hanging on her every word.

Walking home, the serenity of Shabbat permeates the air, filling it with the golden radiance of the afternoon sun. I cannot help but feel hopeful that peace might yet be a possibility.

Back home, my parents announce we are taking a sunset walk in the park before we bid farewell to Shabbat and have dinner. My Aunt Mindale, her husband Tuvye, and my cousins Nadja and Majer are meeting us.

In that last flush of summer, my cousins and I trail the adults as they walk in the park, occasionally greeting neighbors and friends. I look up at the stately chestnut trees, their branches forming a canopy of shade. The path glows with flickering light that cascades down between the leaves, searching for a final resting place on the ground. The rose bushes burst with a profusion of pink, white, and red, scenting the air with their perfume. The park is filled with families escaping the confines of their homes and the barrage of bad news from their radios. Children dash about, their laughter resonating in the air. Here and there, I catch a word or two of the adults' conversation.

"Joel, I think we should prepare for the worst," warns my Uncle Tuvye.

"There is no question that you are right, Tuvye. Temcia and I have stockpiled medicine and food in preparation of an invasion."

"Mindale and I have done the same, though no matter what we store, I am afraid that it won't be enough."

"I feel the noose tightening around us," adds my Aunt, "but I am most fearful for the children. God knows what sacrifices will be forced upon them."

As I try to listen to the adults, Majer grabs my hair, pulling it. "Majer," I scream, "Stop it!"

Letting go and running from me, Majer sprints, as I follow in hot pursuit with fury coursing through my veins.

"Majer," Nadja commands threateningly, "Leave Dina alone!"

Glaring at his sister, Majer freezes in his tracks, kicking at a stone in the path. My sister's arms encircle me, catching me in mid-flight, just as I am about to pounce on my pesky cousin.

"You certainly don't act like a boy who is soon to be a Bar Mitzvah and become a man. Here, come walk with Nadja and me."

Reluctantly, Majer complies with his sister's request. "You always ruin my fun. You're not the boss, you know."

Sighing, Nadja rumples the unruly mass of dark curls framing her brother's face.

Excited to join the older girls, I push myself between my sister and cousin, happy for an excuse to walk with them.

The two Nadjas, who had been walking together conspiratorially, are now forced to part. Linking arms in the dwindling sunshine, we walk. As quiet as a fly on a wall, I listen as the older girls talk, hoping for a juicy tidbit to share with Fela. The girls, well aware of my nosiness, continue with the most mundane of conversation that fills me with boredom within minutes

Saying our good-byes in the growing twilight, the Frydmans and the Finkelsteins return to their respective homes to bid farewell to Shabbat.

We stop at the bakery across the street to pick up the *cholent*[19] that had been left to slowly braise in the massive ovens. On Fridays, the women bring their clay pots filled with different variations of the traditional stew to the local bakeries, where the ingredients slowly simmer for twenty-four hours in the ovens. The flavorful stews of beans, potatoes, meats, and spices infuse the air with an aroma we can smell from a block away. In this way, God's commandment to rest and not work on the Sabbath is kept until the *Havdalah*, a closing ritual that ends the holiday and is performed by all observant Jews.

Evening falls an hour after sundown and we stand in the courtyard of our building as my father searches for the first three stars visible in the heavens.

"There, Tata, there!" Abek points to the darkening sky.

---

19 Slowly braised stew of Spanish Sephardic descent.

"Good, Abek, the first three stars to appear in God's heavens. The hour of farewell to Shabbat has come."

He lifts the wine glass and murmurs the prayer to celebrate the renewal of the spiritual. My father likes to explain the meaning of each ritual so his children will learn to perform the sacred acts and carry their meaning within their hearts.

"You see, children, like the transformation of grapes to wine; we are transformed by our dedication to the ritual of Shabbat, from the physical world to the divine realms. Shabbat is when the Lord opens his arms to his children."

Then my father says the prayer over the spice box filled with cloves and passes it under each of our noses so we can inhale the sweet aroma and fill our hearts with meaning and understanding of our traditions.

"The Kabbalists say that on Shabbat we are given an extra soul, allowing us to reach greater spirituality. When Shabbat ends, this extra spirituality returns to God. By smelling the spices we are comforted in knowing that our extra soul will return when we celebrate Shabbat once more."

In the twilight, my father lights the braided double candle and says the prayer over the brightly burning flame. "Children, according to the Talmud, Adam became distraught on the sixth day of creation when on Friday evening, night descended and the world was cloaked in darkness. The next evening, not wanting Adam to feel lonely, God gave him the gift of fire, the first light of creation so he would know he was not forgotten. In this way, we are reminded of our commitment to God and his commitment to us and we ask for his continued protection and light."

Performing the final ritual, he pours wine into the Kiddush cup until it overflows onto a plate. "You see, children, how the wine overflows? This symbolizes our hope and prayer that the blessing of Shabbat will overflow into our lives and last throughout the week."

As the evening shadows envelope the courtyard, he recites the last blessing of the Havdalah service. We bid farewell to Shabbat with a final "Amen."

Chapter 3

A Threatening Storm

With the daily rhythms of school, work, and household, the days blend one into the other. Calm infuses our household, until one day my father returns from work, his shoulders hunched in dejection, his voice strained with worry. "Temcia, we must prepare for the worst!"

My mother runs to him and they cling to each other. "Joel, what is it? What's wrong?"

We all run to my father, hearing the fear in his voice and the uncertainty it portends. "Hitler is claiming that Polish soldiers crossed into Germany last night in a raid. A bloody battle took place and every Polish soldier was killed! Hitler is raging like a madman that Poland has committed an act of war against Germany."

"Oh my God," My mother and grandmother cry simultaneously, their nervous hands fluttering like the wings of hummingbirds.

"It is a ridiculous manufactured excuse for war. I'm sure the Nazis crossed our borders and captured a group of soldiers and took them back into Germany. Once over the border, they slaughtered the poor men to provide Hitler with a rationalization for invasion."

"Joel, what are we going to do? I am so afraid for the children."

"We must prepare ourselves and keep faith that God will protect us. I think we should bring the entire family together for Shabbat tomorrow night. It is important that we prepare our minds and homes for war. I am going to talk with Tuvye and Chiel and discuss our options. Temcia, you and the girls prepare for a large Shabbat gathering. I only wish that Nachele, Alexander, and David were not so far away in Lodz. Communication is bound to suffer and I would feel better if we were all here in one city."

With the mention of her youngest daughter's name, my grandmother begins to cry. My father's younger sister and the baby of the family, Nachele, is married to Alexander Weintraub and lives in Lodz with their only son David. Alexander owns a successful petrol station in anticipation that Poland will catch up with the growth of the automobile industry altering Western Europe.

My father hugs his tiny mother. "Don't worry Mama, we will survive this together. I will write to Nachele and Alexander and beg them to return to Radom."

My father opens his arms and we rush to find solace in the warmth of his embrace.

The following day, Fela and I are released from school early as worry spreads through our city about the pending threat of the Nazis. We hurry through the streets to my parents' butcher shop to help carry home the provisions for the large family Shabbat. As always, the streets are crowded with shoppers making their last minute purchases for the holiday. We reach Rynek and Rwanska and I stop for a moment to admire the corner building my parents own, with its rental apartments on the second floor and four retail stores at street level. Flanking my parents' shop on either side is a pharmacy and a bakery. The smell of freshly baked bread wafts through the air as people hurry from the bakery, their arms laden with bags.

Fela and I enter my parents' store. Slabs of beef hang from large hooks in the ceiling, awaiting my father's knife. Below stand ice cases full of filleted meat. Behind the counter, my father is speaking Yiddish to a gray-haired woman clearly enamored with him. On the other side of the store, my mother converses in Polish with a customer as she deftly wraps a parcel of meat and ties it with string.

"Froh Gotfryd,[20] this is my daughter Dinka and her friend Fela," says my father in Yiddish to the grandmotherly woman.

"*Ah gitten Shabbos, maidelech,*"[21] says the plump wrinkled face beaming at us.

Fela and I respond respectfully, "*Ah gitten Shabbos,* Froh Gotfryd."

The elderly woman in Yiddish compliments Fela and me to my father. "*Shaine maidelech, gite maidelech.*"[22] For good measure, she repeats her compliments as my father glows with pride.

My father places her purchases in her basket and she nods farewell, walking with her cane toward the door. I run to open the door for her and she smiles with gratitude, "*Ich Dankte.*"[23]

My mother calls us to her and introduces us to her customer, Pani Zdebowa, who smiles as she takes her purchases from my mother. Fela and I curtsy to Pani Zdebowa.

---

20 Mrs. Gottfryd, Yiddish

21 "Have a good Sabbath, girls." Yiddish

22 "Pretty girls, good girls." Yiddish

23 Thank you, Yiddish

"Dinka, you remember my telling you about Pani Zdebowa and what a good friend and devoted customer she is?"

"Of course, *Mamusia,*[24] you always say Pani Zdebowa is your favorite customer."

Pani Zdebowa turns to my mother. "You will have your hands full, Temcia, this one is a charmer. *Wszystkie najlepsze dla Ciebie.*"[25]

The next evening, our spacious apartment seems to burst at the seams with fifteen members of my extended family. Although the gathering is called for a serious discussion among the adults, we still celebrate the Shabbat in festive fashion, following the protocol of blessings and reverence to God. My mother, sister, and grandmother worked hard preparing a traditional Sabbath meal for everyone and all of the girls help with the serving amid the animated conversation. The table is laden with cakes and pies baked by my Aunts Faigele and Mindale.

My grandfather and grandmother had made sure their children are extremely close. My father has three sisters and all but Nachele live in our neighborhood. Faigele and her husband Chiel, a tailor who makes uniforms for the Polish military, live only a kilometer away. Faigele's marriage is not a happy one and providing for their large family of five children puts extra strain on the marriage and their finances. Every day my Aunt Faigele comes to our home, ostensibly to visit her mother. My grandmother, feeling great sorrow for her eldest daughter's predicament, sends her home with baskets filled with our food. Noticing the missing items, my mother accuses my grandmother, reprimanding her for what she considers stealing. My poor grandmother is often caught between her love for her daughter and her hard working daughter-in-law. When pushed to the wall, she seeks remedy from my father, who wishes only peace

---

24 Mommy, Polish

25 "All the best." Polish

between his wife, mother, and sister. My mother is generous and would gladly give food to Faigele and her family, but the deception gets her goat.

My aunt's three sons live at home until such a time as they marry and can afford to move to a home of their own. The two young girls of six and eight study at home and help their mother. Abek, the eldest son, is a professor of languages and history at the gymnasium in Radom. Our spacious kitchen provides him with a quiet refuge to tutor his students in the evenings. My brother and I are respectful of our brilliant cousin, but on occasion I sneak under the table to eavesdrop when he is teaching. Once, I wanted to show off in front of a handsome student who failed to answer a question. I had surprised them both with the answer from under the table. Abek was furious and banished me with a severe reprimand to not interfere when he was tutoring his students. His brother Shlomo works with my uncle Chiel as a tailor. The youngest son Motek is a barber who also is in our home several times a week to shave my father. In Radom, some barbers, like doctors, make house calls. I love to sit and watch while Motek applies the hot towel, my father's face disappearing in the vapors. Then he mixes the thick foamy cream with its scent of menthol, patting it with his brush to the planes of my father's face. Skillful as a surgeon, he deftly shaves away the cream and beard leaving my father's skin pink and glowing. Finally, he pats on the manly cologne that smells like a cross between new leather and cloves. That scent somehow remains on my father until Motek's return and his next shave.

My Aunt Mindale is the most vocal of the sisters and her opinion is highly regarded by all of the men. Always a voice of reason, she is known to stand up to any injustice. Her husband Tuvye is extremely handsome and flamboyant he always dresses meticulously in a fashionable suit and tie. He works as a middleman, selling cow hides to the leather manufacturers that abound throughout Radom. Leather processing is a highly important industry in Europe and Poland's craftsmen are renowned for the beauty and texture of their leather and suede textiles. Polish' leathers are sold and prized throughout the continent. Mindale and Tuvye have two children. My cousin Nadja at sixteen is preparing for gymnasium and my twelve-year-old cousin Majer is preparing to be a Bar Mitzvah.

It is unusual for the entire family to get together for a meal. The adults work hard, whether in business or at home, and the remaining time is dedicated to the demands and needs of their children. This rarc gathering charges the air with electricity.

During dessert, a dozen conversations intertwine as everyone is eager to share everyday family news. My father makes it clear that any talk of the pending war will be saved until after the children are excused from the table. Naturally, the older children will be included in the discussion, meaning Abek, Shlomo, Motek, and the two Nadjas. Majer, Abek, Perile, Risele, and I will be sent to my bedroom to play during the adults' talk. I think about hiding under the table and eavesdropping, but there isn't much chance of my getting away with it.

Suddenly the table falls silent when eight-year-old Perile asks, in childhood innocence, "Uncle Joel, why do the Germans hate us?" The small face, punctuated by quizzical eyes bright as two stars are fixated on my father. Silence grips the air as the adults silently seek an answer in the eyes of each other.

My father clears his throat as he carefully weighs his words. "Perile, people hate for many reasons and not all of them are easy to explain. Sometimes it's fear of people's different beliefs and their distinct customs and behaviors that causes hate. Sometimes it's jealousy of their possessions or their success. People are not born hating, but like a seed, hatred must be planted and nurtured to grow. Hurtful words and actions toward someone who is different than you is the food of hatred. Not all Germans hate us and hopefully we will find a way to change the minds of those that do. Have I helped you to understand, Perile?"

A beautiful smile spreads like sunshine across Perile's face. "Yes, Uncle Joel. I understand. When the Germans come to Radom, I will try to change their minds about the Jews. I will plant seeds of love and hopefully they will grow."

The simplicity of Perile's words and the belief that she can make the difference in the world resonates within each of us. My Aunt Faigele wraps her arms around her eldest daughter, kissing her on both cheeks. "The wisdom of children is like a window opening to the voice of God," she says, her eyes brimming with tears of pride.

"Okay, children," interrupts Mindale, "why don't you go to Dina's room and play for a while so the grown-ups can finish talking and we can all go home?"

In my room, I read to Abek, Perile, Risele, and Majer from my book of fairytales by the Brothers Grimm. Perile and Risele listen with their heads on my shoulders, while Abek, head propped up on his elbows, lies at my feet. Majer listens from a chair in the corner. I don't remember falling asleep, but sometime in the night my aunts and uncles carried my cousins safely home.

In the morning, my sister tells me what was decided. "In the face of the shortages to come with war, our family will remain committed to each other's survival, sharing whatever we have. Also, the adults agreed, if given the opportunity to immigrate and leave, we will all go."

I look into Nadja's eyes with fear and hope. For now, there is nothing to do but wait for Germany's next move.

Chapter 4

Germany Attacks

One week later, during Shabbat, on Friday, September 1st at 4:30 AM, the bombing begins. I awaken to an explosive rumbling that bathes the room in a flash of white light. It is impossible to ascertain whether the shattered peace is raining from the heavens or emanating from the bowels of the earth. At first, I think it is a violent thunderstorm hurling down upon us and sucking the air from the atmosphere. This is like nothing I have ever experienced. As our building shakes to its foundations, I am terrified it will collapse, killing us all. Above the wailing sirens, I hear glass shattering, my mother screaming, my brother crying, and my father in the next room trying to calm them both. My poor grandmother shrieks with each detonation and then regains her senses in the momentary lull. Then she lapses into a mournful combination of moaning and praying in Yiddish to God and my grandfather to intercede and still the firestorm threatening to consume us. Another explosion shakes the building, drowning out the pleas of the inhabitants in my home. I grab my sister. "Nadja, what is happening?"

"I don't know!" Her arms fly around me and we shudder against each other in fear. With her hand clutching mine, we jump from the warmth of our bed and run to the window to see what is happening. Beneath the canopy of stars, we hear the drone of planes overhead. The sky has turned a blistering red from the glow of the fires burning throughout the city.

Gripping the window sill, I look at the scene below. Horses run up and down the street in terror, wailing in fear. They must have escaped their stalls when the bombing began. Adding to the confusion, people are running up and down the street, their arms flailing, trying to avoid being trampled by the disoriented beasts. Every minute, another deafening explosion shakes our home and we hear terrified shrieks from the other apartments. My father runs into our room shouting, "Girls get away from the window! It isn't safe!"

Nadja and I flee from the window to our father's arms. "Tata, what is happening?"

"Come, come with me into the other room. The war has begun. Germany is attacking!"

Staring at my father in disbelief, I begin to cry. Nothing has prepared me for this moment. I feel helpless and exposed as another blast rocks the timbers of the building, sending rivulets of dust-like grainy particles that shroud us in a grayish mist. We run with my father to the safety of our parents' bedroom, where my mother, brother, and grandmother are cowering under the bed. My brother's arms are locked around my mother's neck as he whimpers, "Tata, Tata, make them stop."

My grandmother cries repeatedly, "Please God, help us!" Another explosion shakes the building and the room is filled with a pellucid white light that turns night to day. My sister and I dive under the bed. My mother holds us tight, protecting us with her arms as if they are armor and she can shield us from any harm.

My father does his best to hide his own fear and calm us. "Don't cry children, don't worry it will stop. We are safe; the building is strong. Be brave my darlings."

He is trying to convince himself as much as he is his family. Under the bed, we cling to each other, frozen with terror as the attack continues for what seems like hours.

I feel certain we will not survive the night. Perhaps this is the end. In a terrible final collapse of wood, iron, and glass we will be buried beneath the rubble of our building, forgotten to the world.

Several times during the night, the bombing stops, only to resume an hour later.

We remain prisoners in our home for the next five days while bombs intermittently strike our city. My father ventures out to hear the news. When he returns, we run to him, happy that he has safely returned.

"Tata, Tata, you're back!"

My mother rushes to him, interrupting our questions, "Joel, what have you heard? Is there any hope?"

Looking at our pleading faces, he responds, "Yes, yes, there is good news. On September 3rd, England and France declared war on Germany!"

"Thank God!" my mother exclaims. "What else? Tell us more!" My father weighs his words, "Unfortunately, the Nazis are moving rapidly. The Polish army is fighting valiantly, but they are heavily out-armed and undermanned. Germany is pounding the cities and transportation lines. Thousands of people are being killed. I must be honest with you, I can't imagine any other outcome than the Nazis conquering our country."

"How long?"

"How long what?"

"How long before the British and the French come to our rescue?" my mother asks impatiently.

"I'm afraid… it's likely we will have to endure a German occupation. It will take time for the allies to prepare for war."

My mother's face conveys what we all feel, as her eyes flood with tears.

Protectively putting his arm around her shoulders, he says, "Come dear, let us make some tea and listen to the radio."

We listen to our radio; the steady flow of news is disheartening. The radio waves are filled with the aggressive repetitive voice of Hitler screaming, "We will take Lodz today and tomorrow Kielce, and on and on until we take Warszawa!"

My father turns the dial in search of something other than the hysterical boasting of Hitler, as we sit in misery. Finally, we hear the voice of a Polish reporter crying out his dismal news, "Countrymen, the sovereign nation of Poland is being bombarded. The Germans have thrown an immense force against Poland. We estimate nearly 2,400 tanks organized into six panzer divisions have rolled across our borders, striking with rapid precision through our defensive lines. The Germans are surrounding and destroying our troops with foot soldiers and mechanized infantry. The tanks are scorching the earth and leaving a path of death and destruction in their wake. The only way to describe what is happening is to call it a *blitzkrieg,* or lightning strike. The blitzkrieg is an organized attack of such surprise, speed, and strength, it is impossible to defend against. Pray for our brave soldiers who are fighting for their lives and yours!"

In horror, we hear guns firing and explosives detonating in the background. The announcer's voice fades in and out with the crackle of radio static and interference, until there is only the hiss of a severed transmission.

I sit at the window in my bedroom during a momentary lull, staring down at the street. I had begged my mother to let me go down to Fela's apartment to see her. Her answer was an unequivocal "No!"

My mother, who never raises her voice to scold any of us, now is on the verge of hysteria; her worries overwhelm her usual calm demeanor. The streets are nearly deserted except for an occasional human who darts from doorway to doorway, furtively making his way to some unknown destination.

I stare to see if I recognize anyone that passes, a near impossibility as each one clings to anonymity in the shadows and hides as best he can. The radio in the next room drones its endless blitz of bad news.

We are all suffering various forms of shock and fatigue as we wander from room to room, looking for respite. We hear that the roads are clogged with refugees heading east in a desperate attempt to outrun the Germans who are conquering the towns and cities in their path. I listen at the window and it occurs to me that even the birds have been forced to flee. They vanished when the bombs appeared, flying east to what they hoped were peaceful skies.

How I wish my family and I could take wing and follow them in their flight to safety.

I imagine a procession of overloaded carts filled with the few possessions piled precariously without toppling—accumulations of a lifetime salvaged and grabbed in a few moments of panic, as the fleeing refugees hastily departed. How did they decide what to take and what to leave behind? The carts, pulled by over-burdened horses and oxen, move in a slow exodus, mothers, fathers, and children trying to escape chaos. All the while, thousands of birds fly above, screeching, their wings tearing at the wind in a desperate flight to escape.

My sister comes to sit beside me at the window, hugging me in her arms, offering a bit of solicitude and affection, "So, what do you see, Dinale?"

"I see the end of our world and it breaks my heart," I answer, as tears well in my eyes.

"You mustn't lose hope! There are good people in the world; they will come to our rescue. We will have to be strong and resilient; it is our fate." Her words sound strong, but her face belies her words.

"You don't sound as if you are convinced. And since when do you believe in fate and not free will?" I grumble.

"I'm afraid that freedom for all Poles disappeared when the Nazis crossed our border. I don't know what the future will bring, but I do know we are in for difficult times and Mama and Tata are going to need us in ways that I can't even imagine." She squeezes my shoulders to emphasize her words. "Right now they could use your sunshine smile and maybe you could comfort Abek and play a game with him. He is so frightened and could use a little distraction from his fears. I've tried, but he won't respond to me."

I nod and turn from the window. My brother Abek is playing quietly on the floor with his jacks. I smile at him and tousle his blond curls, asking if I can play jacks with him. He looks at me, his eyes wide with confusion, not sure what to expect from those around him. My once jolly brother, now subdued, hands me the ball. Taking it I whisper, "Are you afraid? It's okay if you are. I know I am."

My question is met with silence as Abek stares down at the jacks on the floor, refusing to look at me.

"Abek, please talk to me. I know sometimes I am not the best sister in the world. I'm sorry; I really am. You know I love you and would never hurt you, not really. Please talk to me and tell me what you feel!"

He leans in to me, his blue eyes glistening with tears. Overnight, my high-spirited brother has been silenced and replaced by this pensive, withdrawn child. My heart is breaking as I grab his hands in mine to reassure him. "Abek, it's okay to cry," I say as I lean into him, our foreheads touching.

No longer able to hide the emotions overwhelming him, he covers his face and begins to sob. My arms envelop him as I try to assuage his pain. Clinging to one another in pent-up sorrow and fear, we tremble as a torrent of tears sweeps our bodies, leaving nothing but barrenness in its wake. With childlike perception, Abek and I sense some inexplicable line has been crossed. No matter how much my parents try to assure us, our world of Radom, and a thousand other cities and villages like it, has vanished. Not for a month, or a year, but forever. We cry without knowing our childhood already has deserted us. Clinging to each other, we hope for an epiphany, an angel from heaven to save us from the fearful uncertainty shrouding the future. We weep in each other's arms for what seems forever. Finally, our tears are spent and I release him.

"Your eyes are all swollen and your nose is all red," he giggles through his sniffles.

"And, what do you think yours looks like?"

Laughing in mutual misery and burrowing his head in my shoulder in a gesture of love, he whispers, "I'm glad you're my sister."

"Me too, I'm glad you're my brother." I hug him so tightly, he is forced to inhale deeply and I feel his ribs expand in my arms.

I think about Nadja's words—being strong and surviving. Each of us will have to be vigilant not to let despair crush us. At that moment, I promise myself that no matter what the future, I will find a way to bear it. I release Abek, pick up the jacks, and throw them across the floor. "Come on Abek, let's play."

Chapter 5

"The New Order"

The morning of September 8th dawns without the usual sounds of military conquest. The streets are empty of pedestrians and the skies hold no sign of aircraft. The barrage of artillery and bombs has ceased. The city seems to be slumbering under a spell, blanketed in an intense quiet, the kind of stillness that precedes or follows a major storm.

Still in my pajamas, I rest my hands on the window sill and stare at the abandoned street. All the while, my sister sleeps. At first, I barely register the tremor beneath my fingertips, but within a few minutes, a visible pulsation increases with frequency and speed. The ground is shaking and I hear a distant rumble, not unlike thunder. Looking up, I see there isn't a cloud in the sky. Within minutes, I distinguish the source of the now deafening disturbance. The first vehicles bearing the flags of red background and black swastikas make their way down our street.

"Dinale, what's happening? What is all that noise?" My sister awakens.

"It's them."

"Who?" Suddenly the sleepiness is gone from her speech and Nadja jumps from bed and joins me at the window.

It's the Germans. Look!" I point to the parade of steel and armor.

"Tata, Mamashy, come quick!" Nadja runs to the door as my parents rush into the room.

We stand in silence, watching the Germans march into Radom. It is a spectacle of unmitigated military might, clearly meant to quash the hearts and minds of the conquered citizenry who hide like ghosts behind curtains. We watch as hundreds of motorcycles, tanks, trucks, and armored vehicles pour through the abandoned streets. A deafening clamor fills the air, dust rising from the ground like a desert sandstorm.

My father's face is as pale as the moon in the sky, a sorrowful look in his eyes as if he were attending a funeral. Unable to bear his unhappiness, I wrap my arms around him and offer up a smile, "Don't worry, Tata. We will find a way to live through this. Please don't look so sad."

He presses me close to his body, forcing his lips to form a smile. "I know, maidele. It just breaks my heart that you, Abek, and Nadja will have to endure this evil."

The Germans quickly occupy the government buildings, sheltering their soldiers and setting up their command posts. A few days later, the SS units and police arrive amid triumphant fanfare. This time, curiosity gets the better of Radom's population and the streets are crowded with onlookers.

My sister and I join the throngs to watch the arrival of the elite officers of Hitler. Many in the crowd are visibly disturbed, tears flowing freely from their eyes, as the conquerors march through the streets laying claim to our city. I look around in shock to see that some of the Poles are actually greeting these monsters like heroes, welcoming them with their hats and handkerchiefs high above their heads waving in salute. I look from the smiling Poles to the scowling faces of the SS, dressed in well-tailored uniforms, black spit polished boots, and cocky hats with the skull and cross bones death insignia. I shiver and whisper to Nadja, "Do the Poles hate us?"

"The Poles have never been our friends. They will gladly feed us to these murderers without a moment's remorse. Look at how they are greeting these monsters. It's as if they are being liberated—not being occupied."

Her words freeze the blood in my veins. I feel the bile rise in my throat as I watch the arrival of Hitler's ambassadors from hell.

In the following days, Nadja's words play out. The Poles adapt to their new masters, groveling with solicitousness in their passion to please. The Nazis regard the Poles with contempt, but at least they are considered human. Not so the Jews. My father can no longer leave the apartment, as the Nazis constantly grab Jewish men off the streets and take them to work details where they are beaten without mercy. The Germans need labor to rebuild the armaments factory razed during the bombings and to repair roads and bridges damaged during the bombings. The expendable Jews are put to work as slaves. Forced to clean the streets and haul coal, the Jews feel the force of blows if they do not work fast enough.

For their entertainment, the Nazis prey upon the recognizable religious Jewish men and rabbis. With their *peius,* long curled side-locks, black long tunic coats, and felt hats, they are easy prey. They bear the initial brunt of the worst cruelties. The Nazis take pleasure in humiliating and denigrating these poor souls. Ripping their beards from their faces, they beat them with clubs and kick them until they are nothing more than a bloodied mass of pulp, unrecognizable as the human beings, grandfathers, fathers, brothers, or sons they once were.

I run with my mother through the streets on a desperate errand for food and supplies. Her hand tightly grips mine as we pass such a scene. I stare in horror as three Nazis shouting obscenities beat an old man as he pleads for mercy. I feel faint as blood gushes from the old man's nose and he crawls in the street, groveling for his life. I look at my mother, her face a mask of fear. I want to protest but she hushes me and pulls me away.

When we are safely away, I ask, "Mamashy, why are they beating such an old defenseless man? What possible pleasure can they get from it?"

She looks at me, her face flushed with compassion. "We are helpless, Dinale. I am sorry, but there is nothing we can do. These people have no decency or conscience. They are filled with the power of their hatred. I need you to be brave, care for our family, and help others when you can." She smiles at me through her tears and hugs me close. "Come, we must get some potatoes for dinner and hurry back home to your father. The streets are so dangerous; he will worry if we take too long."

Jews no longer walk the thoroughfares of the city. Our vibrant neighborhood is a place of fear and mourning for a world now vanished. Many of the businesses remain open and my mama begins opening our store, stocking it as best she can.

My father remains at home with us, listening to the radio for any news of hope. Hitler proclaims he will conquer Warszaw in a week, but has underestimated the valor of the Poles. The fighting is fierce as the German war machine surrounds and squeezes Warszaw in its grip. Yet Warszaw remains free and the Polish army fights on, even destroying the Reinhardt tank division, a pride and joy of Hitler's army. Warszaw is determined to withstand the onslaught of the German blitzkrieg. Against all odds, the remaining patriots fight on, knowing the fall of Warszaw is inevitable.

It is September 13th, the holiest day of Rosh Hashanah. The year 5700 on the Jewish calendar dawns and the "Days of Awe" begin in Radom. I lie awake listening to my parents arguing in the next room, something I have never experienced before from these two respectful people.

"Temcia, I will not allow these interlopers to cower us from keeping faith with God!" My father's voice rises in a crescendo of indignation. "Abek and I must go to synagogue!"

"Joel, I am telling you that you will not go! There is no reason to put Abek or yourself in harm's way when we can all remain here and pray as a family. I have a terrible feeling that the Nazis will wreak havoc on the Jews during our holiest of days."

"Temcia, allow me my dignity. Please don't fight me on this."

Nadja lies next to me listening to my parents arguing. "Is Mamashy right?" I whisper.

"Yes, definitely. Tatashy is being unreasonable. God will hear him just as well in our home as in the shul. Believe me, God has never heard more prayers than will be coming to him tonight and every day and night so long as Hitler is on the march. Mamashy is right and she will prevail and get her way no matter how firmly Tatashy protests."

Finally, my mother uses the ultimate weapon that women throughout history have wielded when all arguments fail; she begins to sob. My father in an instant is powerless as the tears gush from my mother's eyes. My father and brother remain at home and at sundown, we hold hands, greeting the Jewish New Year. We are united in our prayers of peace for all mankind.

My mother is proven correct in her premonition. While we are safely at home, the SS wreak havoc, entering the synagogues destroying the interiors, desecrating the sacred texts and scrolls, and plundering the sacred articles. They patrol the streets, randomly entering Jewish homes and arresting anyone found celebrating the holiday. They drag them from their prayers and force them into work details where cruel humiliations are perpetrated against them. The tales are horrifying. Some Jews are forced to scrub the sidewalks with their prayer shawls, while the Nazis set fire to the beards of others. Meaningless tasks are devised as punishments against the devout. The president of the Jewish Community, Yona Zylberberg, is dragged into the streets and made to walk for hours with his arms raised above his head, carrying a heavy stone, while the Nazi oppressors taunt and beat him with clubs and whips. At least he is alive.

One of the saddest losses is that of a beloved Hebrew teacher, Chaim Shlomo Waks, who is arrested and taken to SS headquarters. There, the Nazis torment him by trying to force him to eat pork. This deeply religious man refuses, so they beat him without mercy as he cries an endless chant of "*Shema Israel, Shema Israel!*" Finding no other way to silence him, they shoot him in the head, silencing his voice forever. The "new order," as the Nazis call themselves, leaves a path of death and destruction on that holy day throughout the city of Radom. Deep into the night the cries of the afflicted can be heard.

Still, the Jewish community as a whole remains strong in the face of persecution, just as they have time and again throughout our history. In an effort to protect the community, our leaders do their best to answer to the continuing demands of the Nazis. The council is required to provide a list of all of the Jews in the city and their occupations. As the Nazi demands increase, the Jewish community tries to manage some semblance of normalcy. People return to work, slipping quietly through the streets to open stores and factories. Jewish charity increases in an effort to care for those already suffering immense losses.

It's a rainy morning in September when we children are allowed to return to school. I am delighted to see Fela waiting for me as usual in our courtyard. She holds her umbrella as a gray drizzle falls from the heavens.

"Fela!" I cry, running to her, our arms enfolding each other as we warmly embrace. Our umbrellas entangle in a mesh of wire and cloth. "I am so happy to see you! Mamashy has been so protective, she hasn't let us out of the house."

"I know," Fela replies. "My parents have been impossible, never letting us out of their sight. Our home feels more like a cage than a home."

I take her arm and we begin to walk our familiar route to school. I am alert for danger, my eyes cautiously glancing around for any signs of trouble.

"I am so afraid all of the time," I whisper. "Bubysy continually cries and prays and everyone else is so jumpy that the slightest noise or complaint sends them into a tizzy."

"It's the same in my house. My mother is constantly on edge and my poor father has nowhere to go to escape her," she giggles.

"I hate the Germans," I exclaim. "I hope God destroys them all."

Fela nods, looking around to make sure I have not been overheard. "Everyone is saying that if we just keep a low profile and do our best to meet their demands, we should be able to endure the occupation and survive."

"I don't believe it. Every day it gets worse. Every day they make new demands and are never satisfied. Their hatred and cruelty seems to grow with each brutal act. I saw them beat an old defenseless man!"

Like a wizened older sister, Fela tries to calm my fears and acts the sensible one in our friendship. "Dynka, we will manage, you'll see. We must manage, we have no choice."

"I wish we could escape to your grandparents' cherry orchard right now," I sigh. "I can taste the sweet black cherry juice; you know how much I love cherries? Remember, when we were there this past summer and we played in the orchard? Remember how big the cherries were and how I looped them over my ears like long beautiful dangling earrings and you said they looked like rubies? It seems like a million years ago. Life was so beautiful. I don't think I can bear this thing called war."

Fela's eyes mist and she wipes away a tear that has made its escape down her nose. "It will be alright. Someday we will return to my grandparents' cherry orchard, and you can eat all the cherries your heart desires. Then we will grow up and go to Palestyne and marry farmers."

I smile at her, my bravery returning as I remember the promise we made beneath the branches of the neighborhood apple orchard. I squeeze her hand. "I know you are right. This will pass."

It is September 17th when Poland's old enemy, Mother Russia, under the iron rule of Stalin's dictatorship and emboldened by Poland's vulnerability, seals its bargain with the devil Germans and invade our eastern border. Poland is like a lamb surrounded by a pack of hungry wolves. Then, on the 27th of September, Warszaw surrenders to the Nazis and the nation of Poland ceases to exist. Within two days, the Nazis and Russians divide Poland with the intention of exploiting her resources and enslaving her people.

With the sealing of this bargain, more than 2 million Jews fall into the hands of the Nazis and another 1.3 million Jews into the clutches of the Russians. The cold and rain have come unseasonably early this year, echoing the misery that envelopes us.

As the days advance, my parents and sister discuss with ever increasing bitterness the continuous commands of the *Judenrat*.[26]

They are trying to mitigate the Nazi cruelties on the Jews while carrying out the oppressive orders demanded on a daily basis.

One of the first of the confiscations is the surrender of all radios. My father reluctantly turns over his precious radio to the authorities, knowing it is a move to isolate us from news on the progress of the war. Newspapers are my father's sole link to the

26 Jewish council

world and he obtains every printed publication available in Polish and German, legally or on the black market. The illustrious Yiddish newspapers are silenced.

I am reading in the kitchen as my father storms in, cursing under his breath, and stuffs his newspaper into the garbage can.

"Tata, what is it? You look so angry."

Quickly composing his anger, my father says, "Nothing darling, it is nothing, just some silliness in the newspaper. Please continue your reading. I didn't realize you were in the kitchen." My father returns to the other room, leaving me perplexed as to what would cause such a reaction. My curiosity gets the better of me. I retrieve the paper from the trashcan and search the front page, looking for any clue to my father's behavior. The newspaper is the German publication *Der Sturmer*. It takes several minutes for me to make sense of the words and figure out which article is the culprit. I carefully read until I am stunned to discover the source of his anger. "The Jewish people ought to be exterminated root and branch. Then the plague of pests would have disappeared in Poland at one stroke." Over and over, I reread the sentence to make sure I am not mistaken as to the vile meaning. The word "exterminated" sticks in my throat. Holding the newspaper as if it is infected with the plague, I run to my father, pointing at the threatening sentences, "What does this mean, Tata?"

My father is in the dining room surrounded by newspapers, his glasses perched on his nose. He looks up and I can see he is loath to discuss the offensive words with me. Patting his knee, he motions. "Come sit, Dinale."

Arranging myself on his lap, I lean back resting my head on his shoulder snuggling into the safety of his arms. My tears fall like rain. "Are the Nazis going to kill us all, Tatashy?"

"Hush, hush, maidele. Don't be silly. They can't kill millions of people; it's not possible," he says, wiping the tears from my eyes.

"But Tata, if they say it, they must mean it. But how? Are there that many bullets in the world, millions of bullets?"

"No, no, no, they would be foolish to destroy such an army of workers. Better to use us for cheap labor. The world is not going to sit by and let this Nazi menace take control of Europe. The Germans tried this once in World War I and they were stopped and brought to their knees by the world's free democracies. They will come to the rescue of Europe again, you'll see. We must stay strong and our resolve to live must be firm. The Jewish People have survived time and again and lived to tell the tale of every tyrant who has tried to destroy us. Remember your Jewish history? Remember Haman[27]? Now, dry your tears and go back to reading your book."

"But, Father, you yourself said that it will take time for the other countries to come and rescue us. How will we live if they wish to wipe us from the face of the earth?"

"These are harsh and hurtful words, but the Nazis will realize what a resource we are. I don't want to hear any more about this and please don't tell your brother. We love you, your sister, and brother so much. We will do everything to protect you, don't worry. Throw the newspaper away. It's simply one man's insane words."

Although my father does his best to calm my growing fears, the newspaper article arouses a mounting sense of foreboding in me. My sleep is plagued by an endless nightmare. I am running from uniformed monsters, lost in a world of darkening terror, screaming, "Stop! Stop! Stop! Leave them alone, please don't hurt them!" My body is soaking with sweat; my heart pounding against my chest.

Nadja shakes me awake gently. "Dinale, Dinale, it is okay," she reassures, rocking me in her arms. "Nothing is going to hurt you.

---

27 The evil antagonist of the Book of Esther who sought to annihilate the Jews of Persia.

You are safe in your own bed. It's me, sweetheart, Nadja, your sister! Don't cry, you are safe, it's only a bad dream."

Gasping for air, I tell her what I can remember of the nightmare. "It was horrible! I saw them dragging you and Mamashy and Abek away. They were pulling you in one direction and me in another. I couldn't stop them. I tried, but I couldn't. It was so unbearable."

She shudders against me and holds me closer to her. "I know how scared you are. We all are scared. It is only natural for you to be traumatized by this nightmare we are living. It's impossible for any of us to understand how anyone could hate us this much. To hate children, the infirmed, and the aged is beyond comprehension. But, we are safe and doing our best. Cry all you want darling, but don't give up hope. Remember I'm here for you always."

I cling to my sister whimpering, "I'm sorry but I can't stop the dreams, they are so frightening and they always end the same! You are taken from me and I am taken from you."

October already shows signs of being a harbinger of an unusually cold and damp winter. The Radom Jews struggle to feed their families and maintain a semblance of dignity throughout the Nazis' onslaught of daily humiliations. Each day brings new orders, called *befehl,* many disseminated with the sole intent of humiliating and reducing community resolve. The new German Mayor Schwizgabel demands that the Jewish community raise a sum of money for the privilege of being allowed to live and work in occupied Poland. They try to blackmail two million zlotys from a population that has already been stripped of its assets. When the community cannot raise that kind of cash, they agree to a lesser extortion of one thousand sets of bedding needed for soldiers and officials. The tailors and seamstresses of Radom, my Uncle Chiel being one of those tailors, sew around the clock to finish the bedding before the deadline. Nothing can satiate the Nazis and soon it is a running joke that "If it belongs to a Jew, it must be good, and we want it!"

At the end of October, a new decree is delivered. All Jews over ten years of age are required to wear a white armband with a yellow Star of David sewn to it. Whenever we leave the house, we are required to wear the badge and if caught without it, we will be arrested and deported to German labor camps. We sit at the kitchen table sewing the armbands symbolic of the punishment for the crime of being Jewish. My brother is on the floor playing with his jacks.

I slip my armband over my sleeve and look in the mirror, admiring my handiwork, "I am not going to allow them to make me feel bad about being a Jew. I'm proud of the Jewish people. I'm proud of our history."

"Silly girl, some pride," says my sister with a hostile grunt. "The Nazi beasts are isolating us from the Polish population. They are dehumanizing us and removing our dignity. Each step is intended to fulfill a larger plan. That's what these armbands are for, to visibly mark us."

"I will not allow them to make me feel bad about being a Jew," I defend.

"Mamashy, I want to wear the star too," Abek chimes.

Cruelly I turned on my brother, "Well you can't, Abek, because you are just a baby, you aren't old enough to be counted as a Jew." No sooner are the words out of my mouth than I regret saying them. Abek looks from me to our mother, his eyes filling with tears. "Mamashy, I am a Jew. Tell her that I am a Jew."

My mother's face hardens into anger as she reprimands me, "Dina, there is no reason for you to say such cruel words. Abek bears our covenant with God upon his person. He is a circumcised male. He can never be anything other than a Jew. You will apologize to him this instant!"

"I'm sorry, Abek, I shouldn't have said that to you," I say feeling downcast and ashamed.

My grandmother sighs, "I don't know what has gotten into all of us. Can someone please tell me where decency and respect has gone?"

In frustration, my sister answers, "Bubysy, the Nazis have made the words decency, respect, and kindness meaningless."

Every day brings a new edict with a new loss of rights. Jews no longer are allowed to walk on sidewalks or take public transportation unless we obtain a special pass from the Judenrat. Many boulevards and squares are illegal for us to use, a sure sign of our degraded status. We are forced to abide a curfew limiting our ability to gather. All the kosher butchers are forced out of business as they no longer are allowed to slaughter animals according to the laws of the Torah. My parents bemoan the end of their much-loved butcher business. Soon every Jewish business in Radom and throughout Poland is expropriated by the Third Reich and German administrators are appointed to run them. In some cases, ex-owners of businesses are still allowed to run the businesses and work for the new German managers. Many of these German managers have no idea how to run the businesses and have to bring in Jews to help them. My Uncle Tuvye becomes a co-supervisor with another friend, a Mr. Berman, at a shoe factory. All Jewish bank accounts are frozen and the few Jewish banks that existed are forced to close, their monies absorbed into the ever-growing bank accounts of the Nazis. Jews are legally only allowed to possess 150 zlotys in cash, which is nothing considering the rising cost of food. Jewish doctors, lawyers, and musicians are not permitted to practice their professions or perform their services for non-Jews. This is quite a problem for the Polish population since they rely heavily on Jews in all of these fields, particularly medicine. They close all of the Jewish schools, but it doesn't really matter. My sister and

I are needed to stand in endless lines that wrap around blocks to procure some bread or other necessity for our family. We are forbidden to walk on Lubelska Street, the main artery of the city, and we are not allowed on Rynek Square where the city hall is situated. Finally, they confiscate all property owned by Jews. We no longer enjoy any rents or income from any of our properties. We have no avenue of complaint as we are denied rights or status as citizens. There is no protection from the courts and, like criminals we are under the jurisdiction of the police.

The practice and celebration of Judaism is expressly forbidden in any public venue or even in the privacy of one's home. With a heavy heart, my father decides to dismantle our beautiful Sukkoth and supply our family with an ample supply of wood for the winter.

I watch with sorrow as he begins to dismantle our *Sukkoth,* a beautiful outdoor room used during the festival of Sukkoth. It still holds the decorations of fruit and vegetables we hung from the slated open canopy. Inside our Sukkoth is a large wooden table where my mother draped a beautiful linen table cloth and placed an earthy set of wooden dishes, symbolic of the primitive tools of our ancient ancestors.

Sukkoth, a celebration of the harvest, is called The Feast of Tabernacles. Sukkoth literally means "hut" and is symbolic of the temporary homes used by the ancient Jews after the Exodus from Egypt. The holiday is a time to thank God for his benevolence in providing for the needs of his people as they wandered the barren desert for forty years. Besides the religious connotations, Sukkoth is a holiday of excitement for children. Our courtyard was filled with at least eight Sukkoths belonging to each of the families in our building.

Each family took pride in hanging the harvested fruit and vegetables from brightly colored ribbons that swayed in the breeze. Together, the many Sukkoths looked like a carnival of colorful pavilions. They provided us with endless entertainment as we played hide-and-seek among the structures. We laughed with unabashed joy as we hid from each other under tables and chairs and behind the posts and drapes of the Sukkoths. Nothing was more fun than the celebration of Sukkoth. It bonded our family and our friends in a love of life and the continuation of the ancient traditions of our people.

I close my eyes and remember how my father took the *Lulav* in his right hand and lightly shook it. The *Lulav* was created with a date palm frond entwined with the *Hadass,* a bough of a myrtle tree and *Aravah,* a willow branch. In his left hand, he shook the *Etrog,* a fragrant citrus fruit perfuming the air with a zest of lemon flavor. Then he brought the two ritual objects together to touch, pointing and shaking them turning in a circle toward the north, east, south, and west while reciting the prayer asking God for his blessings for adequate rainfall for the vegetation of the earth.

In that joyous week, we celebrated God's bounty with outdoor dinners at the wooden table laden with delicacies of fruit and vegetables and traditional foods like *tsimmes* (fruit compote) and cakes laden with apples and cherries, representing the sweetness of life. The holiday meals were followed by singing, dancing, and recounting stories of Sukkoths past and praising God who had blessed us and brought us to this special season.

It takes my father nearly one week to saw apart our precious Sukkoth and stack the wood of its table and chairs for fuel to be consumed in flame. His face is set in repentance to God as he wipes away his sweat and tears with his handkerchief. My brother and I sniffle in misery, lamenting our loss as we watch our father demolish our Sukkoth. This act alone spells the end of a way of life for every member in our family.

Chapter 6

Change is for the Best

The bitter winter of 1939 continues with the Jews desperate to survive the iron rule of the Nazis, who squeeze every last ounce of blood from them. Our home is more crowded as my cousin Dina cannot get home to her family in Brzeziny because of Jewish travel restrictions. She has become part of our family.

Now I sleep with my sister and my cousin, making for unusually close quarters. Cousin Dina, like me, is named for my mother's sister who died in childbirth. She is two years older than my sister and my mother's lookalike, with her beautiful black hair and brown eyes that crinkle when she smiles. She has a hearty laugh that can be heard throughout the apartment, even with the doors closed. Her laughter is so infectious. When hysteria seizes her we all end up on the floor, rolling around, holding our sides. I don't mind sharing a bed with her as she is a wonderful source of lore about my mother's family and she is far more patient with my endless questioning than my sister. She is very much the actress and keeps us entertained with her wonderful impersonations of movie stars and celebrities.

This gloomy evening as we sit by the fire listening to the rain pounding like drums upon the roof, Dina stands, stretching her lanky body, and yawns. "I'm very tired. I think I'll go to bed."

"Goodnight, darling," says my mother, looking up from her knitting. Dina makes her way to the door as the rest of the family calls after her, "Goodnight, Dina." She waves, yawning as she leaves.

Engrossed in our activities, we don't notice a few minutes later that Dina has quietly reentered the room. Thinking she has forgotten her book, I watch. Bending her knees, her tall frame shrinking before my eyes, she begins strutting around the room like Groucho Marx. Mumbling under her breath, she stumbles about like a chicken with its head cut off as she imitates the Fuhrer. The Fuhrer would suffer apoplexy if he could see her goose-stepping and frothing at the mouth, marching around the apartment, mocking his lunacy. Clapping our hands with joy, Abek and I are up in a second, following as she prowls about the room. Dina suddenly turns to Abek, her face nearly touching his. "Excuse me, excuse me, *schveinahund,* she screams, "you vill do exactly as I say, ya?"

My brother's laughter fills the air as she stares at him, twitching her brows, her face as serious as a barking dog ready to attack. Glaring, she waits for his response.

"Ya, ya, mein Fuhrer," my brother squeals, clicking his heels and saluting like a Nazi, all the while trying to keep a straight face.

Feeding on everyone's amusement, Dina scowls and furrows her brows, screaming as she produces two little black drawings from her pocket. She alternates them above her lips first one and then the other and crosses her eyes as she tries to look at the paper moustaches. "*Dumkoff*, when I say that I like my moustache clipped this vay and not that vay you must do it precisely as I say." She brandishes Hitler's little black stub and then the other cutout that resembles Simon Legree's, waxed and curled at the ends. "Do you see vhat I mean?" she shouts.

"Ya, ya, mein Fuhrer," cries Abek, as we all buckle over with laughter.

Dina mumbles to herself, "I am surrounded by idiots, idiot generals, idiot colonels, idiots all of them. Only the Jews are not idiots. Only the Jews are smarter than everyone else."

She walks around in circles, pacing with her hands behind her back, shaking her head. Then, with her finger pointing at her brain, an amazing idea occurs to her. "Hmmm... I know vhat I must do. I must make all of the Jews my slaves and then I vill control all of the really smart people in Europe. Then I von't have to put up with such idiots." At this point, she grabs my mother's hands, pulls her to her feet, and begins dancing around in a circle singing, "And, that's why I am the Fuhrer, because I am almost as smart as the Jews, you see?"

Singing like a child reciting a nursery rhyme and emphasizing every syllable, she pulls each of us to our feet until we are all holding hands dancing around the room. By this time, we are giddy with laughter. Unable to contain herself a moment longer; Dina crumples to the floor in hilarious glee. The sound of that hearty laughter is like a match igniting a flame, sending us into fits of side-splitting merriment. It is such a relief to make fun of the hated Fuhrer and to find moments of respite from the terrible ordeal. The stresses and fears of our lives need this release of anxiety and Cousin Dina somehow finds a way to relieve our tensions. There may be less food to eat and a more crowded home, but Dina Talman brings rays of sunshine to the darkest of our days with her good humor. I love her as if she were my sister. It is early winter in 1939 when another change comes to our household. My grandmother, who has lived with my parents for their entire married life, decides to live with her eldest daughter, Mindale, my uncle Tuvye, and my cousins Nadja and Majer. Aunt Mindale has a large home and plenty of room. My grandmother will have the comfort of living with Tuvye's widowed mother, Chava, a contemporary and friend. And she will be closer to her youngest child Natalia (Nachele), who returned to Radom with her husband Alexander and son David after their gas station was confiscated by the Nazis. They live in the same apartment building as Mindale and Tuvye. Living with her daughters, my grandmother will be well cared for and treated with the greatest of respect. The arrangement is satisfactory for all. For Abek and me, this loss of our grandmother is one more indication that our lives will be altered forever. We cry bitter tears when she leaves.

My grandparents played such an important role in my world. My grandmother was the first to greet me with love in the morning and to give me the last kiss at night. For my mother, it soon proves to be a blessing, as she has never lived without the suggestions and good intentions of her in-laws. Having lived her married life under the watchful eye of my father's parents, my mother welcomes the change. Now she is the sole woman of the house.

My mother adores my cousin Dina's mother, her older sister Hanale, and Dina's presence rekindles childhood memories. It gives my mother the chance to share a cup of tea and reminisce with a relative who intimately knows the history and places of her youth. With the daily hardships and uncertain future, the past replays day after day at our kitchen table and probably at the kitchen tables in all of occupied Europe.

The Judenrat now functions as the intermediary between the Nazis and the Jewish population. They do their best to alleviate the growing hunger among the inhabitants by opening soup kitchens throughout the Jewish neighborhoods. The

Judenrat hands out some 4,000 meals a day at a token charge of 20 *grosz*, which is waived for children and those who cannot pay. They also do their best to organize the labor force needed by the Germans. In this way, they can mitigate the kidnapping of Jewish men from their homes and hinder the practice of randomly beating and grabbing men off the streets. This practice has caused massive panic and fear among us and people hide in their homes, afraid to come out. So we have a vicious cycle of labor being demanded by the Nazis going unfulfilled. In turn, they beat and abduct more Jews.

The Jewish penchant for organization allows the Judenrat to address some of the needs of the most destitute. Much of the forced labor comes from the poorest residents among the Jews, since anyone with resources can pay the Judenrat to remove their names from the forced workers lists. The Nazis pay nothing for labor. The Judenrat uses the sweat money from wealthier Jews to pay the laborers who desperately need the daily 1-2 zlotys to sustain their families. My father says the Judenrat does its best, considering it is forced to do business with the devil and his disciples.

To feed the large occupying army, officials, SS, and police force, the Germans require slaughterers, butchers, and cooks. My father, with a highly desirable skill, is contacted by the Judenrat and ordered to work for the Nazis as a butcher. For this he gets a pittance of money, works long hours, and is supervised by soldiers with machine guns. He returns from a long day's work and jokes about how afraid the Germans must be of the Jews. "They have so many soldiers with guns guarding so few Jews and their dangerous butcher knives."

Although food on the black market is extremely expensive, my mother finds a way to keep our family from hunger. All of her life she has loved beautiful clothing and jewelry. Aside from the investments of our building and store, she knew jewelry would be a valuable asset. Being a business woman and having worked her entire married life, she has been able to indulge in fashion, with her elegant wardrobe, handmade with the finest of wools, laces and silks. These fineries and her ample collection of jewelry are a godsend to us now. Filled with diamonds and pearls, antique watches, necklaces, and bracelets of gold, her jewelry box glitters and fills my eyes with awe. I watch her pick and choose a piece that might bring a hefty price on the black market.

"What do you think Dinale? Which necklace shall I sell?" I watch as she chooses two necklaces from the box.

"Mamashy, they are both so beautiful. I don't know which one to choose."

Placing one necklace back into the case, she holds up the other necklace of delicate white pearls, joined together with two overlapping circles of diamonds. "Let me try this one on you and then we will decide." Fastening the clip she sighs. "There, now turn around and look in the mirror and see how lovely you look. Jewelry has a way of lighting up a woman's face, doesn't it?" Eyeing the sparkling necklace in the mirror, I feel grown up and beautiful. "Oh Mamashy, it is so lovely, I wish you didn't have to part with it."

"I don't mind, Dinale. They are just objects and not lasting. I have enjoyed having them, but they mean nothing to me. All that matters are my children, your father, and the rest of our family. I will gladly sell off all of these baubles if I can keep us safe another day." Smiling, she scrutinizes me in the mirror. "Yes, I think this one will bring a nice price. I will take it to Pani Zdebowa today and she will put me in touch with a buyer."

In this way, my mother sells off her precious possessions, obtaining the best price possible given the times. Secretly, I know she receives a pittance of the true value. But what does that matter? At least she is able to care for those she loves.

Chapter 7

Crisis Strikes Again and Again

It is the winter of 1940 and we are in a daily struggle for the necessities of life. With normalcy unattainable, the worst of times brings out the best in us. My sister and her two friends, Eva and Esterka, patiently continue our education several hours a day at the kitchen table. Each teaches her favorite subject to Abek and me. To tell the truth, I don't miss going to school at all. In addition, my mother has hired a private instructor who comes several times a week. This is a blessing since the teacher has lost all means of employment. To his chagrin, my brother must sit through my lessons, as he is younger and can learn from my more advanced studies. When I am done, I flee outside, leaving Abek to sit and complain how unfair it is that I am allowed to leave. It is a boon, as I am free to play in the park and in the courtyard with Fela and my friends. Fela and I dance in the snowdrifts. Building snowmen and having snowball fights, we feel like children again. We even dare to dream that one day the war will end and our lives will resume where we left off.

The cold winter's days soon present a new crisis. It strikes at the heart of our family with the precision of a thrown dagger. As if my parents' worries were not enough, Nadja comes running into the house as if she is being hunted by lions, her hair an unruly mass of curls and her eyes red from crying. In hysteria, she throws herself into my father's arms, burying her sobs in his chest. My mother runs to her, pressing against her back, her arms encircling her. My parents look like bookends supporting a falling book.

"*Nu*, Nadja, what is it, what has happened?" My mother's voice rises in a frenzied wail. "Please stop crying. We can't understand what you are saying. Tell us what has happened."

My father adds, "Shh... shh... maidele, calm down. It can't be that bad. We can't help you if we don't know what is wrong. Talk to us!"

My sister cannot be quieted and continues to weep; her body is racked with uncontrollable spasms. There is nothing anyone can do but wait for her to regain her composure and tell us what horrible catastrophe has struck. After what seems like an eternity, she raises her head, her face stricken pale with fear, her words indecipherable through her sobs. At first haltingly, like a trickle of water seeping from a dike, she reveals the source of her sorrow.

"I don't know what I was thinking," she stammers, shaking her head. "I... I left the house to meet up with Eva and Esterka. I wasn't thinking, I guess. I forgot to wear my armband. A Polish policeman stopped me; he was walking with a Nazi gendarme and his German shepherd. He asked me where I lived and I said Koszarowa Ulica. Oh my God! I should have lied and said I lived somewhere else. Then he said, 'Isn't that a Jewish neighborhood?' And I said, 'Yes.'"

At this point, my mother begins to cry, which triggers Nadja's tears once more. My father tells them both to stop crying so we can get to the bottom of what happened and decide what to do. Nadja resumes her account of what has occurred. "The Nazi raised his voice and asked, 'You are a Jew, correct?' I said yes, and he began to shout 'Where is your armband, Jew? Where is that gutter symbol of the garbage Jews?' It was so horrible Mama, he kept on shouting at me. *'You are in violation of a directive that Jews are not allowed out of their homes without an armband identifying them as pig Jews!'* He was so angry and so demeaning that I thought I was going to throw up. I was so scared. 'I forgot it sir,' I told him, 'I am so sorry, please, please, I will never do it again! 'The Polish policeman looked uncomfortable and probably would have let me go if he hadn't been with the Nazi, but he had to look supportive in front of him so he remained silent. The Nazi told me to report to Gestapo headquarters tomorrow morning. He said I will receive my punishment when I get there and that I am to come alone. I am so frightened. What will they do to me? What if they deport me? I will die!"

My father begins pacing, his jaw clenching in a paroxysm of tension and his brow damp with perspiration. "We must stay calm. You have to go to Nazi headquarters. There is no way to avoid it. Your mother will accompany you and wait outside.

You will beg them to be tolerant, reminding them that you are a teenager, a child. Do you understand?"

Nodding yes, Nadja resumes her whimpering.

My father continues. "We will wait to see what happens. If they detain you, your mother will return home to inform me and I will go to the Judenrat and beg them to intervene. Don't worry, the Nazis are beasts, but I have not seen them harm any young women or children. I am sure that they will just give you a warning. You will see that I am right."

That night it isn't me who suffers from nightmares. Nadja wakes Dina and me, crying in her sleep tossing and flailing her arms, trying to fend off the monsters that pursue her. We calm her as best we can, whispering words of encouragement that everything will be alright. We sleep wrapped in each other's arms until the morning light.

The next day, even without a good night's sleep, Nadja manages to look startlingly beautiful, her blue eyes rimmed with circles of darkness and her demeanor appropriately subdued. She leaves with my mother and walks to Nazi headquarters. My father has to report to work, so I am left alone with Dina and Abek to await the outcome of Nadja's punishment. We occupy ourselves with reading and games of chess, but our nervousness is getting the better of us. Every few minutes, one of us jumps up running to the window to see if Mamashy and Nadja are, God willing, coming up the street. Finally, after endless hours, we see them turn into the courtyard. Once inside our home and with the door closed, we all rejoice jumping up and down hugging each other, so grateful that Nadja is safe and back at home. My father was correct. The punishment is a severe warning and an added burden of having to report to Nazi headquarters every morning for one week.

Each day, after facing her Nazi persecutor, she returns demoralized, recounting to us what it is like walking alone through Nazi headquarters. "It is so frightening I feel like a thousand eyes are boring into me, filled with hatred and disgust. The yellow Star of David on its white band has its desired effect and most of the people give me a wide berth as if I am contaminated with a deadly disease. Then I am made to stand for hours, waiting to be presented to the same Nazi who yelled at me in the street. No chair, no water, nothing but malicious stares as everyone else comes and goes in the office. Finally, I am called before him and he proceeds to verbally abuse me with every vile name possible. I have to stand there in humiliation, while he publicly degrades and dehumanizes me in front of the worst Nazis, some of whom stand around sniggering with glee at my debasement.

It is terrifying. Once he releases all of his venom, he warns me that if I am ever caught without my armband again, he will see that I am immediately deported and that I will never see my family again. Over and over, he reminds me how lucky I am that he doesn't deport me right now."

The week seems like a lifetime for Nadja, as she endures the daily degradation of cowering before the Nazi. Each day, he inspects her armband, finding fault with the way it is sewn. Each night, she stitches a new armband, only to be traumatized by his dissatisfaction the next day. This goes on for the entire week. By day she is tortured by the sinister Nazi and by night she is terrified with dreams of him. He finally tires of the game and, with little more than a sneer, dismisses her, saying he never wants to see her again. The whole episode has scared us all to death and my parents are now doubly watchful over us. Certainly, no one ever leaves the house without his armband again.

Within a few weeks, after sulking around the house, still smarting from her near deportation, Nadja returns to her old self. My parents have not pressed her, but have allowed her to reflect on the events she has suffered. They know that with time, she will return once more to the confidence and activism that marked her progress since childhood. After a few weeks of silence and pensiveness, our sister resumes our studies with a new urgency. She seizes the reins of our education, easing us forward to what she now predicts will be a bright future. With her natural positivity and poise restored, my brother and I are encouraged to work harder at our studies to please her.

As the deprivations grow with each day, the news becomes even more disheartening, to say the least. The Nazi war machine seems unstoppable. On April 9th, the Nazis invade Denmark and Norway and within days, our northern neighbors surrender. Sadly, we are not the only people suffering from the Nazi menace as it spreads across Europe.

Even with all of the restrictions against any practice of the Jewish religion, most Jews in Radom manage to celebrate some semblance of the Passover Seder. In our home, the story of the Exodus from Egypt and the biblical destruction of pharaoh's armies by the swirling waters of the Red Sea are more poignant than ever. My father leads the Seder with as much joy as he can muster, elaborating and drawing parallels to the evils that plague the Jews of Europe and the Jews of ancient Egypt. At one point, my brother interrupts the story with a question for my father, "But Tatashy, we don't have a Moses. How will God save us without a Moses?" My father stares at Abek as he ponders his question. Lovingly he smooths the errant curls of his precocious son as he assuredly answers. "Don't worry, Abek. He will send us an army to save us. You will see. He will send us a powerful army."

We eat the matzo that has been sent to Poland from the Red Cross and Jewish organizations around the world. We pray that God will send us an army and deliver us from the Nazis, as he delivered us from pharaoh when we were enslaved in Egypt.

Instead, that holiday proves to be the last for eighteen Jewish men and a group of Polish community leaders. The Nazis order thirty-two men to report to the labor recruiting office; fortunately, only eighteen answered the edict. They are taken into confinement and viciously beaten unrecognizable. Then they are thrown into trucks and driven to a suburb called Firley where they are pushed into pits of sand. The Nazis, as if to amuse themselves, play a sport of unspeakable cruelty. Laughing as they perform their grisly task, they blow them to bits with grenades. As word spreads through every home of the awful fate of these innocent men, the entire community mourns.

On May 10th, Hitler becomes even bolder with the invasion of France, Belgium, Holland, and Luxembourg. France fights valiantly for six weeks against the Nazi invasion. Thousands of people flee south from Paris, abandoning the city until an armistice is signed on June 22nd dividing France in half, the Nazis controlling the north and Marshall Petain's Vichy government controlling the south. Belgium and Luxembourg, both neutral countries, surrender within one day, making Hitler's road to France a veritable speedway. Holland battles bravely for two weeks destroying many German aircraft and with much loss of German lives. But in the end, she cannot withstand the massive attack Hitler mounts against her and Holland falls from the incessant bombardment of its cities and people.

The eyes and ears of the world are focused on Europe and the conflagration that is engulfing her. Hitler's army marches across Europe, felling nations as if they are dominoes collapsing one atop the other. Hitler is on an unstoppable run and on September 27th the Axis Pact between Germany, Italy, and Japan is sealed in ink, with the Italians invading Egypt and Greece shortly thereafter. Within months, Hungary and Romania have joined the Axis Powers placing thousands of more Jews within the Nazis' grasp.

My father becomes more distraught and nervous, often hiding the newspapers once he has read them. My sister digs them out of the garbage and reads them, sometimes sharing the news with me. The quotes are terrifying. From *Der Sturmer*, "The time is near when a machine will go into motion which is going to prepare a grave for the world's criminal—Judah— from which there will be no resurrection."

In January 1941, Hans Frank, the German Marshall of Poland, is quoted, "I ask nothing of the Jews except that they should disappear." My nightmares begin again in earnest and long are the nights when my sister and cousin Dina try to comfort me to no avail.

On March 29th, 1941, comes the decree from Dr. Karl Lasch, the Governor of Radom that will change our world forever. Two separate ghettos are to be established, one to occupy the surrounding neighborhood around Walowa Street, a poor neighborhood occupied by Poles, and a small rural ghetto in the suburbs called Glinice. In all quarters of the city, panic strikes, compounded by the fact that we have to leave by April 7th, giving us only ten days to find a place to live and move.

I sit at the kitchen table, staring as a spring storm delivers a steady stream of snowflakes that drift peacefully past the window. I listen as my father begins to detail the forced move from our home to a ghetto. My father's face is pinched and drawn with worry as he begins to explain, "Children, as you know the Nazis are requiring that every Jew in Radom move to one of two ghettos allocated as residential areas for Jews. There are approximately 35,000 Jews residing in Radom, so naturally this displacement is causing great stress in the community. Many Polish families also will be uprooted from their traditional neighborhoods and homes. There are to be two ghettos established. The larger of the two called the Walowa Street Ghetto will hold 30,000 people, making it extremely cramped and crowded. The second ghetto is called the Glinice Ghetto and will hold about 5,000 Jews. It is several kilometers from here and the houses are older, but a bit more spacious. Mama and I have secured a home from a Polish farmer in the Glinice Ghetto where we will be moving. We feel the conditions will be better there as I predict there will be extreme shortages of food and other necessities in the months ahead. Sadly, most of our possessions will have to be left behind and only what is practical for our survival will accompany us to our new home. I will need your help in paring down your belongings to the absolute essentials. Mama and I have already begun to list what will be needed and what will be left behind.

The most difficult adjustment will be saying good-bye to friends and family, at least until the war ends. Some of them will be going to the Walowa Ghetto and I don't know if we will have the ability to see each other."

"But, Tata!" Suddenly it becomes clear to me what sacrifices our moving entails. "You don't mean that we won't be able to visit Bubysy or Fela or anyone?"

"Dinale, it is impossible to say what will or will not be allowed." I feel my heart contract in my chest and the blood in my veins surges in anger. "I won't go!"

"Dinale…," my father's voice becomes sorrowful and compassionate. "Dinale… please, you must understand that this is happening to every family in Radom and most likely every Jewish family in Europe under Nazi rule."

"I don't care!" The injustice of our situation has instilled in me a new-found defiance, "I am going to run away and hide in the forest or the apple orchard! I will not give up my friends and family!"

Tears of frustration fill my eyes and guilt consumes me as I see my father bow his head in dejection. I cannot bear another moment of the emotions that overwhelm me. Jumping up from the table, I grab my coat and run from the house. I run to Fela's house, calling to her from the courtyard. "Fela, come quickly. I need you," I cry. "I need you to come outside so we can talk! *Something terrible has happened.*"

Fela peers from her window, a shadow behind the lace curtains. She waves indicating that she will come in just a minute. I stand there, pounding my feet as powdery snow crystals rise in a cloud around me. Tears fall from my eyes as I ponder the consequences of my insubordination towards my parents. I have never been defiant of them, especially during these times when their burdens are so great. Already my words are echoing in my mind, surrounding me in a veil of guilt and remorse. I have hurt the two people who I love most in the world. As I pace back and forth in the courtyard, Fela finally exits her door and runs to me.

"I can't believe it," I cry as I hug her. "The Nazis are ordering all the Jews into ghettos and we are going to have to leave and move to a small ghetto miles from here."

She embraces me. "I know Dinale, my parents have told us we are going to have to move. Don't worry. At least we are going to the same place, to the small ghetto."

"You too?" I marvel in disbelief.

Taking my hand she says, "Come, let's go to the apple orchard where we can be alone."

Hand in hand, we slip behind our building to the privacy of our childhood haven. We are happy to garner one last chance to escape the realities of a world that slips further and further from our grasp.

With our backs against the solid trunk of our favorite apple tree, we whisper of the pending changes. It is cold and the wind blusters through the leafless orchard, sending snowflakes dancing in the air under the gray skies. I remember the sunny day here, not so long ago, when we made plans for a future. Those dreams seem as farfetched as flying to the moon.

"It won't be so bad, Dynka. We will still be together. Think of it as an adventure. What would Shirley Temple do? She would find a way to make the best of things, never losing her pride. Even in the worst of situations, she manages to look beautiful—even in rags."

I laugh, trying to picture Fela and me wearing rags. The whole idea seems ludicrous and I shake my head clearing the preposterous vision from my mind.

"I know you are right, Fela. At least we will all be together," I say, clasping her hands in mine. "I am just so afraid of what is to come and what will become of us. Why are the Nazis separating us from the rest of the population? What are they planning? Why are they taking everything from us and where is God? Why is He not coming to our rescue?"

"Dynka, you know that God has his reasons for not interfering in the world of men. Believe me, He will eventually see our plight and the evil of the Nazis and He will raise his sword and obliterate them from the earth."

"You are right," I sigh. "God would never forsake his people." Then, remembering my disobedience to my parents, "I have behaved unforgivably. I lost my temper and said the most awful things to my parents. I told them that I was not going to go with them and that I would run away and hide in the forest. They must be so angry and disappointed in me."

"Don't be silly. Go home and apologize to them. They will forgive you no matter what you do or say. We all say things we don't mean. You should hear my parents. They are squabbling all of the time like a couple of mad hens."

The imagery of squawking poultry sends us both into fits of giggles. Simultaneously, we begin to cluck like a couple of hens fanning the air with our wings. I feel light as air as the tension and the cares of the world seemed to fly free from me. My frosty breath hangs in the air as the snow begins to come down in heavier large flakes.

It is time to return to our homes and reluctantly we end our sojourn in the orchard. Fela and I hug and part, running home with the intent of surviving the dreaded move to the ghetto.

I compose myself as I open the door of my home, fully prepared to make amends to my parents. When I enter, they both jump up from the table and run to me, hugging and kissing me. "I am so sorry. Mamashy and Tatashy, please forgive me!"

"It's okay!" they cry, their arms enveloping me. My mother, ready with a towel, rubs my head vigorously, wrapping me in it as she guides me towards the fire burning in the open hearth.

"We wish we could have broken the news to you more gently, but the time to prepare is so short," says my father, following us.

"Yes, and we need you to help us," adds my mother. Respectfully, I nod. "I will do my best to make you proud. Fela also is moving to the smaller ghetto, so at least I have one of my friends."

"That's good darling," says my father. "This is the girl that we are so proud to call our daughter. Now go change out of these wet clothes and let us continue with our discussion. "Nadja, Dina, Abek, come to the kitchen. We must finish planning!"

The days fly by as we pack the belongings we will take with us to our new home. My mother and our Polish maid, Anya, make many trips in advance of our actual departure, cleaning and readying our new quarters. Nadja and I discuss the personal belongings we feel are necessary; winter clothing, summer clothing, comforters, and linens. For me it is my precious balls and books that I could never live without. My mother has the hardest time deciding which of her most prized possessions she cannot part with. Her album of childhood photographs and of course the photos of her children cannot possibly be left behind. Her beautiful furniture will have to be abandoned, as there is no room for it in the small home awaiting us. I watch as my mother wanders around the rooms, talking aloud to herself, weighing the value of objects and whether she needs them. Of course, most of her cooking pots and pans will be needed, but she will only take one set of china, which poses a dilemma for her. She has a beautiful set of Hungarian fine china with butterflies painted in dazzling hues that seem to float across the pure white background. Our beautiful holiday china was passed down from her grandmother. Parting with this treasured family heirloom is like thrusting a knife into her heart. In the end, she makes the decision to leave the dishes behind.

One decision that has been made for her is whether or not to take her paintings that line the walls of our home. She is an avid art collector buying for love and investment from the local art gallery that imports paintings from all over Europe. *Plein aire* oil paintings of landscapes by the impressionists line our walls. She is particularly enamored with the work of a Dutch artist named Van Gogh and has purchased several of his small oils. The Nazis have ordered all art to remain on the walls where it will be confiscated for the benefit of the Third Reich. I watch my mother walk around the rooms of our home, bidding good-bye to her old friends and touching each one with a farewell caress. Anything that can be easily sold such as jewelry and extra clothing are mandatory. The sale of these will provide the money to purchase food and medicines to keep our family alive.

The day before the ordered deadline of our departure, we watch my father remove from our doorway our precious Mezuzah. He whispers a prayer to God, carefully removing this symbol of a Jewish home. Every Mezuzah, whether wood, metal, or glass contains a small piece of parchment inscribed with a passage from the Book of Deuteronomy. Twenty-two lines equally spaced and printed precisely so that they may access the power of God's eternal magic and blessings and keep the dwellers of this home safe. The parchment of the Mezuzah reads,

Hear, O Israel: The Lord our God is one Lord:

And thou shalt love the Lord thy God with all thine heart, and with all thy soul, and with all thy might.

And these words, which I command thee this day, shall be in thine heart.

And thou shalt teach them diligently unto thy children, and shalt talk of them when thou sittest in thine house, and when thou walkest by the way,

And when thou liest down, and when thou risest up.

And thou shalt bind them for a sign upon thine hand, and they shall be as frontlets between thine eyes.

And thou shalt write upon them the posts of thy house, and on thy gates.

And it shall come to pass, if ye shall hearken diligently unto my commandments which I command you this day, to love the

Lord your God, and to serve him with all your heart and with all your soul

That I will give you the rain of your land in its due season, the first rain and the latter rain, that thou mayest gather in thy corn, and thy wine, and thine oil.

And I will send grass in thy fields for thy cattle, that thou mayest eat and be full.

Take heed to yourselves, that your heart be not deceived, and ye turn aside, and serve other gods, and worship them;

And then, the Lord's wrath be kindled against you, and he shut up the heaven, that there be no rain, and that the land yield not her fruit; and lest ye perish quickly from off the good land which the Lord giveth you.

The day of our leave-taking comes. I awaken and go to the window and look down upon the street where I have grown up. Placing my hand on the window, I can feel the cold of the glass. A chill of foreboding races through my body and I shiver.

In the street below I see the leafless chestnut trees, their branches reaching toward the heavens. This gray morning feels more like winter than spring. The street is already bustling with people in various stages of loading a lifetime's worth of possessions into various means of transport.

I hear my parents from the other room as they busy themselves with organizing the boxes and crates that hold the wealth of our lives. I dress and make myself ready for what will surely be a long, arduous day.

Our personal belongings have been brought downstairs and loaded into the dorozka and hired wagon that will accompany us to the ghetto. We have said our good-byes to all of our family and friends, most of whom are moving to the large ghetto.

Solemnly, we take a final walk through the only home my brother and I have ever known the home where we were born. Already Ifeel a stranger in the familiar spaces.

Silently, I bid farewell as I try to burn every angle and surface into my memory. Not just the objects and place, but my childhood. The treasured memories are like paint I brush onto the canvas of my mind. Without further ado, my parents guide us outside and, brushing aside their tears, they shut the door on the past

Part 2

The Ghetto Years

Chapter 8

Life Changes

Once out in the street, we find pandemonium all around us. Carts, horses, dorozka, and people pushing and carrying their belongings have created a throng of humanity that seems not to be moving or going anywhere. Everywhere there are children crying, parents shushing, and the elderly moaning. It reminds me of what the Exodus must have looked and sounded like when, as slaves, our ancestors left the relative safety of their homes for the desert and an unknowable future. The difference between these two momentous events is that as slaves they looked to what they hoped would be a brighter tomorrow and freedom. We however, are moving into what we all know can only be diminished circumstances and slavery. If it weren't so frightening, we probably would laugh at the joke life is playing on Poland's Jews, from slavery to freedom and now back to slavery.

The crowds are overwhelming as people and wagons try to move in different directions in a frenzied swarm of dislocation.

We follow the wagon and dorozka that my parents have hired as it inches its way through the congested streets with everything that is left of our lives teetering perilously atop; we straggle behind, following amid the dust that rises in thick clouds from the wheels of wagons and horses hooves. The poor overburdened horses strain against their harnesses to make headway but are obstructed in every direction. My brother and I each cling to one of my father's hands as he tries to protect us with his body and absorb the bumping and jostling of humanity that buffets us. Now and again someone waves or calls hello to my parents. A man interrupts our progress, thrusting his hand at my father in an effort to shake his, "Joel it is a sad day indeed that we have come to. It is good your father did not live to see this."

My father knows that my brother and I are listening intently to his words and simply replies, "Hopefully we will survive the Nazis and live to rebuild our lives again, good luck, Shmuel."

"You too, Joel, good luck to you and your family," the man calls as the flow of people surges and propels him forward until he disappears into the miasma of humanity.

"Tata," I ask, "Do you think we will ever be allowed to go home?"

"Someday Dinale, someday I pray we will all go home."

Just then, a Jewish Policeman shouts at us, "Keep moving! Keep those children moving!" Interspersed among the river of people and transport walk the newly created Jewish Policemen with their blue and red caps with a yellow Star of David insignia and armbands on which is written *Judischer Ordnungsdienst.*[28] The Nazis have created a special company of unarmed Jews to carry out their bidding and patrol the ghettos and the hapless Jews that will now populate them. I can sense my father's disdain for these trumped up puppets who now wield unbridled power over their own people.

---

28 Jewish Marshalls

With barely a flicker of acknowledgement toward the policeman, my father bids us forward. "Come, children, let's keep moving or we will never reach our new home."

Prior to this move, every Jew has been given an identity card that bears his or her photograph with a large stamped J for Jude on it. These cards, like the Star of David on our clothing, are to be carried at all times. My parents have already informed us that it is illegal to leave the ghetto without a special pass, which is nearly impossible to obtain. If caught outside, the punishment is a severe fine and the risk of being beaten, or worse.

Finally, after hours of navigating the streets and the slow progression of thousands of people and their belongings, we finally reach the Glinice Ghetto, entering through the archway that has been newly built to delineate the entrance and seal us into our new segregated neighborhood. As my father passes through the arch he knows that for him there will be no leaving except under the guard of the policemen that will escort the work details to and from the ghetto each day. I wonder what thoughts my thirty-seven year old father must be pondering as he becomes a prisoner of the city of his birth. He will never be allowed to see his mother or sisters who are moving to the Big Ghetto. The few kilometers that separate the ghettos might just as well be a thousand.

When finally we reach our new home we begin the enormous task of unloading and transferring everything into the house. There is very little time for complaining about the cramped accommodations, as there is so much to be done before we can finally collapse in our beds. The house is very small but we are actually very lucky. It has a large main room attached to the kitchen where we will all sleep, and an indoor bathroom. Upstairs there is another apartment but as of yet no one has been assigned to live there. My sister, Cousin Dina, and I will occupy one bed and my parents and brother will sleep in the other bed. The house previously belonged to a Polish farmer who had a shed in the back where he kept some livestock. My parents have wisely purchased a cow from the farmer and we will have a supply of fresh milk every day, which we will use for our personal needs. The excess milk will be sold or given to our neighbors. My mother has done her best to make the house inviting. Somehow she procured enough brightly colored fabric to adorn the windows with new curtains. We all compliment her on her valiant efforts to cheer up the tired old rooms. That evening when everything has been neatly stored in its proper place, we have a small supper that my mother pre-prepared. After the blessings, with a fire roaring in the hearth, we talk about happy memories and what we hope will be better days ahead. My brother and I must have fallen asleep from exhaustion at the table. Nodding out with our heads on our arms listening to the adults talk, we slipped into the world of dreams for I do not remember my mother and father carrying us to bed and tucking us in under the warm down comforters that made the journey to the ghetto. In the morning I awake in a strange house that is now my home. Both my sister and cousin Dina are up and gone. The room is dark and my nose twitches at the uncustomary dank smell of mildew. The sour odor combined with a hundred years of smoke that emanates from the dark wooden walls accosts my senses. We will soon learn that, no matter how much we clean and scour, the odor is a permanent reminder of the age of the old house and those who have lived in it. My father left early with the police escorts to work as a slave laborer for the Nazis butchering and dressing meats and he will not return until evening. Dressing quickly, I am anxious to explore the confines of the neighborhood. My mother enters the door from the back of the house carrying pails of milk. I run to help her. She smiles and says, "Dinale look at the delicious creamy milk that our fine cow has provided us.

Isn't it wonderful to know that we shall have milk every day? We are very lucky."

"Yes, Mama, we are very lucky," I concur. "Mamashy, where's Abek?"

"Oh, he rose early and is out exploring the street looking for new friends."

"Mamashy, did you milk the cow yourself?"

"See, you didn't know your mama was so talented. Yes, I learned to do this when I was just a young girl. I will teach you how to milk a cow... if you would like to learn?"

"Can you show me now?" I say jumping up and down with excitement. It is seldom that my mother has time to spend with any of us anymore, as she is so busy selling and buying the food and articles that we need and trying to keep us fed and healthy. To be alone with her and have her full attention is like a dream come true.

"Come, let me put these pails down in the kitchen and I will teach you the mystery of milking." I follow as she set the pails down in a cool spot in the room that is both kitchen and bedroom. I watch as she pours a glass of milk, "A cow is one of God's most extraordinary creatures and was clearly created to provide for man and thus should be treated with love and kindness." She hands me the glass of milk as I follow her out the back door and into the cow shed as she continues, "In order for a cow to give you the best milk she has to offer, she needs to be soothed and calmed with gentle words and a reassuring hand."

Drinking the creamy milk, I look at our cow, with her large brown kindly eyes, and she looks at me as she chews on the fresh hay in the bin in front of her. My mother places a small stool next to our cow and motions me to sit beside her on the ground. "I think we should name our cow, what do you think?"

"Oh, yes of course," I nod in agreement. "We must give her a special name."

"Why don't you introduce yourself to our cow and rub her with your hands so that she can get a scent of you."

Placing my empty glass on the floor I slowly approach our cow's large red head. I timidly touch the end of her nose and, gaining confidence, I begin to rub more earnestly. "Hello, dear cow, my name is Dynka Frydman, and I am very pleased to meet you." Turning to my mother, "Maybe we should name her Queen Esther?"

The cow suddenly nuzzles my hand and smothers it in a sticky gooey lick, something like the consistency of moist sandpaper. It tickles and I begin to giggle. My mother laughs and says, "Very good, see, she likes you. Queen Esther..." I watch as she considers the name. "It's a good name. Like the great biblical heroine of our people in ancient Persia, our Esther will be taking care of us too. I like it... so Esther it shall be. Now come here and sit on my lap and I will talk you through the milking of our Queen Esther. Take the udder in your hand and gently pull down and squeeze it ever so lightly." Doing as I am told I try to pull and squeeze but nothing happens. Esther however turns her head and looks at me to see what is going on.

"Mamashy, did I do something wrong?"

"No, no, you just have to be patient and keep trying. Now try again."

I try and suddenly a stream of milk squirts out of the cow's udder, filling the pail. "I did it, I did it," I exclaim with delight as Esther turns her head, looking very pleased indeed.

"Yes, you did," says my mama, hugging and kissing me. I glow with pride and joy at sharing this special moment with my mother. Suddenly the world seems a little brighter. "Now go outside and play, I think I saw a girl who looks about your age. Go and introduce yourself and later you can tell me all about her."

Kissing my mother on the cheek and giving Esther a final pat on her head I run from the shed and around the house onto the street in front. There I see a girl playing with a ball. "Hello," she says, waving. "Would you like to play?"

"That would be great. My name is Dina Frydman. What's your name?"

"Vunia," she replies, "Vunia Greenberg. It looks like we're next door neighbors," she says pointing at the two story wooden house that is nearly identical to the one we now occupy. "I'm twelve years old and I moved here with my sister Lola who is seventeen, my parents, and my Great-Aunt Ruth and Great-Uncle Saul are also living with us. They have two dogs named Winston and Churchill."

I look with curiosity at the almond shaped green eyes that stare appraisingly at me, waiting for my comment. "I'll be twelve in June and I moved with my sister Nadja who is seventeen and my brother Abek who is nine. My cousin Dina is also living with us, she is twenty-one. I've never had a dog, what kind are they?"

"Chihuahuas. Would you like to meet them?"

"Oh, yes!"

"Come on, follow me."

Without hesitation I follow the tall skinny girl with her curly mane of rust colored hair into her home through the low doorway at the entrance. The house is dark and musty like ours, with boxes in various stages of unpacking scattered about the room. Vunia takes the steps two at a time as I follow her to the second floor. She knocks on the door smiling at me with anticipation. "Aunt Ruth, it's Vunia and I've brought a new friend. Can we come in?"

"Of course darling," a woman's voice answers.

The door opens and standing before me is the most exotic woman I have ever seen. Her head is clasped in a golden turban from which wisps of silvery coiled hair fight to escape. The wiry hair reminds me of springs popping out of an old mattress. She addresses me with blue eyes that are lined with a matching shade of smudged cobalt blue pencil that emphasizes the slight protrusion of her oversized eyes. Ruth is dressed in a brocaded caftan that drapes her body in mysterious folds that both hide and reveal her. I cannot take my eyes off the strange creature that stands before me. Her odd demeanor triggers imaginings of Eastern potentates. My gaze travels the length of her, finally resting on the two small dogs that peer at Vunia and me through amber eyes, their little tails drumming the air with expectation.

"Forgive the disarray of our diminutive space." Her honeyed voice has the cadence of someone whose mother tongue is another language. "I guess we are all going to have to get used to a simpler existence, aren't we?" Her rouged lips draw into a smile as the two small dogs wriggle with anticipation of pending freedom.

"This is Dina, Aunt Ruth, she lives next door."

Ruth formally offers her hand, "How nice to meet you dear."

"Dina has never had a pet of her own Aunt Ruth and we are hoping to play with Winston and Churchill."

"Well, I am sure that nothing could make these two mischievous little boys happier than playing with you." Ruth kisses the two Chihuahuas and then bends to release the squirming pups that, upon release, began to spin in joyful circles about our legs, jumping with boundless energy and eagerness for our attention. While Vunia and I play with the two vivacious dogs, Ruth excuses herself, leaving us to our games. Proudly, Vunia puts the compliant pair through a series of tricks that they perform with yelping pleasure. They roll over and dance in circles on their hind legs while Vunia, in an uninterrupted stream of consciousness, shares the story of the Greenberg family with me. I learn that her father was an accountant before the Nazis overran our homeland and installed themselves as our overlords. Now her father is reduced to day labor and her mother, like mine, is forced to sell her fine clothing and jewelry to support their family. As for the intriguing Aunt Ruth, Vunia confides the tale of her avant-garde relatives, which might as well have been a tale from the *Arabian Nights*, so unfamiliar is the reality of it to me. Vunia's Great-Uncle Saul as a young man had moved to England long before the Great War, in order to pursue his education at Cambridge. Through his Rothschild cousins he was introduced to Ruth. They had fallen in love and over the protests of her family Ruth had converted to Judaism and married the foreign Jew. After living as an expatriate for dozens of years, Saul yearned to return to his family. Ever adventurous, Ruth gave him his wish. Theirs is a great love affair that has withstood the caprices of time and they have remained devoted to each other for over forty years. They moved to Poland many years before the current crises and lived in a beautiful home on a wide avenue in the cosmopolitan city of Warszaw. There, amid the wealthy patrons of the city, they lived a wonderful life. Warszaw is considered the Paris of the East with its lively café society and cultural flowering of art, music and politics. Traveling the world, they lived a grand lifestyle, returning often to England and Ruth's well connected relations. The only missing blessing in their lives was Ruth's inability to conceive. Chihuahuas have filled the emptiness and they dote on their substitute children. These two Chihuahuas are the last in a long line of the continuing dynasty of Winston and Churchill Chihuahuas, so named for the great statesman who now leads the British nation as Prime Minister and is Hitler's most vocal foe. Winston is a close personal friend of Ruth's family, hence the Chihuahuas' names. When the Nazis invaded Warszaw, their home was one of the first commandeered by the Nazi elite and Ruth and Saul fled to Radom and Saul's extended family. There they were welcomed in Vunia's family's home until everyone was forced to move to the ghetto. They are elderly people who certainly must now regret having left the safety of England. Through diplomatic channels they are in communication with Ruth's family in England, who are trying to arrange their release. However, there is no sign of the Nazis letting them go and, like the rest of us, they remain prisoners.

Aunt Ruth returns to the room with a tray of cookies and tea that she has managed to scrounge up. The Chihuahuas dance at her feet, overjoyed at her return as she tenderly admonishes them, telling them to behave themselves in front of company. We spend the afternoon sipping tea and feeding cookies to Winston and Churchill while Ruth entertains us with her lively conversation. We listen rapt as she amuses us with anecdotes of her and Saul's travels abroad and of the many escapades of all of the Winstons and Churchills she has fostered. It is as if the real world has disappeared and Vunia and I have found sanctuary in a magical kingdom.

At the end of the day I sadly bid farewell to Aunt Ruth, Vunia and the Chihuahuas. It is the happiest I've been in a long while. Aunt Ruth and Vunia encourage me to return as often as I like and I can't wait to play with Vunia again and, of course, the adorable Chihuahuas.

Living in the ghetto has necessitated many adjustments to our daily routines. We no longer enjoy any of the previous freedoms of movement that were allowed us. In order to provide enough food for our family, my mother is forced to risk life and limb and sneak out of the ghetto to sell her fineries on the black market. Even with our diminished circumstances we have heard that apparently we are the lucky Jews, as word has travelled to us that conditions in the other ghettos like Lodz and Warszaw are far worse than they are for us. Lodz and Warszaw are sealed and there is no escape from the starvation and sickness that is beginning to take a toll on life there. Our ghetto in Glinice is also easier to live in than the Big Ghetto where my aunts, uncles, and cousins live, as we are less crowded and less policed. Although the Judenrat is doing its best, there is a terrible food shortage, as we are allotted only 1.5 kilograms of flour per month for each person. When the winter comes my father predicts there will be massive starvation and widespread disease. The hardships we endure have driven my mother to an obsession with stockpiling food and she ventures out often in pursuit of buyers for her clothes and jewelry so she can store food for the emergencies that will come. Recently the stakes and risks of being caught outside the ghetto have gotten much more dangerous. Last week the German gendarmes caught some people sneaking out of the ghetto and decided to make an example of them. Every man, woman and child was forced to witness the hangings and to stand and listen to the tirade that followed as the bodies swung lifeless in the breeze. The belligerent Nazi shouted at us that anyone leaving the ghetto would suffer a similar fate. I have never seen anyone die and the horror of it haunts me. For several days the three bodies dangled from ropes, their faces blackening with each passing day. The rotting stench was a notice to us all that no infraction of the rules will be tolerated. Although a significant deterrent, the hangings have not stopped the illegal egress, as desperate times require desperate measures and the inhabitants of the ghetto have no choice but to continue to run the risk of death by sneaking out, or else slowly starve to death.

Feigning sleep, I can hear my parents whispering, their heads bent together. Straining my ears, I can just barely make out their conversation. "Joel, I know it's risky but I think Dina will provide the perfect cover."

"I don't know. It is so dangerous now. What if you are stopped? My God, they just hung three people!"

"I tell you Joel, Dina sounds and looks more like a Pole than the Poles. No one would ever suspect her of being Jewish. With her with me, we will blend in and no one will question us."

My father sighs with resignation, "I see you've made up your mind, Temcia. I think we have been married long enough for me to trust your judgment. There is no sense in us arguing. Take her with you tomorrow and may God protect you."

The next day my mother and I slip from the confines of the ghetto. She holds tightly to my hand as we walk purposefully, making small talk in Polish and blending into the stream of people that walk freely through the city. Inconspicuously we make our way to a modest working class neighborhood and arrive at an unremarkable house. My mother knocks at the door, which is opened by a woman I recognize immediately as my mother's customer Pani Zdebowa. She smiles perfunctorily at us, her eyes scanning the street for any irregularities, "Come in, please, come in quickly. I see you've brought your daughter Dina." Pani Zdebowa lifts my chin appraisingly, "Such a pretty child and what rosy cheeks she has."

My mother's face lights with pride. "Yes, she is a treasure, and speaking of jewels, I've brought you a beautiful brooch, something you should have no trouble selling."

"Excellent. Why doesn't Dina sit and I will bring her some milk and cookies and then you and I can do our business."

Pani Zdebowa disappears into what must be the kitchen and returns a few moments later with a plate of cookies and a glass of milk, which she places before me.

"*Dziekuje, Pani.*"[29]

"*Proszem kochanie.*"[30] Pani Zdebowa pats me on the head as she turns toward my mother, "Did you have any problems getting here today?"

"No, thank heavens the streets were quiet. We slipped through when the police changed guard. It was completely uneventful, but I still feel better having Dina with me. A mother and her child is a much better cover."

---

29 "Thank you, Madam." Polish

30 "You're welcome, love." Polish

"I agree completely, Temcia. She is such a beautiful child and the only attention she will attract is admiration. May I see the brooch?"

"Of course," my mother rummages in her purse and takes out a blue velvet pouch. Opening it, she removes a jeweled butterfly brooch with its wings folded. The butterfly encrusted with colored gems looks as if it has momentarily landed upon a single blue stone and might take off at any minute and fly away. "Here, Anya, what do you think?"

"Ahh … yes it is lovely. You are right, this should fetch a decent price. I will take it to my contact. In the meantime, I have good news, I've sold the bracelet that you brought me last week and I have money for you."

"I am very grateful, Anya, for your help, without you I don't know how we would manage."

Pani Zdebowa blushes, "It is the least I can do. I only wish I could do more. I am ashamed of my country and its lack of resolve in helping our Jewish citizens, it is disgraceful."

"You are a good woman, Anya. I wish there were more people like you. Now Dina and I must get back to the ghetto, I've left Abek alone and I shouldn't be gone too long."

"Yes, of course, the sooner the better, let me get the money." My mother stands as Pani Zdebowa hurries to fetch the money. "Dina darling, finish your milk and cookies, we must get back to your brother."

Pani Zdebowa returns and presses a wad of zlotys into my mother's hand and then walks us to the door. The two women hug and kiss each other on the cheek, and then Pani Zdebowa bends to kiss me and whispers in my ear, "Be a good girl, Dina, and take good care of your mother."

On the street a convoy of German cars speeds past and I feel my mother's hand tremble in mine from the mere sight of them. We walk briskly through the neighborhood retracing our route back to the ghetto. People that we pass in the street now and then nod and greet us with courtesy. The contrast between the ghetto and the outside world is unfathomable and I wonder if our fellow citizens ever give a thought to their Jewish countrymen that are now being held hostage.

We turn a corner and it is as if all of the oxygen has suddenly been sucked out of the air. Walking toward us is a Polish policeman, a German gendarme with his German shepherd, and another Nazi whose black boots' sheen reflects the sunlight. My mother nearly freezes in her tracks. I look at her face. I can see the color drain from her cheeks. The dangerous trio hasn't noticed us yet, as they are deep in conversation. We cannot cross the street to avoid them as we will only draw suspicion; we have no choice but to walk forward. I grab my mother's arm to steady her as we continue toward them as nonchalantly as possible. When we are a few feet in front of them I look up at my mother and say in Polish, "Mamusia, tomorrow morning are we going to church?" I speak loud enough that all three of the men peer at me with scrutiny looking me up and down.

My mother quickly regains her composure. "Yes, my darling tomorrow we go to church."

The Polish policeman breaks the awkward impasse as he teases, "Little girl, you make sure your mama takes you to church," his eyes crinkling into a grin as he tips his hat. The Nazis who have been staring coldly at us listening to our discourse break into laughter. When we are safely past them and have turned the corner, my mother, who has begun to breathe again, grabs and kisses me, her heart pounding in her chest. She whispers in my ear, "If it weren't for you and your clever thinking those monsters would've surely stopped us. God only knows what might have happened. You saved our lives, Dina!"

I am exceedingly proud of myself and my mother makes a big point of telling everyone at dinner that evening how smart I am.

My father is now convinced that it is much safer for my mother if I accompany her. From then on I go with my mother most of the time when she ventures out of the ghetto.

The Nazis are obsessed with their lists and now there is a new befehl. The Judenrat has been instructed to compose lists of residents of the ghettos. The lists will comprise everyone's age, sex, and profession. They also want to know how many oxen, horses, carts and animals are residing in the ghetto. I ask my father what this means. "Who knows," he exclaims. "These people are completely insane with their attention to meaningless detail. We are nothing to them beyond names and numbers in columns and rows on endless sheets of paper that they keep in files within cabinets in countless storage rooms. We are no longer human hearts and souls but instead simply livestock to be dispensed with in whatever manner meets their fancy!"

I look at my father in bewilderment, "Tata, I don't understand." Realizing the inappropriateness of his outburst he recovers himself. "I am sorry darling. I didn't mean to release my frustrations on you like that. It's just that the Nazis have made it so difficult to live. I worry how much more we can take."

"We'll be okay Tata, I know we will," I hug him, willing him to believe.

A short time later, at the end of June, I am startled from my sleep by the roar of hundreds of airplanes flying overhead.

"Nadja, Dina!" I scream as fear grips me. "Are they going to bomb us like before?" All I can think about is the horror of the days and nights of endless bombings that accompanied the invasion.

Come… quick, we had better get out of the house!" Nadja yells above the uproar as she grabs my hand, pulling me from the bed as my cousin Dina runs ahead of us. My parents and Abek flee the house on our heels. Outside, the street is filling with people in various stages of undress, shouting and pointing at the sky. Everyone cranes their necks peering up toward the heavens. The planes are flying low toward the East where the first rays of sunlight wash the horizon rose and gold chasing the night from the sky. We stand in the semidarkness like statues, listening to the deafening rumblings of countless engines as hundreds of German planes clear the treetops above our heads. In silence I stare and wonder who will be the next unfortunates to suffer from the armada of enemy aircraft overhead. Soon they will be subjected to the horror of falling bombs. Within days we learn that the German Soviet pact has fallen apart and that the German *Luftwaffe* and *Wermacht* are attacking the Russians. Their first line of approach is to lay claim to the rest of Poland, Lithuania and Belorussia and then to continue on into Mother Russia herself. That Shabbat, my family lights the Sabbath candles and prays for the millions more Jews that now lie helpless in the path of the Nazis.

The leaves have begun their seasonal descent from the trees and with their death the rainy season comes early and the streets are slicked with mud. The effects of starvation are beginning to be felt everywhere and typhoid is now rampant. The streets are filled with gaunt faced children begging anyone and everyone who walks by for any food. Each day brings the carts loaded with dead that have become so commonplace that no one even seems to notice as they wind through the streets on their solemn way. Most likely, many of the poor begging children who roam the streets are the orphans of those who are being buried. In our home the effects are beginning to be felt. We have become a little thinner but my mother has miraculously managed to keep us all healthy, keeping the dreaded typhoid from our door. An important change has brought some relief to our family. My sister has gotten a job working for the Nazis at a factory run by the Germans called A.V.L. Her boyfriend Mikal came to see her and told her that she must come to work for the Nazis in order to protect our family. The Nazis have promised to give special treatment to the families of workers that help with the war effort. The Nazis are packing and shipping everything of value from Poland to Germany, mostly what they stole from the Jews. The ill-gotten gain will now enrich those that are destroying us. They are also shipping blankets, bedding, canteens, medicine and many other items to their soldiers on the front that are now fighting the Russians. The first thing my sister does when she starts working at A.V.L. is to ask if our cousin Dina can also work there. Along with about two thousand workers the two of them are now working every day, which takes a burden off of the food supply in our home, as they are fed a small meal. More importantly, it also gives us a sense of security that we may be afforded some safety from their positions as laborers for the Nazis.

Chapter 9

Adventures in the Ghetto

Our world has lost its color and become a monochromic pallet of endless shades of grey, black and white. The streets are thick with mud and pestilence and the skies seem to mirror the land below with dark clouds that hang forlornly, as if the heavens were covered in shrouds of mourning. A new befehl has been issued to be added to the column of endless wretched orders to which one never becomes accustomed. Any Jew found outside the ghetto will be shot and any Pole who aids a Jew will also be shot. My mother has bought us both small gold crosses to be worn whenever we illegally leave the ghetto. I secretly pray that the luck of the cross is greater than the luck of the Star of David.

We have not heard from our family in the Big Ghetto for several weeks and my father is greatly worried. I have decided to sneak out today when the police change their guards in the afternoon and steal into the Big Ghetto through one of the less travelled streets. Perhaps I can bring my poor father a bit of good news to calm the constant distress from which he suffers. Patiently I wait around the corner of a building, observing the police guard as he smokes a cigarette and then finally grinds it out beneath the black heel of his boot. He paces back and forth and looks at his watch, frowning and anxious to be relieved of his post. I twist the small golden cross between my fingers in nervousness. At last, his patience is rewarded and another policeman strides slowly toward him. I have watched this trading of posts before and know that the two men will probably commiserate for a few minutes while leisurely walking for a block or two with their heads pulled down in their coats and their attention focused on each other. My assumption is correct and when their backs are turned I make myself invisible, flattening myself against the wall and darting and disappearing into the streets beyond. I walk briskly, taking the back streets when possible and avoiding all human contact. The Big Ghetto is several kilometers away and I am forced to cross some crowded areas bustling with people. I garner little attention, as I look just like any other young Polish girl with my blonde hair braided and tied with blue ribbons. No one searches my face in recognition or cares who I am or where I am going.

After an hour I finally reach the boundary streets of the Big Ghetto. Taking a quick look around me and thinking myself safe to proceed, I venture forward. Suddenly, I feel a hand on my shoulder and my heart seizes with fear. Gruffly, the hand hurls me around and I come face to face with a Polish policeman.

Frantically I try to struggle free from his grasp, but he holds me firmly, leaving me no chance of escape. Looking up at his bloodshot eyes, I am completely unnerved. All I can see is his oily uncombed hair and broad peasant face leering down at me and I am suddenly overwhelmed by a wave of nausea. I cannot help but cringe from his sour rotting breath. Please God, I pray, please don't let me faint.

"You seem to be in quite a big hurry to enter the pigsty of the stinking Jews. Perhaps you would like to tell me where you live and why you are here?"

I frantically avoid looking into his leering face, which threatens ever nearer. My heart is pounding in my chest as I strain my mind for a plausible explanation to his questions. "I... I, please let go of my arm, you are hurting me! I will tell you whatever you want to know if you just let go of me," I cry as tears flood my eyes.

"Go ahead, start talking," angrily he jerks my arm. "*I will let you go when I am good and ready.*"

Desperately I try to regain my composure and still my pounding heart. It is all I can do just to breathe. "My grandmother lives in the big ghetto and I miss her terribly. I just want to visit her."

"You are a Jew," he says with disgust. "Where do you live?"

"I live with my family in the Glinice Ghetto. I snuck out without my parents' permission. They do not know where I am. Please, please let me go. I am so sorry, I will never do it again," I cry as revulsion fills me.

"You will tell me the street and address of where you live. I am going to come to your house and talk to your parents. If I don't get any money from your family for letting you go, I will arrest you on the spot and turn you in to the Nazis for illegally leaving the ghetto, which you know is punishable by death! DO YOU UNDERSTAND WHAT I AM SAYING?"

"Yes," I whimper, choking on my tears.

Taking out his pad and pencil with no regard for my terror, he demands, "Give me the address!"

Thinking quickly, I stammer the name of a street that is as far away from my house as I can think of. Writing it down and satisfied with my answer, he lets me go and I run as fast as I can toward my home. "*Remember what I said!*" he shouts after me. With my heart beating frantically and fear egging me forward,

I run through the streets with tears blinding me, oblivious to anyone or anything in my path. I only slow down when I am blocks away and out of sight of that horrible policeman. Once I regain my breath and stem the flow of tears, normalcy returns and I realize how lucky I am. I make a silent thank you to God that he gave me the presence of mind to give the villain a wrong address.

The days pass and I uncharacteristically remain indoors, rarely venturing out to play with Vunia. My parents are perplexed at my new found fondness for home but they don't question my strange behavior, as they are consumed with the everyday problems of our survival. As I fall back into the routines of ghetto life, I draw strength with time knowing that I have escaped the jaws of an awful predator.

I failed in my first attempt to sneak into the Big Ghetto but I feel certain that the next time I try I will succeed. Luckily, the blackmailing policeman has never found me or my home and a week later I decide to test my luck again. Overcoming my fears of capture and certain deportation but unable to suppress the visions of being publicly hung in the square in front of my family, I decide to take another stab at seeing my relatives. Taking the same indirect route, only this time making certain that no one is watching, I slip successfully into the Big Ghetto. With a sigh of relief and gained confidence, I start to walk to the interior streets when I hear a voice behind me yell "STOP!"

I turn, and to my utter disbelief, there is the same vicious policeman running toward me, his arms flailing a club and his shouts ringing in my ears, "STOP! YOU ARE UNDER ARREST!"

This time I am not going to let him catch me and running for my life I flee as fast as I can. He chases me from street to street shouting at me to stop. People jump out of my way while others feign as if to grab and hold me. All I can think about is being hung and dying which only fuels me to run faster; the distance between me and the blackmailing policeman increases. He is slowed by his girth and age and not nearly as fleet of foot as I. Finally, I see a soup kitchen flooded with people and lines that wrap around the block. Pushing against the crowd at the door I rush in, running past the many people waiting in line and those sitting at tables hungrily eating what may be their only meal of the day. Those who are eating barely lift their heads from their bowls to pause and look at me as I look around, desperately seeking a refuge. Seeing a door, I burst in and find myself in the kitchen. A tall bull of a man stands over a large pot of soup, stirring. Beyond the questioning curve of his brows I can see compassion in the brown eyes that stare intently at me.

"What is it, little girl?"

"Please sir," I beg, "please help me, I'm being chased by a policeman!"

He quickly strides to the kitchen door, opening it a crack as he peers cautiously out. Quickly deducing my predicament, he grabs a potato sack from a pile and places it on the floor, opening it. "Get in now!" The last thing I see are his eyes smiling at me. "Be quiet, not a sound!" He lifts the burlap sack and ties it over my head and then gently he picks me up and places me on a shelf containing other sacks of potatoes in similar bags. I hold my breath as the door swings open and the policeman rushes in. "Did you see a blonde girl?" he demands, his voice studded with anger and threat.

I hear the cook continue to stir the pot as he answers, "No, there is no one here but me."

The policeman warns menacingly, "She is illegally in the ghetto. You had better not be lying to me or your punishment will be severe."

"Why would I lie? There is no one here."

"Damn Jews!" The policeman fumes, storming from the room, the squeaking door swinging behind him.

The cook whispers to me, "Don't move; I want to make sure he is really gone."

I hear the door swing open and close as I wait, barely breathing. Returning, his strong arms lift me carefully from the shelf and place me on the floor, untying the strings and freeing me as the sack tumbles to my feet.

"Thank you, sir!" I grab him about the waist, hugging him with gratitude. "That policeman chased me all through the ghetto and was going to turn me in to the SS. I live in the Glinice Ghetto... all I want is to see my grandmother... I miss her so much!"

"Shhh... it's okay. You're safe now; he's gone. But you must see your grandmother quickly and return immediately to Glinice. You are in danger and shouldn't be running around the city alone. Do you understand me?"

"Yes sir, I will see my grandmother and go home. Thank you so much for saving me!"

"Okay, now wait here while I check the street to see that there is no sign of the *mumzer*."[31]

He returns after making sure that the policeman is truly gone from the area, then he walks me to the door and, patting my head, says farewell. The whole experience is a miracle but every now and then miracles do occur. As I leave, everyone in the soup kitchen waves and I am moved by how decent people can be. Each one of them has risked their life to save me. Their silence would have been complicity enough to condemn them.

Once on the street, I get my bearings and begin to make my way to Walowa Ulica. Keeping an eye out for the blackmailing policeman, my mind begins to register the conditions in the ghetto. The stench is shocking and I realize that what I thought were people lying sleeping in the street are actually the bodies

31 Bastard, Yiddish

of the dead and dying. Apparently the carts that collect the dead are unable to keep up with the growing numbers of people that have succumbed to typhoid and starvation. What upsets me the most is that as I look at the faces of the residents of the ghetto that pass me in the street I can see that they are no longer even aware of the bodies they pass or step around. They have become immune to death as they struggle in desperation with their own survival. The streets are filthy and garbage piles are everywhere. I watch as children sort through the garbage, looking for any food that might have been accidently discarded. It sickens me to see these starving little faces and I vow to do something about it. It is clear to me that my parents were right about the Big Ghetto—the conditions here are far more deplorable than in the Glinice Ghetto. The misery the Nazis have wrought is amplified by the overcrowding, the lack of medicine, and rations that are barely enough upon which to subsist. This slow death is not only decimating the population of the Jews, but their hearts and souls as well.

Wiping the tears from my eyes, I finally reach Walowa Ulica and, picking up my pace, I run into my cousin's home, calling out to anyone there. My Aunt Mindale comes running to me with worry and concern on her face. "Dinale, are you all right? Are your parents all right?" Her eyes search the street for the adult that surely must have accompanied me. "Where is your mother?"

"She is at home." Hastily I change the subject. "Everyone is fine, but Tata has been very worried about you, we haven't heard from you in weeks. So I snuck out of the ghetto to find out how you are."

"Do your parents know you are here? Surely, you didn't come alone?"

Lowering my eyes in guilt, I murmur, "I just wanted to surprise Tata with some good news."

"Some good news he would receive if something happened to you! Well, you're here so you may as well ease your grandmother's worries with your visit. Come into the kitchen and see your grandmother," she smiles, hugging me to her.

My grandmother is so happy to see me that she forgets to scold me for risking life and limb to see her. "Dinale, *shayna maidele*," she cries kissing me all over my face. "How are your dear father and mother, Nadja and Abek, Cousin Dina?"

"We're fine, Bubysy, everyone is fine. I just miss you so much that I had to come and see you."

"You have made me so happy, maidele, come... come sit down and tell me about everyone."

My Aunt Mindale leaves to call my other Aunts Nachele and Feigele and any cousins that are about. Everyone crowds into the tiny kitchen to see me. Nadja and Majer are working with their father Tuvye at the leather shoe factory and my other cousins are out working or scrounging up food and necessities. My relatives are all anxious to hear about the welfare of my family and conditions in the small ghetto.

Aunt Mindale looks very much like my father with warm brown eyes, but instead of blond hair like my father, she has black hair that she wears twisted in a braid that sits upon her head like a crown. She is small and curvaceous like my grandmother with a sunny disposition and a mothering, steadfast nature. She is a very devoted daughter and it is clear that my grandmother looks well. Mindale steeps a pot of hot tea and begins to serve everyone as I recount news of the welfare of our family and conditions in the Glinice Ghetto. For a moment it feels like old times sitting around the table, exchanging news over a cup of tea. The subject matter, however, tells another tale. I can't help but reveal how horrified I am to see so many dead in the streets and so many children begging. They nod and agree it is terrible but there is nothing to be done about it. The Judenrat is doing the best it can under the circumstances, but the Nazis become less and less cooperative with each passing day. "Surely, they could do more for the children that are starving," I protest.

"They don't care about the children," my Uncle Alexander, in an angry outburst, rejoins, "They want them to die. They want us all to die."

His words slice like a knife through the room, stunning us into silence. We all know that what he says is true, but hearing the words out loud shatters any illusion we might have of this nightmare ever ending.

My Aunt Mindale gives Alexander a stern look. "She's a child, Alexander. Children need to have hope and believe. We will survive this epidemic of Jew hatred just as we have survived every other period since the destruction of the Temple in Jerusalem 2,000 years ago."

"Amen," we simultaneously rejoin.

My Uncle Alexander keeps his silence, his eyes cast down. I feel certain that he regrets his words in front of his son David and me. The women in my father's family are all strong, opinionated women who never hesitate to call anyone to task.

In defense of her husband, my Aunt Nachele interjects, "Mindale, please forgive Alexander's outburst. He is so distraught over our situation. You know that he loves the children as much as any of us."

"Then he should be more careful about what he says in front of them." Mindale is not to be hushed.

"This stops now!" Feigele icily cuts Mindale off. "Dina is here for a very short visit. I would much prefer we keep a civil tone. She should not return to our brother with tales of bickering and dissension among us."

Again, silence grips the room as everyone respects Feigele's authority as the eldest of my father's siblings. The tension immediately dissipates and the rest of the visit is mainly about my cousin Majer's Bar Mitzvah, which my family, of course, could not attend. Majer performed his *Haftora,* a portion of the Bible which is chanted out loud, at home in the presence of a few friends and family. This sacred covenant celebrates the ancient Jewish rite of a young man's passage into manhood. In a time of so little joy, this ritual was like a spoonful of honey. Majer celebrated his Bar Mitzvah in secrecy, but nevertheless affirmed the commitment of every Jew to the continuity of life by upholding our traditions, no matter how dangerous the circumstances.

All too soon it is time for me to leave, as I need to be back to the small ghetto before curfew. I do not mention my ordeal with the policeman to my relatives, as it would only worry them. One way or another, I have to return home to my parents. We all walk to the door where everyone hugs and kisses me as they send best wishes to my parents, sister, brother and cousin. My grandmother tearfully and reluctantly bids me farewell, collapsing into Mindale's arms at my leaving. My uncle Alexander offers to escort me to the border of the large ghetto. We walk through the streets in the fading late autumn light in silence—my tall, handsome uncle, who it seems is no longer capable of the small talk that had once been his forte. At one time he had been one of the best dressed men in Poland. Alexander eagerly embraced the modern world, like my father, breaking from the tradition of a beard with a clean shaven face and new hopes for the future that reflected his social status, work ethic and economic success. What is left of him is but a shell of the glib, intellectual modern man he had once been—his hands stuffed in his workers pants, his face set in lines of permanent worry. He exudes defeat and disillusionment. His eyes that once burned with life are now empty and lifeless orbs, reflecting the death of his spirit. Like so many others we pass in the street, he has become one of the living dead, their shattered dreams no more than mud beneath their feet.

Trying to distract his melancholy, I remark, "David has grown so, Uncle Alexander. He looks so much like you. You wouldn't believe how big Abek has become, he already is bigger than me."

My Uncle nods, but his face remains impassive. "Yes, David is a good boy; he studies very hard even though there is no school. I hope…" his voice breaks with emotion, "I hope that he will one day go to university."

"I'm sure that one day he will."

My uncle's silence refutes my words as the door shuts on our conversation. We reach the border of the large ghetto and, turning to give me a hug, he says, "Take good care, Dinale," and with that, he turns and walks away. As I continue on my way, I turn once to look back. He is watching me from a corner, lost in shadow, his face hidden in darkness. All I can see is the burning ash from his cigarette and a thin ribbon of smoke rising in the air.

In a daze I walk home, contemplating the events of the day. On the busy streets of Radom life whirls about me as I struggle to reconcile the liveliness of the Jew-free streets and the dying gasps of the Jewish ghetto. Although seeing my grandmother and extended family was wonderful, the grim contrast of life inside and outside the ghetto is overwhelming. The closer I get to the Glinice Ghetto, the heavier my heart becomes and it is all I can do to force myself to pass into the confines of the ghetto and return to my home.

My mother is waiting for me when I return and she is none too happy with me. Her motherly instincts tell her that something is amiss. "Dina, where have you been?" she asks, her hands on her hips.

"I'm sorry Mamashy, but I miss Bubysy so much and Tata has been so sad lately that I wanted to cheer him up with news of everyone. I snuck out of the ghetto."

My mother sighs, "I don't have the energy or will to punish you, Dina, but you must promise me you will never leave

Glinice without me or your sister again. It is too dangerous! Do you understand me?"

"Yes, Mamashy, I understand."

"We will discuss your disobedience when your father returns." That evening I see my father brighten up a bit when I tell him of my adventure. I finally share with him and my mother the whole story of the bad Polish policeman chasing me through the Big Ghetto, both the first time and today. They are wide-eyed with disbelief as I describe being hidden in the potato sack by the cook at the soup kitchen and what a close call it had been. Although grateful that I am safe and relieved to hear about our family, they are highly saddened about the plight of the children and the dismal conditions in the ghetto. Half-heartedly they reprimand me and I am made to promise that I will not leave the ghetto unaccompanied again.

My dreams are plagued with the faces of starving children, their emaciated bodies and outstretched hands begging for food. I awake this morning with determination to do something to help them. Running to Vunia's house, I am eager to engage her in my plan. Vunia is in total agreement with me that we must do something to help the children beyond what the Judenrat is doing. In the small ghetto there are still plenty of families that have enough to eat, like Vunia's and my family. We are going to go to every family we know and plead with them to donate bread, which we will once a week dispense to the poor children of the ghetto. Perhaps we can alleviate some of the starvation with a bread drive for the hungry children. We comb the streets of the ghetto, pulling a wagon and knocking on every door. At first people are hesitant to help us, as everyone is so guarded of their rations and hoarding today what might disappear and be irreplaceable tomorrow. Vunia and I somehow convince many of them that to not help the poor children is a sin against God. *Tzadaka*, charity, is one of the primary commandments of Judaism. Finally they are persuaded by our pleadings, or perhaps they are just amused to hear our argument, but in any case nearly everyone gives us a loaf of bread. These breads are huge, and our wagon is so full and heavy that we can barely pull and push it through the snow. By the time we return it is too late to distribute the bread to the children, so we store it at home with the plan of distributing it in the morning. My father, when he sees the amount of bread we have collected asks, "Can I have a little piece of bread?"

Not sure if he is kidding or not, I say "No, Tatashy, this bread is for the truly poor and hungry children. You are not that poor and you are not that hungry!" Feigning disappointment, he nods in agreement. "You are right, Dinale, there are others who are much more in need than me. What you are doing is wonderful and I am very proud of you and Vunia."

In our charitable venture we have recently been joined by Fela, whom I haven't spent much time with recently. Fela is in love with a boy that lives next door to her, his name is Yaakov. I have managed to inspire her with the "Bread for Children Project" and she has thrown herself into it wholeheartedly, although her conversation consists mostly of 'Yaakov said this or Yaakov said that.' I love Fela and have resigned myself to playing second fiddle to Yaakov. Maybe because I am younger than her I can't seem to share her enthusiasm about the splendors of love, but nonetheless I try to be happy for her, as she and Yaakov are clearly smitten with each other.

Although we can't feed the bread to the hungry children in the large ghetto, there are plenty of hungry children in the Glinice Ghetto. It has become a weekly ritual for Vunia, Fela and me to collect bread before the Shabbat and to deliver it to the needy children. No matter how much we collect and give out it is never enough. It pains us to note that every Friday one or two children disappear from the line that forms in front of our wagon and we can't help but envision the angels that surrender their souls daily in the heavy snows and cold that blanket the ghetto and Poland.

Chapter 10

A Time to Say Good-bye

The severe winter has delivered an added blow to our diminishing hope and resolve. Whereas before the Nazis seldom patrolled the ghetto streets on a regular basis, they now have increased their surveillance of us with daily squads of SS roaming the neighborhoods on foot or speeding down the streets in motorcycles, cars, and trucks. My father is greatly worried by this new mounting exposure and convenes us for a family discussion.

"I know we have all become attached to Queen Esther." My father is clearly distressed and weighs his words carefully. "I want you all to understand that I also have grown very fond of this special cow that has provided us with sustenance. It is time that we consider the possibility that should the Nazis find her, they will take her from us and slaughter her. The danger she presents to us now overrides the benefits."

As he speaks, I look at my mother's face. Her eyes are filling with tears and she avoids looking at me. With a sinking feeling I realize what my father is about to say.

"Dinale, look at me please."

I turn to him with wide eyes.

"Esther can either provide meat for the Nazis or for us. I believe if she could choose she would want to keep us alive and well. We will end her life in a humane way and, God willing, she will keep us alive through the winter months. I am sorry... but..."

Unable to control my tears I flee from the table and out the door to the shed where Queen Esther stands chewing on hay. She looks at me with her wide brown eyes and I touch her cold nose with my hand. I know that my father is right and that Esther must be sacrificed. Knowing something is right doesn't necessarily provide comfort when one is losing a friend, especially when so much has already been lost. "Esther," I stroke the warm red fur on her forehead as tears spill down my face. "I want to thank you for the milk you have provided us. I am sorry your life must be sacrificed. You are a dear cow and I will miss you and remember you always." Queen Esther looks at me as if she understands each word I say. Her large pink tongue licks my hand as if to absolve me from guilt. With a final rub on her forehead, I run back in the house where my family sits in front of the fire trying to stay warm.

Only my father remains at the table, his hands pressed against his face, his elbows resting on the table.

I rush to him throwing my arms around his neck. "It's okay, Tata... I understand that we have no choice. Please don't be sad," my tear stained face shiny and hopeful. My father hugs me to him and I feel his sorrow filter through me. It occurs to me that at times I feel that I am the adult and my father and mother are the children.

Queen Esther is dispatched with compassion for our greater good, and Vunia's and my family have enough meat stored to last several months. Every time we eat meat during that winter we give thanks and blessings to Queen Esther. Like her namesake in the ancient land of Persia, she contributes to the survival of our family when putting food on the table is more and more difficult.

It seems the Nazis must spend their entire days devising new ways to torture and crush the fragile resolve of us Jews. Today a new befehl is announced from the loudspeakers of trucks that make daily incursions into our streets. All pets are to be brought to the main entrance of the ghetto by tomorrow morning, when they will be removed. I cannot imagine the effect this will have on Vunia's Great-Uncle Saul and Great-Aunt Ruth. Winston and Churchill are like their children and I am certain this will kill them. I run to Vunia's to see if I can help relieve the anguish this is sure to cause. Vunia's house is as still as a house in mourning. Softly I call for Vunia, but she doesn't answer. Listening, I hear upstairs the muffled sobs of a woman. Knowing this must be Ruth, I make my way upstairs to her bedroom. I push the door open and find Vunia and her mother on their knees in front of a stricken Ruth. It is a small room with a threadbare woolen carpet and worn wallpaper covered in faded pink roses.

Nothing like the descriptions I have heard of the grand homes in which Ruth and Saul once lived, crowned with vaulted ceilings and crystal chandeliers. In the center of the room is a small bed on which Ruth lies with her eyes staring at the ceiling. Saul stands with his hands leaning on the window sill, his back to the room. His head is bent in either resignation or prayer, I cannot tell which. Winston and Churchill sit at Ruth's side, confused but attentive to her words. She is mumbling indiscernibly to herself as tears flood from her eyes carrying the makeup down her cheeks where it pools and cakes in the deep grooves of her skin, giving her the appearance of a sad circus clown. Here and there I understand a few words of Ruth's garbled sobs, which have become a combination of English and Polish, "No, no I will not give them up. They are my babies, it is too cruel."

Grateful to see me, Vunia jumps up and grabs my hands and whispers, "You've heard the terrible news? Ruth collapsed when she heard the new befehl and has been like this ever since. We are all heartbroken but what alternative is there? We keep telling her that the Nazis will probably fall in love with Winston and Churchill when they see them and someone will want to keep them. She won't be comforted. We are at our wits' end."

Saul slowly turns from the window and, walking to the bed, he sits and takes Ruth's hands in his, his voice hoarse with emotion. "We must be brave, my darling. There are good people dying all around us. It is time for us to help them. Winston and Churchill have been faithful and wonderful pets, they have been like the children we never had and we will always have our memories of them. Perhaps it is time we take in a couple of orphans and offer them a home? I know how much room there is in your heart to love, my dear one, please think about what I am saying." Ruth stares wide-eyed from Saul to Winston and then Churchill. "Oh Saul," she cries. "It is so unbearable. I know you are right but I feel so helpless and afraid. How can I turn over my babies to these monsters?" She looks directly at each of us, her eyes begging us to find some way of avoiding this tragedy. Inconsolable, she reaches for the two Chihuahuas that immediately jump into her open arms, licking her face.

I am devastated—it is not anything like what we thought it would be. Vunia and I plod through the snow on a frigid overcast morning accompanying Saul and Ruth to take Winston and Churchill to the designated staging area where the pets of the ghetto are to be transferred to the Nazis. It is crowded with people clinging to their dogs and cats who are barking and meowing at each other, adding to the mayhem. We stand in a long line that curves around the block and at first we don't see the collection area. Many people walk past us with tears streaming down their faces, having already parted with their beloved pets. Saul and Ruth are each holding one of the Chihuahuas, their free hands in a constant state of motion as they pet and reassure the two little dogs who wear red wool sweaters to protect them from the icy wind that licks at our faces. Finally we turn the corner and can see the trucks that have been brought in to carry away the poor disoriented animals. Ruth is stunned into immobility and Saul is forced to urge her forward until we finally reach the front of the line. Each of us kisses and pets Winston and Churchill, who shower us with eager licks as we say our good-byes.

Ruth, unable to let go of her beloved little dogs, has to be restrained by Saul as she pleads, "Please Saul, don't make me give them up!"

An awful Nazis grabs them out of her arms and throws them into a truck. They bark and whine desperately, their cries tearing at our hearts. It is awful and I worry that Ruth will faint dead on the ground but instead she suddenly regains her composure and, standing tall and proud, she gives the Nazi a withering look of disdain and turns her back on him, walking away. She refuses to give these detestable men the satisfaction of knowing they have brought her to her knees. As we follow close behind her, I hear her mumble under her breath, "I curse all of the Nazi murderers and pray God that they all burn in the fires of hell."

The next day we learn the truth that all of the pets of the ghetto have been murdered. No one is surprised, as we all secretly suspected that it would be the case. Certainly anyone that could treat humans in such a despicable manner would have no compunction killing helpless animals. All that is left of Winston and Churchill are pictures in an album. Often Vunia and I sit with Ruth, looking at the photographs as Ruth reminisces about them—her "gallant lads," as she calls them. With laughter and merriment she recounts tales of their pranks and deeds, sometimes exaggerating their exploits for our amusement. True to their word, Saul and Ruth have arranged for two orphaned children to join them in Vunia's home. Although it has caused them some crowding, it is decisive in helping to heal the wounds that are still fresh from the cruel murder of Winston and Churchill. Just as Ruth had doted on her animals, she now dotes on this abandoned brother and sister, Anya and Jacob, two lost children who fill the empty spaces of her heart. Anya and Jacob lost their parents to typhoid and had been living on the streets, begging. Saul and Ruth assume the role of loving grandparents and the two young children slowly blossom from their love and kindness. The ghetto is full of stories of the human heart rising above the squalor and hopelessness that pervades our day-to-day survival. The will to live is a powerful impetus and each of us in our own way has learned to fight the darkness that seeks to consume us. In countless small acts of humanity we affirm our commitment to life, grasping at whatever joys we can find along the way. In the frigid snow-bound month of December, a tiny bit of hope springs to life and takes root in the gloom and misery of Radom's Jews. The news spreads like a wildfire as it is whispered from ear to ear. Had we not feared terrible reprisals we would be dancing in the streets, giddy with joy that God has finally heard our prayers. On December 8th The United States declared war on Japan after the bombing of their naval fleet in the Hawaiian Islands at Pearl Harbor. Four days later on December 11th Germany declared war on the United States in support of its ally Japan. We Jews are exultant, as this can only mean a future end of the war. President Roosevelt's words resound through the ghetto, inspiring hope in every heart, "Never before has there been a greater challenge to life, liberty and civilization." All over Radom secret discussions commence as to the effect this will have on the plight of occupied Europe's Jews. With the American giant throwing her muscle and vast resources into the war, surely the Nazis will be far too busy focusing their strength on battling the military might that is now intent on eliminating their regime. If we can just cling to our lives and hold on to our hope, our saviors will rescue us from the certain pool of death in which we are drowning. The question is, will we be rescued in time, or will it be too little and too late to save the starving masses.

As each day gives way to another, the glint of light we so desperately cling to is quickly extinguished by the brutal deprivations of food, fuel, and freedom that grow scarcer. Our short-lived euphoria vanishes with the increased tyranny of the Nazis. It is beyond our capacity to understand this hate that is intent on obliterating us from the face of the earth.

The winter months have taken their toll and the pungent sweet smell of death permeates the air in the ghetto. The only populations that are increasing and thriving without abatement are the rats that swarm the streets, running amid the garbage piles and invading our homes at every opportunity. Each evening we endure the ritual of lice picking and I have begun to feel like a monkey as we each take turns inspecting each other's heads and then squishing or burning the disgusting varmints. My sister teases me as she searches my head. "Oh, what a big juicy one I just found hiding in your head, Dinale, hold still while I get it and squish it."

"Wait, let me see!" I squirm grabbing on to her arm trying to see the monster.

"Careful, I don't want to drop it, don't move." Extracting it from my head she shows me the disgusting pest and I shriek in horror shivering with revulsion.

Once the bodily inspections are finished we search the seams of our clothing, coats, scarves, hats and then bedding in search of the blood-suckers that carry the diseases that my mother warns us to be wary of. This evening ritual provides a form of entertainment as we each try to up the ante with exaggerations of the size of each other's pests. It is amazing the amusement and solace that can be found in our misfortunes. Conditions that would otherwise leave us in despair are now the fodder of our jokes.

There has been an *aktion* in the large ghetto, the repercussions of which are being discussed by all. The Gestapo conducted a systematic raid into the ghetto and, using a detailed prepared list, they abducted about forty men from their homes who are suspected of being Communists. The accused dissidents were then taken out into the streets and executed on the spot. Murder has become a daily occurrence.

The Judenrat, which had become useless in curbing the Nazis' appetite for Jewish blood, is virtually dismantled on April 27th, 1942. This day is being called "Bloody Wednesday," due to the immense loss of life perpetrated by the Nazis, who again entered the ghetto with their dreaded lists of victims. They rolled through the ghetto in their cars and trucks, seizing men from their homes and shooting them in their doorways or arresting them for deportation and throwing them into prison to be tortured and beaten. Anyone on that list who managed to escape that day was immediately replaced by a random bystander who was shot in his tracks in order to fulfill the death allotment. These poor people ceased to exist because they were in the wrong place at the wrong time, and of course they had the misfortune of being Jews. Among the hundred or more unlucky victims was Yosef Diamant, the head of the Jewish council and with him the top aides in the Judenrat hierarchy. They and about twenty of the senior members of the Jewish police force were arrested, interned, and marked for deportation. The old saying "No good deed goes unpunished" certainly applies here.

The Nazis have effectively removed the leadership of the ghettos and now we wait in fear without our intermediaries to intercede. Without our leadership we have no idea what will follow next.

April has proven to be a particularly deadly month and even the warmth of winter ended and the subtle hints of spring's rebirth cannot relieve the depression that has descended upon the ghetto. We live with the expectancy of disaster and pray for the intervention of a miracle. My sister is at A.V.L. working and my brother and I huddle together, playing a game of chess. My mother sits in a rocking chair by the fire mending a small tear in my father's coat. For some reason my father was told not to report to work today and he sits at the table reading.

Suddenly there is a loud banging at the door that startles each of us. My father goes to answer. When he opens the door there are heavily armed SS men standing there with their guns leveled, ready to shoot. My mother jumps up in fear, dropping my father's coat and knocking the sewing basket over, from which the spools of thread spill out and scatter across the floor. My mother orders my brother and me not to move as she rushes to my father's side, grasping for his arm. A Nazi officer is yelling at my father and beginning to pull him out the door. It is happening so quickly that I can hardly register what is being said.

"Tata, Tata!" My brother and I have seen enough and begin to scream as we run to our father's side. "Please, please don't take our father," I beg as I cling to my father's leg on one side while my brother desperately grabs the other leg. We are all screaming in panic as the Nazis drag us all from the house, my brother and I manacled to my father's legs my mother to my father's arm, as each of us begs for mercy. My mother is pleading in German that there must be a mistake, that my father is a butcher and is working for the Germans, that he is necessary, that he has a special card.

"There is no mistake. We are arresting all butchers and slaughterers. They are being taken to Police Headquarters where they will be questioned. Orders are that they are to be deported and resettled immediately."

My mother turns as white as the snow that still clings in patches to the ground. She dashes back into the house and quickly reappears with my father's coat. I don't know how she finds the presence of mind to make sure that my father has his coat. Wrapping it about his shoulders she throws her arms around his neck in a quick embrace. "Joel my darling, remember I love you."

"I won't let you take him," I cry in anger at the Nazi beasts.

"Tata, I love you," cries Abek, his face pressed to my father's pants.

"It will be okay children, I will be fine. Remember that I love you all." My father's words, swollen with anguish and emotion, choke from him like the embrace he is unable to give us.

Abek and I cling tightly to my father's legs in a desperate effort to prevent the inevitable. The Nazis yell and curse at us to let go, threatening that they will take us too if we don't release him. Roughly they tear us from our father's legs and throw us to the ground. My mother, sobbing, rushes to protect us. It is awful. My father looks back at us as if to sear the memory of our faces upon his heart as they push him roughly into the truck. The doors slam and in an instant they are gone. Crippled with grief, we sit on the ground, clinging to my mother.

My sister and cousin return from work to find us paralyzed with grief, with Vunia's family trying to administer comfort to us. My mother lies prostrate in bed. She has aged in a few hours, shrunken and diminished from the shock of losing her life partner. Only my sister murmuring secret words of hope is somehow able to rouse her and return her to us from the abyss she has fallen into. "You are behaving as if our father has died," my sister admonishes. "How dare you give up hope, is this what father would expect of us?" She shames us all for our lack of faith and rekindles the hope that perhaps someday we will be reunited with our father. After making inquiries, she takes the initiative and discovers where our father is being held. He has been taken to the police station near the Big Ghetto with all of the other butchers and slaughterers who have been rounded up. Nadja has begged one of the Wermacht officers that runs A.V.L. to issue her a pass so that she might leave the ghetto and inquire as to our father's well-being. With this pass she is able to leave the ghetto unescorted, although even with the pass she is exposed to increased danger. She spends hours waiting for any information as to our father's fate. In order to pass the hours as she awaits word, she takes her journal with her that she has kept since the invasion of the Nazis into Poland. In it she keeps a detailed recollection of all of the events that have occurred to our family and friends, along with her own philosophical bewilderment as to the causes. To fill the time as the hours pass she busily writes in her chronicle. Engrossed in her task, she is unaware as a Polish policeman quietly approaches her and grabs her journal out of her hands. Ignoring her protests, he begins to read the last few pages she has written about the injustices that have been committed against an innocent people by not only the Nazis but also the Poles who have turned their backs on their Jewish countrymen and sought only to benefit from their misfortune. In written anguish she begs someone to explain how this could happen in the civilized world of the 20th century. How is it possible that innocent men, women, and children can be tortured and murdered with no regard to human decency? Apparently, the Polish policeman is so upset by her observations that he sends her away with nothing more than a warning. "Go home now! I don't want to see you here again!" With that warning he hands her back her journal and walks away, allowing her to flee and disappear into the streets.

A few weeks later, we are informed that our father is to be deported. Tomorrow we will be allowed to bring him some food for the journey and say our good-byes. My mother rallies, given the important task of providing sustenance and packing a few belongings for my poor father. She assembles a bundle of food from our dwindling supply, along with my father's heavy coat and some extra clothing in which she has sewn some money. We all go with my mother to say good-bye to my father. He is behind a fence and we can't hug or touch him. All we are allowed to do is hand him the package and speak with him through the wire. We only have a few moments to say everything. A lifetime of love condensed into a few words.

He tries to joke through his tears, "You see the Nazis have decided that we butchers pose the greatest threat to the Third Reich with our ability to dismember a cow. Temcia, you see I was right. I told you that things were going to get very bad for the Jews. Who knows, my darling family, if I will ever see you again?"

"Don't worry, Tata, we will find each other. Remember God is sending a great army to rescue us."

"Yes, of course he is, Abek. His eyes belie his words. "My son, you must remember that you are now the man of the family and you must take good care of your mother and sisters."

"Yes, Tata, I will do my best."

"Joel, you must write to us as soon as you get to wherever they resettle you. Please let us know you are safe."

"Yes, yes, I will write. Children, you must remember the good character of the people you come from. Oh yes, and somebody get word to Bubysy and the rest of the family. Tell them … just tell them that I love them."

"Don't worry, Joel, I will get word to them."

"I bless you all and pray for your safety and deliverance. Temcia, take care of our children and try to keep faith with God."

We all stand there weeping, helpless to do anything or say anything that will allay his fears. "I love you, Tata, don't worry, we will find each other someday," I cry, not knowing if it will ever be so. We bow our heads and pray that God will protect us all.

The next day my father is loaded into a train and shipped to an unknown destination.

Chapter 11

A.V.L.

The *aktions* have produced a quiet panic in the ghetto and there is a desperate press among the inhabitants for jobs in the factories and warehouses that are run by the Germans. Rumors are flying that more deportations are imminent and the only possible safety is in the possession of a work certificate. My sister and cousin Dina both have permits to work at A.V.L., which is a giant warehouse that borders the railroad tracks and is used for staging shipments to Germany and the Eastern front. I have begged my sister to help me get a job there and in June permission is granted and I am issued a certificate. I am so happy when she brings the permit home, dancing through our house, I grab my mother and spin her around. "See Mamashy, we will be able to protect you and Abek now that three of us are employed and there will be more food for you both. Tata would be so proud of me for assuming responsibility and acting like an adult. I hope he is well wherever he is."

My mother, who rarely smiles since my father was taken, tries her best to reflect my enthusiasm. "Yes, my darling, he would be so proud of you. Blessed be the Almighty, I pray that your father is well and not suffering and that one day we will all be united together as a family."

"Amen," I affirm.

Every morning after that at 6:00 a.m. my sister, Cousin Dina and I join the group of workers that are escorted by the Germans to the different places of employment. This morning the dawn is cold and blustery prior to the sun awakening the earth and giving life to a chilly summer day. My sister is always reminding me not to talk during our transfer, as we don't want to incur the wrath of the German soldiers who enjoy nothing more than punishing us with the butt of their rifles. We walk in silence for a couple of kilometers under armed guard to the red brick warehouse where we sort, fill, and box the many items to be shipped out of Poland for the benefit of the Third Reich. Once we have filled the boxes we carry the heavy crates and load them on to the waiting trains. For twelve hours a day we toil with but a few minutes of respite when we are given some weak tea and a thin watery soup that provides little nutrition. It is back breaking labor in a damp warehouse and by the end of the day I can barely stand on my feet. My sister whispers encouragement to me and keeps my spirit up when I complain that I am so tired I feel I can't go on.

"Of course you can, Dinale, look how you've grown. You are no longer a child, but a beautiful young woman. Tata would be so proud of you!"

I quickly wipe away the tears that fill my eyes at the mention of my beloved father whom I miss so much. Just the thought of my proud loving father gives me the strength to continue my efforts.

"Where do you think they sent Tata?" I whisper as I turn over someone's precious samovar, studying it before I load it into a box. In order to tolerate the tediousness of the endless days I dream up stories of the people who once owned the thousands of objects that overflow the warehouse. Prior to their being stolen by the Nazis everything here had belonged to a Jewish family. Each object carries a secret life and past that I try to imagine in my weary mind as I endure the many hours of labor.

"I wish I knew," answers my sister as she finishes tying rope around a box. "He may not even be in Poland. There, help me carry this to the platform where we can get a breath of fresh air." Together we drag the heavy carton to the back of the warehouse where Mietek, one of my sister's friends, rushes to relieve us of it. "*Nu*, so how is our little comrade doing in her new job?" I smile at Mietek, "My sister says I am no longer a child but a woman," I coyly announce.

My sister and Mietek laugh, sharing a knowing wink between them. "Yes, you are becoming quite the seductress, soon none of the men will be able to keep their minds on their work," he teases.

I feel my cheeks burning red and, unable to think of a brilliant retort, I stick my tongue out at him, sending my sister and him into a fit of laughter.

The days wear on in a repetition of conflicting contrasts, the beauty of burgeoning summer and the squalor of the disintegrating ghetto. I yearn for the carefree hours spent with Fela and her boisterous family amid the fruit laden cherry trees of her grandparents' orchard. I no longer have time to play with my girlfriends. Our world of innocence has vanished and all that remains are the ruins of what was once a thriving Jewish community. Without my father's steadfast presence, my poor mother has been forced to assume the mantle of father and mother and the burden has taken its toll on her. Her loneliness for my father is heartbreaking to behold. As she goes about her chores she has begun to talk aloud to herself as if my father were listening. The daily responsibilities weigh upon her, threatening to crush her, and the only way to keep her sanity lies in these make believe conversations between wife and husband. The physical effects are even more drastic to behold. Her dresses, which she had filled with a full and voluptuous figure, now hang like sacks around her disappearing body. You could fit two of her inside her dress and still have room to spare. Before the war, she had maintained her hair a lustrous black by carefully concealing the few gray hairs that had come with her late thirties. No longer concerned with her beauty, and with no access to the chemicals necessary to formulate her special dye, her hair has prematurely aged to a silvery grey. With my sister, cousin and I working at A.V.L., my mother's responsibilities have multiplied as she has to somehow provide the meals, wash the clothes, clean the house, and tutor my brother in his studies. In the evenings she sits darning and mending our clothes, rocking in my grandfather's rocker, all the while conducting a conversation with my father's invisible presence. Not a minute is spent in idleness. As capable of a woman as she is, my sister, Cousin Dina, and I worry at how much more she can take.

I am thirteen today, the 20th of June. I cannot imagine how my mother has found the ingredients to assemble a small cake. I know my father will be thinking about me today on my birthday. Perhaps right at this moment he is dreaming of us and wondering how we are managing. My family, Vunia, Fela, and me hold hands and observe a moment of silence, trying to transmit our love and wishes through space and time, in hopes that he might feel them and know that we are thinking of him. We pray together that God not abandon us and that he keep our father safe from harm. Afterward we light a lone candle, which my mother somehow has procured, and I make a wish for all of us as I blow it out. Even though I keep my wish a secret it is not hard to imagine what it might be. For entertainment my cousin Dina lifts us out of our doldrums with her famous spoof of Hitler with one new addition. At the end of her Fuhrer impersonation, she invites us each to kill her if every word out of her mouth isn't truly spoken. We pounce on her, all of us landing on the bed, as we scream that we are going to tickle her to death and it is a fate far better than what she deserves. Our laughter must sound insane to our neighbors given the misery of our lives. There is so little to remind us of our youth and we crave amusement for our souls just as much as food for our stomachs. This moment of pure laughter and joy releases the tensions that consume us and liberates the hope we harbor that somehow this tortuous war will end and we will be free to live our lives in peace.

As much as the Nazis love to inflict physical torture, they seem to delight even more in spiritual and psychological persecution, which has robbed the Jews of their dignity and will to survive. Just such a cruelty is inflicted upon my poor mother. The Nazis announce that there will be a transport to the work camp where my father is imprisoned and that they are collecting food packages that will be delivered to inmates. Since my father's promised letter has never arrived it is like a confirmation of his well-being and my mother scrambles to assemble a basket of food that she delivers to the designated repository. Cruelly our hopes are dashed when we later discover that it has been an evil ruse. Our desperately needed rations are seized. The Nazis never intended to deliver the packages. Mama laments that she has depleted our precious food stores and with the best of intentions given it to our enemies. She is beside herself with anger at having been duped by their inexplicable cruelty, but more distressing is the reality that we have no idea where my father is or how he is faring.

Chapter 12

An Accident

It is so hot and I am tired and hungry all of the time. The sky is a cloudless endless expanse of faded blue turned pale from the heat that spans from horizon to horizon. Even at this early hour my dress is already soaked with sweat as my sister, Dina, and I walk silently under guard the remaining kilometer to A.V.L. I am in no hurry to get there, as I know the warehouse will be unbearably hot like an oven, perfect for cooking us Jews. Only the German manager of our division, Otto, will keep cool in his small office, thanks to a large fan from which he is loath to stray. Otto is *Wermacht*[32] and not a bad person, really. He is not unduly cruel to us; in fact, one could say he is a decent human being. Pictures of his family abound on his desk and I have seen him gaze at them with love and longing. His wife is a pretty woman with her blonde hair plaited and bound to her head like a crown. Her smile in the photographs is one of a woman whose life has lived up to her expectations. In one photo she is dressed

32 A member of the German army

in a traditional *dirndl* and is flanked on either side by her two smiling daughters, who are dressed in matching attire. The older daughter looks to be about my age, blond and blue eyed like me. When he looks at me he cannot help but think of her. At times I sense his empathy and lingering gaze. Perhaps that is why he looks the other way when I sometimes struggle to perform my job. I am the youngest worker and my physical strength is equivalent with my age.

A creature of habit, he has grown accustomed to my presence among the workers and greets me each day with "*Gut morgan Fraulein.*" Obedient to the good of the Fatherland, he does his duty efficiently and without moral introspection. He is a strong bull of a man who earned this safe and cushy job by surviving the Eastern front with only a minor injury, a permanent limp making him unfit for combat. Of course he can't be too lenient with us Jews, as he has to answer to a brutal SD officer who is even worse than the SS. The SD bully treats Otto with contempt, always questioning his ability to extract the most from his slave labor force. When the Nazi beast is about, we do our best to work like a well-oiled machine in order to make Otto look good and to incur as little wrath as possible. It is a complicity born of necessity and a bond forged from a mutual objective, survival. We know that there are many sadistic men in charge at other forced labor facilities who abuse and denigrate their workers. Some of the poor workers are regularly beaten and sometimes even killed for lack of productivity or some perceived inefficiency. Otto may be strict and appear to be gruff, but he is not without heart. Or maybe he hopes his lack of cruelty will not be forgotten by us or God and it is his own private assurance that, should the war be lost, his family will somehow be protected from vengeance.

As I predicted, the warehouse is blazing with heat when we arrive to begin our labors. Nadja calls me over to the elevator.

"Come with me and Sonja to the second floor and help us carry down twine to tie the boxes. We are running short and there is more in the supply room upstairs." Getting into the elevator, she closes the steel accordion door and pulls the lever. The old machine grumbles to life and slowly ascends to the top floor. My sister and Sonja are gossiping about two of the young men who work at A.V.L. Sonja has a crush on one of them and is filling Nadja in on the details of their courtship. I am too hot to be captivated by the gossip and just want to get downstairs where it is a few degrees cooler. Finally, we reach the second floor and load the boxes of twine into the elevator. Once again my sister closes the door and pulls the lever that starts the old beast of an elevator on its way down. Halfway between the two floors the elevator comes to a sudden stop, nearly throwing us all to the floor. "Damn," says Nadja. "This elevator is so unreliable I don't understand why they don't properly repair it." Opening the metal door, she looks and says, "We are only a few feet from the floor, let's jump and we'll get the men to come and fix it." Jumping down she waits as Sonja makes her escape, my sister offering up her hand as she jumps to safety. Sonja jumps effortlessly. Now it is my turn. I decide to sit down on the edge of the floor and jump from there. Just as I am about to jump, the elevator jerks into motion and with a massive thrust rises, pinning me between the floors. My legs are trapped between the elevator floor and the top of the second floor. I hear screaming and shouting all around me. The world is spinning into blackness and I feel waves of nausea overwhelm me. From far away I hear my sister screaming, "Otto, Otto come quickly. Dina's legs are caught in the elevator, please save her!"

I can't feel my legs or my hand and there is blood everywhere. My last thoughts as I sink into darkness are a prayer to my grandfather and God to save me.

Moments later I awaken in Otto's arms as he runs outside with me. My sister is running alongside offering words of comfort. "Don't worry sweetheart, you'll be alright. We are taking you to the Jewish Hospital in the Big Ghetto."

Otto places me in the bed of a truck with my sister, who cradles my head on her lap. He jumps in, firing up the engine and putting the truck in gear.

"What happened?" I am dizzy from the confusion and the pain.

"The stupid elevator nearly crushed you. You can thank Otto for saving your life. I have never seen such strength. He climbed upstairs and somehow lifted the elevator up just enough for us to pull you out."

"I heard screaming and crying."

"That was you, Dinale. You were screaming for Zaida and God to save you. I ran to get Otto."

"*It hurts so much,* Nadja." I cry, no longer able to hold back the tears.

"I know, maidele, you were badly hurt by the elevator, it slashed open your leg and there is a lot of bleeding. We wrapped you tightly in towels and a blanket."

"Let me see," I beg, grabbing at the blanket.

"No darling, let's wait until we get to the hospital and let the doctor do it," restraining my hands firmly in hers. "Otto was very nervous when the accident took place and he notified the SS that a young girl has been hurt and he is driving her to the hospital. I hope they don't stop us."

Just as she says this the truck comes to a sudden halt. Nadja carefully lowers my head to the floor of the truck and peers out to see why we have stopped. Otto's superior, the beastly SD officer known for his cruelty and abusiveness, has stopped us and he is shouting like a mad dog at Otto. We listen, crouching in fear as the SD officer yells at Otto. "How dare you leave the factory for a damned Jew? Our men are dying at the front and you dare to care about the life of one shitty Jewess?"

Otto, holding up under the onslaught answers, "*Yavol, mein commandant,* you are right. She is only a Jew but her sister is an excellent worker and very smart. Let me take the girl to the hospital." After delivering a furious tirade, the vicious Nazi finally stops screaming and berating poor Otto.

As Otto pulls away the SD yells after us, "Put her in the hospital and you get back to A.V.L. immediately!"

My sister, holding me close, sighs with relief. "Thank God for Otto, he is a good man to take such a risk for us and stand up to that monster."

"My leg is numb, I can't feel it. Am I going to die Nadja?"

"Don't be silly, of course you aren't going to die. You probably will need stitches and have to stay in the hospital for awhile. Mamashy is going to be furious with me for letting this happen to you."

"Don't worry, Nadja, I will tell her it wasn't your fault."

Finally we reach the hospital and Otto gently picks me up and carries me inside while he calls authoritatively for the doctor in charge. A nurse rushes to get the doctor while another nurse escorts us to a room with a bed. Carefully, Otto lays me on the bed. I am soaking wet from the heat and moaning in pain. Otto is also drenched with sweat, probably a combination of heat and nerves. Nadja nervously clings to my hand that is unharmed as she soothes me while watching wide-eyed for the doctor. Finally he arrives, deferring to Otto and ignoring me.

"There was an accident at A.V.L. and this young girl was hurt, she probably will need stitches."

The doctor finally looks at me, acknowledging my presence with a nod. It is obvious that my arrival came at an inconvenient time. Indignantly, he removes the blanket and towels and looks at the wounds on my leg. I gasp when I see how deep the cut on my leg is and the amount of blood that is oozing from the open gash. I am gripped with terror wondering how I will be able to work if I am crippled. Feverishly I fret that they will kill me if I am no longer useful. The doctor lifts my right hand, which is cut open between the thumb and my first finger. "Yes, well this is not too bad, she will need stitches though. I have some other patients to attend to first and when I am finished I will stitch her up."

"*You can't just leave me here bleeding and in pain*," I begin to sob uncontrollably. Otto's face turns red as a beet and he glares at the doctor. Exploding with anger, he grabs the doctor by his lapels and screams in his face, "NO, NO, YOU'RE NOT GOING ANYWHERE, YOU ARE GOING TO TAKE CARE OF HER RIGHT NOW! DO YOU UNDERSTAND ME?"

The doctor, visibly shaken and completely confused by a German showing concern for a Jew, stutters "Yes… er… yes, whatever you say commandant. I will take care of her immediately!" Turning to the nurse he orders her, "Nurse, go fetch my surgical tools and prepare this young lady for me, now!"

The nurse scurries away, "Yes doctor."

Nadja and I look at each other and then at Otto. "Thank you, Otto," I whisper.

Otto shrugs off my thanks and turns to Nadja. "We have to leave and get back to A.V.L. right now! Your sister will be well taken care of. Am I right doctor?" He again glares at the doctor. "Yes, of course, don't worry, I will make sure she receives the best of everything."

Nadja brushes my cheek with a quick kiss, "Don't worry, you will be fine." She whispers, "Mamashy and I will come see you tomorrow, be brave." Kissing me again, she is gone, with Otto leading her by her arm out of the hospital.

I am alone and petrified with fear. Although my sister has tried her best to dispel my uncertainties, my mind is overcome with dread of what my injuries portend. My leg is throbbing and I beg the doctor for something to alleviate the pain as he begins to stitch the large swollen gash.

The hospital is poorly supplied with medications but the nurse returns with some pills that I eagerly swallow. The doctor, who must have resented his treatment by Otto, wordlessly stitches my wounds with little care as to my suffering as I bear the pain without any anesthetic. When he is done stitching and bandaging he tells the nurse to apply icy compresses to my leg and hand. "You will remain in the hospital for a week or two. I don't want any infection to take hold." Then turning to the nurse he orders, "Nurse, I want these bandages changed once a day and the wound cleaned."

"Thank you, doctor," I murmur.

"You are a lucky girl, young lady, that the German isn't SS, otherwise the outcome would have been much different. Now if you don't mind, Princess, I will return to my duties." With a slight bow he takes his leave of me.

Chapter 13

The Jewish Hospital

It is impossible to describe how depressing and frightening my first night at the Jewish Hospital is. The screams and cries of the afflicted patients begging for relief echo through the halls, making it impossible to sleep. The hospital has only the most basic remedies and most of the patients suffer through their maladies without hope for cure or proper medical intervention. I sleep fitfully from the pain of my hand and leg, which throbs unmercifully. I miss my mother, sister, and brother and feel completely abandoned. I want to go home to my old house and my old life before the ghetto. I yearn for my father, my grandfather, and for the war to end, for the Nazis to vanish, and for the world to return to a way of life that exists no more. I am a child whose childhood has ceased to be. It is impossible for me to understand. I lie alone in pain, feeling sorry for myself. The adult I have too soon become is angry and filled with hatred. My childhood is gone and I will forever be forced to contend with the world through the eyes of lost innocence. Where is the God that I have been taught to revere?

Why has he abandoned us? I feel guilty even thinking such irreverent thoughts, but the questions plague me throughout my waking and sleeping hours.

The next day my mother and sister come to see me. Mamashy has baked me a *kugl*[33] sweetened with apples and kisses me a thousand times with grateful tears in her eyes that I am going to recover from my wounds. My sister tells me that Otto took quite a bit of abuse from the SD officer for daring to save a worthless Jewish girl. "You could hear the shouting throughout the factory."

Otto and his family are now included in my mother's daily prayers. Otto is a true *mensch,* a decent human being, which is a rarity among the Nazis, who thrive on inflicting pain and misery. He has even issued my sister a pass to visit me, which is strictly against the rules.

"Nadja, I am so scared that I won't be allowed to return to work at A.V.L. What if they tell me I can't come back?"

"Don't be silly. Otto didn't save you just to abandon you later. You will have your job back, don't worry. Just get better. Everyone at A.V.L. wishes you a speedy recovery. They call you 'A.V.L.'s good luck girl' because Otto was so upset over the elevator accident that today he called in an engineer and crew to fix it. I heard him say that he won't have his workers injured and his shipments delayed and efficiency compromised. At least something good has come out of this terrible accident."

It is a short visit but I am so grateful to see my mother and sister. My mother says she will come every day to see me and that cheers me immensely. Nevertheless, I cry when they leave, as I know my sister will not be able to come and see me as often. She

33 A casserole, usually made with noodles, fruit, and cottage cheese

has to work at A.V.L. and Otto cannot be expected to issue her a daily pass. I cling to her last words of reassurance to me. "Dinale, don't worry about anything, just relax and get better. Be brave and remember you are strong and the strong survive."

I am going crazy lying in this bed and as soon as I can put weight on my leg I begin to roam the halls of the hospital, peeking with curiosity at the patients and staff. As I limp through the corridors I come across a section of the building that houses a group of young women who all look relatively healthy. They laze around in various stages of undress, brushing their hair and applying rouge to their lips. I can't figure out what they are doing here since none of them looks ill. It takes me a few days to find out, but apparently they are Jewish women who earn a living for their families by being whores. I can't believe it and I ask who the customers are. Surely not the Nazis, who are forbidden to fraternize with any Jews? Certainly it could not possibly be Jewish men, who have barely enough money to care for themselves and their families. Who, then? Finally my pestering produces an answer, the customers are Polish men who dare to risk entry into the Walowa Ghetto and are not frightened by the signs outside the Ghetto that read "Contamination" and "Beware Typhoid." I try to hide, hoping to see what kind of Polish men visit these women, but one of the prostitutes sees me and gives me a tongue lashing. Furiously she scolds me, "Do you think this is a circus? How dare you hang about spying on us? Get back to your room or I will give you a spanking you won't soon forget!" I would have run if I could have but my leg won't allow it. I feel ashamed for myself and for these poor women. Some of these women are not much older than me. What a tragedy to be degraded to such a low and desperate vocation. I now realize that they are much like the walking dead in the ghetto. They have no future. They are ostracized by everyone and will never be acceptable to any society. Seeing their ruination makes me ponder my sister's parting words. "Remember you are strong and the strong survive." Is this what it means to be strong and a survivor? Aren't these women survivors? Perhaps, but I swear to myself that no matter what the future might hold I will never succumb to selling my body for any compensation, not even if it means my survival. The values and ethics my parents have instilled in me are the one thing that no one can ever take from me.

That evening when my mother visits she brings a surprise visitor. I am overcome with joy to see Vunia, whom I miss desperately. I am so happy to listen to her babble on about everything that is going on in the ghetto. "Dina you should see Fela and Yaacov, they are like an old married couple holding hands and strolling through the ghetto. Poor Fela's leg hasn't completely healed from her fall and she limps terribly, but Yaacov doesn't seem to notice. He supports her the whole way when they walk. He and Fela have been helping with the 'Bread for Children' drive and I even saw him sneak a kiss from her," she giggles. "She is so lucky to have met Yaacov. He is so handsome and seems completely devoted to her. I bet they will get married someday, when the war is over. Oh, she sends her love to you and can't wait to see you return home and healed."

Vunia's words are restorative to my spirit. It is as if there is no war, hunger, or disease. She paints the world with the colors of hope, future, and normalcy. "How are Anya and Jacob doing?" I ask.

"Aunt Ruth and Uncle Saul have accomplished a miracle with them. Anya and Jacob now address them as Zaide and Bubby. Guess what? My sister has started a school for Anya, Jacob, and me. Every day we spend a few hours with her, studying Polish, math, and whatever else she can muster up for us to learn. We have to write a paper each week which she grades, oh, and memorize a poem. The best part, though, is when she reads out loud to us. As soon as you are better and can come home, you must join us. When are you getting out of here, anyway?"

"I don't see how I can study with you, I have to work at A.V.L. and they haven't told me yet when I'm to be released."

"Don't worry, we will figure something out. At least you can study on Sunday or after work sometimes."

Just then the nurse comes in with a tray to change my bandages. When the nurse removes the bandage from my leg, Vunia gasps in awe at the crude uneven surgical seam that runs across the wound, "My God, that is really ugly!"

"V-u-n-i-a, that's not nice to say." I am healing but I know I will carry these scars for the rest of my life. "Does it really look that bad?"

"Sorry. No, it's not that bad. You are really lucky that you didn't lose your leg, though."

"Yes, I suppose you're right. I just want to go home."

My mother now intercedes, "Speaking of home, girls, we have only a few more minutes and then Vunia and I must return."

We laugh and hold hands, delighting in each other's company, but too soon it is time for them to go. Watching my loved ones take leave of me is a difficult moment, as I have only the company of family and friends to distract me from the long lonely days and nights. Vunia promises to return as soon as possible and grudgingly I bid her and my mother farewell.

It is ten days since I arrived at the hospital. My mother is here and I notice she seems particularly distracted and nervous. I am healing well and I expect to be released from the hospital in the next few days so I can't understand her distress. "Mamashy, what's wrong?"

"Oh nothing, I am just tired," she sighs, brushing my hair and deftly braiding it. "It's becoming more and more difficult to buy even the most basic food on the black market. Your brother is so thin it worries me and no matter how I try I can't seem to get any fat on his bones. Sometimes I just feel the struggle is more than I can bear. I will be fine, don't worry about me, you just continue to gain strength, my angel." Finishing my hair, she kisses the top of my head.

Unsatisfied with her answer, I prod, "What's going on in the ghetto, anything new?"

"No, nothing much, just the usual day-to-day struggles." Fidgeting, she begins straightening things around my room. "Oh... yes, I forgot, the Nazis have been very busy installing searchlights throughout the ghetto."

"Why would they do that? Have you heard anything?"

"No, no, you know the Nazis they are constantly thinking up better ways to round up workers, they probably plan to come at night and remove more men for work."

I begin to shake with fear, "I don't like when they do something out of the ordinary. Maybe they are planning deportations. There are rumors circulating like crazy in the hospital that deportations are imminent."

Hugging me, she assures, "Remember, your sister and Dina have work permits, they will protect your brother and me. I don't want you to worry."

Refusing to relent, I whine, "Mamashy, please stay with me just tonight? I don't want to be alone. You could sleep here right next to me in this bed. Just one night, please? Tomorrow you can take me home. Please, Mamashy?"

"Dinale darling, please don't ask me to stay, you know I can't. Your brother can't be left alone, and your sister and Cousin Dina will come home from A.V.L. hungry and tired. I must be there to feed everyone. I promise tomorrow I will come and bring you a special treat."

Reluctantly I accept the inevitable and allow my poor mother to return to the ghetto where duty calls her. I make her promise that first thing in the morning she will return to the hospital and ask the doctor if I can be released. I kiss and hug her, holding back the usual tears that overwhelm me when she leaves. Instead I give her my biggest sunshine smile and beg her to be careful and to send love and kisses to Nadja, Dina, and Abek from me.

Sometime after midnight I am startled from my sleep by the sounds of gunshots and screams. At first I think it is a summer thunderstorm. I lie in my bed, straining to discern where it is coming from or whether it is real or a dream. Rubbing my eyes, I realize that what I hear are guns, something terrible is happening. Everyone who can get up out of their beds is running about the hospital. The main doors of the hospital are locked at night and no one can get in or out of the building. I sit up, terrified. It is impossible to tell where the gunfire is coming from. Please don't let it be Glinice. I feel helpless, the only thing I can do is pray to God that he will keep my family safe. The rest of the night is an endless series of frightening sounds, gunshots, Germans screaming from loudspeakers, and the anguished cries of victims. The reverberations echo through the city and I can't tell if they are near or far away. Sleepless, I huddle with a group of patients as we all try to imagine what is happening. Fear spreads among us like a contagious disease. Sometime after two in the morning the sounds seem to be getting closer to the hospital. I can hear the thunderous sound of a large convoy of trucks moving in the streets outside. Again, we hear the Nazis braying through loudspeakers, a barrage of gunshots firing and the blood-curdling screams that follow. Running to my bed I curl up in a fetal position, clinging to my blanket, alternating between praying and crying. Exhausted, sleep finally claims me. No one comes to comfort me that night.

Chapter 14

Nadja Tells a Tale

I wake in the morning in a sweat with my sheets soaking wet. The hospital halls are teeming with activity. Those that can walk are gathered in small groups throughout the hallways discussing the previous night's events and speculating on what might have transpired during the night. Whatever has occurred, the streets are basically silent now as if nothing ever happened. A short time later, a few doctors and nurses report for work at the hospital and rumors begin to circulate that there has, in fact, been a deportation and that the Glinice Ghetto was targeted. How many have been taken and where they were sent is unknown. I wait anxiously for my mother's promised arrival. I know that she will make every effort to get to me or at least to send me some reassurance of her safety. The morning wears on and still there is no word from my mother or my sister and I become increasingly more upset and desperate for news. I cling to the belief that my sister's and Dina's work permits will keep my mother and brother safe. Without any word, I lie in my bed, tortured with visions of the worst possible outcome. My fear is beginning to turn to anger at my sister for not finding a way to come to me. How dare she let me worry like this, doesn't she know how scared I am? I feel trapped in this hospital, as I have no proper clothing with me and even if I wanted to escape, I can't. All I have to wear is a hospital gown and slippers.

My mother left emergency clothing for me at my Aunt Mindale's, which isn't too far from the hospital, but how am I going to get them? Presciently, she wanted me to be able to call on family, just in case she had trouble getting to me in the hospital. I will go crazy if I don't do something. I must find a way to get out of this place.

I have a beautiful traveling mirror that my mother bought for me when I visited my grandparents in Brzeziny the summer before the war. It has a cameo on the front with a button that opens up the case to a mirror. I saw one of the nurses admiring it. When that same nurse comes to my room to check on me, I beg her to go to my aunt's house and ask one of my aunts or cousins to bring me my clothes. At first she refuses saying she doesn't have time to do errands for me, can't I see how busy the hospital is, and what a panic everyone is in since the previous night's terrors. She doesn't have time as it is to care for her own family, let alone outside requests from patients. Refusing to accept defeat, I beg her and picking up my treasured mirror, I offer to give it to her if she will just help me. I know immediately by the glint in her eyes that temptation has won her over. She reaches for the mirror, agreeing to help me. It is amazing to me how the greed of possessing a little bauble alters her priorities. I store this information for future reference, knowing it will serve me well in my dealings with people in the future. Hesitating but having no real choice, I surrender the mirror to her, trusting that she will do as she promises.

An hour or two pass as I anxiously wait for a member of my family to come to my rescue. Finally, my cousin Nadja appears alone with the clothes that will provide my freedom. My beautiful eighteen year old cousin looks haggard and worn, her brown eyes circled in blackness. She is disheveled and nervously her eyes dart around my room as if she is worried someone may have followed her. Rushing to me, she crushes me to her and immediately a torrent of tears and cries of sorrow flow in a steady outpouring of suffering.

"Dina, it was awful, you can't imagine what has happened. I'm so sorry for you, for me, for Mama. I can't bear it."

What she says is nonsensical to me and I pale with each word, my own tears silently streaming from my eyes in disbelief. "What are you saying?" is all I manage to utter. Desperate for news, I restrain myself from interrupting her and allow the ugly tale to enfold me.

"At around two a.m. the Nazis rolled into the Walowa Ghetto with what seemed an endless line of trucks. They quickly set up searchlights and unloaded hundreds of armed Nazis and their dogs surrounding each street with a guard of madmen. The loudspeakers screamed that everyone was to line up outside their homes in five minutes. The angry voices threatened that anyone who was found in their home after five minutes would be shot immediately. They began banging on all the doors and emptying the houses of all occupants. We were terrified and dressed in seconds, my parents urging us to hurry. Fear gripped us all. The poor grandmothers were crying and praying for God to intervene. We came outside as Nazis bludgeoned, kicked and cursed us as we crossed the threshold of our homes. We were blinded like deer held frozen by the lights in our eyes. The vicious dogs barked bloodthirstily at us and the Nazis held guns trained on us. Anyone who protested or even asked a question was shot dead on the spot. A cold blooded killer from the SS, his lightning streak insignia blazing brightly in the light, walked in front of each person, sneering with disgust, and with malicious amusement he divided each family. Choosing randomly husband, wife or children, we were separated and torn from each other's arms." Unable to continue Nadja collapses in my arms, violently sobbing. My tears join with hers in a river that flows soaking into the crisp white linen of my sheets. Holding my breath, I wait for her to continue as my heartbeat pounds in my chest. I try to comfort her as best I can as I stroke her head, trying to calm the sorrow that knows no relief. Finally her sobs subside enough for her to continue. "It was beyond anything you can imagine, a nightmare that had no end. It happened so quickly, I don't know if I even had time to say good-bye! They took my mother, Bubysy Surale and my Bubysy Chava, Aunt Feigele, and the girls. They drove them like cattle through the streets with a hail of bullets at their backs randomly targeting anyone who didn't keep up the pace. The streets were running with blood. Dinale, it was hell come to earth. What we witnessed was enough to drive one mad. We saw babies, infants ripped from their mothers arms, held by their feet by these monsters who laughed as they smashed their small skulls against building walls while the poor mothers watched, begging for mercy. Some of those mothers, seeing their babies murdered, begged the Nazis to murder them, too. Sometimes the Nazis accommodated them with a bullet to the head, other times they just laughed and forced them back into the crowd heading for the train station. Those that survived the slaughter in the streets were taken to the railroad tracks and crammed into cattle cars. Hundreds of people packed like sardines into cattle cars. *Oye,* there is no way our grandmothers could survive this horror. All we know is that this was repeated earlier in the evening in the Glinice Ghetto and that nearly everyone there was deported. Thank God you were here, it is a miracle."

"No, no! You are wrong, my sister and Dina have permits, they couldn't have been taken. They are probably all at A.V.L. safely waiting for me. I must get out of this hospital *now* and go to them. I'm sure my sister found a way to save my mother and brother. Yes, yes, I'm sure Otto the manager at A.V.L. would have helped her. He saved my life! I know he would help my sister!" Nadja looks at me with pity in her eyes. "Dinale, Dinale, you have to face the reality that they are probably all gone. Thank God you were here in the hospital. Now you must get out of this hospital before something bad happens. There is no way the Nazis are going to maintain a bunch of sick and crippled Jews. Come home with me, there is nowhere else for you to go. The Glinice Ghetto is no more!"

"No, no, you go home. I will be alright! I'm going to A.V.L. I know my sister is waiting for me. I know she is there. After I find her we will figure out what to do.

Give my love to your father, Majer, Aunt Nachele, Uncle Alexander, and David. Tell them how sorry I am and that I will see them soon. I must find out what has happened to my family!"

Nadja reluctantly leaves in a daze, drained by the telling of the night's horrors. As I dress I carefully avoid the bandages that cover my wounds, still raw and painful. I try not to think of my Aunt Mindale's face; this woman who has spent her whole life in dedication to her family and community. Poor Nadja, to lose her mother, my heart is breaking. What of my sweet bubysy and her talent for healing, how will she survive such a traumatic experience? It is all more than I can bear. Silently I pray that God will protect them from the evil fiends who hold them captive. My worries spin a tight web around me, threatening to asphyxiate the hope to which I still cling. Exiting the hospital, I enter the world outside, where the summer heat is already promising another hot and humid day. Absentmindedly, I touch the braids my mother had lovingly plaited just yesterday. They are still bound neatly and I can almost smell my mother's scent on them. Is it possible that only a few hours have passed since I last kissed her good-bye? Is it possible that everyone I have ever loved could be gone? I look around, desperate to get my bearings. Those who survived the night have returned to the streets, pursuing the daily rigors of life and its necessities. Suddenly, around the corner from the hospital, I spy a group of A.V.L. workers walking. Rushing to them, my heart pounding with joy, I nearly knock them down in my excitement. "I am so happy to see you. Thank God I found you! I was going to try to get back to A.V.L. on my own. Where's Nadja, where's my sister?" I search each face, looking for reassurance, "Why isn't she here with you? Why didn't she come to get me? Are my mother and brother safe, and my Cousin Dina?"

Delighted to see me recovered, Jacob, one of the young men, takes my hands and, looking into my eyes, says, "Listen to me Dina, we have been ordered to collect our things from our homes in the ghetto and return to A.V.L. where we are now going to live." Quickly casting his eyes around the group with furrowed brows he adds, "Don't worry; your sister is waiting for you back at A.V.L. They are all safe. They wouldn't let your sister come with us to the Big Ghetto because she is from the Glinice Ghetto and has no valid reason to come here. Now you must gather your things, don't forget your work permit, and wait for us in front of the hospital." He commands, "Do as I say and you will see your sister again, okay maidele?"

I am so happy I throw my arms around his neck and kiss him. "Yes, Jacob, I understand and I will be waiting for you here." Waving good-bye, I would have danced across the street if my injuries had allowed me. I am elated, my prayers have been answered; my sister is safe and waiting for me. I walk up the steps of the hospital, anxious to grab my belongings and inform the nurses that I am leaving. Although it takes me only minutes to gather my things, when I tell the nurse that I am leaving she insists that my bandages be changed once more and that the doctor give me a final examination. I wait impatiently for the doctor as the nurse changes my bandages and cleans my wound. The seam of my stitches is crooked and ragged and I know that I will have ugly scars on my hand and leg. In my less than expert opinion, the doctor did a terrible job, but at least I am healing and I will be able to work. After what seems like eternity, the doctor arrives and gives me a clean bill of health. He is anxious to be rid of me, and tells the nurse to give me bandages and a salve so that I can change my own dressings.

I nervously wait outside in front of the hospital, scanning the street for Jacob and the others. Minutes pass by and there is no sign of them. I become more and more agitated that maybe I have missed them. Finally, I see one of the girls, my sister's friend Sonja hurrying up the street in the direction of A.V.L. I call to her, halting her progress as I limp across the street. She tells me that she has missed the group and is on her way back to A.V.L. alone.

"That means I too have missed them, the stupid doctor wouldn't let me go. Please, take me with you?"

"Of course, I am going to take you with me." Taking my arm she scans the street for trouble. "We must not waste a minute, let's get out of here!"

As we hurry through the streets I nervously chatter about how excited I am that I will soon see my sister and family. Over and over I reiterate my joyful expectation without any reaction on Sonja's part.

"I can't wait to see my sister, Nadja," I reaffirm as I limp beside Sonja trying my best to keep up with her hurried pace. "I am really angry with her, though, for not getting word to me. When I see her I am going to give her a piece of my mind."

Nodding in agreement she says nothing.

"Did you talk to my sister at all?" I query her.

"No, I didn't."

Finally her evasiveness brings forth fear I can barely contain. I begin to sob uncontrollably, "She is there, isn't she? My sister is at A.V.L.? Please tell me she's there!"

"Dina, stop crying, if a Nazi comes along you are going to get us arrested." Nervously she looks around. "I'm telling you the Nazis will surely stop us if you don't stop this wailing! Your sister is fine; she is waiting for you, okay? Now stop your sniveling. I'm just very nervous walking alone like this after such a night."

"I'm sorry, Sonja, I didn't even ask if your family is okay. Are they alright?"

Her eyes swell with tears, which she brushes aside, "No, they are gone. My mother, father and brother were deported last night."

Feeling her anguish, I clasp her hand, "I'm so sorry, it was selfish of me to pester you about Nadja. Please forgive me."

Sonja nods, silently accepting my apology as she picks up her pace in the direction of A.V.L.

I try my best to believe her and control my fears as we walk the final kilometer to A.V.L., but she refuses to look me in the eyes as she repeats over and over that my sister is waiting for me. By the time we reach A.V.L. my leg is throbbing but I run inside, forgetting my pain, "Nadja, Nadja, where are you?" I run to a group of workers standing together, their heads bent deep in conversation. "Jacob, where is Nadja? I don't see her?"

He takes my hands, his eyes filling with tears. Pulling me into his arms he whispers in my ear, "Dina, I'm so sorry. Forgive me for lying to you. Neither she nor your cousin is here, they never showed up at Kosna Street where workers with permits were told to assemble. They must have stayed with your mother and brother, not wanting to abandon them."

I look at him in disbelief, unable to suppress the uncontrollable shaking that overwhelms me. "NO, NO!" my screams pierce the air. "IT CAN'T BE TRUE! THEY CAN'T BE GONE! NO, NO, MAMASHY, NADJA, ABEK, DINA!" My world crumbles about me and I feel it spinning out of control. Falling to my knees, I sink into oblivion. Unable to bear the pain that engulfs me, I faint.

Part 3

I Am Alone

Chapter 15

The Hands of Friends

When I wake they are all standing over me, even Otto is there, concern written all over his face. They carry me into a small room with mattresses on the floor. I am numb with grief and my head is throbbing. My ears are deaf to their sympathy. Once Otto sees that I am awake he insists that everyone get back to work. He tells Sonja to stay with me and he tells me to just lie quietly for as long as I like. "Dina, I am sorry, little one, for your loss. Take your time and heal, don't worry, as soon as you feel up to it you can resume your work."

In silence I receive his kind words but they make no impression on me. I feel dead. I have no will to go on living. All I can think of is my mother, Nadja, Abek, Dina, Fela, Vunia, their families, and my aunts and cousins. A world without them is a living death.

Another day comes and goes as I lie prostrate with grief. I refuse to eat or speak. I am barely aware of the steady stream of workers who come to my bedside to offer some form of encouragement or hope to my world that lies in ashes. I go from delirious days to nightmarish nights. The voices of my family ring in my ears, their faces appearing like ghosts; they haunt my waking hours and plague my restless sleep. Finally, my sister's friend Mietek comes to my bedside. Clasping my hands in his, he begins to share his memories of the awful night of the destruction of the Glinice Ghetto. He speaks to me in a quiet voice, "Perhaps by walking through hell with me, together we can find some meaning that will allow us both to fight to live another day. It seems we are in the same boat, you and me," he whispers, his voice hoarse with emotion. "We both have lost everyone we hold dear. In fact, nearly every person who survived the selection on August 5th has lost some or all of their families and friends." He pauses, gathering his thoughts, his eyes fixed on some distant horizon only he can see. Pain is clearly visible in his face. In order to bear the enormity of what he is saying, I force myself to focus on the movement of his mouth. I concentrate, watching his lips as I listen to his tale. He grasps my hands like a lifeline. "That evening I was with your sister and Vunia's sister, Lola, outside of your house in the street. We were discussing the usual topics that consumed us—politics, the war, and our dreams of one day immigrating to Palestyne. Even in this living hell we all have clung to our dreams and hopes. Your sister was vibrant and animated as usual." His face lights up with a smile as he remembers. "It was a warm evening, a beautiful evening, a star-filled summer's night that reminded us of how bittersweet life is. Even the Nazis have not been able to quash the desires of youth. It was magical until Nazis arriving in trucks came through the ghetto announcing over loudspeakers '*Go into your homes! You are not allowed to be on the street!*' Reluctantly, we bid each other good-night and went to our homes… at around midnight it started. We were startled from our sleep with banging on our doors and loud speakers shouting for us to immediately assemble in the street. It was unbelievable. We were blinded by lights and clubbed as we exited our homes. The sounds were heart-rending, children crying and people screaming, the prayers of the elderly, it was pure chaos. They ordered us to dress. We had fifteen minutes to pack a few basic belongings and food. All Jews with labor cards were told to report to Kosna Street and those without were to report to Graniczna Street for immediate resettlement. In my family my brother and I were the only ones with a labor card and my family urged us to go to Kosna Street. At first my brother and I refused to go. We argued with my parents that we would never be separated from our beloved family. We wanted to go with them regardless of the consequences and face the future together as one. My mother began to tear at her hair and began to scream, 'NO, NO, you will go to Kosna Street. We will be fine! We will write and let you know where they take us. You will do as I say; you will not disobey your mother!' My brother and I reluctantly gave in to her hysteria. In the street there were thousands of people, we embraced my mother, father, and sisters and then they were gone, pushed forward by the crying mass of humanity that inched its way toward Graniczna Street. The slow flow of the distraught crowd wasn't fast enough for the Germans. They arbitrarily shot into the mass of people, aiming mostly at the elderly and children that lagged behind and hindered departure. The streets were bathed with the blood of the innocent. I sent my brother on to Kosna Street and took a dangerous chance and ran to your house, hoping to find Nadja and your cousin Dina so that I could take them with me to Kosna Street, but I was too late. When I got there they were already gone, the street had been emptied. All that was left were the bodies of those that had been shot on the spot. It was eerie and ghostly, just doors left ajar and candlelight from within that flickered in the night. Running from the destruction that was everywhere around me, I prayed that Nadja and

Dina had gone ahead of me and would be at Kosna Street when I got there. When I got to Kosna Street, they lined us up in rows of ten and the SS surrounded us with rifles leveled and aimed. I looked for your sister and Dina in the crowd but I couldn't find them. You could smell the fear from the crowd; the telltale smells of fear—piss, vinegar, and human waste. It impregnated the air and hung about us as we stood waiting, our lives hanging in the balance. Then the selections began and I watched as the Nazis chose the strong and healthy, dividing us from the mothers with children and the weak. Helplessly we watched the Nazis terrorizing those chosen and marching them away to Graniczna Street. It was heartbreaking hearing the crying children clinging to their mothers who desperately pleaded for mercy as they slowly wove their way down the street. Members of families separated continued to call their good-byes until moments later you could hear the machine guns and rifles as they ceaselessly emptied their bullets. The air was filled with the screams from the dying and those who loved them. It was a nightmare beyond anything the human mind can imagine and many a soul mercifully lost his mind that night. It is clear that the Nazis mean to soak the ground with our blood and annihilate us from the face of the earth. There can be no delusions among us. Dinale, I don't know where our families have been taken, but I can't imagine it is anywhere good. We the survivors must fight to live so that the world will know what took place here. You and I must live to testify and to remember. We are all that stands in the way of the extinction of an entire people. Help me find a reason to live! You are the youngest and you are strong. Your people need you. You must live for your mother, your father, Nadja, Abek, and Dina!"

The tears stream down Mietek's face as he lowers his forehead to my hands. The effort he has exerted to describe the horrors of that inexplicable night has taken its toll. Now it is my turn to save a soul. The tears that have failed me now pour freely down my face as I bend to kiss his head. My voice barely above a whisper, I speak for the first time since my collapse. "Mietek, Mietek, I cannot bear the pain, I feel so alone."

Lifting his head, his face shiny and wet from the tears that drench it, he hoarsely whispers, "You are not alone, we are a family, a family of lost souls. Anger will keep you alive Dinale. We must nourish our anger until the day we are set free and then vengeance will be ours."

"You are speaking of hate. I know nothing of hate. I have lived surrounded by love and taught to respect human life. Even now, knowing that I may never see those I have loved again, I feel only misery and guilt that I was not with them; that I am alive while they may not be. Hate will not bring them back to me."

"Hate and revenge will nurture your will to live, which in itself will destroy the Nazis. Dinale, you cannot lie on this mattress indefinitely and not work. Even Otto cannot protect those that don't work. Get up, PLEASE! It is time to return to the living."

Chapter 16

We, the Living

With Mitek's encouragement I returned to the world of the living. I rose from my pallet and threw myself into the work at A.V.L. Otto seems relieved to see me back on the floor fulfilling my labors. I am a shadow of who I was; daughter, sister, friend, these are descriptions that hold no meaning for me; they no longer represent who I am. My young healthy body strains under the tasks assigned to me, but these burdens only seem to strengthen my physical and mental determination. As Mietek suggested, I nurture my anger and direct it at those who destroyed my world. At least in my thoughts and prayers I beg God to wipe the Nazis from the face of the earth. With each curse my resolve to live grows stronger.

Confirmation of our worst fears comes but a few days later.

The conductors of the trains that carried our loved ones to what was supposed to be resettlement returned and word spreads like a wildfire as to their actual fate. The endless line of cattle cars which had each been crammed beyond capacity with hundreds of people had traveled to a destination called Treblinka. A trip that should have taken six hours from Radom had taken twenty-four hours before finally arriving in Treblinka, a small village near the Bug River. The train was then held in limbo and sat on the tracks for two more days in the brutal heat of summer. The cries of the innocents entombed in the cars could be heard pleading for water and food throughout the days and nights that followed. The SS did nothing to alleviate the suffering within. In fact, they perpetrated unspeakable cruelties by occasionally shooting randomly into the cars to silence the prisoners and tormenting them with promises of water and food that were never delivered. On the third day the train was finally allowed to enter the camp itself. When the doors were opened the unfortunate masses were greeted with blinding lights and Nazis yielding whips and guns who screamed "RAUS!" "RAUS!" "HURRY!" "HURRY!" "GET OFF THE TRAINS!" The German shepherds were barking incessantly, accompanied by the cries of the frightened children. The train was also emptied of the many who had died in transit and the pile of bodies grew to massive proportions on the platform. Immediately the men and women were separated, young boys were pulled apart from their mothers and young girls from their fathers. From there they were marched off down a long narrow path that led to some buildings. Beyond the buildings were smokestacks that filled the night air with noxious fumes and a cloud of ashes that blocked the moon and stars from the sky. Once they entered the path that looked like a tube they were never seen again! The witnesses had no idea as to what might have happened to these thousands of Jews. It was as if they had vanished into thin air.

It is too much to fathom. I can't breathe as the news is whispered from ear to ear until I myself listen in horror as the nightmare is repeated. I can't begin to imagine the agony of my family's last hours on earth. Visions of them play before my eyes like an endless movie. My dear Grandmother Surale and Grandmother Chava, did they survive that tortuous journey in the train? I can see my grandmother, her eyes closed so as not to see the depravity around her, praying to my grandfather and God for mercy. Then the arrival in hell; my poor brother being torn from my mother's and sister's arms as they screamed and tried unsuccessfully to stay together, in the end being sent with strangers to his death at age ten. My pain is unbearable as I envision my dearest girlfriends Vunia and Fela and their entire families being marched to their death. All the promises and dreams of youth unfulfilled and ended. Fela and I will never keep our promise of a new life in Palestyne. All gone and lost forever. I imagine my mother hysterical, holding tightly to my sister's hand as they are beaten and driven to where? Did they know that death awaited them at the end of that road? Did my mother think of me in her last moments? Did she wonder if my father had suffered the same fate? Or was the unspeakable cruelty of being separated from her beloved son all she could think of? The horror must have been crippling and, I pray, mercifully numbing. Perhaps she, my sister, and Cousin Dina just kissed and said good-bye, clinging to each other as they walked to the end of the tunnel. I will never know. I pray to God that they didn't suffer too terribly, that death came quickly. Please God that my dear ones are all in heaven together, no longer in pain.

As for those that remain in the Big Ghetto, they are now of two schools of thought: those who believe in a facility that exists for the sole purpose of annihilating human life, and those who refuse to believe. Many of the Jews that remain in Radom choose not to believe the tales of a death factory at Treblinka. For us at A.V.L., there can be no doubt; and we pray and say *Kaddish*, the prayer for the dead, for our loved ones as we try to reconcile the fact that we will never see them again. My grief is bottomless. I am thirteen and entirely alone. I will never see my beloved family again.

Eleven days after the destruction of the Glinice Ghetto, I am visiting my cousins in the Walowa Ghetto on a warm summer day. It is Sunday. My girlfriend Dora Rabbinowicz suddenly arrives out of breath at the door of my relatives' apartment. She has run to get me. Our stay in the ghetto has been cut short. Otto has sent word that all A.V.L. employees are to report immediately to the entrance of the ghetto and are to return under guard to A.V.L. There will be no exceptions and those who do not report immediately will lose their work permits. It is all too mysterious but I hurriedly bid farewell to my Aunt Natalia, Uncles Tuvye and Alexander, and my cousins, promising I will return as soon as I can. I angrily remark to Dora as we run to the designated assembly point that can't the Nazis even let us have one day to spend with our families in peace? I am so distressed that at first I don't notice the Polish electricians working in the ghetto. Astonished, I stop running and grab Dora's hand, forcing her to stop in her tracks as I point at the Poles.

"What are they doing?"

Dora's face pales as she realizes that they are wiring and hanging spot lights. "This is just what they did the day they liquidated the Glinice Ghetto."

I begin to shake uncontrollably. "I need to go back and warn my relatives."

"No, we have to go now, we don't have time. Don't worry, word will spread quickly, there are plenty of people about. Come on," Dora urges. "We have to get out of here NOW!"

Numb and trembling, I allow her to lead me on to our rendezvous with the guards that escort us back to A.F.L. Once more, fate has intervened.

The destruction of the Glinice Ghetto and its eight thousand inhabitants who were deported and murdered at Treblinka was nothing compared to what the Nazis would endeavor to carry out on August 16 through August 18. I will never be able to know with complete certainty, but it is highly likely that Otto, Hans, and a few of their fellow supervisors at A.V.L. may have saved our lives by cancelling our visit to the ghetto and recalling us back to A.V.L. I don't know if Otto knew of the Nazis' plans, but it seems likely he was tipped off. None of us were forced to report to the Walowa Ghetto on that fateful night or in the ensuing days, while many other workers at other factories were forcibly marched to Walowa and their probable doom. While we slept in relative safety in our beds at A.V.L., in the big Walowa Ghetto a massive *wysiedlenie,* or deportation, took place under cover of darkness beginning at midnight. The rumors had been circulating for days that further deportations were inevitable and absolute panic ensued when Polish electricians entered the ghetto on the sixteenth to install powerful searchlights on every street. Dora had been correct—the population was quickly alerted to the coming disaster. The ghetto was completely sealed with no escape and the Nazis employed their mightiest forces against the unarmed frightened inhabitants. The ghetto was surrounded with armed S.S. troops and Ukrainian militia dressed in S.S. uniforms, gendarmes, and Polish and German police. Machine guns were poised on the rooftops, prepared to mow down any and all who tried to escape or didn't proceed as quickly as ordered. For three days and two nights, twenty-five thousand people were systematically removed from their homes. Each building was thoroughly searched with dogs and their handlers to assure the meticulous Nazis that no one was left behind, somehow eluding detection. There would be no escape or commuting of sentence. Anyone found remaining was quickly dispatched with a bullet to the head. Whole families were liquidated in the streets as they were driven from their homes. Street by street, apartment by apartment, the buildings were emptied of Jews, who were led under fire to areas for selection and there made to stand in endless lines while enduring degrading verbal and physical abuse. After many hours they finally reached a Gestapo arbiter who barely scrutinized the work permits of those who were fortunate to have them. One can imagine the desperation that enveloped the crowds as they stood awaiting their verdict before a heartless adjudicator who, with a swift motion of the hand, decided the life and death fate of each innocent man, woman, or child as he uttered the words of finality—"right," which meant to stay in Radom and live another day, or "left," being sent to deportation and crammed into the waiting cattle cars of trains standing ready to leave immediately to destinations unknown, or worse, Treblinka. Even the precious work permits were no guarantee of safety as many of the factories were designated to be closed and their slave employees were now easily expendable.

Too soon I learned from my cousin Majer and Nadja that they and their father Tuvye had been spared. Not so, my beautiful Aunt Natalia, who was wrested from her beloved husband Alexander's arms as her distraught son David screamed and cried for them not to take her. The Nazi plan to divide, conquer and destroy was brutally put into motion by their willing accomplices. All this was clearly done to family after family in order to inflict the worst possible pain and destroy and crush any hope of life or the will to live it. Who could possibly rally the will to fight when all human decency is fodder under the boots of the monstrous murderers who control your loved ones destiny?

Twenty-thousand Radomers were deported over those three days of hell, leaving but a scant remnant of survivors of what had been the Walowa Ghetto. The Nazis quickly set about ransacking the homes of the vanquished. For this disheartening task they utilized the remaining Jews, who were given the unenviable task of emptying and sorting what was left of the lives of the vanished. From there the plunder was distributed to shipping warehouses like A.V.L. We that remain are granted life in order that we can categorize, crate, and ship the belongings of our expelled brethren to families in Germany and the soldiers on the Eastern front. We are all that remain of our once thriving Jewish community. We struggle on, knowing that our days, too, are probably numbered. Each day the sand pours through the hourglass of time, bringing us closer to our fate.

Chapter 17

When Love Comes

A false sense of safety wove its way into the tapestry of our days at A.V.L. following the destruction of the Walowa Ghetto. We are lulled by the decent Germans like Otto who barely harass us and run the large complex of assorted buildings that provide the war effort with needed supplies and we hope our work will assure us a modicum of safety. The shared tragedy of having lost some or all of our families and living and eating where we work forge ties between us that begin to resemble something of a family. In our small community any sign of normalcy and a commitment to life is welcomed, rejoiced, and celebrated, albeit quietly. At A.V.L. we eat our meals in a cafeteria that services the entire complex. At long communal tables we share our brief respite from hard labor; together we whisper any news of the war effort that can be ascertained from conversations overheard between our German overlords. Although we experience hunger, we are not starving and each day brings enough soup and bread to keep us functioning. I have noticed a young handsome teen who always positions himself in my path as I enter at meal times. His serious blue eyes seek me out and once he holds my gaze, his eyes crinkle up into a smile that lights the room. I can do nothing but return that big open grin and nod my head in recognition of his friendliness. I have no experience with boys and certainly I am not used to getting any attention from the opposite sex except in a brotherly manner. I feel awkward and inept in his presence but there is something about his smile that disarms me. It is but a short time before he finally works up the nerve and approaches me.

"Hello, my name is Natek Korman, what's your name?" he asks, as he thrusts his hand toward me to shake. His penetrating eyes unsettle me, they seem to be seeking answers to questions not yet spoken. I am reluctant to open my soul to him or anyone, for that matter. I fear what he might ask of me. Shyly, I shake the firm hand that grasps mine. He holds my hand, not releasing it as his eyes burn into me with the fury of a thousand candles. Those eyes stand ready to judge every evil perpetrated since the beginning of time and every cry of innocence that has ever been swept away by the deaf embrace of the wind.

"Dina Frydman," I stammer unable to meet his gaze. "I am pleased to meet you." Quickly I remove my hand from his, stuffing it into my pocket. I can feel my cheeks burning red with embarrassment. I look around for someone I know to provide me an escape, but I come up empty handed.

"Well Dina Frydman, would you mind if we eat our meal together?" Again, that marvelous smile beguiles me and I can hardly resist such a well-mannered proposal, but still I search my mind for a plausible excuse as my heart flutters within me like a bird trapped within the sights of a gun. I hesitate a moment too long and Natek pronounces, "Good, let's sit over here." He leads me to a table and before I can protest we are sitting and I am gazing into his serious blue eyes.

Natek quickly launches into the tale of his young life and tells me that both he and his brother Benjamin survived the liquidation of the Glinice Ghetto. He turns and locates Benjamin sitting at another table and waves, flashing him that mischievous grin that somehow conveys an assurance that life is a game of sport that can be won with an equal dose of risk and luck. Natek is like a book in the making whose pages are crisp and white, awaiting the glorious story that will be written with the days of his life. Hopelessly idealistic, he carries within him a firm faith that his is a story that cannot be denied and that he will live to tell his tale, no matter what the obstacles. As tears fill his eyes, he talks nostalgically of his parents and sister who were not so lucky on that fateful night and I listen patiently as he speaks of his loss. Then it is my turn to recount the simple twist of fate, my injury in the elevator and subsequent hospitalization, which saved my life and led me to safety at A.V.L.

"There is nothing glorious about me," I express forlornly. "I don't understand why I am alive. How is it possible that while the Glinice Ghetto was being liquidated and my family taken to their deaths, I was safe in a hospital room suffering from nothing more than a cut and stitches? Saved by Otto, a German no less?

Now the Walowa Ghetto too is no more and again I am spared the sight of evil and its enormity. I was here in Radom, yet I saw nothing of the slaughter and the streets that flowed with blood. I heard nothing of the cries that were born to the heavens, pleading for mercy. I did not see the lives of children extinguished like a flame in the gust of an evil storm. I cannot comprehend what has happened, and so I suffer and mourn; the lone surviving fruit on a tree that winter has lain bare. I feel tormented by the guilt of the living. In my heart I don't believe I deserve to live—why should I be the one chosen to continue my family's lineage? It should be my sister, with her strength of purpose and her brilliance. It should be my younger brother Abek, with his rabbinical wisdom. I feel as if there has been a terrible mistake."

Natek nods his eyes full of compassion and, taking my hand, in his he kisses it. "Dina, I have asked myself the same question over and over again. Some say it is God's will and man should never question the will of God, but my belief in God is no longer strong or important to me. God has abandoned us in our hour of need and I can no longer pray to him for our redemption. The only God left to worship is the God of survival. All I want is to live and I will do anything and everything to stay alive until the end of this war. You, too, will survive, of this I am sure. You are a compilation of all that your family was and is. You are the hope and future of our people. More precious than a mine of gold, you dazzle the eyes with beauty and goodness." He smiles as my cheeks blush and turn a vivid red. No one has ever spoken to me like this. Natek's words confuse me. In my heart I am grateful to have a new friend, someone to care for and share my thoughts with. His words kindle a flame in my soul and allow me to begin to believe that perhaps I am meant to continue and carry on the torch of my family.

At only sixteen, Natek has a command of himself that is far beyond his years and I feel great pride that he has singled me out as his girlfriend and confidant. He becomes my shelter from the storm that rages around us. Ours is a relationship of total purity born out of the debris of devastation. In a barren landscape, our love is a seed of hope. Natek is my first love and I am his and we make many a promise to each other that we hope we will be able to keep. Our courtship mainly comprises of hand holding and an occasional kiss. That is the beginning of a routine that becomes the heart of my day. Natek and I meet for every meal and we sit close together, sharing our dreams, hopes, and of course, all of our food. The world and its troubles seem to disappear when he holds my hand. Always trying to cement our ties to each other, he comes up with a silly but endearing idea to share our bowls of soup; eating one before the other. Our two spoons clicking in the bowl until it is finished, our faces intent upon each other. Then, fetching the second bowl, we consume it in exactly the same manner. It is a silly ritual, but it forges a bond between us that seems as unbreakable to me as the barbed wire that surrounds us. It feels good to love again.

The remaining Jews of the Walowa Ghetto are now squeezed into the Szwarlikowska. Camp and surrounded by a wall and barbed wire. They work in the various industries around Radom that continue to function after the *wysiedlenie* of August. I am anxious to learn the fate of my remaining family, so it is with great relief we learn a few weeks later that we will be allowed to visit Szwarlikowska Camp on Sundays. With me I smuggle in some special treats I have stashed away—some jam, fruit, and German *Neufchâtel* cheese, which we have at A.V.L., but which is not even imaginable in the Szwarlikowska Camp. My relatives are delighted with these treasures and I am happily united with what is left of my dwindling family—Nadja, Majer, their father Tuvye, my distraught Uncle Alexander, and my cousin David. When I visit, we once more recite the *Kaddish,* the prayer for the dead, for my Aunt Natalia and all the others that have so recently been murdered.

My cousin Majer works with his father at the shoe factory repairing and making boots and shoes for the Germans, an indispensable industry, for what good is an army if their soldiers have no shoes on their feet? His sister Nadja has recently been reassigned to work in a warehouse separating what remains of the now defunct Glinice Ghetto. There she categorizes and sorts the spoils of those sent to Treblinka, much of which will be sold to the Poles for fractions of what it is worth, providing a tidy income for the Fatherland. The rest of the plunder is bound for German families who eagerly await the bloody gains.

With tears in her eyes, she recounts that the work is nearly more than she can bear. "It seems everywhere I look I recognize something that belonged to someone I knew. Sometimes it is my imagination, I am sure, but I hear the voices and feel the presence of the owners of this property. They haunt my waking and sleeping hours. All the photographs that I sort through… the marriage and birth certificates, so many happy occasions; fading photographs are all that is left of these lives. All of it gone, and for what? Why? In the end, the pictures and the lives all destined to end in a pyre of flames. In the end, not even a graveyard or a stone to show that they once walked the earth."

We all stand there, sentries of silence, guardians of the truth, without any answers and nearly without hope, knowing that we, too, are probably destined for a tower of smoke.

Like a wound that reopens and festers anew, painfully I remember my mother's precious photo albums as I turn the pages in my mind. What I wouldn't give to see and hold them again! Now the photos that marked the important occasions of a lifetime, though lost, are forever seared in my memory. I will carry the faces and voices of my loved ones with me for the rest of my life. I make a promise to myself that each day I will remember the colors of eyes and hair, the cherished smiles, and hopefully by remembering I will keep alive something of the family I love and have lost.

Natek calls for me at my cousins' home to meet my family and to escort me back to A.V.L. Proudly, I introduce him as my boyfriend, which makes his broad handsome face radiate with joy. Nadja and I serve tea to our guest in an attempt to preserve the age old custom of decorum when receiving a guest into one's home, a hospitality that even in these destitute times is not to be forsaken. Natek speaks with confidence and optimism so infectious that even my downcast family finds they dare to speak of the future and an end to the conflict that holds us prisoner.

He argues single-mindedly that the Nazis cannot possibly win the war. Now that fighting has commenced on the Eastern front between the Germans and Russians and the Americans have joined the skies in the bombardment of German held Europe, they will lose. Natek is sure that a two-front war will take its toll on Germany's fixed resources of men and the commodities that sustain an army. "Every day brings us closer to freedom," he advocates.

In Alexander's eyes I note skepticism, defeat, and loss. Resignation has crushed this once thriving man. It seems to me that only the young have the indefatigable belief that tomorrow will ever come. Alexander replies, "Natek, the question is not whether the war will end, but when it will end and who will have survived to celebrate it."

"I shall be there, I promise you that!" Taking my hand and kissing it. "Dina will be there with me, I know it!"

Even Alexander's pessimism is stayed by the positivity and belief that Natek embodies. For a moment I see hope rekindle in his eyes as he looks from Natek to David, who is enthralled by Natek's words. "See, Father, you and I too will survive the war. We must do it for Mother."

Alexander throws his arms around his son, hugging him to him. "You are right, David, we must live for your Mother." Tears fill the once handsome face of my uncle at the mention of his beloved wife, Nachele.

It has been a wonderful visit, and as Natek and I walk back, arm in arm, to our designated rendezvous with the rest of the A.V.L. workers I cannot help but glory in the warmth of the sun that bathes my face and revel in the miracle that I am alive to enjoy it. As we walk towards the gate, a woman comes toward us and stops dead in her tracks. She stares at me in disbelief as the blood drains from her features. She looks familiar to me but I cannot place her. I feel the odd sensation of seeing someone out of context, of recognition without placement. Natek and I stop in front of her as I smile quizzically at her, "Do I know you?"

"You are alive?" From her ambiguous intonation I cannot tell whether it is a question or a statement.

"Why shouldn't I be alive?"

"You were in the Jewish hospital, were you not?" Her gaze searches mine.

"Yes," I answer now recognizing her. "You were a nurse at the hospital while I was there." Not wanting to be rude I turn to Natek and introduce him. "This is my friend Natek Korman, I am sorry I don't recall your name."

Nodding her acknowledgement at Natek, she answers, "Anna Greenburg, nice to meet you." Turning back to me she continues, "Shortly after the destruction of the Walowa Ghetto, the Nazis came to the hospital and ordered all of the patients to be given food and clothing to last for twenty-four hours and they assured the doctors that the patients were being transferred to another hospital. Dr. Walchovicz complied and the patients were transferred to the SS and the hospital was emptied. They dismissed the doctors and nurses and simply told us to go home. I remember you because you were one of the youngest in the hospital and before I left I searched for you. I couldn't find you in the confusion of that desperate hour when the patients were being taken away. I hoped that you had already been removed and somehow I had missed you. Thank God you were not there. The next day the Nazis took all of the patients to Pentz Park and executed them with a bullet to the head, each and every one. I have felt terrible guilt that I didn't save you, how did you escape? I thought I was seeing a ghost when I saw you walking toward me," tears fill her eyes as she reaches for my hand.

Squeezing her hands, "I am no ghost. I left the hospital the next day after the Glinice Ghetto was destroyed and ran to where I thought my sister would be at A.V.L." My voice chokes as I remember my beautiful sister, "She wasn't there, but I was safe."

"I am very happy that you are alive," she says. "I have seen my share of miracles in this life and you are one of them." She hugs me, "I must go now, there are some sick people waiting for my help." Turning she calls over her shoulder, "Stay well and good luck!"

Natek and I watch her as she slips around a corner, disappearing from our sight.

I grasp Natek's arm tightly and shudder. "Again luck and fate have stepped in to save me. Natek, I should have been in the hospital when it was liquidated and I should have been in the ghetto when my family was taken. I feel like a cat with nine lives that has no more to spare. How much closer to the fire can I get without getting burned?"

He smiles and kisses my cheek. "I told you that we are both meant to survive, we will walk through the fire together unscathed."

Chapter 18

Burnt Offerings

Natek is my pillar of strength during the days that follow and for a time there are no *aktions* and our work proceeds uneventfully. Time has lost all meaning for me and it is difficult even to remember the order of the days and months. The weather and its seasonal changes are the only clue that the world continues its eternal progress unhindered by the detrimental activities of man and his eternal quest for power. The rains and snows come early with a vengeance unsurpassed in our collective memory and turn the roads and fields to mud and ice. We cannot imagine how the heavy machinery of war will overcome the natural obstacles of nature and we take comfort in the knowledge that the Germans are suffering in their effort to dominate the world. At the same time we are well aware that the allied forces will also be bogged down by the icy hand of winter.

We surmise that the war on the Eastern front is not going as planned when a few Wermacht soldiers return and are assigned to A.V.L. These men bear the scars of the harsh realities of combat. Gerhard, a young steely eyed warrior, returns from the front having lost an ear and fingers to frostbite. Bitter and disheartened from his war experience, he has a short fuse when angered. None of us has the inclination to run afoul of our wardens and a careful watch is kept as to their whereabouts at all times. As if by magic, word spreads quickly through the work stations when any of the foremen are on the prowl and inspecting the environs of the factory. Immediately everyone assumes their most diligent work ethic, hoping not to catch any rancor and reprisal from our overlords. Having been alerted of Gerhard's pending approach I am busily emptying a carton that had been damaged during shipment from Germany. My job is to rebox the contents, which are destined for the Eastern front. It is with great effort I keep my face a mask of indifference when I place the contents on the table before me. Stacks of photos of the Fuhrer Adolf Hitler stare at me, filling me with revulsion. I am caught unawares and my first reaction is to tear them into pieces in a symbolic act of destroying the man whose goal is to eliminate me and my race. This is the face of the devil incarnate, the man who has destroyed my innocent family. My heart pounds in my chest, my cheeks flush red, and hatred threatens to overcome me when I feel the warm breath of Gerhard at my back as he exhales smoke from his cigarette. I am frozen immobile like a deer caught in the glare of a light.

"Well, what have we here?" he asks aloud, as much to himself as to me. I stand motionless, paralyzed with fear, afraid to even breathe. The cigarette dangles from his lips and he sneers as he lifts the photos to take a better look.

"Yes, our esteemed Fuhrer, what an excellent likeness." I cannot help but notice the sarcasm in his voice. I watch as he takes the stack of photos from the table and with his cigarette burns out the eyes, nostrils and mouth of Hitler. Smiling with satisfaction he watches the photos burn waving away the ashes that swirl around us. "This son-of-a-bitch has destroyed Germany. He will be the end of all of us; we will follow him to our graves! You of all people know that I am right. By the time he is done there will not be a Jew alive in Europe!"

His palpable anger physically shakes him with a tremor that I can feel as he stands next to me, though we do not touch. His hatred is consuming and flows from him like a current of electricity. The act of burning Hitler is a complete breach of protocol. Never have I witnessed a German break with authority or show any uncertainty as to the objectives of the Third Reich. I dare not acknowledge his words. I fear when he recovers himself and realizes what he has said and done in front of me his retaliation will be swift. Instead, the symbolic act of defacing the photos of the Fuhrer eases the frustration and anguish of a young man who has clearly seen his fill of war.

"Now you can continue to box these lovely pictures of a madman. We will send them for morale boosting to our gallant soldiers. I wonder if they will find solace in death as they clutch to their hearts a picture of our fine Fuhrer." He pats my cheek unaware of the profound effect his actions provoke in me. Straightening his uniform and composing himself, he walks away in a trail of smoke. "Don't worry, Fraulein, this incident never happened. Our secret is safe between us. Now carry on!"

This is the first chink I have seen in the mighty armor of Germany's war machine. Is doubt spreading among the ranks as to Hitler's goals and aspirations for world supremacy? How odd that I somehow feel sorry for Gerhard. I am the prey, yet I feel sorry for the hunter. With this small act of insubordination I realize the impossibility of the Germans succeeding in their march to glory. Certainly if he feels this way there have to be many others who sense that the path ahead is one of total destruction. I know now with certainty that they will lose the war and evil will not prevail. The question is, what will the final cost be and how many Jews will survive to see the end of this deadly regime?

With a touch of satisfaction and grateful that he has moved on and left me in peace, I return to the task at hand, which is boxing and shipping the now eyeless Hitler photos to the Eastern front. I cannot wait to share this incident with Natek.

Chapter 19

Escape

It is freezing outside but I need a breath of fresh air and a change of scenery. It's Sunday and the factory is closed. My breath hangs frostily in the air as I pace back and forth along the fence, trying to exercise my limbs. As I walk I notice a Polish man across the street leaning against a building. Tall and blond, his handsome face draws my attention. Dressed in typical worker's clothes he stares intently at our building, watching for someone or something. Our eyes meet and after watching me for a time, he approaches the fence. I look around to make sure I am not being observed as I lean my back against the fence and whisper to him, "I see you are looking for someone, can I help you?"

In Polish he asks, "Do you know Lola Freidenreich, I am a friend of hers and I would like to speak to her. Can you ask her to come outside?"

"Yes, I know her, she is my roommate. What's your name?"

"Tell her Yannick Karzynswki is here to see her."

I hurry in to get Lola, who is in our small bedroom, an off-shoot space attached to the factory floor. It is Sunday and the girls are clustered about in small groups chatting. Sundays are spent washing our few garments and resting for the week ahead. I find Lola in our room with the rest of our roommates. We are all the best of friends so I don't hesitate to tell her about the handsome young Pole that is looking for her, "Lola, there is a young man outside asking for you. His name is Yannick Karzyn-swki and he wants to talk to you."

Lola's face takes on a radiant glow and I assume that she and this Yannick are more than friends. Everyone in the room looks inquisitively at Lola for some explanation. "I… I will explain everything after I speak with Yannick," she exclaims as she darts downstairs to see him. We all run to the window, hoping we can see something of this unusual occurrence of a Pole asking to speak to a Jew. Downstairs we see Lola and this Yannick engaged in a lively conversation. Lola returns a few minutes later, trembling, "Girls, I need your help. The man outside is my brother who is living as a Pole in Warszawa. He has brought me clothing and identity papers to assume an alias of a Christian widow who is in mourning for her dead husband and child. Yaacov, that's my brother's real name, says the new identity will provide me with a perfect cover. The Nazis will not be too scrupulous in their questioning of a woman in mourning. He says everything has been readied for me. All I need to do is get out of here."

"Oh, Lola, we are so happy for you. How can we help?"

"Yes, Lola, what can we do?" Dora and I are beyond excited and would take any risk to help Lola escape to freedom.

"I'm not sure exactly how to manage it, but I thought that you and Dora could distract the guard downstairs long enough for me to sneak past the gate."

"Yes, of course, I will pretend to fall and sprain my ankle and start crying in pain."

Dora, catching the gist of my plan, offers, "And I can run to get the guard and beg him to carry Dina inside. That should give you ample time to make your escape. The other girls can keep watch and coordinate everything from the window."

"Dina and Lola, you are so clever. How can I ever thank you?" Lola throws her arms about us in a bear hug. The other girls also join us in a communal embrace. Instantaneously, our joy turns to tears as we realize that this is good-bye and that it might be the last time we will ever see each other again.

As Lola readies herself, gathering her few things, we all watch the guard from our window, whispering different strategies in case of unforeseen problems. In order for our plan to work we need to wait until just before the end of the guard's watch, when he will be less cautious about abandoning his post, knowing that his replacement will report momentarily.

Just before the changing of the guard we go into action with our daring plan. Dora and I go outside for a breath of fresh air. As I block her from view, Dora pours a cup of water on the ground which immediately begins to ice up in the frigid air. It is like a scene in a movie. Our upstairs roommates keep watch and coordinate the timing and implementation of our ploy from our bedroom window. On a given signal, I throw myself to the ground and begin to cry in pain. Dora runs to the guard. "Herr Rummel, one of the girls has slipped on a patch of ice and may have sprained her ankle. She is in terrible pain. Please, can you help me get her inside?"

"Where is the clumsy girl?" Slinging his rifle behind his back, he follows Dora to where I sit, my heart pounding with excitement. Adrenalin races through my veins and I give a command performance. Like Sarah Bernhardt, I cry like a baby as I feign pain, clutching my ankle looking up at the guard. "I slipped and twisted my ankle; I don't think I can walk on it."

The guard curses me under his breath. He picks me up and carries me inside as I watch over his shoulder. With no one on duty, Lola has no trouble slipping through the gate. Lola runs to her brother who is waiting nearby and they disappear behind a building.

The guard lowers me on my bed while all of the girls crowd about fussing over me. "Don't worry, we will take care of her."

"Yes, she will be fine; she just needs to rest."

The guard, anxious to return to his post, is gone in an instant. We all run to the window. Lola promised that she will wave good-bye to us. Moments later, Lola and Yaacov appear around the corner of the building. Lola is now dressed in a black dress of mourning and a heavy veil. Lifting the veil she looks up and sees all of our faces pressed against the glass. She waves while her lips form the words of 'thank you'. She waves, sending a kiss, her face flushed with joy. Yaacov, smiling and nodding his head in salute, takes her hand and they disappear once more from our view. It is like a fairytale in which the Princess is rescued by the handsome Prince. We are all elated as we dance around the room with joy.

We have helped our friend escape to freedom. Lola's escape is like a personal victory over the Nazis for each of us. At least one of us has a chance of surviving. Lola's disappearance goes unnoticed or at least unacknowledged. No one at A.V.L. ever asks about her or any other prisoners that vanish. The Wermacht that supervises A.V.L. does not want any SS scrutiny and chooses to turn a blind eye rather than be held accountable.

Chapter 20

Moses Comes

The snows continue to blanket Poland and we continue to pack and ship the last vestiges of the Jews of Radom to Germany. Natek and I worry over what the Germans will do with us once every scrap of wealth has left Radom. What use will they have for us? What reason to prolong our lives? Through the particularly nasty winter, we fret over our future of which we have no control and warily watch the Germans, who also show signs of apprehension. Sometimes we can hear them drinking together, they listen to records and sing trying to amuse each other. They seem to be drowning in bitterness and melancholy and we assume and pray that the war is not going as planned. The Lagerfuhrer who oversees A.F.L. is a soldier named Hans who is maybe forty years of age. His eyes are the blue of a mountain stream and he stands a head above everyone else, but it's his eyes that have earned him the sobriquet of *Moishele,* or Moses, among the workers. When he enters the shipping department the whispers seem to travel on the wind, "Moishele is coming!"

"Moishele is coming!" Quickly all conversations cease and we all bend our backs over whatever task we are performing, the only sounds to be heard are those related to our efforts. We are all experts in disappearing, it is as if we shrink from the space of our bodies and become invisible in our clothes in an effort to draw as little attention as possible to our existence.

Today Hans enters the shipping floor and before any of us can telepath his arrival he shouts with laughter, "*Moishele bist comen! Moishele bist comen!*"

Everyone is frozen speechless. How did he discover his nickname?

Hans continues to laugh and repeat, "*Moishele bist comen! Moishele bist comen!*"

Then a group of workers bursts into laughter and soon we are all laughing with Hans. None of us is immune to the hilarity of the joke. It is an unusual lightheaded moment, this sharing of intimacy between master and slave, and it relieves some of the tensions and fears that permeate the air.

Not long after the Moishele incident, a male voice wakes me, whispering in my ear, his hand caressing my hair. Stunned, my eyes snap open in fear; sitting on my bed is Moishele. It is as if a specter has appeared before me and I rub my eyes, thinking him a dream. It is after midnight and there are six of us who sleep in the small room adjacent to the main floor of the warehouse. Suddenly the apparition before me begins to speak, "*Dina, komm mit mir in mein stuben.*" I am mute with fear, desperately trying to organize my thoughts, and he must think that I don't understand him, for he repeats himself somewhat louder. "Dina, you are coming back with me to my room."

Anxiously trying to control the panic that envelops me, I plead, "Herr Lagerfuhrer, I don't understand, why do you want me to go to your room?" I begin to cry. "I am just a young girl. Don't you have a daughter my age?"

"Nein, I have no daughter and you are old enough!" His voice rises in pitch with irritation, "You will do as I say and come with me!"

My roommates cannot help but hear my crying and protests and are beginning to stir. I am only thirteen and a half but I can't tell him my real age or I will be in terrible danger, as workers at A.V.L. must be sixteen. His breath holds the unmistakable scent of alcohol. I cringe from his hands that paw at my hair and face. Cipa, an older girl who sleeps next to me comes to my defense. She knows Hans fairly well, as she has the chore of cleaning his rooms. Standing, she commands him in a quiet controlled voice, "Herr Lagerfuhrer, please leave Dina alone. Let me take you back to your room, it is okay, I will go with you."

He fixes his drunken bloodshot eyes upon her, which causes me to shudder, but Cipa stands firm. "Come, Herr Lagerfuhrer, you don't want to bother with this child. Come I will take you back to your room."

I don't know what changes his mind. Perhaps he considers the repercussions of sexually assaulting me. For a moment he just stares at me, his eyes narrowing, and then for whatever reason he stands and throws his arm around Cipa, allowing her to escort him back to his apartment. Cipa has saved me from a molestation that I could not have borne. What price she paid to protect me is never discussed between us. The incident is forgotten. Only Hans never forgives me for the humiliation of that evening. For the most part, he avoids me. Sometimes though, I turn to find his eyes boring into me, glaring. I shun his gaze, grateful to have avoided disaster. Hans holds my life in his hands. Thankfully, his animosity hasn't caused him to take any revenge against me. Once more, the hands of good fortune have intervened between me and a dangerous situation.

In January we learn of the next tragedy to befall the dwindling Jews of Radom. It becomes known as The Palestinian Aktion. In a climate of complete hopelessness rumors abound, and one of possible freedom spreads like a wild fire through the ghetto. Jews with relatives in Palestyne can sign up on a list for resettlement in the Holy Land. Hope springs anew and everyone lines up five deep in the field at Szwarlikovska as their names are checked and rechecked against the list to make sure that no one sneaks on that isn't listed. The desperation for freedom is immense and everyone tries to get out in hopes of going to Palestyne. In the end, sixteen hundred of the so called lucky are marched under heavily armed guard and are loaded on to trains. Too late they realize the true destination, which is a direct route to Treblinka and awaiting death. Many try to escape but are gunned down or crushed beneath the wheels of the moving death train. A few escape and return to the ghetto to relate the horror stories. Some try to join the Polish partisans in the forest in their resistance against the Germans but find that the Poles' hatred and distrust of them is so consuming that instead of welcoming the additional fighters, they attack or murder them or just drive them away. Apparently it is better to die and lose against the Germans than to fight side by side with a Jew. Those that survive their encounter with the partisans return to the ghetto with their spirits broken and disillusioned. It is a crushing blow to the remaining Jews as once more hope is quashed beneath the boots of the Nazis and depression descends upon us.

The Nazis, however, are not through with the ghetto survivors and at the end of January they once more line up the spiritually broken remnants of Radom's Jews. I am visiting my cousins in the ghetto shortly after the incident when Majer describes to me the grizzly event. "Fear gripped us as we were forced to line up for another selection in the brutal cold. We stood apart from our families, hoping to increase our chances of making it through the selection. We have learned that it is far better to show no family ties, as the Nazis delight in dividing families, so we interspersed throughout the crowd awaiting judgment. This time, the Nazis had a special plan in mind. They played a game of Russian roulette as they walked behind the rows of frightened detainees. We dared not move a muscle or even our eyes. It was as if they were playing a child's game. They walked behind the rows counting off ten of the unsuspecting, and when they reached the number ten they shot the tenth man or woman in the head on the spot. It was surreal, a gunshot followed by their barbarous laughter filling the air, as if Satan and his minions were among us. The monsters tortuously dragged out the suspense, counting, walking, teasing, they amused themselves. Then without warning another shot from the luger pierced the air and the next body fell to the ground. I felt certain I was going to die that day. Once the desperate crowd realized what was intended, every man and woman took the hand of the person beside them. You could sense desperate prayers being silently murmured. It was all we could do to remain standing and not crumple to the ground in terror. Helplessly we stood and awaited death. To break and run would have been suicide, or worse, it would have meant death for everyone lined up. The game was played out and the Nazis continued their cold blooded murders until every tenth Jew lay dead. Then we were made to drag away the bodies of our friends and relatives. Somehow, what is left of our family survived the death squad massacre." Tears slip silently down my cousin's cheeks. There is nothing I can say to ease his disconsolation. It is heartbreaking and impossible to take comfort in knowing that you have survived when many others were murdered in such a callous monstrous fashion. It is hard to find joy in living when guilt eats away at your soul.

After the slaughter at Szwarlikovska, hope takes a holiday from the ghetto. It is as if we are sleepwalking, going through the motions of living without being alive. Then, like a match struck in the gloom of a starless night, a tentative spark of hope returns to the faces of the ghetto inhabitants. Good news comes amid the day-to-day persecutions and boosts our flagging morale. It races through the community like a raging forest fire spread by a wind of words. First, there is great reason for us to be proud; an uprising has begun in the Warszaw Ghetto and Jews are fighting. Like the *Maccabeus* of ancient Judea that waged a resistance against the Hellenistic oppressors, we are fighting an armed resistance against the Nazis. With young leaders who are willing to fight to their deaths, the rebels have organized an underground army and Jews are inflicting casualties against the mighty Nazis. We also overhear our guards at A.V.L. commiserating that Germany has suffered a massive defeat at Stalingrad. They surrendered their Eastern offensive and are in retreat, with the Russians in hot pursuit. We quietly rejoice that the Nazis have suffered their first major defeat of the war. Even if we cannot cheer out loud, our eyes are burning with a new brightness and hope.

Each day, what is left of the belongings of Radom's Jews grows smaller and the shipping backlog lessens, and so it comes as no surprise to us when one day our German supervisors line us up to tell us that A.V.L. is to be closed at the end of the week and we are to gather what little we have, as we are being moved to the Szwarlikovska Street Ghetto. After the massive deportations of August, the shrunken Walowa Ghetto, now called the Szwarlikovska Street Ghetto, is only a few streets enclosed by barbed wire and sealed off. None of the Germans look pleased to inform us of these changes. They know that with the closing of the factory, they too face reassignment. We soon find out that Hans, Otto, Gerhard, and the rest of the German Wermacht that run A.V.L. have been ordered to the retreating Eastern front and active war duty. The future looks grim for our taskmasters.

I manage before leaving A.V.L. to thank Otto for everything he has done for me and to wish him well. I still firmly believe that Otto saved all of us when the Walowa Ghetto was liquidated and

I will never forget him. In a world of darkness, he alone showed humanity. Besides, I could never hate these men that only seem to be following orders. They are not killers like the SS or Gestapo and have never struck or abused us.

I watch Otto's jaw clench as he bids me farewell, shaking my hand. "Dina, we each have a road to travel. You and I are but pawns in the hands of others. I wish you well on your journey. May God look after you."

Part 4

Szwarlikovska Street

Chapter 21

The Workers' Camp

All in all, A.V.L. has been a safe and decent place to work and we are all apprehensive about what this turn of events will mean for our future. Natek and I walk together in silence as I ponder Otto's last words to me, his future probably as bleak as mine. Our death warrants are surely seared into the metal of two bullets that, at this moment, are being forged in an armaments factory. We walk under the watchful eye of an SS unit that supervises our transfer to Szwarlikovska. I wonder if this is our last walk on earth. Maybe when we reach the ghetto they will simply shoot us in the head and throw us into mass graves as they have so many others. Greedily my eyes sweep the landscape. I cannot help but notice that the signs of spring reborn abound everywhere around me. The land is a verdant green and flowers burst from unexpected fissures, extending outstretched leaves and petals to the sun. The brutal winter now lies in the past. All that is left are small patches of snow that are disappearing in retreat of the warm sunlight. Hungrily they claw at the ground, tenaciously trying to repossess the land that winter's grasp has owned. With great trepidation, we pass under the sign at the gate that announces "Forced Labor Camp Szwarlikovska Street." It seems that as slave labor we still have some use to the Nazis, for they assemble us in a field along with the remaining residents of the ghetto and stamp our ID cards with new numbers. Those that don't have any family still alive in the ghetto are assigned a place to sleep and the rest of us will crowd in with whatever family or friends have survived the death squads and deportations. I have my Uncle Tuvye, Majer, and Nadja to stay with, but Natek and his brother Benjamin are allocated housing. We are told to report to the front gate at five a.m. on Monday, where we will be assigned work and escorted under guard to different locations outside the ghetto. Afterward they tell us to immediately disperse and go to our designated housing. Natek hugs me good-bye and assures me he will pick me up for work bright and early at five a.m. tomorrow. I watch him and Benjamin round a corner, their shoulders hunched together in determination, as my cousins and I walk home together discussing the practicalities of our day-to-day existence and what is expected of me.

There is a comfort in being with family, a familiarity that provides a sense of security and love, but each familiar face of my relatives is a painful reminder of all those I have lost. Still, I manage to adapt to my new circumstances with little or no complaint. Besides the duties of cleaning our cramped quarters, I assist Nadja as she tries her best to prepare an evening meal from the meager food or lack of food available. Everyone in the house is employed in some manner. My cousins Abek and Motek Madrykamien, my Aunt Fela's sons who are the only survivors of their immediate family, work at the armaments factory Wytwornia and are housed there. My Uncle Alexander and cousin David who live upstairs work for the Waffen SS at a garage maintaining and repairing their cars and other vehicles. I am joyful to be united with my uncles and cousins. Even under these terrible conditions we all try to make the best of a desperate situation. Our food rations are so meager and hunger and malnutrition wreak havoc with our bodies leaving our tempers short, but still we cling to life in whatever way is possible.

The days that follow are shadowed with death's presence; we live doggedly committed to our endurance while around us our world continues to deteriorate. We are slowly starving while being worked to death.

It takes only one day for me to realize how lucky I was to live and work at A.V.L., where I received enough hot cooked food to abate hunger and maintain strength. Our allotment of rations has plummeted to near starvation levels. Every ten days each person is apportioned a few meager grams of bread, a little sugar, jam, and now and then a piece of soap. From the soup kitchen within the ghetto we sporadically are able to get our hands on a few grams of meat, some potatoes, margarine, grits, and a few vegetables. The aching of our stomachs is only enhanced by the brutal conditions of our labor. Natek, Benjamin, and I are assigned to the peat bogs where we cut turf for fuel. It is the worst job in the ghetto—a back-breaking twelve hour ordeal in which we sink knee deep into swamp-like marsh, cutting turf into bricks that we load and carry to awaiting trucks and wagons. Turf is naturally formed from concentrated vegetation and plant life that never dries up or decomposes in the swampy land. Once shaped and dried into bricks, it can be burnt like coal and is readily available and cheaply harvested by slave labor. It is a primary source of heat for the Germans and the people they dominate. Every day many of those that slave in the mire and muck die from added exposure to colds, fevers, and heart attacks, and some days I am certain that I will not live to see another day. Natek works always with one eye on me and one on his brother. He slaves beside me whispering words of encouragement, always seeing the bright side when no one can possibly imagine one. "At least, Dinale, we get to work outside and inhale the goodness of the air which is good for our bodies, and behold the sky and scenery which is good for our hearts and souls."

"Natek, you are an eternal optimist," I grumble. "How you can find good digging in dirt and filth is beyond me."

A huge smile like a ray of sunshine spreads across his mucky grime-smeared face. "You will see I am right. You become stronger and more beautiful every hour of every day."

"Yes, I must look like a princess with my cheeks and hair caked with black mud. I am sure that I am irresistible." As I brush a blackened tendril of hair from my face I can't help but smile at his determination to lift my spirits.

Benjamin, who is by far the moodier of the two brothers, snarls, "Natek, the peat must be growing in your brain. We are all going to die in this muck and as far as I am concerned, the sooner the better!"

Natek's muscles tense as he grabs Benjamin's arm. "Don't ever let me hear you speak like that again! How dare you resign us all to death! Think of our mother and father, our sisters! We must live for them, for everyone who has been murdered! Who are you to extinguish that hope?" He releases Benjamin and pats him on the back, the sudden tempest of anger vanishing in a grin. "Look at Jacub, you don't see him complaining every minute."

Jacub is the nephew of a Jewish policeman who has assigned him to work in the peat bogs in order to preempt any complaints of nepotism. Natek's innate leadership is appealing to the disgruntled youth, who resents being forced into hard labor while the rest of his family enjoys the fruit of protected status. He has joined our band of three in order to be close to Natek, who does his best to counsel the rebellious young man. Trying to clear the air, Jacub suggests, "Come, Benjamin, let's get a drink of water, I need a break from this cesspool."

Natek watches as Benjamin and Jacub walk to the trough for water. Satisfied that the incident is over, we bend to resume our labor. "Benjamin worries me sometimes."

"He's just tired and hungry like the rest of us. Not everyone can be as optimistic as you are."

"I have no choice!" Natek's face is forged in determination as he shovels a large block of turf into the wheelbarrow.

My cousin Nadja has been reassigned to work at the Korona Warehouse, which is one of the last shipping centers that sorts and packs what remains of the stolen possessions of the Jews that were plundered after the liquidation of the ghettos. There she separates the mountains of burnished leather, fur, snowy goose feathers, shoes, eyeglasses of every prescription, glittering jewelry, clothing, hats, woolen scarves, toys, children's dolls, and other precious bits and pieces of the lives of those who have been murdered. She says her dreams are haunted by friendly ghosts that live among the relics of their past. It was much the same for me when I worked at A.V.L. I often felt the presence of spirits as I packed and shipped away the lives of the dead.

One of the most disheartening realities of our impossible existence is the difficulty of remaining clean. At A.V.L. we had access to showers, sharing the factory's attached accommodations. Now, our home has no shower and minimal water access and the only way to stay clean is to cleanse ourselves at a bucket outside, exposed to the elements and with little or no privacy. Even in the frigid temperatures of dawn we brave the pelting spring rains, standing in the mud, taking turns and doing our best to sponge ourselves off with water that must serve a multitude of needs. Adding to our frustration is the lack of soap, so meagerly rationed it has become nearly as precious as gold. Regardless of the temperature outside and using the same water for all of us, we try to cleanse ourselves. Naturally, after slaving in the turf I am filthy and it has become a losing battle and a running joke as each of my family tries to beat me to the bucket. There is no respite even in sleep to escape the terrible hardships of the day. I wake in the middle of the night aching with hunger and dreaming of my mother's brisket, or sometimes I dream of languishing in a hot tub of perfumed water and the wonder of a thick clean towel awaiting me when I rise pink and radiant from my hallucinatory bath. The unconsciousness of sleep provides an exquisite torture as our body's cravings become relentless dreams of what had been so keenly satisfying in our prior lives, a complete contrast to our waking hours and the tortuous reality of what is. During these quiet moments when no one can hear, as I listen to the steady breathing of my cousin Nadja, I allow myself to succumb to silent tears.

Chapter 22

Jacub

Jacub hasn't shown up at work for a week. Natek and I are sick with worry for him, envisioning all sorts of illnesses and accidents. When I recognize the unmistakable long gait walking a block away, I run after him calling, "Jacub, Jacub, STOP! Where have you been? Have you been ill?"

His face lights with pleasure when he sees me. "Dina, how are you?"

"Never mind how I am, why haven't you been at work?" I ask in my most authoritative voice.

"I'm tired of the filthiness of the swamps and I decided to take a break. Tell Natek I will see him soon."

In shock I warn, "Have you lost your mind? If you don't show up for work they will come after you. You can't just decide not to go. It is forbidden and the punishment will be brutal. Everyone has to work or they become worthless to the Nazis. Promise me you will come tomorrow, please Jacub. Natek and I have been so worried about you."

He shrugs off my warnings with a laugh, "My uncle is the head of the Jewish Police, he will protect me. Don't worry, Dina, I will be fine. He will find me another job. I've slaved long enough in that filthy swamp. I am going to see my uncle now, he will help me. Maybe I can get you and Natek reassigned to a job where you won't be sloshing in mud like a pig."

"Natek and I will be fine. Please don't take any chances and either resolve this with your uncle or come back to work."

Hugging my carefree friend I remind him as we part, "Remember, Jacub, straighten this out with your uncle immediately or come back to work!" With a last glance I look back at his retreating figure. I can't help but wonder at his foolish daring.

Several days later as I return from work Nadja tells me that she has heard some bad news. She knows that I work with Jacub and that he has become good friends with Natek, Benjamin, and me.

"Dina, you know your friend Jacub?"

"Yes, he hasn't shown up for work in two weeks. I haven't seen him since last week when I saw him in the street, why?"

"The Nazis rounded up everyone today who hasn't shown up for work and brought them to the Ukrainian guards' station. Jacub was one of them. He, along with twenty or thirty other men, were hauled in and lined up. Then, suddenly, the Ukrainian guards started shooting. Jacub tried to run away, but he was shot and killed in the street. One of my friends saw the whole thing and she said she heard Jacub pleading for mercy as he ran. He kept shouting that his uncle was the head of the police. It didn't do him any good; they shot him like a dog in the street."

"My God, poor Jacub, he was so sure that his uncle could protect him from anything." I begin to cry and Nadja wraps her arms around me, trying to comfort me.

"He was foolish; there is no protection against these murderers. May God rest his soul!"

"Amen," I whisper.

Executions take place nearly every day for the merest of reasons or for no reason at all. Jacub was one of thousands who meet their fate with a bullet. Two of my friends that worked as tailors were executed in front of their homes just down the street from us. They were accused of sabotage. Their crime was leaving an iron on unattended at the factory where they worked. Because of a little piece of burnt fabric and a table with some scald marks on it they were shot in the head.

The weather has turned warm and breezy as it ushers in spring. Forgotten is the fierceness of winter that felt as if it might never end. March has arrived and with it the joyous holiday of Purim, which is celebrated on the fourteenth day of *Adar* on the Jewish calendar. It is a celebration of redemption. The Persian King Ahasuerus married the beautiful and clever Esther and made her Queen, setting aside his first wife Vashti. Queen Esther kept her Jewish identity a secret at the urging of her Uncle Mordecai. Mordecai's enemy, Haman, a minister of the King, persuaded the king that the Jews of Persia should be exterminated for plotting an alleged conspiracy. Esther risked life and limb by revealing that she was a Jewess to her husband, King Ahasuerus, and pleaded with him to save her people. She revealed Haman's treacherous lies and secured his death warrant, and in so doing saved the entire Jewish population of Persia. The parable of the story is clear; those who seek to eliminate the Jews will find themselves eliminated. Naturally we live with the hope that once again this will hold true for Hitler and his Nazis.

Instead, great sorrow again envelops us. The Germans devise a cruel lie that negotiations are underway for an exchange of Jews for German prisoners held by the allies. In celebration, the Jewish Elders produce a list of academics and intellectuals who will be freed. In a desperate attempt to save their children and facilitate them out of Radom, a group of families convince the lucky chosen to take about fifty children with them by pretending they are their own. On the happy day of Purim we celebrate on the streets of Szwarlikovska as the lucky ones arrive at the gates surrounded by family and friends. The children, with wreaths of flowers in their hair, wave as they are loaded onto trucks and are driven away to what they hope will be the beginning of a new life. Within seconds the true intent is clear. Instead of heading toward the train station, they head in the opposite direction. The few that survive return to tell what unfolded as the trucks arrived at the Szydlowiec cemetery. A contingent of SS and Ukrainians followed the trucks. At the cemetery a massive open grave, freshly dug, lay waiting for the crying children and pleading adults, who were stripped naked and pushed into the graves by waiting Polish police. Without pause the Ukrainians threw grenades into the hole, silencing the screams of protest, and with rifles they shot any who managed to survive the explosions. It was mass murder. The next truck of intended victims, seeing what happened to the first, made a valiant effort to escape and fight. They attacked the SS and Ukrainian murderers and refused to die without a battle. Nearly all were killed in the end, either clashing with the death squad or trying to escape over the cemetery fence. Thirty survived, having convinced the SS officer in charge that they were mistakenly placed on the list. Where once the voices of our children filled the air with playfulness and hope for the future, now there is only silence.

The Warszaw Ghetto is no more and the brave rebellion of its valiant Jews is stilled forever. Word comes that on the eve of Passover, the Nazis, using a full thrust of tanks and intending to overpower the fighters in three days, entered the ghetto with a mighty assault. Burning and emptying each building street by street, the SS waged a war on the Jewish resistors. The ghetto fighters, using guerilla tactics, managed to stop the deportations and hold out for more than a month, frustrating the Germans with their determination to resist. Their heroism has become an inspiration to us all in our struggle to survive and there is a new resolve and faith among us that our freedom will come in time.

Chapter 23

Farewell, My Love

It is a scalding hot summer day and I search the horizon for the thunder storm that would bring relief. The air is heavy with an oppressive humidity that clings with beads of moisture to my body. My family and I have received word that we are to be transferred from Radom to work in a village called Pionki. Dazed, I run to Natek's apartment with the hope that he too is being sent to Pionki.

Arriving at his door, I begin pounding on it, "Natek, Natek, it's me, Dina, please open up."

His brow furrowed with concern, he opens the door admitting me, "What's wrong Dinale?"

My arms fly around him, hugging him to me as I lift my chin, searching his eyes. "We are being moved, all of us, I have very little time. The Nazis are sending us to a place called Pionki, and they have told us to gather our things and report for immediate transfer. Please tell me that you too are being sent to Pionki?"

He turns pale as the color drains from his face and I know immediately that he is not going with me. "Oh Natek, I can't bear it, how will I live without you? You have been my strength, my dearest friend."

"Dina, we knew that this might happen, that we could be separated. I will find you, I promise. When the war is over I will find you, no matter what."

"No, no, I will never live… I'm so afraid. What is Pionki? Why aren't you being sent there with me? Fela promised me that we would live in Palestyne one day, and now she is gone. I can't lose you too. Nearly everyone I have ever loved is gone!"

Holding me firmly against him, he kisses my eyes, my cheeks, and my neck until finally he finds my lips and tenderly he presses them. Huskily he murmurs, "I will find you, I promise!"

Weeping I surrender to his kisses as we try to turn minutes into hours. With a thousand promises on our lips, our parting inevitable, he again vows to find me and insists that I must take no chances or unnecessary risks. Again he reassures me that it is our destiny to survive and I try my best to believe him.

We leave Szwarlikovska Street with a knapsack of belongings and the clothes on our backs. My cousins Majer and Nadja, Uncle Tuvye, Uncle Alexander, and Cousin David are with me. Each of us is lost in our own thoughts. Silently we walk to the gate and the awaiting trucks. Our hurried good-byes of Abek and Motek have numbed me. My two cousins are not being transferred. I wonder if I will ever see them again. The sun glares overhead and I feel trickles of sweat run down the sides of my dress as we walk. It seems I have no more tears left; my parting with Natek has drained them all from me.

The truck begins to move and I am grateful for the breeze that catches my hair as I watch the city of my birth slip away. Outside the gates of the ghetto life goes on in normalcy. People hurry along the streets, knowing that their families are alive and well cared for, even though they must suffer through shortages and the difficulties of war. I wonder, as I probe the faces of the Poles we pass, what they think when they look at us, their former neighbors and countrymen. They glance impassively at us, quickly averting their eyes. Bitterness descends on me as I silently pray for the Jewish citizenry of Radom that have been wiped from the face of the earth and those we leave behind to face an uncertain future. With Natek and his brother Benjamin in my thoughts, I make a promise to myself that, should I live, I will never return to Radom or Poland. My ties to this country are severed forever.

Part 5

Pionki, Poland 1943

Chapter 24

Slavery

The trip to Pionki from Radom takes approximately three hours. The caravan of trucks bounces over the rutted roads as we drive through lush grassy pastures and fertile farmland. Mute with worry, each of us contemplates what can only be a dismal future as we wrestle with our fears of what lies ahead. Finally, we arrive in Pionki, a tiny village in central Poland where an ammunitions factory is hidden deep within a forest of towering trees that completely blocks its view from the skies and aerial assault. The largest armaments factory in Poland, it contains a series of factories and large separated living quarters. When we arrive in the summer of 1943 there are approximately three thousand workers slaving for the Germans. Pionki is an *arbeitslager*[34] and is divided into various factories where different weapons and ammunition are assembled. It had been a thriving arms factory before the war, built in a solid brick construction adjacent to the railroad tracks. Once conquered by

34 Work camp

the Germans, it has become vital to the war effort and the trains are loaded daily with gunpowder and munitions that supply the waiting armies of the Fatherland on the Eastern front. The compound is completely fenced with barbed wire and our sleeping dorms are built contiguous but set apart from the factories. The SS patrols and guards the outer perimeter of the camp, but inside where we work we are supervised by Polish overseers. There are also a group of Ukrainian workers that are supervised by Ukrainians. Upon arrival, we are assembled and given ID cards and then assigned to jobs and sleeping quarters. I share a room with about seven women, Dora being one of them. I am grateful to be with my girlfriend, someone with ties to my past. After the filth of the ghetto it is heartening to have cleanliness. We sleep two in a bunk bed, with mattress, blanket, and pillow. The room is kept clean and the wooden floors are well swept. Of course, we are slaves with no freedom, bound by the barbed wire that surrounds us. We can only gaze with longing through the fence at the beauty of the forest and freedom beyond.

I am very lucky to once more be assigned to *haufcolonie*[35] which, although extremely hard labor, is one of the safest jobs to be had. I work with a crew of women, filling bags with black gunpowder, which we then pack into crates and heft onto waiting railway cars. The crates weigh nearly twenty-two kilograms and we stagger under the weight of them as we carry them on our backs. At least there are no physical beatings or unspeakable cruelties, but I am bent with exhaustion after the twelve hour days. The routine of the week continues without abatement until Sunday, when we are allowed to rest. On Sundays we launder the few garments we possess and walk around the camp enclosure, enjoying the fresh scent of pine needles that fills the air. Sometimes near collapse and exhaustion, my muscles aching from the week's exertion, I simply take pleasure in a few hours of

35 Shipping

much needed rest as I daydream of freedom and Natek. I wonder if he is thinking of me.

There is quite a bit of illegal trade going on between the Polish workmen and the Jews. The Poles are eager to trade bread for jewelry or money. Of course, the consequence if caught is only a reprimand for the Poles, but for a Jew it is certain death.

Today is not like any other as we wake to the shouting of a German officer ordering us to assemble outside for an immediate roll call. We are driven from our barracks and forced to line up outside where a gallows has been newly constructed. We nervously stand in a dense eerie fog that shrouds us in a thick mist that licks at our faces and bodies. Before us the death-ropes sway as if ghosts are hanging in them. I watch the SS Lagerfuhrer's face materialize and dematerialize as he shouts at us. "It has come to our attention that a group of you Jews has been smuggling unauthorized contraband into the camp. This is explicitly prohibited and has been pointed out to you time and time again. *We will not tolerate these activities!* Just such a group has been caught red-handed. To emphasize the seriousness of this crime, these offenders will be executed before your eyes as a warning to you all that the same fate awaits each of you if you disobey the rules."

In silence we watch as three males and three women, their arms tied behind their backs, are marched out as the guards punch them forward with the muzzles of their rifles. One of the accused is a teen who looks to be but a few years older than me. Tears run down his cheeks and his eyes dart around with fear. When the poor young man sees the gallows a visible tremble assaults his body as he struggles to remain standing.

The Nazi wastes no time delivering the sentences and the condemned are quickly forced to climb the steps and a noose is slipped around each of their necks. The young man, who has regained his bravery, looks out at us and through his tears he fearlessly shouts, "*Fellow sisters and brothers, do not forget what you have witnessed and do not forget me!*" No sooner has the final "me" escaped from his lips than the floor beneath the condemned opens up and they all drop. It is horrible to watch them kicking and swaying as life ebbs from their bodies until they move no more. It is a numbing experience, as any show of emotion is dangerous. When the condemned no longer struggle and the Nazi feels that his lesson to us has been properly absorbed, he dismisses us. I leave as quickly as I can, unable to look another minute at the horror before me as the bodies of the victims vanish into a cloud of white. For one week we are forced to march past the bodies, which are left to dangle and rot as a reminder to us all of what awaits us for any infraction of the rules.

After the hangings a black depression hangs over the camp. It is impossible to erase the image of our comrades' deaths from our minds. Work defines our hours and days and time seems to slow to a nonexistent pace. The Polish foreman who monitors my work area is named Pietr and one day as I am loading a canvas sack with black gunpowder he approaches me. "Dina, I want you to report to my office after work today."

"What do you want with me, sir?" I shrink from his gaze, knowing that this can only mean trouble but not knowing why I have attracted his antagonism.

"You'll find out when you get there," he barks, as he walks away. I have developed a sixth sense when it comes to men and Pietr's evasiveness triggers an instant alarm. When we are excused from our labors I rush to find Hannah. One of the youngest inmates at the camp, she is a lovely child whose parents were accused of smuggling in the Warszaw Ghetto and then shot. A Polish policeman intervened on her behalf and somehow she was sent to Pionki. With no friends or family, she has attached herself to me like a shadow. Her skeptical dark eyes and wary manner have not endeared her to many of the other prisoners but for me she is like a younger sister. Although invisible, the scars that her losses have etched into her heart are raw and oozing. Her smiles are as rare as moonbeams in a cloud-filled sky. Often, I awake to find her lying beside me snuggled into my back, her thumb in her mouth. In repose her face is that of an angel. The first time I noticed her trailing me I told her, "Hannah, never leave me. Stay as close to me as you want. I don't mind. In fact, I rather like having a little sister." From that day forward, wherever I am, she is never far away.

Shrugging off the personal risk, Hannah accompanies me to Pietr's office. When we arrive I knock softly on his door and his gruff voice orders my admittance. I enter with Hannah trailing behind me like a lost puppy. Pietr is sitting at his desk and when he looks up he sees Hannah standing there with me, his face turns red as a beet and his eyes grow large as saucers. "What is she doing here?"

I smile, trying to look confident as I take Hannah's hand. "She goes everywhere with me, we are like sisters." His anger explodes like a volcano and furiously he shouts. "Get out this minute and take that little brat with you! The next time I tell you to come here, you had better be ALONE!"

"Yes, sir." My knees trembling, I pull Hannah with me as we run from the office.

"Why is Pietr so angry?" she asks.

"I think he wanted to get me alone and do something evil to me. He is angry because I brought you with me and he wouldn't dare touch me with you there."

"I will never let you go to him alone, no matter what he says or does," she answers bravely with the adult voice that loss and tragedy have bestowed upon her. I am reminded that the war has destroyed any signs of childhood. We have seen too much to ever be children again. As soon as we are safe within our room I hug Hannah to me, kissing her until I finally win a smile from her brave little face. Thanking her a thousand times for going with me, I know my little friend has saved me. I have no illusions of what Pietr wanted from me.

The next day, in retribution, Pietr orders me to a day of labor that nearly kills me. I am given a shovel and a bucket and told to empty an entire railroad flatcar of its coal. By myself with only a bucket and shovel I struggle to complete the task. From dawn until midnight in the rain I toil until my back goes numb and I am as black as the coal I unload. Normally this is a job for several men. When I finally finish, I collapse in my bed. In the morning I lie prostrate, unable to get up. I tell the other women in my bunk that I don't care if the Nazis kill me for insubordination, I can't move. When I don't show up for work Pietr comes and inquires as to where I am. My roommates tell him I am half dead from my exertions and sick from the coal dust that I inhaled. It takes me three days to return to the living. Fortunately, Pietr leaves me in peace and allows me time to recover. He must feel guilty because he never bothers me anymore and has even begun to treat me with a new found respect.

The winter in Pionki is unbearably cold and in order not to freeze we wear all of the clothing we own when we work and when we sleep. Dressed in our layers, we look like an army of overstuffed bears. Today we line up shivering in the snow and a Nazi asks which of the Radomer prisoners would like to return to Radom to work. I volunteer with the hope of seeing Natek again. I miss him so much and would rather return to the deprivations of the ghetto than remain in this frozen tundra. A group of about forty of us is scheduled to leave.

The trucks arrive to transport us to Radom. Just as I am leaving my quarters with my knapsack on my back and with Hannah beside me, I find the Polish foreman Pietr waiting for me outside. "Go back in your room and put your things away, both of you! Neither of you are going to Radom."

"I would like to go, please Pietr, I want to go home, please don't stop us."

"No, you are not going anywhere and don't let me catch you even mentioning the thought of leaving or I will break your neck! You are staying right here!"

He is adamant, even my tears don't move him as I stand there with Hannah, who also begins to cry.

"I don't understand why you are preventing us from going, you should be glad to be rid of us!"

"I don't have to give you an explanation. I need you here working in transportation. You don't have to understand, you just have to do what I say!" With that he walks away, leaving Hannah and me with no other choice but to return our belongings to our room.

Outside it is freezing and the trucks blow white plumes of exhaust into the frigid air as the Radomers are loaded on. I run to say good-bye to a mother and daughter who have befriended me. They are very excited to be returning to Radom and the family they left behind. I hug them and wish them well, slipping a small piece of paper into Tosha's hand as I beg her to give it to Natek Korman.

"Don't worry, Dina, I will find him and give it to him," she promises me, her face glowing with hope.

A group of us stand and wave good-bye as the trucks pull out of the gate. Two hours later the trucks return empty of Jews. Pietr sends a group from the shipping department to go outside to unload them, specifically pointing at me to join them. We are heartbroken when we realize that the truck is full of clothing that belonged to the Jews that left this morning for Radom. Inside, as we sort through the piles, I find Tosha's coat. Picking it up, I reach in the pocket and find the note for Natek that I gave her. My tears fall silently, cascading in rivulets down my face, quickly absorbed into the coarse wool. The horrible deceit is revealed. I can only imagine the agonizing last minutes of my friends' lives, the terror that must have seized them when they realized the deadly ruse. The Nazis must have driven the trucks into the woods and made the poor Jews undress naked in the freezing snow, executing them before the edge of a mass grave. I imagine each person falling upon the other in a ditch, their hope ended with a bullet. Once more the Nazis have played a despicable trick on us, replacing even the smallest of hope with death. I realize now that Pietr must have found out about what the Nazis were planning and he saved Hannah and me. If I survive this war it will not be by resilience or luck alone, but by the conscience effort of a few who cared and intervened.

Chapter 25

"*Chervonutka*"

The head supervisor of the Ukrainians is enamored with me and never fails to smile or address me in an affectionate manner. His name is Dutchko and all of the women say he is very handsome. I try not to encourage him in any way but cannot avoid his probing catlike eyes; pale gold luminous orbs set deeply beneath his solid black brows. His hair is blonder and straighter than mine, if that is at all possible. His cheekbones and forehead are broad like mine but where my lips are full and pronounced, his are thin and sculpted. In some ways his features remind me of my dear brother Abek, which pains me whenever I look at him. Towering above me, he loves to call me "*chervonutka*," an affectionate Ukrainian endearment. He has told me that I remind him of his sister who he obviously adores and twice he could not resist pinching my cheeks. He constantly embarrasses me in front of the other workers just to see me blush. It is very unsettling to me, as he willingly works for the Nazis and can be no friend of the Jews.

In order to get to and from the factories and our housing each day we must wait in line and pass through a security checkpoint where we are counted and our IDs are checked against a master list. The Nazis are meticulous in their scrutiny of us, checking and rechecking to make sure no one escapes or goes missing. Occasionally they pull someone out of the line and search them more thoroughly, which only slows the process. They are always searching us for stolen goods or food. This is exactly how the poor unfortunates were caught smuggling food into the camp and then hung from the gallows as an example to us all. The bitter damp cold of the evening as we wait in line to return to our housing is numbing and we shuffle in place in order to spread some warmth to our frozen extremities. Dancing around in circles trying to keep warm, I notice two sisters who look extremely nervous. Their mouths are pinched as their eyes dart left and right in fear. We are all so tuned to be on the lookout for any behavior that is out of the ordinary that I know immediately that something is wrong with these two. I slip back in the line to where they are standing and whisper, "What's wrong?"

"We each have a loaf of bread hidden under our skirts and the Nazis seem to be checking everyone more carefully than usual. We are frightened that they will catch us."

"I have an idea, don't worry. Just come when I call you." Resuming my place in the line I maneuver toward Dutchko, who is checking IDs.

"Hello, Dutchko." I smile my most winning smile and hand him my ID.

"Chervonutka, how are you this evening?"

"I am fine, Dutchko, but my girlfriends Ella and Talia are not feeling well. I am afraid they are going to become deathly ill standing out here in the cold."

He looks up as I wave to the sisters, who are shaking as much from fear as from the cold.

Pinching my cheek, he directs me, "Go, go get your friends and pass through the gate. I see no reason for you to stand in this awful cold. Go now!"

I wave at Ella and Talia and they run to join me as Dutchko waves us through the gate.

Hurrying to our dorms, we embrace and Ella and Talia thank me for saving them from a possible search and worse. Ella reaches under her coat, pulls out a loaf of bread, and breaks off a chunk.

"Here, Dina, enjoy this bread, you deserve it."

Handing it to me, they both reiterate their gratitude once more as they rush off to their building and I go inside to share my extra ration with Hannah.

The next day Dutchko calls me over and tells me that from now on I don't have to stand in line with the others. He instructs me to come to the front of the line and he will send me through. I smile and thank him. Of course, he cannot help himself and pinches my cheeks, which flame red with embarrassment. I realize that it is good sometimes to trust strangers and that not everyone has bad intentions.

Chapter 26

Farewell to Arms

Thank heaven spring is here and winter has yielded her icy grip on the land. The warm temperatures are melting the snows drifts that have encased the camp. Here and there a sprig of greenery can be seen outside the fence, reaching like fingertips to the sky. Rumors abound that the war is not going well for the Nazis and that the Russians are advancing into Poland. We wonder how much longer we will be held prisoners at Pionki, maybe one day soon the Russians will liberate us. Obviously the Germans are still committed to their fatal mission, for the drudgery of our work continues and the trains leave daily, filled to capacity with the fruits of our labor—an endless supply of bullets and weapons. Each day brings a new mishap in one of the factories. Detonations are common when you work with explosive materials. I know I am lucky to work in shipping and transportation, as it is relatively safe. Just yesterday there was a loud bang coming from another building that shook the windows, breaking glass. We found out later that a woman was wounded when a blast occurred. The fingers of her hand were blown off and she is in the hospital. She will live, but how will she work without fingers? Without a useful position there can be no assurance that the Nazis won't find you expendable and decide to kill you. Every day the weak and worthless are removed from the camp to destinations unknown, most likely a bullet to the head and an unmarked grave in the forest.

The days proceed unhindered by the capriciousness of man. War has no effect on the march of time or the seasonal evolution as the sun continues its approach toward the summer solstice, warming the earth. Ours is a struggle to preserve body and mind in the face of inhumane conditions. The riches of the world are valueless when hunger is your only companion.

All I have in this world that is of monetary value is a Doxa Swiss watch that belonged to my cousin Dina; that I have it is a miracle. Right before the annihilation of the Glinice Ghetto, Dina had given her watch for repair to a young man who had been a jeweler before the war. He worked at A.V.L. and repaired watches as a sideline for the Jews. Unlike my cousin, he survived the *wysiedlenie* of Glinice and had hidden the watch at A.V.L. When I returned to A.V.L. he returned the watch to me and told me to take good care of it, as it is very fine. His honesty overwhelmed me; he didn't have to return the watch to me. I didn't know anything about its existence. I had assumed that it—like all of my family's other possessions, including my mother's jewelry, which she kept hidden—was left in the ghetto when my family was deported to Treblinka. Tearfully I had thanked him. I have kept it hidden all this time. It is the last material link to my dear family. For me it is a treasured heirloom, the last that I possess. Today I arranged to sell it because the Nazis have informed us that most of us are being evacuated to an unknown destination. We suspect that we are being moved to a work camp somewhere in Germany, as the Russians are within Poland and advancing. The Germans are in a panic to get us out of here; they have already begun to dismantle the factories and ship everything toward the west. Although it breaks my heart, I sold the white gold Doxa to one of the polish foremen for a hand full of zlotys and a brown bread. The bread will keep Hannah and me from starvation on our journey.

We are leaving tomorrow on trains that stand ready to depart at dawn. I have packed my knapsack with what little possessions I have. I sit on my bunk with Hannah close beside me as I braid her hair into a single plait down her back. The Polish foreman, Pietr, has suggested to me that he could arrange for me to stay at Pionki where a small group of workers will remain. He came to my barracks and asked for me tonight, pleading with my roommates to get me to see him. I refused to come and speak to him alone but sent word through Dora that I wish him well and thank him for all of his decency to me. I cannot stay. My surviving relatives are being transferred and I wish to remain with them and face whatever fate has in store for them and me. Pietr means well, I am sure, but I am afraid of his intentions and could not bear the thought of being beholden to him for sexual favors. Dutchko, too, has indicated that I should stay, that he will protect me, but I am also afraid of what his kindnesses might represent.

It is difficult to trust anyone under such circumstances. I am too young to make these decisions. Certainly, I will never give up the religion my family died for or the morality and integrity I was taught to adhere to. They are the remaining treasures I possess of the world that vanished. If I survive, I must stay true to the past. My future is not with the Poles or the Ukrainians. If I live... Natek will find me and we will build a new life in Palestyne.

We leave with a bit of good news to hold on to on our journey. One of the workers has overheard on the office radio that the Allies have landed in Normandy. The noose is tightening on

Nazi Germany and hopefully we are being moved closer to our liberators.

In the early morning's light we march under guard to the train. The supervisors and foremen stand apart, watching us as the Nazis goad us into the cars. Pietr and Dutchko are among them. Sending a last smile their way, I hold tightly to Hannah's hand as the Nazis urge us into the crammed enclosed stock cars. Once they are fully loaded, the doors are shut and locked, throwing us into darkness. There is little ventilation and we are packed body against body. I pray that the journey isn't long, as already the car is stifling. There is a smell of collective fear, sour as mildew and acidic as vinegar, which envelops us along with the sound of whispered prayers that hang in the air as the train jerks into motion, sending us reeling one against the other.

Chapter 27

A Train Journey

It is amazing what the human body can endure and how it can replenish itself in any circumstance. Hannah is asleep beside me, standing up, propped up by the bodies that hold her in place. She is suspended upright without any of her muscles being engaged. I am fascinated and distracted from the putrid human smells that assault my nose as I focus on the arc of her brows and the peaceful repose of her face. Inconspicuously, I reach in my pocket and break off a piece of bread, carefully stuffing it into my mouth. Barely chewing so as not to draw attention, I slowly suck the nutrients from the bread. I also slip a small piece into Hannah's mouth, which she accepts and chews in her sleep. I watch the motion of her small mouth chewing, her eyelashes flutter in concentration. Wherever we are headed, we will need our strength. With nothing to do but contemplate the passage of time and the clickity-clack of the railroad car as it eats up the track, I wonder if I have made the right decision leaving Pionki. Maybe this is the fork in the road that has decided my fate; to the left, Pionki and life, to the right, a train to oblivion. Perhaps it is reversed, and to the left, Pionki and death, and to the right, a train to liberation. If only Natek were here to tell me what to do. I resign myself to the fact that I am but a pawn trapped in a game without any rules, or worse, one in which the rules keep changing. My head begins to nod from the monotonous motion of the train until it rests on the top of Hannah's head and I too am weightlessly pressed between bodies. Hours pass, I snap awake as the wheels of the train commence to slow and the whistle blows mournfully to announce our arrival. Whatever our destination, we are here. I am not sure, but I think it is my fifteenth birthday.

Part 6

Arbeit Macht Frei

Summer 1944

Chapter 28

What is This Place?

The train stops and we can hear male voices barking orders in German outside. The train again begins to inch forward, slowly rolling through a large imposing gate. One of the women reads the words that are cast in metal above the gate, "*Arbeit Macht Frie*," Work Makes You Free. I whisper to Hannah, who is now awake, that it sounds like we are at a work camp. Minutes later the doors slide open and we are greeted with the snarling orders "*Raus! Raus! Alle Raus!*"[36] The deafening barking of vicious dogs who strain against their chains eager to tear us to pieces paralyzes us with fear. "*Schnell! Schnell! Macht schnell!*" Faster! Faster! "*Schnell laufen*" Run faster! We are herded off the train as Nazis spew venomous words at us and crack our backs and heads with their whips. Everywhere I look there are trains being unloaded and hundreds, if not thousands, of Jews being beaten and ordered into lines. It is utter chaos, yet eerily organized and impossible to describe. Above our heads is a tower

36 "Everyone out!" German

that dominates the skyline with black smoke billowing toward the heavens. It reminds me of a fire breathing dragon. We are ordered to leave whatever belongings we have on the platform. The Nazis are separating us, men from women. There is no time to say good-bye as we are pushed and shoved apart. I have already lost sight of my Uncle Tuvye and Majer. Dora is gone. I have not seen her since we left Pionki. I am not even sure if she was on the same train and sent to the same camp as us. It breaks my heart to think that I never really said good-bye. Nadja and Hannah are still with me as we are made to line up. All around us they are selecting people and dividing them, some to the right, and some to the left. It is clear which side you don't want to be on. On the left are mothers, wide-eyed and desperate, with children crying and clinging to them. Here, too, stand the elderly and crippled. I cannot bear to look at them and my stomach seizes with nausea. Nadja, Hannah and I are sent to the right with a group of workers from Pionki as a Jewish man dressed in blue and white striped pajamas approaches us and in Yiddish urges us to follow him. As we follow him and leave the nightmare behind; he tells us he is a *kapo*.[37] "Don't worry, you are going to the barracks and not to the gas chambers."

Nearly in unison we all implore him to tell us where we are. He looks at us with eyes that burn with madness. "You don't know? You are at Auschwitz."

37 A Nazi concentration camp prisoner who was given privileges in return for supervising prisoners, to whom they were often brutal.

Chapter 29

Auschwitz, Birkenau II

The little kapo shuffles forward, offering no more than odd snippets of ambiguous information that we assume to be the ranting of a madman. We follow like a line of ducklings behind their mother until we come to a building. The kapo delivers us to a long line that slowly inches its way to the front, where three Ukrainian women stand next to three small tables. As we get closer to the head of the line I can see that as each prisoner reaches the front, she extends her arm. At first I can't discern what they are doing until it is my turn to offer my arm. The woman holds a pen with a sharp needle point and she begins to alternate between stabbing my arm and dipping the needle into a bowl of blue black ink. I wince in pain, trying to pull away, but she holds me firmly in her grasp as she repeatedly stabs me. Tiny drops of blood trickle down my arm as I cry in pain. When she is done, I tear my arm away, looking at what she has etched in blue ink, A-14569.

I watch as she scribbles the number into a book. “From now on you no longer have a name, Jew, you are only a number,” she gloats, her eyes disappearing into the fat folds of her face.

Once finished, a group of Ukrainian women leads us inside a building and order us to remove all of our clothing and leave all of our belongings behind. The stench of fear is palpable as we undress. Nadja turns so as to block the prying eyes of the Ukrainians and presses something into my hand. I open my fingers and look at the diamond ring she has placed there. “What is this ring for?”

“Do you think you can hide it somewhere?”

“I don’t know.”

“Well if you can’t, just throw it away.”

“Stop talking,” a large Ukrainian guard orders us. “Take a piece of soap from the basket, you are going to the showers!”

Grabbing the soap, I press the ring into the bottom of it and go and stand in the inspection line. When I get to the front the guard searches my mouth to make sure I haven’t hidden jewelry in it. She motions me through, and after thoroughly searching Hannah and Nadja she orders them to follow me. We have two minutes to shower and I am thrilled to wash away the grime from our journey and feel the water, cold and refreshing. Afterwards, they spray us with a chemical for lice and tell us to go in the next room. Laid out on tables are piles of blue and white striped *pashaks,* dresses that hang like bags when we put them on and are identical to the pajamas worn by the little kapo that delivered us. The texture of the material is coarse like burlap and scratches and irritates our skin, which now itches from the toxic insect repellant. Next to the prison clothing with only three choices of sizes are the most horrible shoes I have ever seen, with thick inflexible wooden soles and thin leather tops, or maybe they are cardboard. When we put them on we can barely walk, which now explains why the kapo shuffled ahead of us. We immediately become an army of shufflers, unable to move the heavy unbalanced boats that weigh on our feet.

"Here, Nadja." I press the diamond ring into her hand.

"How did you get it through the inspection?"

Lifting my brows and smiling, I shrug my shoulders. "I am a child, no one suspects cleverness from a child."

Another woman comes in and begins to select certain of us and tells those that are chosen to follow her. Nadja and Hannah are selected. Hannah refuses to let go of my hand but I whisper to her, reassuring her that I will find her. Truthfully I am scared to death as Nadja and Hannah are led away. Maybe they are going to kill me now. Those of us that remain wait silently in fear until the guards return and lead us to another room. The room is buzzing with the sounds of scissors snipping and women weeping as they cut away the hair from the prisoners that falls, floating like feathers to the ground. Panic fills me as I look about and realize that everyone who has been selected has beautiful hair. Blonde, red, and brown piles of hair are being separated and gathered into sacks and stacked against the wall. One of the guards shoves me forward and pushes me into a chair. When the barber grabs my hair I yell, "NO, NO, LEAVE ME ALONE!" I latch on to her wrist, throwing the full force of my weight on her arm as I try to pull the scissors away from my head. Slapping my face, she wrenches my hair so hard that I scream.

"If you do it again, Jew, I am going to pull out every hair from your head!"

Covering my face with my hands, I sob helplessly. She takes her revenge and instead of cutting my hair short, she shaves my head bald. She couldn't have cared less about me and intentionally nicks me with the razor, sending small red rivulets of blood down my back.

This final humiliation and degradation drains me of the will to live and resist. Dazed and numb, I am led to a massive barrack packed with women. I wander from bunk to bunk until I find Nadja and Hannah. We are crowded into bunk beds, four on top and four on the bottom, crammed together in forced intimacy. The room is lined with rows of bunks, enough for more than a hundred women. It is like Babylon, everyone talking in a different language. French, Hungarian, Danish, Romanian, German, Polish, the melting pot of women have only one thing in common, we are all Jews. Though Hannah tries her best, I will not be consoled. I sob uncontrollably at the loss of my beautiful hair. Finally, after an hour of relentless crying, Nadja cannot bear it anymore. She is so annoyed with me that she threatens, "Stop crying, you're not dying, your hair will grow back." She pauses for emphasis, "If you live!" Her message is clear that if I don't stop crying I won't have to wait for the Nazis to kill me, she will do it herself!

To greet the day in Auschwitz is like waking up in Hell. A catastrophe of unparalleled proportions, the nightmare replays itself through all of our waking and sleeping hours. The Nazis have delivered the Jews from slavery into the executioner's hands for extermination. They created Auschwitz, the death factory, the unimaginable. Nothing grows in this wasteland, not flowers or trees, not the human body or soul, not children and their dreams, not hope or sanity. Death and only death ripens and blooms in a self-perpetuating cycle of evil. Day and night the smokestacks belch their poisonous tendrils to the heavens, challenging God to intervene. Day and night the gas chambers silence the voices of the young, the old, and the innocent with toxic fumes. Day and night the ovens bake the corpses, the smell of burning hair electrifying the air. The inescapable choking sweet smell of incinerated bodies and bones transformed to ash is lifted by the air currents. A thousand years from now, the ashes of the Jewish people will still lie upon this land begging for retribution.

We have no idea why we are alive, as we serve no useful purpose. There is nothing to do here but die. We are awakened at dawn by a bugle and like cattle are driven outside. There we form lines for roll call, *appell,* and stand for hours while the Nazis count us, over and over again. Sometimes unsatisfied with the first count, they start over and count us again. I cannot imagine why they count us every day except to torture us, or maybe for entertainment. It is insanity. Where do they think we are going to go? It is best not to move or draw any attention to oneself or the lash of a whip will bring you to your knees, or a vicious killer German shepherd will sink its teeth into you while Satan's emissaries standby, grinning with bloodlust in their eyes. While we stand in misery, the kapos are busily searching the barracks for all the spoils that the Jews must have hidden in their lice-infested beds. After hours, our minds now numb, we are fed crumbs of bread and a thin watery soup that often has living roaches and insects swimming in it. Every day someone crosses the line into madness and hurls themselves on the electrified fences that surround us, unable to bear another moment of this hell.

Hannah has disappeared. I can't find her. One minute she was beside me and the next she was gone. I have searched everywhere, asking anyone who will listen if they have seen my little sister. Most of the women look at me as if I have lost my mind. People disappear into thin air regularly here, while others just lie down somewhere and die, their bodies quickly collected and fed into the furnaces that belch day and night. Please God that she has made a friend somewhere that can feed her and care for her better than me. She mentioned to me that she saw some women from Warszaw that recognized her. I hope she has found safety with them. I pray that she was not picked up in some infernal roundup and delivered to the gas chamber.

One of the first things to disappear when humans are treated as less than animals is all trace of decency and the capacity to care for others. People revert to instincts that were better forgotten, they become animals. In this place, daughters turn on mothers and mothers turn on daughters, sometimes even stealing food from a family member. Their screams pierce the blackened night. The weak become the prey of the strong. If we live through Auschwitz, it is the disintegration of compassion that I shall never forget.

Friendships do not grow when the only thing one can think of is food. Miraculously, I have found a friend, a new bunkmate, Lusia. She is a sixteen year old dark haired beauty from Krakow and I have nicknamed her "*Krakawyanka*" for her feisty spirit.

Like me, she is now an orphan, her family murdered. Lusia and I pledge to care for each other like sisters. Cleanliness is impossible at Auschwitz. There are only three sinks that must service hundreds of women. We can never get close to the sinks so Lusia and I decide to go during meal times when no one in their right mind would think of cleaning themselves, as we are all starving to death. We both would rather feel clean than eat the poison they feed us anyway. If we are quick, we figure we can clean ourselves and still make it back for the bottom lees of the kettle of watery broth that masquerades as soup. Together we sneak to the sinks during feeding time and, as expected, we are alone. The water feels like heaven. We wash sparingly, using our small precious sliver of soap. Delighted, we congratulate each other for our cleverness while we quickly wash the filth away. Finishing, we race back with plenty of time to get a cup of the dregs of pigswill.

Chapter 30

Kaddish

Sometimes when I lie in my bunk, I fear I won't have the strength to rise again. It would be so easy to just lie down and die. Instead, I force myself to move and to think of something other than food. I try to think of Natek's face and our last few moments together, but it seems so long ago and more like a dream than reality. Who knows if he is even alive any longer? I must not think of that possibility. I must believe that somehow he still breathes and that we will be united.

The wind has changed direction and it looks like it is snowing. I put my hands out and white flakes land on them. Fixated, I stare at my hands, perplexed until I realize that what I am holding are ashes. The ashes from the crematorium of lives extinguished are floating around me and suddenly I am filled with immeasurable sadness. I close my eyes and begin to whisper the prayer of *Kaddish* for the dead.

May His great Name grow exalted and sanctified
Yit'gadal v'yet'kadash sh'mei raba
in the world that He created as He willed.
b'al'ma di v'ra khir'utei
May He give reign to His Kingship in your lifetime and in your days,
v'yam'likh mal'khutei b'chayeikhon uv'yomeikhon
and in the lifetime of the entire Family of Israel,
uv'chayei d'khol beit yis'ra'eil
swiftly and soon. Now say Amen.
ba'agala uviz'man kariv v'im'ru: Amein.
May His great Name be blessed forever and ever.
Y 'hei sh'mei raba m'varakh l'alam ul'al'mei al'maya
Blessed, praised, glorified, exalted, extolled,
Yit'barakh v'yish'tabach v'yit'pa'ar v'yit'romam v'yet'nasei
mighty, upraised, and lauded be the Name of the Holy One
v'yet'hadar v'yet'aleh v'yit'halal sh'mei d'kud'sha
Blessed is He,
B'rikh hu,
beyond any blessing and song,
l'eila min kol bir'khata v'shirata
praise and consolation that are uttered in the world. Now say: Amen
toosh'b'chatah v'nechematah, da'ameeran b'al'mah, v'eemru: Amein
May there be abundant peace from Heaven
Y 'hei sh'lama raba min sh'maya
and life upon us and upon all Israel. Now say: Amen
v'chayim aleinu v'al kol yis'ra'eil v'im'ru Amein
He who makes peace in His heights, may He make peace,
Oseh shalom bim'romav hu ya'aseh shalom
upon us and upon all Israel. Now say: Amen.
aleinu v'al kol Yis'ra'eil v'im'ru Amein.

Opening my eyes I find that a small group of women has surrounded me. Their thin weakened voices join mine in offering up the prayer to God. We stand apart yet together as we repeat the words of mourning. It occurs to me that there is no one who will say the *Kaddish* when I die. It matters not. I have said the prayer myself with a small group of strangers for all those who have perished and for me when it is my turn.

I have learned of my dear father's fate. A kapo from the men's camp named Isaac came looking for Nadja and I, Uncle Tuvye sent him. Isaac told us that when he learned there was a shipment from Pionki and that there were Radomers on it, he searched among the men for a familiar face and found Nadja's father Tuvye, Majer, and his own father and brother. It is a miracle. He has been very helpful to Uncle Tuvye and Majer, as the kapos receive more food and have more freedom than the rest of us. Isaac is the son of Mr. Berman, who was Tuvye's partner in the leather factory they ran for the Nazis at Szwarlikovska Street. Isaac disappeared and was presumed dead and his family mourned terribly for him. He vanished one day from the ghetto and was never seen or heard from again. It seems he was kidnapped off the street of the ghetto during one of the frequent Nazi raids. They shipped him here to Auschwitz and he has risen to the status of a kapo. I can't believe that he is an "elder," one of the longest living survivors of Auschwitz. He arrived at Auschwitz at the same time as the butchers, with my father. He remembers seeing my father here. At first I am overcome with joy at the possibility that my dear father might be alive, but my hopes are quickly dashed. Gently and tenderly he answers my questions. As he speaks, his words extinguish the fragile flame of hope I have held close to my heart. Apparently, my father became immediately ill when he arrived. I can imagine his horror upon seeing a facility dedicated to the extermination of European Jewry. With no hope for the future and no ability to save his loved ones, he must have prayed for death. Isaac remembers only seeing him for a very short time and then he disappeared. Having been weakened by his prior heart attack, he could not endure and Isaac said that only the young and the strong can withstand the cumulative effects of the starvation of body and soul. My father was only forty-two years old, God rest his soul. He died completely defeated with the awful realization that his wife and children were destined for the chimneys of Auschwitz. The extermination of my family is complete, I am an orphan. Once more I say *Kaddish*, my heart broken, praying that my father can see that at least one of his children still lives.

"Dina, come quickly, you won't believe this story." Nadja stands talking to a group of Radomers, their faces pinched with starvation. I walk to where they are gathered and listen to a woman named Sonia repeat her tale. "Yesterday, when my work unit was sorting through the belongings of a newly arrived transport that had been sent to the gas chamber, another train arrived. It was a transport from France and we were ordered to the platform to remove their baggage. I noticed a good looking man staring at me from the new shipment. His eyes were filled with incomprehension and I couldn't bear to meet them. I knew that soon he would be no more, as the entire transport was doomed to be fuel for the crematorium. His penetrating gaze disconcerted me and finally, seeing no harm, I smiled, trying to convey comfort to him in his last hour on earth. Then the man and his group began their final walk of life toward the gas chambers, totally unaware of the horror that awaited them. For some reason the line stopped and the Nazis leading them were called away. The prisoners were ordered not to move and, without supervision, I took a risk and wandered a bit closer to the man. Perhaps sensing the hopelessness of his situation, he threw a bag toward me. His eyes met mine and he smiled and nodded. Snatching the bag from the ground and hiding it in my dress, I nodded my thanks and ran back to the platform. The Nazis returned and led the transport away. I watched him until he disappeared," Sonia pauses, remembering.

I wait spellbound for her to continue, but when no words are forthcoming I find I am unable to bear the suspense and whisper, "Sonia, what was in the bag?"

She hesitates before she answers, "Can you imagine my shock when I opened the bag and saw that it contained a pouch filled with diamonds? It was unbelievable. He must have sensed what was coming and decided that it was better to give it to a Jew than let the murderous Nazis have it. May his soul rest in peace."

"*Amen,*" we murmur in unison.

In a desperate final act, a man throws a bag of diamonds. Without knowing it, he delivered a lifeline to another human being. Fate has intervened and one life will be prolonged while another ceases to exist.

The days crawl by and we waste away our bellies aching with hunger. The heat of the summer sun depletes what little strength we can muster as our pores empty of nutrients. The stench of unwashed bodies permeates the air with human odor and the sickly sweet smell of death lingers in the barrack from those that lie dead, waiting to be removed. It is nearly impossible to sleep. The night echoes with the cries of the forlorn and the incessant coughing and rasping of the sick and dying. Death waits in the shadows ready to claim us, our one constant companion.

Chapter 31

Run as Fast as You Can

It is dawn and a kapo has come to tell us that we have been ordered to come to the *platz*[38] naked for a special appell. Surely the end has come and we will be marched straight to the gas chambers. There is a relief that seizes my heart knowing that the fight to live will soon be over. We line up, maybe five hundred women, naked in front of a platform where a high ranking Nazi accompanied by two other Nazis glare out at us. The tall man, as handsome as a movie star, is a vision in his finely tailored immaculate uniform jacket embellished with medals and ribbons of military valor. He wears riding pants that are tucked into his freshly polished black boots and wears his hat dashingly off center, completing the picture of perfection and confidence. I am struck by his white gloved hands, which would be more appropriate if worn by someone attending a dance instead of one about to make a selection of who will live and who will die. I hear one of the women whisper that it is Mengele, the infamous

38 Square

doctor and master of Auschwitz. We all have heard what a cold blooded murderer he is and of the secret diabolical experiments he is conducting on Jewish prisoners who, upon arrival, are given a choice of being his guinea pig or going to the gas chamber. It is difficult to reconcile his reputation for indescribable cruelty with the good-looking man that stands before us.

We stand shivering not from cold, but with fear at what is about to come as the three Nazis proceed to walk down the rows of women. Some of the women, in vain, try to cover themselves in modesty. Stopping now and again to inspect the teeth of a woman he clearly relishes the moment when he makes his selection of "right" or "left."

After what feels like an eternity, he stands before me. I can smell the luxurious spicy scent of his cologne. He is so close to me that I am tempted to touch his perfectly coiffured hair that is brushed back off his high forehead, every hair in place. His blue eyes drift down my body with a penetrating gaze, inspecting me for imperfections. He looks me over with a final perfunctory glance and motions me with his crop to the right. I hear him whisper under his breath "dirty whores." Lusia and Nadja, who are beside me, are also told to go to the right. At long last Doctor Mengele finishes the selection and those that were sent to the "left" are marched away. There are about two hundred of us that remain. Returning to the platform, he begins to address us.

Pointing in the direction of the entrance gate of Auschwitz he raises his voice so that we may all hear his words. "Do you see that gate there? You are all very lucky; you are the first Jews that will be leaving through that gate alive." He then points at the smoking chimneys of the crematoria. "Everyone else, your mothers, your fathers, your sisters, your brothers, and your children will leave through the chimneys. You have five minutes, go back to your bunks, get dressed, and report back here."

Running naked, our hearts pounding, we race to get dressed. In minutes we return to the platz where a group of SS officers marches us out the gates of Auschwitz and loads us into a waiting convoy of trucks. None of us can believe our good fortune. I can't hear myself think as everyone is talking at once trying to make sense of what has just occurred. Over and over again someone says what is on all of our minds. "Wherever they send us, nothing can be worse than Auschwitz!"

As I look out the back of the truck, I read the words on the gate, "*Arbeit Macht Frei,*" and it occurs to me that a more appropriate motto would be "Death Makes You Free." This place, an inferno of death, will forever burn in my memory, just as the tattoo that I bear will remain indelibly etched into my arm. As we drive away, my eyes are fixed on the chimneys that disgorge plumes of smoke and ash into the autumn sky. This residue of countless human lives is the only thing produced at Auschwitz—death and only death!

Oświęcim – Brzezinka, dn. 31 maja 1984 r.

L. dz. IV-8521/1688-1689/84 /84

PAŃSTWOWE MUZEUM OŚWIĘCIM BRZEZINKA

NBP OŚWIĘCIM KONTO 718-92-7

CENTRALA TELEF. 20-21 – 20-24

MUZEUM CZYNNE CODZIENNIE W GODZ. 8-15 OPRÓCZ PONIEDZIAŁKÓW I DNI POŚWIĄTECZNYCH

PRZYJAZD ZWIEDZAJĄCYCH NALEŻY WCZEŚNIEJ ZGŁOSIĆ

Pani Miriam N o v i t c h
Kibbutz Lohamei Haghetaot D.N.
ASHERAT 25220, Izrael

Odpowiadając na zgłoszenie, Państwowe Muzeum w Oświęcimi uprzejmie informuje, że w posiadanych aktach byłego obozu koncentracyjnego Oświęcim-Brzezinka /KL Auschwitz-Birkenau/ są następujące dane o niżej wymienionych :

FRYDMAN Dina oznaczona numerem A-14569 imiennie nie figuruje.
Muzeum może jedynie ustalić, że więźniarka oznaczona numerem A-14569 /nazwisko brak/, została przywieziona do obozu KL Auschwitz-Birkenau w dniu 31.7.1944 r. transportem RSHA Żydów z Bliżyna. Pod datą: 27.10.1944 r. notowana jako przebywająca w podobozie KL Auschwitz III – Hindenburg.
Innych danych brak.

FRYDMAN Joel ur. 14.9.1904 r., został przywieziony do obozu KL Auschwitz w dniu 6.6.1942 r. transportem z Radomia. W obozie oznaczony numerem 37474.
W dniu 25.6.1942 r. zginął w obozie KL Auschwitz.

PODSTAWA informacji: akta więźniów obozu KL Auschwitz-Birkenau.

Muzeum w załączeniu przesyła 2 sztuki fotografii obozowych więźnia numer 37474 FRYDMAN Joela.

Załączniki: 2

D Y R E K T O R
/mgr Kazimierz Smoleń /

ZGPT Oświęcim, zam. 210 4. IV. 75 50.000

This letter from the museum at Auschwitz cites Dina's arrival on July 7, 1944 and her transport to Hindenburg on October 10, 1944. It also describes her father Joel's arrival on June 6, 1942 and that he has ceased to exist by June 25, 1942. The photos of Dina's father Joel were taken on his arrival at Auschwitz.

Chapter 32

Satellite Camp Hindenburg

After a full day's journey of no food and water, we cross the border into Germany and finally arrive at the village of Hindenburg. About a mile from the actual village is where we will live. There is nothing here but a fenced plot of land that lies in a gully in full view of the trains that come and go throughout the day and night. Upon arrival, we are informed that we are going to dig the foundations for our own sleeping barracks. The Germans plan to bring in pre-fabricated buildings once the foundations have been laid. Then we will be used as slave labor at the different armaments factories that are scattered throughout the town and surrounding areas. For now, we sleep in the open on the ground with night watches of armed SS to insure that we don't escape. Fortunately, the fall weather is mild and a small blanket is enough to keep us warm.

There has been an accident and I am lucky to be alive. The pain is awful and my face has swollen to the size of a soccer ball. I can't open my eyes and they are completely black and blue. We were digging the earth from a large tract of land to make way for the cement that will be poured to construct the foundations for our barracks. Some women are assigned the job of digging the holes while others carry away the dirt and debris in buckets. My job is to take the buckets filled with the dirt that is shoveled out of the hole and deposit it to another area. I had just finished filling a bucket when one of the prisoners inadvertently swung her shovel and hit me with the sharp edge, splitting open my eyebrow. Blood was everywhere and I was knocked out by the force of the blow. When I regained consciousness I found myself in the infirmary where a doctor and his nurse were administering to my injury. It is a miracle that I didn't lose my eye, another inch and I surely would have. It would be quite a ridiculous folly to die by the hand of a Jew when it is the Nazis that are annihilating us. Had this kind of injury happened at Auschwitz, I would have been sent straight to the gas chambers. I am lucky that there is a capable doctor here who stitched me up and applied salve, but there is nothing to alleviate the pain and throbbing that tortures me through the night as I toss and turn on the hard ground. In the morning I have no choice but to get back to work. Wearing a patch over my eye and my head in bandages I return to my labor of dirt removal. What vision I have is blurry, as my eyes are nearly swollen shut, but at least I am alive and I can still work.

It takes six weeks for my swelling to go down and for the barracks to be built. I will bear the scar of this injury for the rest of my life, however long that might be; but what is one more scar?

Our barracks are simple prefabricated wooden buildings with small windows to let in the light and they are kept immaculately clean by a crew of prisoners. The only furniture in our barrack are the double bunk beds that line the room in which we sleep six to a bed. Our pashaks are freshly laundered every day and it is good to feel clean after the filth that was Auschwitz, with its epidemic of fleas, lice, and typhoid. Each evening we are allowed to clean ourselves at a communal shower. There we are given a heavenly ten minutes to wipe away the filth of our labors.

It is not surprising to see the people of the town stare at us as we walk past on our way to work. They look at us as if we are aliens from another planet. What a pathetic sight to see a shabby group of gaunt women shuffling and stumbling down the road in our blue and white pashaks and our clumsy wooden shoes. At least they have given us pretty colored scarves to cover up our baldness.

Hindenburg is an industrial town with immense factories that support the German war effort. The unit that I work in specializes in parts for the Navy. They have taught me to be a welder on an assembly line where I weld a door handle shaped like a wheel to a steel central turning bar. It is dangerous work but at least I have gloves to wear and an eye shield to protect my eyes from flying sparks. I hold the glass shield in one hand as I weld with the other. I have become an excellent welder.

Our day begins at 4:30 am when we line up outside for appell and are counted. The Germans never tire of counting us. All of this takes place before the eyes of the SS-Unterscharfuhrer Taube who was reassigned from Auschwitz to supervise us here at Hindenburg. He is young, perhaps twenty-nine years of age. Tall and burly with dark slicked hair, a good looking man with navy blue eyes. At Auschwitz he was known for his sadistic cruelty during selections, but his reassignment to Hindenburg has mellowed him. One of the reasons for this change in behavior is he is clearly in love with one of us Jews. Her name is Esterka Litwak and from the first moment he saw her he has been unable to take his eyes from her. Only nineteen, she is the most beautiful woman any of us has ever seen. With heavily lashed turquoise blue eyes set beneath black arched brows and thick black wavy hair that frames her oval porcelain skinned face, she is perfection. Her womanly body is obvious even under the ugly pashak that we wear. Esterka sleeps on the lower bunk beneath me and I have seen the Unterscharfuhrer enter our barrack before dawn, quietly standing as though hypnotized as he watches Esterka as she sleeps. Leaving before she wakes, it is obvious that he is completely obsessed with her. He assigns her the easiest task of keeping his quarters clean. Esterka tells us that every day when she cleans his apartments he shows up at some point to see her. He sits in a chair and watches her, completely speechless except for his greeting of "Gut Morgan Esterka, how are you today?" or his farewell of "Auf Wiedersehen Esterka, I hope you have a pleasant evening." She laughs at his buffoonery, the way he savors her name on his tongue. She detests him and can barely keep her disdain from her eyes as she performs her work, doing her best to ignore his gaze. Hopelessly in love, he sees only what he wants to see. Fortunately for her he is forbidden from any intimacy with her and so far he has behaved with propriety. I don't know what punishment he would suffer if he ever gave in to his lust, but one thing is for certain, he would never be able to see her again. It is probably the fear of being separated from the object of his desire that keeps her safe from his advances.

Each morning following roll call we are given some bitter ersatz coffee and marched off under guard to our assigned work locations. My factory is about a mile away and it is pleasant to walk through the countryside and see the leaves of the trees turn to rust and gold in the fall light. I try to enjoy the mild fall weather, as I know the icy grip of winter will come soon enough and this walk will instead become a tortuous journey in our inadequate clothing and footwear.

There are about five hundred female and about seventy male slave laborers at Hindenburg. There are other laborers employed at the factories that are not Jewish and are paid a salary. These workers are free to come and go, most board in the town. The war has displaced and disrupted the lives of not only the Jews but the lives of so many people. There are quite a few young male workers that are French, Ukrainian, Polish, Hungarian, and Czech who work for the Germans, probably sending home money to support their families. Every day when I arrive at work there is a group of Frenchmen that are welders who work close to my station. One of them smiles and winks at me each morning and sends me a kiss through the air. He is very cheerful and friendly. I don't mind his flirtation. It feels good to be treated like a human being. Anything that reminds us of normalcy and life, that there are ordinary pleasures and decency that still exist somewhere in the world, is welcome. I always return his kiss with my own grand gesture of a kiss that sails through the air landing on his happy, grinning face.

At the factory we are guarded by an old German who usually falls asleep warming himself at the stove, snoring. Aside from the Unterscharfuhrer, most of the German guards that work at Hindenburg are older. The Nazis have reassigned most of the young soldiers to active war duty against the Allies and have replaced them with the most awful SS women that are designated *Aufseherin,* or overseers. These women are even more zealous in their cruelty than the men. One of these monsters is a small middle-aged ugly witch named Juana Bormann who walks around with a vicious German shepherd dog that is nearly as large as she is. I have seen her without the slightest provocation unleash the beastly dog on a prisoner in a brutal attack, the unfortunate victim suffering terrible bites and forced to cower in pain and fear until the mad animal is called off by Frau Bormann. She also carries a whip that she uses frequently on women for the slightest infraction. This Aufseherin Bormann has noticed the Unterscharfuhrer's attraction to Esterka. We were standing at appell one morning when I heard her warn him that if he doesn't keep his eyes off that female prisoner she will report him to headquarters and make sure that he is transferred. Esterka has told us that Aufseherin Bormann often barges into the Unterscharfuhrer's rooms when she is cleaning them. She assumes that she is checking to make sure that the Unterscharfuhrer keeps his distance. Esterka thinks the ugly little witch is secretly in love with the Unterscharfuhrer is and jealous that his attentions are directed elsewhere. For the Unterscharfuhrer's part, I cannot even imagine there being a question. It would be like choosing between beauty and the beast.

A wonderful thing has happened today that will hopefully ease the hunger of Lusia and me. One of the Ukrainian workers came over to my station when our guard left the floor to go to the bathroom. He speaks a little Polish and I have picked up a little Ukrainian thanks to Dutchko and we had no trouble in communicating. "These are very pretty scarves that you wear. If you can get more, I will give you bread in trade for them."

The thought of an extra ration of food is tantalizing. "Yes," I answer, "that would be something I can manage. I will bring you this scarf tomorrow and leave it here under my table. You can take the scarf and leave me bread in trade."

"We have an agreement," he nods and offers his hand, which I shake to seal the deal.

Lusia is so excited to hear what the Ukrainian has suggested. It is all she can do to restrain herself from dancing around the room. We have come up with a plan that we think is foolproof. We will take Lusia's scarf and cut it in half and each of us will wear half a scarf. You can't even tell that it has been cut and no one will notice. Then we can trade the full scarf for bread from the Ukrainian. Once a week we can get new scarves by saying that the sparks from the welding torches keep burning holes in the scarves and ruining them.

We are exhilarated with our cleverness and feel as if we have mounted a battle and won the war. The plan works like a charm and a big beautiful loaf of brown bread is under my work station.

When the guard goes to the bathroom I motion the Ukrainian to come over.

Thanking him for the bread, I waste no time making my proposal. "I have a plan that I can probably get one scarf per week for you, if you want it?"

"You have a deal, just let me know when you want me to bring the bread."

"Don't you worry, I will let you know."

With that, he walks quickly back to his station. That evening Lusia, who is a little on the plump side and more developed, sneaks the bread back to our barrack under her pashak. We feast together on our bunk. Bread has never tasted so good! Lusia and I are like sisters, we share everything together. We are always hungry and this bread is like manna from heaven.

The winter blizzards have begun and the morning appells are tortuous. We stand half naked, trembling, while they count and recount us. Our walk to the factory has become an ordeal to survive. Shivering in knee deep snow that fills our wooden clogs, with no coats to warm or protect us, we drag ourselves forward buffeted by the icy shrieking wind. Today it is so cold and blustery. The snow is falling as we stand at appell. I can't feel my fingers and my hands are frozen numb. Unable to bear the icy temperature I rub my hands together, blowing hot air from my blue lips in an effort to warm them as I thrust them in my pockets. I am in the back row with my head hunched down into my shoulders, shifting my weight, trying to keep my feet from freezing. I'm not paying attention to the roll-call and haven't noticed Aufseherin Bormann and her German shepherd walking through the rows of lined up women until she suddenly stands in front of me. I pull my hands quickly out of my pockets and stand at attention, but it is too late. She raises her black gloved hand and slaps me so hard across my face that my entire head feels like it is going to fall off and I see stars dancing before my eyes. I fall to my knees unable to breathe, my cheek burns like fire and tears fill my eyes turning to icicles as they slide down the sides of my nose.

"How dare you put your hands in your pockets, Jew? If I ever see you do anything like that again I will turn my dog on you and then you will have something to regret."

As she says this, the dog is growling and barking inches from my face, straining against the chain leash, ready for the command to attack. I can smell the warm moist animal breath and feel the foamy saliva hitting my face.

"Get up now!" she orders.

Shaking and crying bitterly, I stand. "Yes, Aufseherin Bormann, I am sorry, I will never do it again."

"See that you don't!" She walks away, pulling the dog as it continues to bark viciously at me, angry to be dragged away from its sport. Silently I pray that God will strike her and her beast dead.

My cheek balloons and I bear an angry red welt from the force of that cruel blow. I know that I am lucky that she didn't turn her killer dog on me. Lusia makes me a snowball and tells me to hold it against my cheek as we walk to work. She tries to console me but I cry most of the day, even as I weld. Somehow it is even more demoralizing to receive such cruelty from a woman, someone who could be a mother.

The allies are winning the war and a decisive battle has begun. We learn this from our co-workers that are not Jews, who secretly keep us apprised as to the progress of the war. The Germans have mounted an offensive in the forested mountain region of the Ardennes where Belgium, France, Luxembourg, and Germany meet. The Germans have officially named this operation "*Unternehmen Wacht am Rhine,*" which means "Guard on the Rhine."[39] It is an aggressive surprise attack that commenced on December 16th and it will have lasting consequences as to

39 The Battle of the Bulge

the outcome of the war. We are all praying that the allies will be victorious. We also learn that the Russians are gaining ground in Poland and are at the gates of Warszaw in the east and we pray that Auschwitz cannot be long after that. We have seen the allied planes flying low overhead and pray that maybe they will bomb the gas chambers of Auschwitz, bringing to a halt the extermination of an entire people. The Nazis at Hindenburg have become increasingly nervous as we are just over the border of Germany in a corridor of disputed land that has changed hands innumerable times between Germany and Poland. Every day brings the Russians closer and we suspect that our time here is limited and that soon we will be moved somewhere deeper into the heart of Germany.

A hush has fallen over the factory with the arrival of a most unwelcome and unusual visitor. The Unterscharfuhrer is here to inspect our factory and is spending time examining our work. Out of the corner of my eye I can see him making his way from station to station accompanied by two other Nazis and the plant supervisor. He is serious and unsmiling, his mouth set in a thin line of contempt. Occasionally he asks a question and nods in understanding at the explanation of what each person is doing on the assembly line. Eventually he makes his way to me. Nervously I weld as the sparks fall around me, intent on my work.

As he starts to walk away he suddenly turns back to me and yells, "*Komm her!*"

I nearly drop my welding torch and the wheel I am working on. My immediate response is panic as I scramble to comply. I am in trouble and I don't know why. Impatiently he taps his gloves against his pant leg and scowls at me as I quickly turn off my torch and approach him my head bowed in submission.

"Where did you get that rouge on your cheeks?"

Shocked at his ridiculous question, "*Herr Unterscharfuhrer, das ist naturlichen,*" this is natural.

Handing his gloves to one of the other men I flinch as he raises his hand, expecting a slap. He grabs my arm with one hand and proceeds to roughly rub my cheek with the other. Then he inspects his fingers, his face frowning. Anger floods his face with color as he brusquely releases me, throwing up his hands as if to beg God for an explanation as he screams, "*Diese verdammten Juden haben alles naturlichen!* These damn Jews have everything natural! Go back to work! *Raus! Raus!*"

As I walk back to my station I can see the shock on everyone's faces before they quickly avert their eyes and resume their work. The moment is pregnant with meaning. Under my breath I whisper as I light my welding torch. "Go to hell, you bastard!"

That evening, safely ensconced in my bunk, I relate the day's event to Esterka who knows him better than any of us. She laughs knowingly. "He is frustrated because he cannot have me. His love is driving him mad. I hope it drives him to suicide. He hates the Jews because he is told he should and this allows him to rationalize the evils that he perpetrates against them. It kills him that the woman he is infatuated with is a Jewess. He is transferring his dissatisfaction with me to you, Dinale. I am sorry you had to be the object of his frustrations. He is a pathetic bastard."

"Be careful, Esterka, you know what evil acts he is capable of. In Auschwitz he selected and killed thousands."

"You do have the rosiest cheeks." She smiles, patting my cheek tenderly. "Don't worry about me, I am always the giver of smiles coated with sugar when I am around him. It makes me sick to act in such a false manner but someday he will get just what he deserves. I just hope I survive to see it." Esterka's eyes blaze with determination which only emphasizes her remarkable beauty.

Chapter 33

The Last Christmas

Tonight the Nazis are treating themselves to a splendid party in honor of Christmas. The sounds of music and singing fill the air drifting on snowflakes to our barracks. The performers are all Jewish musicians and vocalists. One voice that sounds like an angel pierces the winter's night, melodious and perfectly pitched. An operatic soprano, her high notes tear at the strings of our hearts as we sit in silence straining our ears to catch each perfect note. The finale is a startling choice. The heavenly voice, in a daring act of resistance, cries out "My Yiddishe Mama" in German. Nothing could be more poignant. We all weep in memory of our own lost mothers as we savor the beauty of that moment and pray for those we have lost.

It is over, our safe haven at Hindenburg is finished. We are being relocated because the Russians are closing in. The trains have arrived and we leave tomorrow morning. We have not been told our destination but we are certain it will be behind Nazi lines deeper into the heart of Germany. Today I traded our last scarf with my Ukrainian friend and bid him farewell. Our business would have ended regardless, as the supply of scarves has run out. Tonight Lusia and I will eat well, which will give us the strength to sustain us on our journey.

In the pale light of dawn we are marched from our barracks. The trains are being filled beyond capacity. The Unterscharfuhrer looks like a lost boy as he stoically watches Esterka and the rest of us as we load into the waiting trains. The sound of the slamming door is like the finality of a casket being sealed. Is this our last journey, I wonder? The wheels screech into motion and a cloud of steamy vapor drifts by the tiny windows as we roll into motion towards the south. It is freezing. Lusia and I huddle together as the countryside flies by. I cannot help but appreciate the beautiful brilliance of the snow white landscape that reels past the tiny window. In the distance the mountains push their thorny spines toward the sky like a cathedral that God has fashioned to remind man of his inconsequence. Every minute the mountains loom nearer, growing larger as the train lumbers ever closer. Nestled in barren groves of trees, farm houses can be seen, their chimneys working to provide warmth to all who lie within—children snug and cozy with parents who provide for their every need, surrounded by love and security, barely aware of the storm of war that rages around them or the train of sorrow that slowly trundles past.

Many hours have passed since we left Hindenburg and we have no food or water. It is the lack of water that is the most debilitating. Some of the women moan from thirst and dehydration. Lusia and I and a few other women come up with a solution. Of our few possessions is a handled tin pot which we tie to a long string and can drop out of the railroad car window and drag in the snow. If everything goes perfectly, when we pull it up it is filled with snow which we share with everyone in the cattle car. Everyone grabs for the pot in desperation but we manage to somehow see that everyone gets a little as we repeat the process over and over again.

Meanwhile, we are beginning to climb into the Hartz mountains and the train has slowed to a crawl. The landscape is rugged and snow packed and the switchbacks cause a tremendous amount of unbalance from the shifting of the human cargo as everyone is forced to lean into each other. We can't imagine where the train could be headed, or why?

We are slowing and the whistle announces our arrival as we pull through the gate of a camp. We are at a camp named Nordhausen. They are keeping us in the train and some of the women are going completely insane, banging on the railroad car doors and screaming to be let out. Hours go by and we are desperate to be released from this prison. There is only a bucket to be used for a toilet and it is full and stinking.

Finally we hear the doors being unbarred and the Germans screaming "Raus! Raus!" We fall out of the cars as we are being pushed from behind by anxious women desperate to get out. They line us up and tell us that we are staying at Nordhausen for two nights and then we are leaving for a camp called Bergen-Belsen. There is no explanation of why we are here and none of us knows what or where Bergen-Belsen is. Nordhausen is enormous and completely fenced in with barbed wire with vast buildings that we are told were airplane hangars and now house the inmates. It is not an extermination camp, at least in the normal sense of the word, like Auschwitz. There is no gas chamber or crematoria.

Without food or water, we are abandoned to a small shrunken man who greets us. It is Leo, who we follow into the enormous concrete building where our eyes behold a gruesome sight. This is a camp of walking dead, skeletons with skin that hangs as they move, their eyes bulging with the knowledge that death awaits them. Leo explains that this is a sub-camp of Dora

Mittelbau, a secret arbeitslager, a work camp complex where the slave laborers toil under subhuman conditions. Nordhausen is a *vernichtungslager*[40] and contains mostly Germans, French, and Poles. These *haftlinge,* or non-Jewish political prisoners, many of which were resistance fighters, had dared to stand up to the Nazis. Here they are treated to a living death. Once captured and sent to Dora, they are forced to build massive underground tunnels into the mountains for the development of the V-1 and V-2 rocket program, what Hitler calls his *vergeltungs waffen,* or weapons of retaliation. The unfortunate captives are rewarded with disfiguring beatings and starvation as they are forced to carry heavy equipment and excavate mile long tunnels under the earth. Within these living tombs they die like flies, overwhelmed by the gas, dust and explosions that are a daily occurrence. With no medical attention and a starvation diet, their bodies quickly succumb to death or, once beyond usefulness, they are sent to Nordhausen to die. The dead are everywhere, mountainous piles of tangled legs, arms, and hands, rotting. The stench is unimaginable, the visual atrocity unforgettable. The dead stare out at us, their hollowed eyes and emaciated faces begging for burial, a testament to the crimes committed against them. They lie wherever they collapsed, in amongst the living. Our hunger and thirst forgotten, we realize how lucky we have been compared to these poor human beings that barely resemble men. Exhausted from our journey, we huddle together on the ground as we stare in disbelief at the nightmare around us. We are surprised to find that even in this valley of death human decency somehow clings to life. Those that have nothing, that can barely walk, bring us a bit of food and water. They share what little they have with us and we are humbled by their generosity.

One of the women asks, “Leo, do you know anything about Bergen-Belsen?”

---

40 Nazi extermination camp for ill prisoners

His forlorn eyes gaze on us. “I have heard of it. It is north of here maybe 200 kilometers near Celle.”

“But what kind of camp is it, is it a work camp?”

“I don’t think so.”

It is clear he is reluctant to share what he knows of Bergen-Belsen, which sinks our hearts, but we persist in our questioning.

“Please, Leo, tell us the truth. Tell us what you know?”

Sadly he looks at our eager faces, the last vestige of hope contained within our eyes. “Bergen-Belsen is a concentration camp, a death camp, like Auschwitz,” he whispers.

Like mourners at our own funeral, we stare at Leo in shock, silenced, as the grim realization of what lies ahead penetrates our thoughts. Painfully Leo watches the transformation as our bodies sag in resignation. Hope flies from us like a bird escaping on the wind.

Chapter 34

Death Has a Name

For two days we remain in Nordhausen, sleeping on the ground in an airplane hangar. The non-Jewish prisoners kindly share what little they have with us. The Germans, true to their obsessive punctuality, inform us that we will leave in the morning. We bid Leo and the other men good-bye, but our words of good luck ring hollow in our ears. There is no question that few of the Nordhausen internees will survive. Death walks unhindered and will easily lay claim to hundreds if not thousands of the victims at Nordhausen.

The train, filled beyond capacity with its cargo of women, lumbers north towards Bergen-Belsen. Once more we are able to gather enough snow in our small pail to abate the thirst and dehydration that become an unquenchable desire as we sadly proceed through the countryside. Fear grips us and mutes our voices as we each worry about what awaits us when we reach our destination. The hours pass in silence except for the rhythmic rattle of the tracks that fly beneath the train's wheels, and the mournful sound of the whistle that pierces the quiet winter's air and announces our passing.

The train's wheels squeak as we slowly come to a stop just beyond the gates of what must be Bergen-Belsen. Here we sit, contemplating our sorrowful fate until the whining wheels cry out, announcing the arrival of our train and its human cargo inside. Once more we are greeted by "Raus!" "Raus!" "Raus!" Then it begins, the endless obsessive routine of which the Germans never tire... counting Jews. This is our first introduction to concentration camp Bergen-Belsen. The freezing cold assaults our bodies as the moisture of our breath hangs in the air. Underdressed, shivering in our pashaks, we stand at attention starving and thirsty while the commander of the camp, SS Hauptsturmfuhrer Kramer, addresses us. He informs us of the rules of our new prison. Finally, near exhaustion, we are led away to our barracks. Nadja and I part as she follows some older girlfriends to the barrack next door. It is fine with me, she is twenty and I cannot blame her for wanting to be with girls her own age. I have Lusia and there could not be a truer friend or sister. Upon entering the barrack we stand for a moment, blinking, as our eyes adjust to the dim light. The nightmare vision we behold is what Hell must look like. Lusia and I, gripping each other's hand, enter a building that defies description. It is massive and filled with at least five hundred, maybe a thousand women, crowded together lying on straw mats on the floor. There is barely room to walk without having to step over a body. Lusia and I inch our way forward. Coughing, crying, and moaning in every language assaults our ears. The stench of the unclean, the sick, and the dying accosts our sense of smell. Numb with exhaustion, we walk to the furthest point in the back of the building searching for a place as far away from the sounds and smells as possible. Finding a small patch of straw, exhausted, starving, and in despair we collapse to the ground in hopeless exhaustion.

An hour later, careful not to step on anyone, we make our way out of our prison to see if we can find some water to wash ourselves. What we find is the unimaginable. As far as the eye can see in either direction for what seems like miles is a mountainous wall of contorted bodies, their arms, legs and torsos melting one into the other, their faces frozen in a last tortuous grimace of death. Terror seizes me. Gripping Lusia's hand, I moan with despair as I gag with nausea. With no food in my stomach to vomit I am racked by dry heaves that convulse my body. Lusia holds me in her arms as we sink to our knees together, unable to control the misery and revulsion that overwhelm us.

"Lusia," I gasp, unable to breathe. "*This can't be real. So many bodies, there must be thousands of them.*"

Lusia's eyes are round like two full moons filled with tears, unblinking in the vast sky of her face; her voice on the brink of hysteria, "*Why haven't they buried them?*"

"*This is the end! We will never survive this place. Everything that we have been through is meaningless. We will never live to tell the world the evil that has been done to us. The Nazis have accomplished their goal; Europe will be free of Jews! I don't care anymore; I don't think I can go on. No one cares about whether we live or die. What did we do to deserve this? God has turned his back on us.*" I begin to sob uncontrollably. "*This place is Hell on earth!*"

"Dina, please don't cry. We did nothing to deserve what has happened to us. We will survive, we have to! You have to try, please promise me you will try? Please don't leave me alone in this place!"

We sit there rocking, terrified, clinging to each other; afraid to give up and afraid to go on. Our future as dead as the thousands of bodies that lay outside the door of our barrack.

Night comes early in a concentration camp. The blackness enfolds you as you lie awake remembering all you have lost. Women weep all night long, awake or asleep, their sorrow wrenching at your sanity and tightening the space between your heart and your chest. Between the thousands of tears that fall in the night there are the piercing screams of "*EN KENYER!*" MY BREAD! All through the long night with heartrending sorrow they shriek, "*EN KENYER!*" We are awakened from our nightmares by the desperate cries of a Hungarian woman whose precious piece of bread has been stolen while she sleeps. Starvation will drive a person to murder for a piece of bread. Who am I to condemn these poor souls that are driven to steal from those that are weaker than them? The closer we get to death, the more we resort to madness and animal instinct, our humanity is obliterated.

The morning appells continue unabated. They line us up next to the wall of death as they count us. It is as if the Nazis are blind, as if the wall of death is invisible. If they ignore it then it must not exist! The counting is an opportunity to bludgeon us with clubs and whips or to turn on us their foaming mouthed German shepherds that lust for our blood. Haupsturmfuhrer Kramer and his crony SS Aufseherin women clearly glory in sadistic behavior. After being counted for the umpteenth time we are returned to our barracks. It is just as well that they don't feed us anything until noon, as now our single chore of the day beckons. Those that still breathe must remove those that died in the night. Lusia and I, along with any that have the strength, drag the bodies outside and toss them on the growing pile. We are only one of endless rows of barracks that all perform the same unenviable task of clearing the dead from our midst. The wall of dead grows with each passing day as does the realization that we will not survive this inferno. We have become emotionally numbed to the pyramid of bodies that reaches toward the sky. Our tears have long dried up with our hopes. Like the sand pouring through an hour glass, our time is running out and we know that soon we too will be a link in the chain of death that surrounds us.

There is a sweet girl from Krakow who lies beside us, her name is Lena. She is suffering from typhoid and her frail feverish body trembles through the night as she talks incoherently in her delirium. Lusia and I care for her, bringing her water and a bit of bread, forcing her to drink and eat a few mouthfuls. Sometimes when she gains consciousness she tells us of her dreams. Smiling, her eyes flooded with the glow of fever, she tells us that her sister is living as a Christian in Krakow and that she is coming to save her, to take her home. She keeps repeating "Manya is coming to save me. She will take me out of here. Have you seen her, is she here yet?"

The typhoid madness is consuming her, poor thing; we reassure her that it must be so. "Yes, Manya is coming soon. Don't worry, we will bring her to you when she gets here. You must hold on Lena, Manya is coming."

She smiles, slipping into a world of fever racked dreams. Her parched dried lips flutter like butterfly wings as she thanks us for our kindness.

This morning we woke and Lena was gone. Lusia and I drag her body outside to her last resting place on the wall of death. It is the first time I have cried since our arrival. I try not to care, to distance myself. What is one more death amid so many, but my heart breaks.

A few days later I too come down with typhoid and for several days I hover somewhere between this world and the next. Lusia is vigilant in her care for me, forcing me to drink water and eat a little bread. Sponging my forehead with dirty rags and whispering encouragement in my ear, she begs me to live. My feverish sleep is filled with dreams of my family. Last night I dreamt that I had survived the war and so had my father. In the imaginary landscape of my dream my father had a girlfriend and I was furious with him. I cried to him 'How could you have a girlfriend already when my mother has just died? How can you be so heartless?' Pained at my accusations, he begged me to understand,'Your mother has been dead a long time. I am so lonely. I need to feel love again.' Lusia woke me from my delirious cries and rocked me in her arms like a baby. "Shhh, shhh Dina, it's just a dream, please don't cry." Of course the memories of the dream flooded me with sorrow and I only cried more when I remembered that my father is dead, that they are all dead.

The fever has broken. I will live another day. The icy grip of winter has begun to release its hold on the bleakness of our barbed wire prison. The sun grows warmer with each passing day and with it the putrid smells of death grow stronger. We have no news, but there is desperation among the Nazis that can only mean their days of power are numbered.

Today I am surprised to see Unterscharfuhrer Taub from Hindenburg. We are in line at appell and I watch as he walks down the rows eyeing each woman. He immediately recognizes me and stops, ordering me out of the row to question me. It dawns on me that, whatever his reason for being at Bergen-Belsen, the real object of his unusual appearance is his obsession. "Have you seen Esterka Litwak? You are her friend you must know where she is? I must find her!"

"Nein, I haven't seen her since we arrived at Bergen-Belsen. I don't know where she is." My face is as blank as an empty page. I see my opportunity to wound him and I inject, "Probably she is dead. Maybe you should check the wall of bodies?" His eyes blaze with madness as he registers my words, my heart beats stronger. Even if I knew where Esterka is I would never tell him. Most likely she is here at Bergen-Belsen, but there are so many, thousands of us, it is impossible to know. We die like flies here with no one to note our deaths.

"I will search every barrack until I find her. Go back to the appell."

"As you wish, Unterscharfuhrer."

As I slowly walk away he cries, "Halt!"

Turning, I stare defiantly into his eyes. I am expecting to hear some obscene declaration of love. To my surprise, instead, as if speaking to a comrade or friend with a similar agenda he feels obliged to confide, "I cannot believe that we are losing the war. Can you imagine what has happened to Germany?"

I am too stunned to reply and I stare blankly back at him. An uncontrollable hatred wells up within me, but I say nothing. Recovering himself with a last worried glance at my face, he turns and walks away and I return to my place at the appell. Under my breath I curse him. "You have lived too long!"

Today they march us for no apparent reason to the men's camp. We are forced to parade through the grounds as if on spectacle. Meanwhile the Nazis entertain themselves with a barrage of blows to our heads, beating us unmercifully. Maybe they want to torture the men by reinforcing their feelings of helplessness? It is impossible to understand the Nazis' motives. Mystified, I implore Lusia to explain why. "How can we possibly live through this insanity?"

As always, she answers, "We must!"

As I leave our barrack today on my way to appell I have to step over two dark haired sisters. The older one is suffering from typhoid and looks near to death. The younger sister cares for her tenderly, her large expressive brown eyes fraught with worry. In Dutch she begs her sister Margot[41] to hold on. I notice them only because there are so few of us who are lucky enough to have any family to cling to. It saddens me, reminding me of my own sister. How I wish that Nadja were here.

41 The two sisters were Anne and Margot Frank.

My cousin Nadja is dying and has sent a woman to find me. I heard her calling my name through our barrack. She is taking me to Nadja now. The woman tells me that Nadja can't eat and can't walk. I brace myself for the worst.

I find my cousin in a lifeless heap. Her body, like mine, has wasted away to almost nothing. Using every ounce of strength within me, I drag her across the ground wrapped in her ragged blanket back to my barrack and find a space for her near to mine. There is fear in her eyes as I ask, "What is it that hurts you?"

She can barely speak and I must lower my ear to her lips to discern her words. "I can't swallow, my tongue is in agony," she rasps.

"Open your mouth and let me look inside," I order her. Her tongue is covered in white pus-filled sores. She can't swallow anything and is in excruciating pain. I am not a doctor but I must try my best to save her. I fetch some water and take my only possession, my toothbrush, and begin to scrub out her mouth. She screams in pain the whole time as I continue to scour away her sores which gush puss and blood.

"You're killing me!" she wails.

"What are you doing to her?" asks a woman nearby who can't stand the screaming.

"I am saving her life," I answer determinedly. "Hold still, Nadja, or I will slap you. If you want to live you had better let me scrub away these sores." Finally, when I can rub no more, I clean her mouth with water. Pleased that I have removed the poison that is killing her I tell her to sleep for a while and later I will bring her some food. I sink to my straw pallet, exhausted from the effort.

Nadja sleeps for two days, drifting in and out of consciousness. She awakes only long enough for me to spoon some soup and water down her throat. I check her mouth daily and find that the sores are beginning to heal and that the pus hasn't returned. I have saved her life and she is very grateful. Lusia says that when Nadja is awake she doesn't take her eyes off me. She stares in wonder at me like a child might stare at its mother. I am grateful to God that I could help her.

It feels like years since we got here, yet I know it is only a few months. Starvation has taken its toll and my body has shrunk to that of a small child. My pashak swims on me, I have no breasts and my menstruation has never come. Death lurks in the shadows for all of us, but lately I feel the cold hands encircling me in an icy embrace. I eat less and sleep more, happy to slip into the darkness of dreams where I relive my childhood. I dream of my mother's cooking, of holiday meals with my family. The dreams are so real that sometimes I wake in pain having bit my tongue, my mouth pungent with the metallic taste of blood.

I know that I am dying and I feel tranquility... peace. Sometimes my soul rises out of my body and I see myself lying below. All the pain and hunger have left me. I am nearly free of the ties that bind me to this life. *Like a butterfly I glide across the sky, now and again lifted by the fingers of the wind. I barely hear Lusia, who calls to me in my stupor. Her voice is a distant echo from far away, calling me, but I pay her no heed. I am soaring toward the sun.*

Someone is shaking me! "DYNKA, DYNKA, WAKE UP! WAKE UP! YOU HAVE TO GET UP! WE ARE LIBERATED! THE ENGLISH ARMY HAS LIBERATED US. THE WAR IS OVER!"

"Let me sleep, Lusia, why are you telling me lies? Go away and let me die. Please, do not tease me!" *I am falling from the sky, plunging to Earth.*

"Get up, we are free! The English are sharing their food. We are moving into the Nazis' housing in Bergen. I swear, Dynka, the war is over! You are not going to die! Not now!"

Pulling me to my feet with her arms supporting me, she leads me outside. Now I am surely living in a dream. Everywhere I look I see handsome men in uniform smiling at me. No one ever smiles in Bergen-Belsen. Perhaps I am dead already. All around me everyone is smiling, laughing and crying with joy. It is surreal, I am still not able to comprehend the reality of the moment until I see a group of Nazi SS women being led away, their hands on their heads, fear in their eyes. With whatever strength I have left I pick up a stone and throw it in their direction. I hit Aufseherin Bormann squarely on her temple and she winces looking at me, her face now hideously grey and lined with fear. Suddenly I am filled with strength as my blood soars through my veins. With the joy of revenge pulsing through me, I spit in her direction.

Part 7

The Road to Recovery

Chapter 35

Castle Langdenberg

The war is truly over. The English have tried their best to help the starving inmates of Bergen-Belsen. Nothing could have prepared these brave soldiers for what they found when they liberated us. Their faces express everything, they smile with encouragement when they look at us, but their eyes are fused with horror and tears. Not knowing what to do, they feed us whatever they have, trying to stem the epidemic of death: powdered milk and Bully beef, soldier's fare. The result is catastrophic. Our bodies so debilitated are unable to digest the proteins, having shut down most functions. The sudden infusion of food ravages us with diarrhea, which only escalates the cycle of death. Nadja, Lusia, and I are all sick with diarrhea but we refuse to go to the hospital. The English move us into German military school barracks that were formerly occupied by the Nazis, who are very busy dragging to mass graves the wall of bodies that surrounds the camp like a decomposing funeral wreath. They are helped in this grizzly task by the German occupants of Bergen who are being forced to assist. It is fitting that these compatriots should bear witness to the horrors their country has perpetrated. Ten thousand bodies lay dead on the wall. At liberation on April 15, 1945, sixty thousand survivors were found barely clinging to life at Bergen-Belsen. Sadly, that number shrinks every day as we continue to die from the effects of malnutrition and disease. All in all, another thirteen thousand of us will die in the weeks ahead. Five days after our liberation what is left of the survivors of concentration camp Bergen-Belsen gather within the camp for a memorial. Our long captivity is over and it is time to pray for those who did not live to see this day. In a gathering of strength and hope for the future, our voices unite in a song based on Naphtali Herz Imber's nine stanza poem, *Hatikva.*

As long as in the heart, within,
A Jewish soul still yearns,
And onward, towards the ends of the east,
An eye still looks toward Zion;
Our hope is not yet lost,
The ancient hope,
To return to the land of our fathers,
The city where David encamped.

It is finished; it is time to rebuild our lives. Many countries have begun to open their doors to offer us a safe haven for rehabilitation and resettlement. Nadja is not recuperating quickly.

Sweden is taking about 6,000 survivors for convalescence and she is going to go there for additional medical treatment and rehabilitation. She wants me to go with her, but I can't. There is no way that I will live in Europe; for me it is just one massive graveyard. Besides, there is a promise I must keep. If Natek still lives, I must wait for him until he finds me. Wanting my dear cousin to recover and begin a new life, I encourage her to go to Sweden. She needs to feel young and alive. A lovely family is sponsoring her and she will go to school, which she is desperate to do. Four days later, she leaves. Amid a waterfall of tears and a thousand hugs and kisses, we promise each other to write every day.

Now it is just Lusia and me who remain at the DP camp at Belsen. Lusia, who is two years older than me, has reconnected with some survivors from her native city, Krakow, and more importantly she is keeping company with a young man named Szymek, whom she met in Pionki. Szymek is wonderful and is mad about her and I suspect that they will marry before too long.

We all spend a great deal of time together eating our meals communally and socializing. Love is blossoming everywhere around us. It is as if we had been in a coma for six years and just awoken. Each of us is trying to cram all the lost years into a single moment. We eat too much and too fast. We laugh too heartily and too loudly. We are desperate to feel emotions that have lain dormant for so long. We run from the abyss that was the war as if we could put it behind us and never think of it again. Europe lies in a pile of ashes that have been scattered by the winds of war. Displaced families, Jewish and non-Jewish, are everywhere. Orphaned children are given priority by social agencies from around the world that join together to find and unite missing family members. Everyone is in a frenzy to register the names of their family members that are missing. Every day I go, with great hope in my heart, to check the lists of survivors that have been found. Every day I walk away in tears not finding a single name. Can it be that no one from all my many aunts, uncles, and cousins has survived except Nadja and me? Not one Frydman, Topolevich, Talman, Erlich, Madrykamien, Pomirantz, or Finkelstein?

Dina's cousin Nadja after the war in Stockholm Sweden, 1945

I have mail, thank you God, a letter has come from Majer. He is in a DP camp in Italy. With this joy comes sadness, as I learn that his father, my Uncle Tuvye, did not survive. Majer writes that he was sent with his father to Mauthausen after Auschwitz and from there to a sub-camp of Mauthausen called Ebensee in Austria. Conditions at Ebensee were terrible. The inmates suffered from beatings and starvation and were worked to death. The commandant was a particularly vile and sadistic creature who took great pleasure in torturing and shooting his prisoners for sport. Like Dora Mittelbau, Ebensee was a secret site for rocket development and Majer slaved in the underground tunnels performing back-breaking labor. One day he left for work in the morning, leaving his father behind in the barrack. When he returned in the evening his father was gone. No one knew what happened to him, he simply vanished. Two weeks later Majer was liberated by the Americans. I write back to him telling him how sad I am about his father, but how happy I am that he has survived and I give him Nadja's address in Sweden. Now there are three of us that have withstood the Nazi storm and, God willing, there will be more.

Photograph of Dina's cousin Majer Finkelstein in Italy, 1946

Lusia has left with Szymek for Krakow to search for any family members that may have survived and returned. I remain, the last of the three of us who went through so much together. I have three new friends and roommates, three sisters that survived together, a miracle by any stretch of the imagination. Rosa, who is twenty-one years old, Fela, nineteen, and Rachela, the youngest, is my age. Miracle of miracles, they have gotten a letter from their older brother Shlomo who, has also survived and is on his way to Bergen. Imagine, four from the same immediate family, it seems impossible. What I would give to see my brother and sister! It is so painful to contemplate a future knowing that I will never see them again. They live only in the landscape of my memory, cherished and preserved forever, nineteen and ten, forever young.

Shlomo has arrived and the girls are beyond excited to be reunited with their older brother. He is twenty-four and survived in the forest fighting with the partisans. Very tall and thin, the premature lines on his face are a testament to what he has witnessed and make him seem far older than his age. Clearly, he adores his sisters and their reunion is poignant to watch. Within moments I can see that he has completely assumed the mantle of responsibility for the family. The girls hang on him, his arms tightly embracing them in a huge bear hug. My eyes well with tears, it is so beautiful to see.

Thinking that I should leave them alone and give them some privacy, I quietly turn to leave.

"Who is this little girl?" asks Shlomo, as I reach for the door handle.

"Oh, Shlomo," says Rachela, "This is Dina, she is from Radom. Dina is our roommate and she is wonderful!"

"Yes," interjects Fela, "Shlomo, she hasn't found any of her family yet, she is alone."

"Not anymore," says Shlomo. "She is coming with us."

"Where?" asks Rosa. "Where are we going?"

"We are going to the American Zone, to a castle near Heidelberg in Baden-Wurttemberg. The Americans are much better supplied than the British and there are many more opportunities."

"Oh Dina," Rachela squeals. "You must come with us, it will be wonderful. Can you imagine a castle for us to live in?"

"I don't know. I don't want to be a burden to you, and the British have been so wonderful to us."

"Don't be ridiculous," insists Shlomo. "I will not leave without you. It is decided, you are coming with us to Langdenburg."

Lusia and Szemek, taken after the war.

Within a few days we leave for Langdenburg, which lies between Heidelberg and Stuttgart. This train ride is far different from the prior journeys as prisoners of the Nazis, when we rode with only death keeping us company. Now we are treated respectfully and with honor and can ride anywhere in all of Europe for free. We are seated in first class where the stewards pamper and coddle us. Langdenburg is a fairy tale castle dating from the 12th century that sits on a promontory overlooking the Jagst Valley and it is the most beautiful place I have ever seen. The first blush of summer sun has worn away the tired colors of winter. The expansive lawns, which have slumbered all winter, have turned a verdant green and the gardens are bursting with flowers that cascade out of their beds on to the walking paths in a symphony of vibrant color. The fruit trees are filled with ripening fruit and vineyards slope up against the dense old Swabian forests that pierce the landscape like spears. Rolling hills like waves of green water stretch all the way to snowcapped mountains that can be seen in the distance. This is the land of Hohenlohe royalty. For the time being we will live like kings and queens with a large staff of servants who will see to our every need. Untouched by the war, it is truly heaven on earth, but in some ways it is very disconcerting. Even with all the astounding beauty, it is impossible for me to grow comfortable in Germany; the language alone assaults my ears, as it echoes with a thousand reminders of unforgettable cruelty. I cannot help but feel resentment in every German's eyes. Perhaps it is my own paranoia that disturbs me and I should just relax and enjoy this dream vacation that has been given to me, after all it is a small compensation for the ruination of our lives.

Natek has found me. I am holding his letter in my hand as I read it aloud to Rosa, Fela, and Rachela, who are shrieking with excitement. Natek and his brother Benjamin survived. I am shaking with joy as I crush the paper to my heart, tears roll down my face soaking the fragile sheets. The girls wrap their arms around me, nearly crushing me in their embrace. Natek is coming immediately, maybe even tomorrow or the next day. My God, I can't believe it! My prayers have been answered and soon I will see Natek!

The warm summer day is crystal clear and I am outside basking in its glory. The gardens are filled with aromatic flowers and the bees busily buzz from flower to flower drinking in the sweet nectar and yellow pollen. Lost in a daydream, I hear my name being called. Looking up, I see Natek running toward me, his arms open wide, "Dinale, Dinale!"

"Natek!" I cry. "Is it really you?" I jump to my feet, dropping the book I was reading as I run to greet him.

"Dinale!" He picks me up as if I am a feather, spinning me around, my laughter pealing like a Sunday church bell. "I told you that we would outlive the Nazis and their evil. It is just as I said it would be. You and I have endured, our lives a testimony to our will to survive."

Greedily my eyes take in the wonder of him. He is thin but strong, his face years older than his age, but his grin is still that of a young boy who has been caught with his hand in the cookie jar.

"Natek, isn't this place like a dream? I am so happy to see you! I have so much to tell you and I know you have so much to tell me. It has been so long since we parted in Radom."

"I don't care about this place. I only have eyes for you. Look at you! You are more beautiful than I remembered. You have grown into a woman."

His eyes feasting on me, blushing, I take his hands in mine. Seeing the redness of my cheeks, he heartily bursts into laughter. "I'd forgotten what marvelous rosy cheeks you have."

"Stop embarrassing me." I pull him to a bench. "Come, sit and tell me everything."

"There are not enough hours in a day to tell you everything."

"Never mind, I don't really want to talk about the war. There will be plenty of time for that. I just want to enjoy being alive and having you here with me. You must be hungry and tired from your trip. Let's see if the kitchen can make us a picnic and we can walk down to the clearest stream you have ever seen."

"I am starving," he admits. "I would welcome a little food." Arm in arm, we stroll back to the castle where the staff eagerly stuffs a basket with roasted chicken, fruit, and sweet pastries. We dine in a meadow at the edge of a stream, a scene as perfect as an impressionist painting. After we eat our fill, we take a walk by the stream, our toes digging into the coal black mud as we wade in the water holding hands. Small fish and pollywogs dart in and out between our legs as birds chirp in the trees that curve along the shoreline. I stumble and Natek catches me, his arms encircling me and pressing me to his chest. He kisses me and my head spins. These are not the urgent kisses of the boy that I remembered, but the commanding kisses of a man full grown. My knees buckle as I surrender to the warm rush of heat that envelops me. I can feel his manhood swell against me and hear the soft moans that escape his lips as he kisses my neck. My own breath is coming in shallow gasps and I know that what I am feeling is overwhelming. I realize if I don't stop him now, I may not be able to. "Natek, Natek, please... please stop. We mustn't go any further, please."

"It's okay, Dina, just let me hold you, please! I promise I won't force you."

Both our hearts are pounding, one against the other, as I whisper in his ear. "Maybe we should take a swim. You know, to cool off."

Natek looks into my eyes and kisses me on the forehead. "I think that is a very good idea."

As intended, the cold water of the stream extinguishes the heat of our kisses. We fill the void of our youthful passions with laughter as we splash in the shallow stream. After our swim we lie on the bank, basking in the sunlight as our clothes dry. Gently Natek prods me to tell him what happened to me after I left Radom. I try to compose myself and relate all that happened as dispassionately as I can, but I am soon overwhelmed by emotions. Again, he holds me and kisses me tenderly, but this time they are the kisses of a brother and not a lover.

Now it is Natek's turn to share his and Benjamin's story of survival. He breathes deeply and all of the joy in his eyes fades. "You left in July 1943 and after that Benjamin and I were assigned to Szkolna camp, which in January 1944 became a full-fledged Konzentrations Lager with all of the enforced rules and security of any other camp, minus the gas chambers. The labor was backbreaking, the food minimal, the appells interminable, but we still considered ourselves lucky to be alive and in Radom. Then in March the Nazis abducted about 600 of us to the extermination camp Majdanek near Lublin. I don't need to tell you what it was like there, much like Auschwitz except that by the time we arrived, the Russians were advancing and the Nazis had stopped using the gas chambers. Benjamin and I were young and healthy and the Nazis used us for hard labor until in April the Russians were nearly at our door and they shipped us to Plaszow Camp near Krakow, where a nasty bunch of SS ruled. Things were really bad there, the beatings and torture…" Natek's eyes darken with anguish as the excruciating memories flood him. I watch as his jaw clenches and the mighty effort it takes to subdue the tortuous memories. I squeeze his hand, waiting for him to continue. Wiping the tears from his eyes as he fixes them on some distant horizon, he fights to gain control. "They evacuated us finally to Mauthausen, and even at the end, with the Allies closing in, the Nazis were fixated on their goal of eliminating every Jew. One day Benjamin and I were rounded up and taken into the woods. I knew it was the end that they were going to shoot us. My thoughts were in turmoil. I couldn't believe that I was going to die; that I was never going to see you again. I hadn't kept my promise to you and it was devastating. Suddenly I heard machine gun fire all around us and I grabbed Benjamin and pulled him to the ground. With the Nazis' attentions focused on preserving their own lives, we crawled away into some brush. Fierce fighting ensued until every single Nazi bastard lay dead. Within minutes we were liberated by U.S. Army troops. It was a miracle and now I am here. I've found you and I've kept the promise I made to you so long ago." Lifting my hands to his lips, he kisses each one lovingly.

When we return to the castle I introduce Natek to Rosa, Fela, Rachela, and Shlomo. An instant friendship is forged between Natek and Shlomo and the girls. Natek thanks Shlomo for taking such good care of me. Everyone is so happy and eager to leave behind the years of tears and begin anew. Natek remains at Langdenburg and the month is spent in the pursuit of simple pleasures that have so long been denied us—joyous picnics and walks through the countryside. Hungry to learn, we watch American movies in the evening and try our best to mimic the English words that are so foreign to our ears.

After not being able to bathe for six years, I cannot get enough of the magnificent bathtub at Langdenburg. The bathroom alone is as big as our whole home in the ghetto, with vaulted ceilings and solid gold fixtures and special racks for warming the towels that hiss as the steam circulates through the pipes. Sometimes I lay for an hour languishing up to my ears in hot sudsy water, daydreaming about the miracle that I have survived against all odds. That I managed to live when so many have not is a constant reminder to me of the great responsibility I now shoulder. I know I must create a life of purpose in the image of the family and community I was born into. Soaking in the bath is recuperative and I linger in it until one of the girls pounds on the door begging me to hurry up so she too can bathe in such splendor.

Today, June 20th 1945, I celebrate my birthday for the first time since the Glinice Ghetto. I am sixteen. Natek and the other members of our survivor cadre arrange a lovely party for me and the staff even provides bottles of champagne for a toast and a beautiful cake embellished with my name and age. We are all giddy with hope for the future and embrace the opportunity to proclaim our dedication to life and rebirth. The tears and laughter flow freely as we clink our champagne glasses with a toast to the future and we try our best to forget for a moment all the devastation we have endured. Natek never leaves my side and has asked me to marry him. I beg him to be patient and not to press me. I am only just sixteen and I am not ready to make such a life-changing commitment.

It has been a dream, but unfortunately our idyllic sojourn at Langdenburg has come too quickly to an end. The Americans have notified us that they are moving us to Stuttgart, where a displaced person facility has been opened. We are all sad to leave, but reality had to call eventually. It is a time for good-byes, as some of us are going on to other places. Many are returning to the cities of their birth and others to DP facilities that have been set up throughout Europe as they continue to search for any surviving family.

I have learned that people come and go through your life. Some leave having altered the future forever, while others just pass through for a moment, barely leaving a sign, much like a footprint in sand washed away by the rising tides of time.

All of these people are woven in some way into the tapestry of your life, and even when they have passed through and are gone forever, they are never forgotten. It is time for us to move on in our lives and figure out what kind of world we want to build for ourselves and where we want to build it.

Chapter 36

Stuttgart Displaced Persons Camp

Stuttgart is one of the largest cities in Germany and is the Capital of Baden-Wurttemberg. It must have been a beautiful city filled with music and art before the allies bombed it into submission. Much of it has been destroyed, yet it still retains its essential character and charm due to the beautiful natural landscape. It lies in a lush valley surrounded by hills, fertile farmland, vineyards, and thick woodlands that show little or no effect from the war. Parks and lakes abound throughout and it is rich in cultural patrimony and history. Interspersed here and there are neighborhoods that stand intact, but everywhere you go the signs of war are obvious, as buildings lay in piles of rubble and ruin. The DP Camp is situated on the outskirts of the city in an area that was untouched by bombs. The Germans who lived there have been moved out to other areas to accommodate our housing needs. The large complex of buildings is fairly new and is comprised of four-story brick apartment buildings that are clean and charming with garden beds planted with colorful flowers that weave throughout the grounds. The apartments provide comfortable quarters for our living and transition. Again, the happy sisters Rachela, Rosa, Fela, and I are roommates sharing laughter, secrets, and the normal dreams of youth. Each apartment in the complex has its own kitchen and we are encouraged to cook for ourselves so that we can acquire the skills of normal independent life. Across the street is a restaurant that provides breakfast, lunch, and dinner if we choose not to cook. The food is delicious and I am packing on weight. Six years of starvation has had a profound effect on all of us and food is a constant craving in which we revel to indulge. Eventually we will normalize and be more cautious with our intake, but for now we eat as if there is no tomorrow. During the day we take classes in English and several other languages, which are being provided to prepare us for immigration to the countries that are opening their doors to us. We are dedicated to embracing all aspects of freedom—going to the movies, having picnics, and taking the trolleys to different destinations throughout the city. Last week a group of us journeyed to the mountains and visited an alpine spa where the fresh mountain air and nature's beauty were completely restorative. However, the primary focus for all of us is to find any family and friends that might still be alive. The ebb and flow of people is constant at the DP facility as people come and go every day in search of relatives. Natek and I check daily the lists the Red Cross posts for any members of our families that might be somewhere among the displaced masses of Europe. I read the lists, finding no one. My hope receding, I cry on his shoulder in disappointment. As always, Natek is my tower of strength. His arms surround me protectively as he tries to absolve me of my sorrow.

A group of survivors in Stuttgart, Germany after the war. Second from left standing is Natek, third from right standing is Dina.

Each new day brings a new group of survivors seeking relatives, everyone immediately crowds around them anxious to see if perhaps they have seen or know what happened to any of their relatives. Occasionally we learn the fate of someone we knew, but more often than not it is the indefinite sentence, "One day I saw them and the next day they disappeared." Usually the truth affords no consolation and generates only a larger mystery, giving rise to fantasies that perhaps that dear one is still out there waiting to be found. Perhaps they are ill or amnesiac. We know now that millions of Jews were murdered in the death camps and by firing squads. These are the facts. These are the results of genocide. These are the tears that we will spend a lifetime shedding.

My heart is broken. I have learned the tragic fate of my dear friend Dora Rabbinowicz. Beautiful Dora, whose first words to me at A.V.L. after I returned from the hospital in Radom and found that my sister and cousin Dina were gone were, "Dinale, don't cry darling, I am going to be your sister." So many memories, frozen moments in time. I see her face smiling at me, beckoning me to remember. I can hear her voice as clear as a bell telling me that her older sister had fled to Russia when the Germans invaded Poland, and her anguish when she spoke of seeing her father shot in the street by the Nazis. Dora was my sister's age, a very pretty petite girl with a mane of black curly hair that she would carefully brush into a long braid that touched her small waist. Her large luminous brown eyes were like magnets inviting you to explore the secrets behind her gaze. The warmth of her personality was attractive to anyone who beheld her, but it was the childlikeness that she exuded that resulted in men wanting to protect her. Men fell for Dora and one in particular tried very hard to ease her burden during our time at A.V.L. Karl Rumuel was a warm, good looking man, a bit on the heavy side. Like many large men, there was a joviality about him that was very attractive and he was very well liked by all of the workers. He was one of the Wermacht supervisors at A.V.L., a kind man that treated us with decency. He fell madly in love with Dora and did everything in his power to ease her burden. He even went so far as to share his own food with her, presenting her with special treats when he could. I remember how upset I was when Dora told me that she was a little in love with Karl too. I knew that Karl was, like Otto, a good man forced to do the bidding of the Nazis; nonetheless, he was still a dutiful co-conspirator. I was only thirteen and I felt Dora was acting like a traitor and I told her so. She laughed, saying one day I would understand the dynamics between men and women and I would not be so condemning. At the time, however, I was greatly disturbed by her confession of caring for Karl. How could she fall in love with the enemy? Now, in retrospect, I realize that I should not have judged Dora for grabbing a few moments of happiness. She was eighteen and longing to experience life. When A.V.L. closed, Karl was sent to the Russian front and we were moved to Szwarlikovska Street Camp. Dora moved into an apartment with a group of young people. One day as I walked home from the peat bogs, one of the other Wermacht supervisors from A.V.L. called me over to the fence. Nervously I approached. He asked me if I could bring Dora to him, that he had a message from Karl for her. I ran to get her but she refused to come, telling me it was over between Karl and her. There was no point in continuing, Karl was at the front and she was a prisoner. I ran back to the fence to convey Dora's message but the soldier had disappeared. Within a short while Dora had conquered another heart, a young Jewish man that lived in the apartment with her. They had fallen in love with each other and had promised to marry when the war ended.

Standing before me telling me my girlfriend's fate is Motek, Dora's betrothed. Searching for her after the war, he learned her fate. After surviving Auschwitz, during the frigid winter in January she had been marched to Danzig on the Baltic Sea, just ahead of the Soviet army. There the Nazis, desperate and trapped, with the Russians about to conquer the city, had executed a ghastly crime. They had forced Dora's group of women into the icy sea. Standing there with rifles trained on them they had watched until every woman had drowned. Bitterly, my heart broken, I weep on Motek's shoulder at the sadistically cruel fate of my dear friend. Darling Dora, I pray and promise I will never forget you!

The story of Dora's fate has left me depressed. Even Natek is unable to revive my enthusiasm for life. I feel lost at sea without a clear plan of action of what to do with my life. My dreams are restless journeys through the past, peopled by familiar faces that no longer live. Over and over again in my dreams I picture Dora forced into the sea and over and over I watch her drown. Sometimes I wake gasping for air as if I too am drowning.

Natek again has asked me to marry him. Again, I beg him to be patient, pleading that I am too young and need more time.

Today there is a new sign posted on the message board inquiring if there are children under the age of sixteen who want to go to school. The sign says that a Major Sperry will meet with anyone interested in front of the building tomorrow at 9 a.m. Suddenly I am flooded with desire. This is what I want to do. To go to school and recapture some of what I missed during the six dreadful years of the war. To continue my education and achieve something that would make my parents proud.

When I arrive in the morning there is a group of teenagers surrounding Major Sperry. Mrs. Sperry is a Major in the United States Army. I wait while the others finish their interviews with Mrs. Sperry and her translator. Finally, it is my turn. I explain briefly to Mrs. Sperry some of what I endured during the war. I tell her that I turned sixteen in June, but that I want desperately to go to school. I try to use the few English words that I have picked up from the movies and here at Stuttgart. She listens attentively, barely interrupting the tale that spills from me in a torrent of emotion. Breathlessly I wait while the translator relays my words. Then, looking at me with a large mothering smile and taking my hands in hers she says, "Dina, you are going to Aglasterhausen, you are going to school. I want you to pack up your belongings and meet me here tomorrow at 9 a.m. I am going to personally drive you to Aglasterhausen."

I listen to the translator as she transforms Mrs. Sperry's words into Polish. When she finishes I am so excited that I throw my arms around her neck, hugging her in gratitude. I am beside myself with joy.

Now I must face the most difficult part of my decision. I dread the moment when I must tell Natek.

It is worse than I thought it would be. Natek is completely dejected and angry when I tell him my plans.

"How can you leave me after all that we have been through? I love you Dina and want to take care of you for the rest of your life. How can you abandon me?"

"Natek, if you love me you would want the best for me. I need to go to school and find out who I am. We have lost six years of our lives, we have lost our identity and we have suppressed our emotions during all of this time. Who are we, you and I? How can we even know what we want? We need time to heal to rediscover who we are. How can I be a wife without an understanding of the world at large? What kind of partner would I be?"

"I know that I love you and that we have survived the fires of Hell. I know that we promised each other we would live in Palestyne if ever we survived the Nazis. I know that I am willing to face the world and whatever it throws at us as long as I can be with you. I know that now you want to leave me."

"Natek, Aglasterhausen is less than an hour by train from Stuttgart. You can visit me as much as you want. It is a school for war orphans who want to continue their education. It is an opportunity to recapture some of the years that were stolen, a chance for normalcy, to study languages, mathematics, science, and literature. I need to do this; you have to give me this chance to find myself." I fling my arms around him pressing him to me, my face buried in his chest. "Please, Natek, please do not be angry with me."

Sighing with resignation, "I cannot be angry with you, at least not for long."

His arms surround me protectively. Turning my face up to meet his, my hands cupping his face with tenderness, I whisper, "Thank you Natek, thank you." As always, he kisses me with an urgency that takes my breath away.

With great difficulty I say good-bye to Rosa, Fela, Rachela, and Schlomo Cooperschmidt, who have shown me such devotion and friendship. Schlomo has made the decision that they will immigrate to Palestyne together. To get to Palestyne is a dangerous endeavor, as the British run and enforce a blockade in effect barring the entry of desperate refugees to the homeland they now rightly consider their only choice of haven. Jabotinsky's dream is now becoming a reality, although the price exacted of millions dead in a Holocaust was far too dear. The Jews in Palestyne are facing a war with the Arabs. The British are only allowing a trickle of refugees to enter when there is a building flood of Jews who want in. Even after the near annihilation of the entire Jewish population of Europe the world is still indifferent to the necessity of a Jewish homeland. Clandestinely, through various underground operations, the displaced and surviving Jewry of Europe are being smuggled into the Holy Land. I myself still have every intention of making *aliyah* to Palestyne when fully recuperated. Nearly four months have passed since liberation and I still suffer intestinal problems from my ordeals. Natek knows that I am still unwell and for this reason alone he is patient and undemanding of me. My leaving of Natek is an outpouring of tears, of promises said and unsaid. I promise to write every day and Natek promises to visit soon. He has decided to make the journey with his brother Benjamin back to Radom to see if any of their relatives have survived and returned. He will travel back to Stuttgart by way of Aglasterhausen after Radom. By then I will certainly be missing him terribly. Nervously, I take leave of him, his ardent kisses smoldering on my lips. I don't know how much longer I can resist his passion or if I even want to. I wonder if I am making the right decision leaving Natek.

Major Tommy Sperry in Heidelberg, 1945.

Chapter 37

Aglasterhausen International Children's Center

Major Sperry greets me with a smile at the wheel of an Army Jeep. My English is minimal and she speaks no other languages so our communication is mostly conveyed through our eyes and hand movements. The day is bright and hopeful and Major Sperry keeps up an endless chatter, her smiles filling me with confidence as we make our way through the fertile countryside.

Transportation throughout Europe is intermittent at best. Buses are few and trains sporadic and overcrowded as thousands of people crisscross the borders of Europe, entering and exiting the zones that are now controlled by the different Allied forces. Along the way we pass a group of hitchhikers and I am suddenly besieged by panic. Sometimes a face will trigger a memory of a Nazi and my stomach will seize up in fear. I grab Mrs. Sperry's arm and repeat "No, No, No!" shaking my finger and head to indicate that she should not stop to pick them up. Mrs. Sperry understands me perfectly and reassures me. "No, don't worry, Dina, we are not going to give them a ride. I can understand perfectly how you feel. Let them walk."

I don't understand exactly what she says but my fears dissolve as we continue down the road. Relaxing again, I begin to enjoy the scenery and try to use my English. I point at trees, the sky, cows and barns along the roadside and Mrs. Sperry responds with the words in English, which I repeat after her. The terrain is a series of hills covered with thick groves of trees that roll in and out of valleys devoted to farmland. Sparkling rivers and streams punctuate the open spaces, their blue-green veins slicing through the landscape. One thing cannot be denied, Germany is breathtakingly beautiful. Like a fairy tale kingdom from a Brothers Grimm story peopled by knights, princesses, and ogres, the countryside spans vast as it butts up against ancient forests and castle-crested mountains.

Postcard of Aglasterhausen School. Dina's bedroom, third floor center windows.

After a couple of hours of driving at a leisurely pace, we arrive at a series of buildings nestled within a meadow surrounded by open farmland with cows contentedly grazing. Nearby sit stately off-white four story stucco buildings crowned with tall slanted red tile roofs. The whole complex lies at the edge of a knoll surrounded by pastureland. Tall birch trees surround the property that is bordered by a stream, a large vegetable garden and an expansive soccer field. We are greeted by the warbling of birds and the babbling of water cascading over rocks and pebbles in the stream. It is breathtaking to behold this pastoral setting and I whisper a prayer of thanks to God for leading me here.

Aglasterhausen International Children's Center is maintained by the United Nations Relief and Rehabilitation Administration, better known as UNRRA. Before the war, in a previous incarnation, it had served as a home for mentally challenged children. When the Third Reich became all powerful, to enforce their ideology of Aryan superiority and perfection, they had given lethal injections to all of the child inmates at Aglasterhausen. How distinct the differences between the Nazi murderers that committed the murder of innocent children at Aglasterhausen and the good people that now only wish to rehabilitate children here. Located near a small town called Neunkirchen about 100 kilometers from Heidelberg, one of Germany's most beautiful cities, Aglasterhausen is the perfect facility for recuperating and teaching the rescued children of Europe. We number at any given time approximately two hundred children, ranging from babies to eighteen years of age. The children of Aglasterhausen are a smorgasbord of nationalities, ethnic origins, and religions. There are Polish, French, Hungarian, German, Estonian, Lithuanian, Romanian, and Russian children. The school is administered by a tall statuesque woman named Rachael Greene, a social worker, who demands propriety and respectfulness from her charges. If in her good graces, one can expect to receive deep affection and kindness from this compassionate woman.

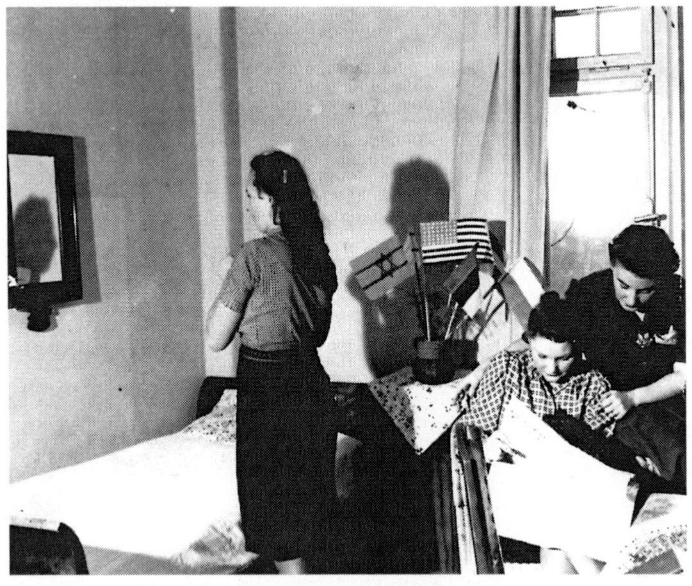

Publicity photo taken at Aglasterhausen school by UNRRA. Dina is seated reading the newspaper.

My room is on the top floor with a window that faces a pasture where cows lazily graze on plush grass. That window niche will become one of my favorite places to relax, read, and daydream of the future. There are two beds, two nightstands with lamps, and a roll-top desk and swivel chair. The walls are papered in a beautiful blue toile wall covering depicting the French countryside, which mirrors the views from the windows. The room even has an attached private bathroom with a large free standing tub with claw feet. I am thrilled to meet my only roommate, Haneczka Handelsman, who was originally from a small town outside of Radom. A tiny bit of a girl with green eyes and rich brown hair, she is the only survivor from her family. We become instant friends. She also has a boyfriend at the Stuttgart DP Camp named Rakocz. Haneczka and I immediately begin to plan the fun we will have when Rakocz and Natek come to visit.

Our day begins at 7:30 a.m. for breakfast in a huge dining hall where we naturally congregate with people from our birth countries. Our English is minimal and we mainly speak our native tongues when we aren't in class. Our table is next to a table of Estonians. The Estonian boys are terribly handsome and we can't help but flirt with them. After breakfast our rigorous classes begin at 9 a.m. and continue until 1 p.m., our break for lunch. Our studies include World History, Geography, English, Mathematics, and our native languages, in my case Polish and Hebrew. Even Yiddish is offered for the Jewish children. The curriculum includes religious classes from Catholicism to Judaism. After lunch we play sports outside or simply walk among the tall birch trees and gravel paths. At Aglasterhausen the walls literally breathe with life as children's laughter echoes through the halls. It is a far cry from the putrid death wall that surrounded us at Bergen-Belsen. Except for the boisterous sounds of youth, it is peaceful here, the complete opposite of everything that we have suffered.

The clouds lie heavy in the blackened sky as I stare out the window watching and listening to the rain. Winter is approaching and the trees have changed from the greens of summer to the bright orange, red and gold of fall. In a last desperate effort to live, they array their beauty to the world before the winds tear them from the branches and they are no more. As I look at the whirling leaves I can see that those of us that survived share a close affiliation to the natural world. We who cheated death now dress ourselves in the splendor of life. We dance before the wind without fear. The war devoured our formative years and then spit us out, bare without roots, yet we fight to live again and plant ourselves firmly among the living. We have suppressed who we are for so long that we are lost in a darkened room unable to find the light we know must be there. Today I overheard one of our teachers, Jadzia, make a derogatory remark about the Jews. She said that Jewish greed brought about the war. I could not believe what I heard her say. I was incensed and immediately went to Mrs. Greene to report the incident. Mrs. Greene's face turned crimson, fused with anger. Mrs. Greene is not a Jew, but she has seen the effects of bigotry. Apologizing to me and promising she would investigate, I left her fuming in her office. Several hours later I returned to her office expecting to hear that Jadzia had been fired and told to pack her bags. Mrs. Greene, without judgment, told me Jadzia's story and asked for my decision as to her fate. She has placed Jadzia's destiny within my hands.

Jadzia *is* a Jew! She spent the entire war pretending to be a Catholic, hidden with a family in Poland. So ingrained is this deception that her true identity was lost to even herself. All around her the anti-Semitic words of the Church, her Polish neighbors, and the Nazis penetrated her psyche and she completely became one of them, a Jew hater, and in so doing a self-hater. Even after the war, the habits of six years are not easily abandoned. She has continued the lie, afraid to be a Jew, afraid to claim her history. On her knees, sobbing, she pleaded with Mrs. Greene to please not send her away.

My anger dissipates when Mrs. Greene tells me of Jadzia's ordeal. Who am I to condemn the poor girl, we are all damaged in different ways. Feeling only pity I simply demand her apology and that she admit to everyone that she is a Jew. Mrs. Greene tells Jadzia that if she ever speaks ill of the Jews or anyone else again she will be sent away without another word. "You will do well to remember, Jadzia, that Aglasterhausen is a place of healing for children who bear the ugly scars of hatred and discrimination. I will not allow you or anyone else to deepen the scars they already bear."

Jadzia comes to me, her eyes swollen red. She begs my forgiveness and apologizes. Feeling her sincere shame and contrition, I forgive her. "Jadzia, you must come to terms with who you are. You of all people know what it means to be hated. I have lost enough to this hatred. I will lose no more."

It is Christmas and everyone has thrown themselves into the holiday season. A group of boys went on an expedition to the forest and returned dragging a tall evergreen tree. After much ado we finally heaved it into the assembly hall where everyone set about decorating it with ribbons and hanging bulbs of silver and gold. The younger children are stringing popcorn to drape around the tree while the older girls are busy helping in the kitchen, preparing a feast of traditional Christmas and Chanukah fare. The cook is stuffing geese with spices, dried berries, and bread and I am frying hundreds of *latkas* with a group of girlfriends.

Natek and Rakocz are coming today and will stay for the weekend to enjoy our Christmas dinner and party. I knitted Natek a blue sweater to match his eyes and I can't wait to see his face when he opens his gift. Everyone is so excited to celebrate our first holiday since the end of the war. Tonight we will light the first candle of the menorah and sing Chanukah songs and Christmas carols. Natek has been very patient with me but I know that once winter has passed he will be insistent that we make arrangements to go to Palestyne. Major Sperry is encouraging me toward a different path. She says the United States will soon open its doors to many of the survivors of Europe. She emphasizes that I have seen enough war for one lifetime. In America I would be able to continue my studies. She insists that the opportunity of going to the United States is a great one. Soon I will have to make a decision that will change the course of my life forever.

I know that Mrs. Sperry has grown to love me like the daughter she never had and only wants the best for me and her arguments are sound. She has had her own series of misfortunes that have given her a sense of wariness with the world. She was married to an attorney and was very much in love. After several years of trying, she finally became pregnant. Sometime during her pregnancy, she and her husband had a terrible fight and he hit her. Tragically, she lost the baby. Soon after they were divorced and she enlisted in the US Army. As a trained social worker, the army through the United Nations assigned her to Aglasterhausen to rehabilitate and resettle the orphaned children of Europe. She is devoted to the children of Aglasterhausen, they are her children.

"What about Natek?" I ask her. "Can he come to the United States too?"

"I don't know," she answers. "He must apply for asylum. Certainly with time he will be admitted."

The more I think of it, the more I realize that Natek would never come to the United States; he is set on playing a part in the birth of a Jewish state. I am completely confused as to what I should do. On the one hand, the thought of fulfilling my sister's dream burns like a fire in my soul, but is it my dream? Even the contemplation of fighting a war immobilizes me. I just want to live in peace, go to school, and one day get married and have children. I haven't the stomach to spend the rest of my life surrounded by hatred and fighting a war. I love Natek in every way imaginable. When he touches me all I can do is surrender to his passion with the force of mine. If only I had more time to decide. Perhaps there is too much water under the bridge, too much shared misery between us to ever build a successful life. In the privacy of our room, Haneczka and I discuss our dilemma until we are blue in the face. She also wants more than anything to immigrate to the United States. She and Rakocz are madly in love with each other, but all of her arguments with Rakocz are over this one issue of Israel versus the United States. Rakocz, like Natek, is determined to make any sacrifice to build a new country out of the desert and swamp that is Palestyne. "That is where we belong," he argues. "We can trust no other country to our safety and future."

So it goes, around and around, we argue as to the merits of whether it is Palestyne or America that is best for us. At least for the weekend there will be peace.

"Natek, I am so happy to see you!" I rush to his arms as he lifts me in the air, his eyes never leaving my face.

"Dina, you look so pretty."

As always, Natek's compliments cause me to blush. "I don't know how? I think I cooked a thousand *latkas* today." I take his hand, pulling him behind me. "Natek I have something for you." His eyes light up with the old glimmer of mischievousness that I remember so well from when we first met at A.V.L.

"What is it?" he asks, his face filled with pleasure.

The menorah stands on the upright piano surrounded by gifts wrapped in cloth. I pick one up and hand it to him. "It is nothing special but I hope you like it. I can't wait a moment longer to give it to you."

We sit on the piano bench as he carefully removes the sweater from the wrappings. "You made this for me?" he asks incredulously.

"Yes, of course I did. Look, see the blue matches the color of your eyes perfectly. Do you like it?"

"I love it!" He throws his arms around me, hugging and kissing me.

I beam with pride knowing that our weekend has started off on a wonderful note.

Outside the snow is drifting down in a powdery shower of crystal flakes veiling the countryside in a virginal gown of white. Mrs. Greene has arranged for a villager to take us for sleigh rides. Natek, Rakocz, Haneczka, and I all bundle up and squeeze into the sleigh, covering our legs with a thick red blanket. The driver takes off at a brisk clip and the air is filled with the music of sleigh bells as our words and laughter echo in the crisp winter wind. We ride through pastures where the cows barely lift their heads to acknowledge our passage. The low winter sun does its best to pierce the gauze-like clouds but barely manages a golden shimmering film that washes the sky in splendor. From a distance we must appear like a holiday card, young and happy, without a care in the world, flying through billowy clouds of snow.

Our faces flushed with color from the invigorating sleigh ride, we return to the festivities in the dining room. Everyone gathers around as we light the menorah and sing the traditional Chanukah song, *Maoz Tzur*, for the first time since the war. We sing the song in Hebrew the traditional way and then one of the American soldiers sings it in English.

Rock of Ages, let our Song
Praise Thy saving power;
Thou, amidst the raging foes,
Wast our sheltering tower.
Furious they assailed us,
But Thine arm availed us,
And thy Word
Broke their sword
When our own strength failed us.
Children of the martyr race,
Whether free or fettered,
Wake the echoes of the Songs
Where ye may be Scattered.

Yours the message cheering
That the time is nearing.
Which will See
All men free, Tyrants disappearing.

The words could not be more profound or apropos and there is not a dry eye in the room when he is finished.

This is a time for celebration and the phonograph is quickly turned on and music pours forth, reinvigorating the party with "White Christmas." Everyone begins to dance and return to a jovial mood. Paul Hodys, a wonderful dancer, asks me to dance and we spin around the room as Natek watches his face alight with a glimmer of a smile. Mrs. Sperry and Mrs. Greene are both dressed in red and are chatting, sipping glasses of holiday punch. I have noticed that Aglasterhausen is proving to be a fertile ground for love. Mrs. Greene has an admirer, a Jewish survivor named Samuel, a man in his thirties, a few years younger than her. Whenever he is near her face takes on the radiance of a young girl. I think they are both very cautiously tiptoeing toward courtship. Their attraction is powerful and I suspect that soon they will be running toward each other with open arms. Our nurse Marjorie, a beautiful Mulatto woman with skin the color of amber honey, is also testing the waters of love. John, our school bus driver, seems to be in constant attendance to her. They are both wonderful dancers and are teaching us to dance the swing, which is the new popular dance in America. They are sensational and once they really start kicking up their heels we all stand around applauding with encouragement. Most of us are pretty inept on the dance floor but we certainly are willing to make fools of ourselves as we whirl around the floor emulating Marjorie and John. I am happy to see that Mrs. Sperry has found a dance partner. A nice looking man dressed in an American army uniform, another social worker. Tommy Sperry, it turns out, is quite a good dancer herself, surprising us all. There are a few military men in attendance at our party and they aggressively lose themselves in the spirit of the holidays, dancing with every girl in the room. Everyone is having such a good time. The world is at peace and is beginning to heal from the conflagration that almost consumed it. Lives, cities, and countries are being rebuilt and hope illuminates the horizon. Tonight we toast the future that shines brightly. Tonight all things are possible.

Everything is perfect and somehow the staff even manages to procure a small gift for everyone. I receive a bottle of cologne. I have no possessions except for the clothing that is donated from charities around the world. The cologne is like a gift of precious jewels and I sparingly touch my pulse points with the floral scent, raising my arm to Natek for his approval. He inhales the fragrance and attacks me, hungrily showering me in kisses up and down my neck as I squeal with laughter.

Natek and Rakocz return to Aglasterhausen to celebrate the New Year with Haneczka and me. We manage to stay up half the night dancing to music. At midnight we toast the end of 1945, a year that was nearly our last. 1945 is the year of our liberation and of our rebirth and we join the world in toasting the victory of good over evil. At breakfast the festivities continue, as we learn that John has asked Marjorie to marry him and she has accepted. Now we have a wedding to look forward to as they are planning to be married in March right here at Aglasterhausen.

Natek, in a last effort to kindle a flame beneath me, has announced that he and his brother Benjamin are leaving for Palestyne. Haneczka and Rakocz are going with them. Haneczka has lost her battle with Rakocz and all her dreams of the United States have been set aside. Rakocz is firm and her deep love and devotion to him has decided their future. Only I have not committed myself to Palestyne. Mrs. Sperry, well aware of my trepidation, is strongly pressing me to wait and see if the United

States opens its doors. She predicts that it will be very soon and that I could be one of the first to be granted immigration status. In the meantime, a representative of the new Jewish government in Palestyne has come to Aglasterhausen to encourage immigration. I speak with him and he questions me as to why I don't want to go to Palestyne. I explain to him that I want to go but I don't think that I am physically able to endure another war. He completely understands and assures me that whenever the Jewish state is born I will always be welcome as a citizen. Unbelievably, the next country that shows up encouraging immigration, in my case return, is Poland. The gentleman asks me if I would like to go back to Poland and without hesitation I respond, "NEVER!" I tell him that for five generations my family lived in Poland and that they gave everything to Poland. All they asked in return was to live in peace as good citizens. The Poles have always been consumed with anti-Semitism and their true colors were proudly displayed during the war. "Although not all," I remind him, "the majority of the Polish citizenry couldn't have cared less what the Nazis did to the Jews." I have seen the worst of Poland and, for me, the last of Poland. I ask him, "Why would I want to go back and give anything of myself to a country that hates me and my kind?" To this he is only silent; he knows that what I say is true.

Representatives come from Sweden, Switzerland, France, and England to offer asylum, but I can't bear the thought of living in Europe, where my whole family was murdered. Europe is a graveyard buried in a layer of Jewish ashes.

I have made my decision, though difficult it may be. I will go to the "golden medina" America. As much as I love Natek, I know that I am not ready to marry. I am too young and the dream of going to America is too tantalizing. My leave taking from Natek is one of the most painful of my life. He comes to say good-bye, sadness written in his eyes.

"Dina, you know that if you change your mind I will be waiting for you."

"Natek, this street runs both ways. You could make application and join me in the United States. We could both go to school and with time... who knows? At least we will have the time to find ourselves."

Stubbornly, he resists. "No, there is only one place that I wish to call home, one place where my children will be born."

Taking Natek's hands in mine, I try my best to smile, though my heart is breaking. "You know I will always love you, Natek. I could never have lived through the war without your strength urging me on to fight. Even in my darkest hours, it was your smile that sustained me. I lived knowing you had commanded me to, that we had promised each other. I will never know a truer friend."

"Yes, well... I too lived by keeping your face before me. There were many times that I lived another day knowing that I must find you; that I had promised."

Wrapping my arms around him, my tears flow in a steady stream as I whisper in his ear. "Thank you, Natek. Please forgive me?"

His eyes crinkle in the smile that I will always cherish and, repeating the words that he has so often said to me, "Dinale, you know that I could never stay mad at you."

Dinka's roommate Hanka and new husband Rakocz after arriving in Israel, 1946.

Natek is gone, Haneczka and Rakocz with him. The first few days are filled with regret and uncertainty. Have I made the right decision? Sometimes you have to step off a cliff into the unknown and trust that you will land softly on solid ground. Time will tell if I shall land safely. At least I know that I have time to find out who I am. Time is my biggest asset. School fills my days and reading fills my nights. My English is beginning to improve and Mrs. Sperry spends a good deal of time encouraging me and correcting my sentences. She promises that in the next couple of months the United States will open its gates and welcome us to the "Land of the Free and the Home of the Brave."

Winter's cloak of snow is giving way to spring and a sea of cornflowers and field poppies blanket the meadows in vibrant color. The warming of the sun awakens a warming of the soul. Marjorie and John are to be married this weekend and everyone at Aglasterhausen is busy preparing for the event.

The wedding day dawns with a drizzle of rain that washes the air clean like a new beginning. A multicolored rainbow sweeps the sky as it pierces through large puffy cumulus clouds. The sun promises to warm the earth enough to keep the ceremony outside. An Army Chaplain has arrived to officiate and Marjorie's brother, a tall handsome man, has flown in to represent her family and give the bride away. We all assemble on the lawn to the beautiful sound of flute, guitar, and cello playing music by Wagner, Vivaldi, and Bach. Marjorie is a vision dressed in a white brocade suit with a pencil thin skirt that accents her narrow waist. Her jacket has a low cut bodice and she wears a string of pearls that rest on her amber skin. John and Marjorie have written their pledges of faith to one another and their words inspire a rush of tears from everyone. When the Chaplain says "You may kiss the bride!" an enormous hoopla breaks out among the men in uniform and we all rush to congratulate the bride and groom, their faces aglow with excitement. Indoors, the dining hall has been draped in white with splashes of pink roses that scent the air with the perfume of an indoor garden. The party swings into motion as we abandon ourselves to the music with John and Marjorie leading the charge to the dance floor. We dance with abandon, our hearts keeping rhythm to the drums and our faces gleaming from exertion, we dazzle with our youth. Then we drink champagne to a myriad of toasts to the couple who teeter against each other, intoxicated with joy. Weddings are new beginnings and we all feel our own lives touched with the magic of the moment. John and Marjorie leave amid a shower of rice and the rattling of tin cans that are tied to the jeep that will take them to Heidelberg for a honeymoon weekend. I cannot help but think of Natek and wish that he were here to share this special day with me. Today all things seem possible and I hope that one day I will convince Natek to follow me to America.

The spring days blossom one into another. I sit under a large birch tree enunciating my English aloud as I listen to a spotted woodpecker busily tapping out a love letter to a future mate on a tree. I look up and see Mrs. Sperry walking toward me, beaming.

"Dina, do you know what today is?" "April 15th."

"Yes, and today the United States approved your immigration status and you are going on the first ship of immigrants to America! You sail May 11th, it has all been arranged. We have been told that the President of the United States, Harry Truman, plans on meeting your ship when it arrives in New York Harbor." "I can't believe it!" I am so excited that I throw myself into her arms. "Thank you, thank you, Mrs. Sperry!"

"Dina, I know you are worried, but believe me your life is going to change for the best. New doors are going to open for you. America is the greatest country in the world and you will find happiness there."

"I am very grateful to you, Mrs. Sperry, for all you have done for me." I press my lips to her cheek and feel her wet tears. This dear woman loves me and has mentored me and now she is going to have to say good-bye to me in a few weeks. "Will I see you again?"

"Of course you will. I'll be back in New York when my work here is done. You will write me and let me know where you are."

"It is like a dream," I sigh.

"Yes, and the dream is about to come true. I have to get back to my desk, but I will see you at dinner." Hugging me one last time, she leaves me to ponder my future.

For all of my words to the contrary, now that the moment has actually arrived, leaving the continent of my birth fills me with apprehension. My entire family lies buried in ashes, forever part of the soil of Europe. Will they hear my prayers from a world away? Will I quickly adapt to a new homeland and find acceptability, or will I stick out like a weed in a rose garden, my foreignness isolating me from everyone around me? It is unlikely that the familiar traditions of the Old World will serve me in the modernity of America. With no family to protect me or guide me I will have to rely on myself; the prospect both terrorizes and excites me. I have lived a lifetime of pain and seen more than enough horror for any life, but six years of disrupted childhood will never be recovered no matter how hard I try. I spend the ten days leading up to our departure on a pendulum swinging from ecstasy to misery. The nights pass restlessly as I toss and turn in my sleep, lost in dreams that play like newsreels. In these dreams I find myself running through Radom searching for my mother, father, sister, or brother. Sometimes I catch sight of one of them but just when I am about to reach them they vanish. Continuing to run, I suddenly turn a corner and find myself running toward the gates of Auschwitz, unable to stop. Before me towers the chimney, spewing the life of European Jewry in a blast of smoke. Then the scene changes and Auschwitz becomes Bergen-Belsen and I am running beside the wall of bodies that seem to be reaching out to touch me. Over and over, night after night, I wake up drenched in sweat and shaking with fear. Then one night my grandfather comes to me in my dream and stands before me. His presence shimmers, exactly as it did that night so many years ago when I sent him away. This time I reach out to him in my dream. Although I cannot feel him, when I touch him he smiles reassuringly. I feel his love wash over me, his eyes filling with sadness. I hear his voice in my head telling me that I will be fine and not to be afraid. "Live, Dinale," he says. "Live and know that your family is watching over you. We are wherever you are, wherever you go. Sleep, maidele, you have a long life ahead of you. You have nothing to fear. One day we will all be reunited." When I wake the next morning I am filled with a sense of peace and new hope. Remembering my dream, I am filled with courage. I know that my grandfather and the rest of my family are with me. I know that I will never be alone.

Chapter 38

Lady with a Torch

The days fly by like the springtime clouds that glide across the sky. Our departure day has arrived. John is driving us to Bremerhaven to the USS Marine Flasher which will sail her cargo of immigrants to the hallowed shores of America. Sixty students from Aglasterhausen are sailing as are many of the teachers. Our dorm parents and teachers Fred and Franka Fragner, concentration camp survivors from Czechoslovakia, will be our chaperones, continuing their dedication to the orphaned children they call "our children." The buses are lined up to leave, our small cache of belongings stowed in the storage racks on top. Tearfully we bid our good-byes to those who will remain. Soon Aglasterhausen will be filled with the voices of a whole new group of children. In fact, Aglasterhausen, under the astute guidance of Rachel Greene, will remain open until February of 1948, rehabilitating the lives of orphans who lost everything during the Nazi era. Rachael Greene, Tommy Sperry, and Marjorie are outside, along with the rest of the staff that will remain, to wish us bon voyage. With my heart pounding in my chest, I take a tearful farewell from these women who have showered me with love and affection. In some ways I feel that I am losing my family again and I am overwhelmed with emotion. The death and losses from the cataclysmic war trail like a shadow, impossible to lose. It is like walking in and out of sunshine. Sometimes the sun dispels the gloom with its bright rays of happiness until the cold shadowy grasp of memory plunges me back into darkness and sorrow. Aglasterhausen has been transformational. It has cast light on the dark recesses of my soul, and leaving the safety of this haven cannot be more poignant to me as I wave through the window of the bus. I listen to the sound of gravel crunching beneath the tires and the words of good-bye repeating from our lips as the bus makes the turn and a grove of birch trees block the familiar buildings from our sight.

We sail from Bremerhaven into the North Sea with a crisp breeze at our stern forcing us forward with a thrust. Don't look back, the wind coaxes, look forward to the future. We are over eight hundred refugees from every corner of Europe and most of us stand on deck as the shoreline gradually shrinks from view. Our eyes remain fixed on the invisible shoreline that recedes until we are surrounded by only the deep blue of the sea. Overhead the sea birds that command the skies swoop, diving into the water and emerging with silvery fish. The Marine Flasher is a naval troop carrier and this is her first mission moving civilian population. I feel Mrs. Sperry's influence when I see my assigned cabin, which is on the top deck next to the Captain's quarters. Most of the passengers are crammed four or more to a room, but somehow Mrs. Sperry has arranged for me to share a cabin with one older woman who is coming to America to join her son. It is just like her to provide me with a surrogate mother. Seas of calm prevail and we spend our days parading the decks and inhaling the clean salty air. I have two girlfriends from Aglasterhausen on the ship, Hanna Starkman and Hankah Sajkiewicz. Both girls are from Poland and we have become very good friends. Most of the day we spend sunning on the decks and flirting with young men. I suppose that if we had inclement weather and rougher seas our journey might take on a whole new meaning. Seasickness would have fostered our worst fears. Instead we sail under idyllic conditions, balmy sunshine and clear black evening skies that glitter with millions of stars. The expansive horizon that appears one with the sea gives buoyancy to our dreams as we inhale the sweet perfume of freedom like an aromatic therapy. During the day we attend a class where they are teaching us to sing American patriotic songs. We learn "The Battle Hymn of the Republic," "The Star Spangled Banner," and "My Country, 'Tis of Thee," all of which we will sing on our arrival when we cruise into the mighty harbor of New York. In the evenings we are entertained by the crew, who double as performers, showcasing song and dance numbers or we watch American movies. My favorite film on the voyage is from 1945, "A Tree Grows in Brooklyn." It is the story of a teenager, Francie Nolan, and her family. They live in Brooklyn, New York, which I think is very close to where we will be living in the Bronx. In the film, the Nolan family struggles against poverty to make a better life, but the father is an alcoholic and can't keep a job, which condemns the family to an endless cycle of disasters. He dies, forcing Francie to quit school in order to help support the family. Francie never loses her faith or determination and in the ends falls in love with a wonderful man, Ben. The film is an anthem to hope and a better life and we all come away from the movie inspired. After all, if Francie can find happiness, so might we. Nothing can dampen our spirits as we sail into the future.

Our passage across the Atlantic seems to fly by and the night before our arrival the Captain gives a wonderful speech wishing us success in our new lives in America. He announces that we will be arriving in the morning and encourages us to get a good night's sleep so we can all be topside when we arrive. That evening we are so excited that I don't think any of us sleep a wink.

Dina aboard the Marine Flasher arriving at New York harbor on May 20, 1946.

I am on deck just as the sun begins to rise out of the sea, a dazzling orb of gold that lights the eastern horizon like a candle in the dark. I hold tightly to Hannah's and Hankah's hands as we look out over the water. Everyone is on deck, squinting into the distance, trying to make out the outline of the city of our dreams. Slowly we approach the harbor, which even at this early hour is a whirlwind of activity. Ferryboats and tugboats stream in and out of the sea lanes as they move about the many ships that ease their way through the lower bay. We enter the upper bay and the Captain blows the ship's foghorn with its deep resonant sound while overhead fly hundreds of seagulls that keep up a constant squawking, as if to herald our arrival. As we approach, like a vision, the lady with a torch rises up from a star pedestal on Liberty Island. Eight hundred voices rise in shouts of awe and every arm reaches toward her, everyone pointing as if they are the first to see her. "Liberty!" "Liberty!" "Liberty!" we chant. She glints in the morning sun, her coppery green robes seeming to move in the breeze as her foot steps forward to the future. To every immigrant that has ever come to these shores, she has represented the dream personified of freedom and democracy. Regally crowned, she towers above the bay with her arm held proudly baring a golden torch; the light of freedom known the world over. Behind her stands the greatest city the world has ever seen, with its outline of pinnacled skyscrapers spiraling toward the sky. Now, we the survivors of the worst genocide in the history of the world have arrived to seek our fortune and live in peace in this Promised Land, like so many immigrants before us. Without America the war would not have been won and Hitler would have fulfilled his dream of annihilating all of the Jews of Europe. Suddenly I remember the last Passover my family celebrated in Radom. I can hear my brother, his young voice asking my father how God would save us without a Moses. My father hesitated for a moment, perhaps stumped by the probing mind of his son. Then with the confidence of one who knows that evil cannot triumph, my father pronounced that God would send a great army to save us. Little did he know how prescient his words really were, not only did God send us a great army but he also sent a great nation to rescue us and to offer his own daughter asylum and a new home.

Silence descends on the ship as we anchor in front of the Statue of Liberty. Each of us has traveled through so much to reach these shores. Our emotional and physical scars, still raw and painful, for this moment are forgotten. A hush falls over us when over the loudspeakers a voice breaks the silence, reciting the poem that Emma Lazarus, a Jewish girl, wrote long ago:

Not like the brazen giant of Greek fame,
With conquering limbs astride from land to land;

Here at our sea-washed, sunset gates shall stand
A mighty woman with a torch, whose flame
Is the imprisoned lightning, and her name
Mother of Exiles. From her beacon-hand
Glows world-wide welcome; her mild eyes command
The air-bridged harbor that twin cities frame.
"Keep, ancient lands, your storied pomp!" cries she
With silent lips. "Give me your tired, your poor,
Your huddled masses yearning to breathe free,
The wretched refuse of your teeming shore.
Send these, the homeless, tempest-tost to me,
I lift my lamp beside the golden door!"

I am not sure that we understand every word of that poem as we prepare to enter the gates of Ellis Island and our new lives. What does that matter really? The emotional impact is clear to all of us as we cheer and wipe away the tears. I know that I have made the right choice for me and kept the promise of survival. America stands before me, the antithesis of all that I have lived through. I know already that I will cherish this grand land in my heart and from this moment forward I will love her and be loyal to her until the day that I die. I look at the goddess of freedom that towers before me with wonder and amazement. The incredible journey of war that has brought me to her shores is nearly at its end. Taking a deep breath, I inhale the promise of a bright and beckoning future. With my eyes open and focused on the soaring city beyond, I realize that I am home.

Epilogue

The journey through my mother's Holocaust experience has taken 72 years, a lifetime; the writing of this novel has taken two years. From my earliest childhood my mother shared her stories with a truly inquisitive child who probed ever deeper into the world of darkness that was my mother's teen years, 1939-1945. Unable to comprehend how such horrors could have happened, over and over my young mother was made to explain. This constant retelling of the nightmare seared the memories like a branding iron into both her skin and mine. Neither of us could ever forget. Although reliving those years is still as painful as a new wound, I knew that the time had come to share that historical journey through Hell. My mother is one of the youngest survivors and their numbers dwindle as I write this. The witnesses/victims/testifiers will all too soon be gone and the deniers will spew forth their venom as they try to alter the historical record. Only these personal accounts from the flesh and blood survivors will stand firm in the face of evil.

After the war and through the ensuing years, the fate of some of the characters in the novel has been learned. The names have been changed where necessary to protect privacy but the events have been unaltered and are as true now as the day they occurred.

Mrs. Felzenszwalbe, my mother's teacher in Radom, lived in a primarily Christian neighborhood. After the German invasion and after the Jews had been resettled into the two ghettos, my mother ran into Mrs. Felzenszwalbe in a pharmacy on one of her illegal excursions out of the ghetto. There for a few brief moments they reunited and conversed. My mother learned that Mrs. Felzenszwalbe and her daughter had not been forced to move into the ghettos. A German officer had commandeered their home and the two women were allowed to remain cooking and cleaning for the officer. He must have known that they were Jewish but he chose to look the other way, pretending they were not. As far as is known both mother and daughter survived the war.

Dina's maternal family in Brzeziny, except for her elderly blind grandfather, were all resettled in the Lodz ghetto and perished in Auschwitz. Interestingly, the Nazis declined to murder or resettle her fragile blind grandfather, a saintly old man who was revered by his Polish neighbors. Taking everyone else, they left him in the care of these same Polish neighbors who pleaded for his welfare and purportedly cared for him until his death of natural causes sometime shortly after his family was taken to Auschwitz.

Dina's girlfriend, Lola Freidenreich, who escaped from A.V.L. with her brother Yaacov (Yannick), assumed a false identity as a Christian in Warsaw. She joined her sister, who had previously assumed a Christian alias. The sisters worked for a wealthy Polish family as live-in maids until one evening Lola overheard her employers in a conversation. The mistress of the house suggested to her husband that she suspected the sisters of being Jews. In fear that they would be denounced, the two sisters fled the home in the middle of the night. Their brother Yaacov worked as a construction laborer. The three siblings paid a Christian family to hide their mother and the husband of Lola's sister. They would visit regularly and one day when Yaacov was visiting his mother the SS surrounded the building and emptied it of all the occupants. All of the Polish residents, Lola's brother Yaacov, her mother, and brother-in-law were forced into the street where the Nazis (having probably been tipped off that there were hidden Jews in the building) proceeded to execute everyone. Lola's brother Yaacov, her brother-in-law, and mother were all murdered on that day. The sisters, although, devastated by their loss, continued to work in Warsaw as Christians until Warsaw's liberation by the Russians. After the war, the sisters immigrated to the United States. Lola married another survivor who had also lived as a Polish Christian during the war. They had one daughter and lived in California until her death.

Hannah, Dina's young friend from Pionki, who disappeared in Auschwitz, survived the war and immigrated to the United States and lives on the East Coast.

Esterka Litwak, the beautiful Jewess who captivated Unterscharfuhrer Taube, survived the war and was liberated at Bergen-Belsen. I have searched the archives for information regarding the fate of Unterscharfuhrer Taube (commander at Hindenburg) but unfortunately his fate is unknown. He was never captured or tried. However, this was not the case for Hauptsturmfuhrer Josef Kramer, Commandant of Bergen-Belsen, who was tried and hanged on December 13, 1945.

Dina's dear girlfriend Lusia married her boyfriend Szymek and immigrated to the United States. They settled in Philadelphia and had two daughters. Dina and Lusia kept up contact until Lusia's premature death.

Dina's cousin Nadja who went to Sweden after the war ended up immigrating to the United States where she married another survivor, Morris, who was from Lodz. They had three children, Theodore, Larry, and Sharon, and seven grandchildren. Dina and Nadja remained close until Nadja's death.

Dina's cousin Majer also immigrated to the United States, where he met and married Helen, who spent the war hidden as a Christian on a farm. Helen and Majer have two children, Abe and Mindy. Dina and Majer have remained close to this day.

Dina, Majer, and Nadja were the only survivors of their immediate and extended families.

Hanezka Handelsman (Dina's roommate at Aglasterhausen) and Rakocz immigrated to Israel where they married and had two daughters and a son.

Natek Korman immigrated to Israel and participated in the birth of a nation. He married and had children. Dina visited Israel in 1981 with her daughter Tema and future son-in-law Joe Merback and enjoyed a wonderful reunion with Natek.

Dina, after her arrival in New York, was placed with a family in Philadelphia where she attended Overbrook High School. She left Philadelphia for Los Angeles, where she found a relative, Pauline Solow. Pauline was the daughter of Dina's grandfather's brother, who had immigrated to the United States in the early 20th Century. Dina finished High School at Roosevelt High School in Los Angeles but was forced to go to work and was unable to attend college. Dina married Leo Balbien a kindertransport survivor from Vienna, Austria. Leo spent the early part of the war at a trade school outside of London. When he turned eighteen, he followed his parents to the United States and enlisted in the US Army. He served in the Philippine Islands until the end of the war. Dina and Leo have four children, Tema, Joel, Joshua, and Sarah. They are also blessed with seven grandchildren. Dina lives in Thousand Oaks, California, devoted to her children and family. She is vibrant and healthy and often speaks at schools, Temples, and other organizations of her experiences during the Holocaust.

Acknowledgements

I wish to thank Jennifer Livingston, editor extraordinaire. She took my unedited first edition with all its grammatical errors and has made of it a masterpiece. I will always be eternally grateful and honored to have had the good fortune of working with someone of her professional caliber. Beyond her brilliance she also possesses the spirit and soul of a *mensch*!

I also wish to thank my husband, Joe Merback, sounding board, critic, editor, and biggest fan, who patiently read and re-read the many drafts.

Dina and Leo Balbien on the occasion of their 50th Anniversary, with their children and grandchildren.

About the Author

Tema Merback is the wife of Joseph Merback and the mother of Ben and Natasha. She attended Bryn Mawr College and resides in Malibu, California.

CPSIA information can be obtained at www.ICGtesting.com
Printed in the USA
BVOW070835150513

320757BV00001B/164/P